"Some books are meant to be read. *All Manner of Things* is meant to be lived in. The pages enfolded me into a raw and beautiful family journey that touched me on a soul level. This exquisitely rendered portrait of hope, courage, and love in a time of war is a triumph and a gift. Susie Finkbeiner at her finest."

Jocelyn Green, Christy Award winning
author of *Between Two Shores*

"Susie Finkbeiner has created characters so real in *All Manner of Things,* you may want to write them a letter to find out how they are doing once you've turned the last page of the book. You'll cheer them on in the good times, weep with them during the hard times, and be glad you got to live their story with them. Definitely a story and characters you will remember."

Ann H. Gabhart, bestselling author of *River to Redemption*

"*All Manner of Things* should be at the top of everyone's reading stacks. Readers will love Finkbeiner's graceful prose about an overlooked but important era. With intimacy, a poetic voice, and an ever-present grip on hope, Finkbeiner writes with breathtaking admiration for the common American family in the throes of unbearable circumstances. Beautiful. Honest. Artfully written. A winning novel."

Elizabeth Byler Younts, author of *The Solace of Water*

all
manner
of
things

all manner of things

SUSIE FINKBEINER

Revell

a division of Baker Publishing Group
Grand Rapids, Michigan

Published by Revell
a division of Baker Publishing Group
PO Box 6287, Grand Rapids, MI 49516-6287
www.revellbooks.com

Printed in the United States of America

Library of Congress Cataloging-in-Publication Data
Names: Finkbeiner, Susie, author.
Title: All manner of things / Susie Finkbeiner.
Description: Grand Rapids, MI : Revell, [2019]
Identifiers: LCCN 2018055474 | ISBN 9780800735692 (pbk.)
Subjects: | GSAFD: Christian fiction.
Classification: LCC PS3606.I552 A78 2019 | DDC 813/.6—dc23
LC record available at https://lccn.loc.gov/2018055474

ISBN 978-0-8007-3634-7 (casebound)

19 20 21 22 23 24 25   7 6 5 4 3 2

For my parents

All shall be well, and all shall be well, and all manner of things shall be well.

—Julian of Norwich

Prologue

SUMMER, 1955

We sat at the end of the dock, my father and me. Early morning fog hovered over Chippewa Lake, so thick I couldn't see to the other side. As far as I could tell we were the only two awake out of all the people in Fort Colson. It wouldn't have surprised me to learn that we were the first up in the whole state of Michigan.

My father was having a good day, I'd known from the moment I came out of my bedroom. For one, he smiled as soon as he saw me. For two, he asked if I wanted to sit on the dock with him. Last, he'd poured two cups of coffee, his black and mine mostly milk and sugar.

"Don't tell your mother," he'd whispered, his voice soft and deep, his dark eyes full of mischief. "Promise? She wouldn't approve of a six-year-old drinking coffee. She'll worry that it'll stunt your growth."

"Will it?" I had asked, pushing my cat-eye glasses up the bridge of my nose.

"I guess we'll see."

Loose shoulders, easy smile, teasing words, sparkle in the corner of his eyes. He was having a good day, all right.

Good days didn't come along very often for him, not since Korea.

Melancholy was what my mother called it. When I asked her what that word meant, she told me it was a longer word for sad. When I asked why my father was sad, she told me that war made people that way. When I asked her how war did that, she told me I'd understand when I got older.

It little mattered that morning, though. I was beside my father, sitting Indian style on the dock and listening to the loons call to each other. Their trilling and yodeling filled the air, echoing off the trees that lined the shores of the lake.

"You know what she's saying?" my father asked.

I shook my head.

"She's calling out to another loon. Maybe her mate, maybe her chick. Either way, the other has strayed off and she's searching for him." He sipped his coffee. "She says, 'Hey, where are you?' Then the other one answers, 'Don't worry. I'm right over here.'"

"Then they find each other?"

He nodded, looking out into the first-of-the-morning fog.

"Dad?" I whispered.

"Annie."

"What if the lost one doesn't call back?"

He hesitated, nodding his head and pushing his lips together the way he did when he was thinking.

"Well, I suppose the first one yodels out louder, 'You get back here, you loon!'"

I laughed and he smiled and I thought I saw a glimpse of

how I imagined he'd been before the war. I'd been too small then. I couldn't remember.

We sat in the quiet a few minutes longer, the loons still calling back and forth through the fog that thinned as the sun brightened, burning it away. We drank our coffees, the bitterness of mine cutting through the milk and sugar just enough so I'd know it was there.

That night, while the rest of us slept, my father packed a few of his things and drove away in his Chevy pickup truck. I waited for him the rest of that week, sitting alone on the dock with my feet dangling over the edge, toes disturbing the stillness of the water. He hadn't left a note, and I was sure he'd come back any minute. I wanted to be there when he did.

The next Wednesday his letter came with no return address.

Gloria, I can't be who you need me to be, it read. *I have to see if I can walk off the war. Tell the kids I'm sorry. —Frank*

After that I stopped waiting for him. We all did. It was easier that way.

1

JUNE, 1967

When God created the world, he only afforded Michigan just so many good-weather days. He caused the bookends of the year to be winter and the months between to be warm enough for the earth to almost thaw before it was to freeze solid once again.

And somehow, in his infinite wisdom he had chosen to call it good.

In the deepest of winter, I often questioned the soundness of mind that made my ancestors think that Michigan was a good and fine place to settle. But it was in spring, when the whole world came back alive and I forgot the cold, that I swore to never leave my home state. Leaves turned the forests back to green, and flowers speckled bright red and yellow and orange across the lawns and fields. Purple lilacs bloomed on the bush below my bedroom window, smelling like heaven itself. Finches molted tawny feathers to show off their brilliant goldenrod. Robins returned with their trilling song, and just-hatched chicks peeped from their nests, discarding pretty blue shells on the ground.

Every year it caught me by surprise, the return of life to Fort Colson. But by June I'd fallen into the routine of longer days and leaving my jacket at home, letting the sun warm my bare arms.

I certainly would have liked to enjoy the sunshine. Instead, I stood looking out the big window of Bernie's Diner, dripping washrag in hand, wishing the view was of something other than the five-and-dime across the street. It was the perfect day for sitting on a dock, dipping my toes into the waters of Chippewa Lake.

Old Chip. That was what my brothers and I called it. Where we all learned how to swim and row a canoe and catch fish. Growing up without Frank around hadn't been a walk in the park. But having a mother who was unafraid of getting muddy and hooking a worm on the line made it a little bit easier. Especially for my brothers.

The sound of clattering pots or pans from the kitchen snapped my attention back to my job. I wrung the extra water from my rag and scrubbed down the tabletops, wiping away the breakfast crumbs to make way for the lunch plates. A couple of girls I knew from high school walked along the sidewalk past the diner window, wearing minidresses and bug-eyed sunglasses that seemed all the rage that year.

Using my knuckle, I pushed up my plastic-framed glasses and hoped they wouldn't notice me. Bernie's dress code only allowed white button-up shirts and slacks—no jeans. On my own I was a certifiable L7 square. The uniform didn't help matters at all.

The girls looked in through the window. Sally Gaines with

the perfectly coiffed auburn bouffant and Caroline Mann with her diamond engagement ring sparkling in the sunshine. Sally's mouth broke into an impossibly perfect smile and she waved, her fingers wiggling next to her face.

I knew that it was not meant for me. As far as girls like Sally and Caroline were concerned, I was less than invisible. I didn't even exist.

Turning, I saw my brother behind the counter, lowering a crate of freshly washed glasses to rest beside the Coca-Cola fountain. The glasses clinked together, but delicately, sounding just a little bit like chimes.

"You have an admirer," I said, stepping away from the window.

"Great," he said, thick sarcasm in his voice. Not looking up at the girls, he took one of the glasses and put it under the fountain, pulling half a glass of pop for himself. "They're good tippers at least."

"For you." I watched him take a few drinks of the Coke before moving on to setting the tables with silverware wrapped in paper napkins. "I don't have the advantage of flirting with them."

"You've got a point," he said. "I am charming."

"And I'm a nerd."

"Nah, you're peachy keen."

"Well, thanks." I looked back to where the girls had stood. They were already gone.

"I have my meeting today," Mike said, finishing off the last of his pop. "The one I told you about."

"When?"

"After lunch. Bernie told me I could leave a little early."

"Did you tell him what it's about?"

"No." Mike put his empty glass on the counter. He lowered his voice to just above a whisper. "I kind of gave him the impression that it's a doctor's appointment."

"And he bought it?" I asked. "You know you're the worst liar in the world, don't you?"

"He didn't seem to doubt me." He poured himself another half glass of pop and drank it all at once. "I didn't want him trying to talk me out of it."

"Do you really have to do this?" I asked.

"Yeah," he answered, covering a silent burp with his fist. "Unless you have any other ideas."

"Canada's only a few hours away."

He raised his eyebrows and made a humming sound. "I'm not sure that's a great option."

"What did Mom say?"

Shrugging, he walked around the counter, checking the ketchup bottles from the tables to see which needed refilling. He carried the half-full ones back to the counter in the crook of his arm.

"You told her, didn't you?" I asked. "Please tell me you did."

"Not exactly." He lined the bottles up on the counter.

"What do you mean by 'not exactly'?"

He cringed. "Not at all."

"Golly, Mike," I said, hoping it didn't sound too much like a scold. "You should have asked her about it. She might have had some ideas."

"I'm almost twenty, Annie. I'm an adult," he said, making his voice deeper. "It doesn't matter anyway. They're sending me whether I like it or not. I might as well just volunteer and at least have some say over things."

"I guess."

"She's going to be furious, though. I know she will be." He moved behind the counter again and wiped the bottles down with a wet rag. "I don't know how I'll tell Joel."

In the thirteen years since our baby brother was born, Joel loved no one as much as he did Mike. If he ever tired of such undying admiration, Mike rarely let on. He took to the role of big brother near perfectly.

"Why haven't you told him?" I asked.

"Gee, I don't know," Mike answered, uncapping the ketchup bottles. "I tried. I just didn't have the heart."

"You aren't abandoning him, if that's what you're worried about."

"Maybe that's it."

"Still, you have to tell them sometime."

"I will," he said. "Don't worry."

"The sooner the better," I said.

"I'll know more about what's going to happen after my meeting with the recruiter." He sighed. "It's a pickle, that's for sure."

"Maybe they won't want you."

"Come on, buddy, you're going to hurt my feelings."

"Oh, get out of here."

"Soon enough, sis." He turned toward the kitchen. "Soon enough I'll get out of here all the way to Vietnam."

●

If there was any consolation to be had for missing out on summer, it was that Bernie let me read during the lulls of the day, provided I had all my silverware wrapped and tables clean. I'd just settled onto the stool behind the cash register with book in hand when the bell over the door jingled with the arrival of someone. Regretfully, I shut the book and put it back on the counter. Scout Finch would just have to wait a little bit longer.

My mother stood just inside the door, purse hanging from her bent arm, and looking every bit the lady in her red blouse and tweed skirt. She'd worn her hair down that day with the ends in upturned curls.

She'd never been one to lie about her age. In fact, I'd heard her more than once brag about being over forty. "Just over," she'd say. The conversation inevitably turned to how she looked so young.

"My secret?" she'd say with a conspiratorial wink. "A hair-dresser who can keep my secrets and a strong girdle."

My mother, Gloria Jacobson, ever the charmer who turned heads anywhere she went. And me, her beanpole of a daughter who hardly took the time to twist a braid into her hair most mornings. It was a wonder she never tried to give me beauty tips, as much as I sorely needed them. Then again, I'd never asked. Never much cared to, either.

"I can't stay long," Mom said, making her way to the counter. "I have a few other errands to run before going back to work."

"Late lunch?" I asked, checking my watch.

She rolled her eyes. "Mrs. Channing was in for a checkup today, and you know how she can go on."

She lifted her hand, making a puppet out of her fingers, opening and closing them like a mouth.

"Did she ask again about you and the doctor?"

Mom sighed. "Of course she did."

After Frank left us, Mom found herself in need of a job for

the first time in her life. She'd put on her most professional-looking dress and walked over to Dr. Bill DeVries's office to ask him to hire her. She'd said he owed her. For what, I'd never had the courage to ask. The doctor, though, just happened to have a position open at his office. She'd worked as his receptionist ever since.

If rumor could be believed, the good doctor had held a torch for my mother since they were young. He'd even invited her to prom, but a day late. She'd already accepted Frank's invitation.

Most of the women in town waited for a romance to bud between Mom and Dr. DeVries. They'd waited more than twelve years with no sign of giving up hope. I wasn't sure if theirs was an act of sheer determination or utter stubbornness.

Either way, Mom could outlast anyone, even the old biddies of Fort Colson.

"I told her that I'm still married and, as far as I know, that won't change any time soon," Mom said, instinctively touching the gold wedding band on her left ring finger.

When I'd asked her years before why she still wore it, she told me it was to "discourage any interested parties." I wondered if it was also to keep certain chatterbox busybodies from speculation.

A small town like Fort Colson was fertile soil for gossip to take seed.

"Is Bernie here?" Mom asked.

"He's in the office," I answered. "It's bookkeeping day."

She reached into her purse, searching for something. "I'm sure it's putting him in a foul mood."

"Well, no more than usual," I whispered.

"He's not being grumpy to you, is he?" She arched one of her eyebrows. "You don't have to put up with his moods, you know."

"He's my boss."

"And he's my cousin."

"Second cousin, Mom." I rolled my eyes. "Everyone around here is your second cousin."

"Still." She went back to digging through her purse. "You don't have to take it from him. You'd get treated better working in an office somewhere."

"You know I'd hate that." I leaned my elbows on the counter. "I'm horrible at typing."

"You'd learn. Besides, there's more money in it." She tilted her head. "Or you could go to college."

"I don't mind his moods," I said. "Besides, I can't afford college."

"We could work something out." Her hands stilled and she looked up into my eyes. "I could work more hours. Maybe get a second job."

"You don't have to do that." I slid my book off the counter. "I wouldn't want to go anyway."

She gave me a sharp look—eyes narrowed and mouth puckered—that told me she didn't believe a word of it. The look didn't last long, just enough so that I'd see it. Then she turned her attention back to her purse.

"If you say so. Ah," she said, pulling an envelope from the depths of her handbag. "This came today."

Red and blue stripes colored the edge of the wrinkled envelope and a darker blue rectangle with white letters that read "BY AIR MAIL PAR AVION." It was addressed to me, the sender was Walter Vanderlaan, Private First Class.

"Any idea why he'd be writing you?" she asked, tapping his name with her long, red fingernail.

"No." I shrugged one shoulder. "I haven't a clue."

"You're sure?" She turned her head, giving me the side-eye.

I picked up the envelope, tapping a corner of it against the counter. Walt and his parents had been our neighbors when I was small. Our folks would play cards some Friday evenings, letting us kids stay up late to swim in the shallows of Old Chip or watch *Ozzie and Harriet* on television.

Walt had been my friend even though he was Mike's age. When he knocked on the door to ask for a playmate, he sought me. When we picked teams for a game of tag, he'd call my name first. More than once I'd overheard our mothers talk about writing up papers for an arranged marriage.

He was my very first friend and I was his.

But after Frank left and we moved, we didn't talk much anymore. And the older we got, the more Walt hated me. At least that was how I interpreted his name-calling and dirty looks.

I tried my hardest not to grimace, looking at my name on the envelope written in Walt's handwriting. "He's hardly spoken two words to me since we were little."

"Well, apparently he wants to talk to you now."

"I can't imagine why." I pushed up my glasses. "I'd think he has plenty of other people he could write."

"People change. Being at war can make a boy get ideas." Her eyes widened, she nodded once. "It makes them take notice of things they might otherwise overlook."

"Mom, no. He wouldn't—"

"Annie, you aren't getting any younger. You're eighteen,

after all. And I know you are probably in a hurry to get married." She leaned over the counter toward me. "I'm sure you think he's a nice boy, but . . ."

"He's not nice," I interrupted. "I already know that. I've always known that. Besides, I'm not in a hurry to get married."

"Honey, he's at war. I'm sure he's lonely." She sighed. "I guess I just want you to be careful."

"Careful of what?"

"I don't want you getting your heart broken."

"Mom, I harbor no secret affections for Walt Vanderlaan. I promise. Besides, he's been engaged to Caroline Mann for ages." I stuffed the letter in between the pages of my book. "Don't worry. I won't write him back, if that's what you want."

"You can if you would like." She let out a breath and leaned her elbows on the counter. "Just don't keep any secrets from me. Can you promise me that?"

I nodded, squinting at her, trying to figure out what she was up to. She never sighed that way unless she had something up her sleeve. Then, her blue eyes sharpened, as if she was trying to see through me. I'd never in all my life held up under her X-ray gaze.

"Is there anything that you'd like to tell me?" she asked. "Any secrets about Michael?"

"What do you mean?"

"I know he's keeping something from me."

"Gosh, Mom, why would you think that?" I widened my eyes, hoping to look puzzled instead of guilty.

"What's this appointment of his?"

"How do you know about that?"

"Mothers always find out," she answered. "What's this appointment?"

The door to the diner opened, letting in a handful of girls who wandered to the window booth, whispering to each other about this or that. I let them know that I'd be right with them, and they nodded as if they were in no hurry.

"You know, don't you?" Mom asked. "Is he in some kind of trouble?"

"Mom."

"It's not about a girl, is it?" She touched my hand. "Please tell me it isn't."

"Mother."

"I understand, times are different than when I was his age." She stood upright, smoothing her blouse. "With the music and the movies now, I know that it can all be so confusing . . ."

"Mom, I swear to you it has nothing to do with a girl," I said, trying to stop her from saying something that would make me blush.

"All right," she said, putting her hands up in surrender. "I'm just worried is all."

"It would be better if he told you."

"Okay." She snapped her purse shut. "I should get back to work anyway."

I nodded.

She touched my cheek with her fingertips. "You're getting so grown up."

"If only I looked it." I pushed up my glasses. "I'm tired of people thinking I'm twelve."

"Someday you'll be glad you look younger." She winked at me.

"Maybe."

"Trust me, you will." She turned her attention to the pastry case, where we kept the desserts from the Dutch bakery down the road. "See if Bernie will let you bring home some leftover *banket* for dessert. Tell him I'll pay him back next week, all right?"

"Sure."

"And your *oma* is coming for supper. She might like it if you walked with her."

She picked up her purse, putting it back over her arm, and walked out of the diner, hips swaying with each step.

Mike reminded her of Frank. She never said it in so many words; still I knew. The way his brown eyes were unable to hide his mood, how his dark hair curled when he let it get long, his deep voice, his dimple-cheeked smile. All of Mike was all of Frank.

The girls at the booth ordered a glass of Coke each and a plate of french fries to share. The whole time they stayed, they watched everyone walk past on the other side of the window, giggling and gossiping.

While they ate, I sat behind the counter, my book unopened with the envelope peeking out, begging me to find out what was inside. I told myself I'd toss it in the mailbox at the end of the street with a big "RETURN TO SENDER" scrawled across it.

But stuffing the book into my purse, I knew I'd do no such thing.

Dear Annie,

I'll bet I was the last one you expected to get a letter from. I hope it was a good surprise, seeing my name on the envelope. No doubt the only reason you opened it was to find out why in the world I would be writing you.

Anyway, I found this feather on the ground over here in Vietnam and thought I'd send it to you. I hope you still like birds. Don't worry, I cleaned it really well. Isn't it pretty?

Wish you could see the birds here. They're like nothing at home. I tried taking a picture of one of them for you, but the ~~tiny~~ thing flew away just as I snapped the shot.

Do you remember when we were kids and we'd watch the hummingbirds flit around the feeder in my front yard? You said they were magic and I wouldn't believe you. You cried, remember, when we found the one that died after it flew into the window. I think about that sometimes, you know. I felt bad that you cried that day. It was so small—impossibly small—and weighed almost nothing at all.

I never told you, but I buried it under my mother's hydrangea tree and marked the grave with a fieldstone. It's still there. When I get home, I can show you if you want.

Your friend,
Walt Vanderlaan

PS: You can write back to me if you'd like. I hope you will.

2

My *oma* lived in a small cottage on Sunny Side Avenue, just a block or so away from our house. She and my *opa* moved into it soon after immigrating to Fort Colson from Amsterdam. They had little more than what could fit into their steamer trunk. But what they lacked in material possessions they made up for in hope.

Hers was a house of yellow siding and white shutters. There was hardly a porch to speak of, and the two bedrooms were barely big enough for the beds and small dressers they contained. The stove in the kitchen was narrow and the counters short. If one wanted to take a bath, one would have to fold in half to fit into the tub.

Everything about the home was tiny. But Oma didn't mind.

"It's just me here now," she'd said. "What do I need a bigger house for? Just to clean it all day long?"

I couldn't imagine her being happy anywhere else.

I rounded the corner to her road, not in a hurry and glad to be outside. The neighborhood was a peaceful kind of quiet that afternoon. The breeze rustled through the leaves, and a cardinal made a *chip-chip-chipping* sound from across the street. I turned to see its bright red feathers where it rested on the branch of a maple.

The creaking of a screen door opening and the clunk of its closing stole my attention. Oma stepped onto her porch, two halves of an orange in her hand. She put the fruit on the small railing and rubbed her hands together.

When she noticed me, she waved me over and I walked along the edge of her yard, breathing in the subtle sweetness of the flowers that grew in well-maintained beds, wishing the tulips would last more than just a few more weeks before they'd be done for the year.

"How are you, Annie?" Oma said, stepping off her porch and meeting me in the yard. "Did you have a good day?"

"I did," I answered, bending to kiss her cheek. "How about you?"

"I can't complain," she said, smiling. "Did you hear that Mrs. Martinez had her baby?"

"I haven't."

"A little girl. They named her Donna," she said, looping her hand through the bend of my elbow. "I haven't seen her yet, of course. But Mr. Martinez told me she has a headful of black hair. Can you imagine? What do you have there?"

She nodded to the paper bag dangling from my hand.

"Some banket from Bernie's."

"I could have baked."

"That's all right," I said. Then pointing at the oranges, "Are the orioles still visiting you?"

"Oh yes. I have to put out an orange almost every day." She smiled. "They strip it perfectly clean."

"Maybe they'll stick around a little longer this year if you keep spoiling them."

"I do hope so."

A neighbor, Mrs. DeJong, walked by, a paper bag of groceries on her hip. Oma gave her the news about the Martinez baby and then the two of them exchanged pleasantries in Dutch. I caught bits and pieces of what they said. But my grasp of the language was embarrassingly bad, despite Oma's efforts to teach me.

"I told Mr. Martinez I'd bring some *saucijzebroodjes* just as soon as they bring the babe home," Oma told Mrs. DeJong. "But for the life of me, I couldn't remember what you call them."

"Pigs in a blanket," I answered.

"That's it. Do you think they'll like them?" she asked.

"I should think so," Mrs. DeJong answered. "Whoever wouldn't?"

"That, I don't know." Oma smiled at Mrs. DeJong. "And will you bring a meal to them too?"

"Of course." Mrs. DeJong nodded and smiled. "I would love to."

Oma had a brand of kindness that involved pure butter, almond paste, and hours of baking in the kitchen. Not a sickness overtook a family in Fort Colson that didn't find its cure in a bowl of her chicken soup. No celebration met a family without a plateful of her cookies wrapped up on the porch. A funeral didn't pass without her arriving in the church before anyone else to cook and leaving last to ensure that all the pans had been scrubbed and put away.

If there was to be crowned a queen of benevolence, it would be my Dutch grandmother, Tess Pipping.

The ladies said their good-byes and Mrs. DeJong asked me to give her love to my mother. Oma took my arm again and whispered to me.

"She has come around," she said.

"I'm sorry?"

"I don't like to be a gossip, but I will now," she said. "When the Martinez family moved into the neighborhood, Mrs. De-Jong was against it. I'll let you guess why."

"Because they're Mexican?" I asked.

She opened her eyes wide and raised her eyebrows to let me know that I was right.

"But I told her that we would welcome them." Oma nodded. "I was a stranger in this land once. It is not easy, being new in this country."

My oma was a good woman. But I didn't tell her that because I knew it would have embarrassed her. Besides, she would have turned it around, reminding me that she could do no good thing without God.

So, instead, I put my hand on top of her fingers that were curled around my arm.

"Should we go?" I asked. "Mom will be waiting for us."

"Yes, I think that's a good idea, dear."

We made our way down the sidewalk, Oma holding on to me not because she needed the support but just because she liked to be near. I didn't mind it at all.

"Now, what's this I hear about you getting a letter?" she asked. "Don't look so surprised. The mailman isn't good at keeping secrets, is he?"

I sighed, conceding that she was right. "It was nothing, really."

"Is it from a sweetheart of yours?"

"No. Just Walt Vanderlaan."

"Oh, him?"

I nodded.

"When I was a girl in Amsterdam, I had a boy at school who wrote me letters. He'd put them in my coat pocket for me to find." She shook her head and laughed softly. "I cannot seem to remember his name at the moment. Old age is the thief of certain memories."

"That's okay."

"Do you know that I kept those silly notes tied in a red bow for years? I would take them out and read them sometimes when I was feeling down." She sighed. "Of course, I threw them out when Ruben came along."

"Didn't Opa ever write you love letters?" I asked.

"He wasn't one for such things." She patted my arm. "Your opa was a practical man. He wasn't much of a romantic."

"Did you ever wish he was?" I asked.

"In the early years, perhaps. I wanted proof of his love, I suppose," she said. "Over time I learned. All I needed was to open my eyes. He lived his love for me every day we were together."

In quiet we walked past the flowers that grew wild against the white picket fence of the house at the corner. Stopping, she touched a sprig of spiky green with little purple blossoms among the nettles that grew up wild beside the whitewashed slats.

"Rosemary," she told me.

"'That's for remembrance,'" I said.

"Shakespeare, eh?"

I leaned over to smell of the plant, its piney-mint aroma

tickling my nose. My book toppled out of my purse, the envelope still peeking out from between the pages, the top edge ragged from where I'd torn it.

Oma noticed and gave me a smile that said she understood.

3

Less than a month after Frank left, Mom put a "for sale" sign in the front yard of the house that backed up to Chippewa Lake. Three days later she signed the papers with the new owners. A week later she had all our things boxed up and packed in the back of our station wagon. Mike and I sat with her in the front bench seat, Joel squeezed in between us.

Three minutes after that, she pulled into a neighborhood across town and told us we were home.

It was a smaller house. Mom called it "cozy." It needed a bit of fixing up. Mom said it had "charm." It was set in closer to the other houses than we were used to. Mom said it was "neighborly."

The day we moved our belongings into that house was the first she'd smiled in too long.

There was little trace of Frank there and only new memories to be made. Memories that wouldn't include him.

The only trouble was that the old days weren't so easy to forget. Still, she did her best.

Oma and I hadn't even reached the front walk before my little brother Joel rushed to the screen door to hold it open for us. At thirteen, he'd grown nearly as tall as me, and I tried to think of when that had happened. It seemed he'd sprouted up overnight.

"Thank you, *lieve*," Oma said, reaching up and patting Joel on the arm.

"Well, you're welcome, Oma." He leaned down and kissed her on the cheek. Then he turned his attention to me. "Did Walt Vanderlaan really send you a letter?"

"How did you hear about that?" I climbed the steps, handing him the paper bag. "That's for dessert, by the way. Don't eat it yet."

"I won't." He tried peeking into the bag to see what I'd brought home. "Is it true? Did he?"

"None of your beeswax," I said. "And try not to tell half the town, all right?"

"Jeepers, Annie. You know I'm good at keeping secrets."

"Don't let Mom hear you say 'jeepers.' She'll make you bite a bar of soap for cursing."

My kid brother was like a tall, lanky teddy bear. A bit of heaven's mercy for Mom. He did not possess an ill-tempered bone in his body. If ever he did get himself into trouble, it wasn't out of mean-spiritedness. Usually, it was more that he was one part naive and another part goofball.

Mom had often said, "I can deal with naughty. What I can't handle is mean."

In all his thirteen years, I had never known Joel to be mean.

I let him hold the screen door for me, and we found Mom in the dining room, a stack of plates in her arms. Oma had gotten to work already, folding the napkins and putting them at each seat.

"Well, I had to send Mike out to pick up supper," Mom said. "I hope nobody minds. It was just too hot to cook."

My mother could do just about anything. She could hem a pair of pants faster than anyone I'd ever met. She kept the doctor's office organized and running without a single hitch or double-scheduled appointment. Never did she leave the house without every hair in place and her makeup done just so. And she'd brought my brothers and me up with a gentle strictness that kept us in line.

Her one failure was in the kitchen. No matter how hard she tried, she never developed a knack for cooking. She could stick to every instruction of a recipe and somehow still get it all wrong. If she had any insecurity, it was in the fact that she could burn a pan of water even if she kept her eye on it.

"Don't worry about it, Mom," Joel said, taking the remaining plates from her and setting them on the table. "We aren't picky."

As if on cue, Mike came in, a bucket of fried chicken in one arm and a bag of sides in the other. The mingling aromas of grease and potatoes and biscuits made their way through the room, and I could have sworn I heard Joel's stomach grumble.

"Hi, everybody," Mike said, smiling. "Hi, Oma. I didn't know you'd be here."

"Give that here." Mom reached for the food, taking it to the table. "Let's eat it while it's still hot."

Mike and I met eyes in the hallway before taking our seats at the dining room table. I raised my eyebrows at him, hoping he'd know what I meant. By the way he nodded, closed his eyes, and smiled, I knew he did.

He mouthed, *I will.*

The five of us sat around the table, eating fried chicken and coleslaw off Mom's everyday plates. Conversation hopped from one topic to another. Weather, last night's church baseball game, stories about the day's work. Mike, however, didn't say much, and when asked a question he gave nothing more than one-syllable answers and he hardly ate more than a drumstick and half of his potatoes.

Mom watched him from her seat on the other side of the round table. Her eyes moved from his downturned face to the way he crumpled the napkin in his left hand. It was something he only did when he was anxious, the crumpling of napkins.

"How did your appointment go, Michael?" Mom asked, narrowing her eyes at him. Somehow she kept suspicion out of her voice.

"Huh?" He lifted his eyes to her as if he was surprised to see her sitting there. "My what?"

She smiled and nodded. "You had an appointment today."

"Right." He sat up straighter before noticing the wilted napkin in his hand. "That. I was going to tell you . . ."

He trailed off and Mom leaned forward, putting her elbows on either side of her plate and lacing her fingers together.

"I have something to tell you," Mike said, looking at her and swallowing hard. "You're going to be mad."

Joel put his fork down, a pile of potatoes still on it. "What's going on?"

"Mom, promise you won't get too upset or worried," Mike said.

I kicked him under the table to let him know he wasn't starting things off so well.

"What?" he asked, turning toward me.

"Michael Francis Jacobson, what have you done?" Mom

asked, her voice stern and eyebrows lowered. "Is it something to do with that Gaines girl? I told you she was trouble."

"No, Mom. No," he said. "Golly."

"Don't curse at the table." She pushed her chair back and shifted to the very edge as if she was preparing to pounce. "I just want to know. What was this appointment about and why didn't you tell me?"

They locked eyes from across the table. His jaw tightened and he breathed in through flared nostrils. She raised a brow and narrowed her eyes even more. It wasn't the first time they'd engaged in such a standoff. I nudged Mike with my elbow, hoping to break the seal of tension.

"I enlisted." He said it so quietly, yet we all heard it like a shout.

"You did what?" Joel asked, turning and squinting at Mike.

"Should I excuse myself?" Oma whispered to me.

"No, please stay," I said.

"I enlisted in the Army," Mike said again, his voice stronger.

"Why'd you go and do that for?" Joel's mouth hung open.

"I was 1-A," Mike answered. "You know what that means?" Joel shook his head.

"It means I would have been drafted anyway." He threw his wrinkled-up napkin onto the table. "I figured it made better sense to join up. At least this way I have a little more choice in how it goes."

He put his hands in his lap, and I wondered if he was trying to keep the rest of us from seeing how they shook.

"This is why I wanted you to go to college," Mom said. "You were accepted and everything. You could have avoided all of this. Do you know how many boys would kill to be in that position?"

"I know."

"How many times did I tell you we'd work the money out?" She waited for him to say something.

"I know you're angry," he said. "You have a right to be. Just know, I didn't see another good choice."

She leaned into the back of the chair and rubbed at her temples with her fingertips. All the fight had fallen from her face. Eyes softened, she looked at Mike the way she had whenever one of us had skinned up a knee when we were little.

"Mike." She sighed his name. "Sweetheart, I'm not mad at you."

"I told the man at the office that I was an Eagle Scout," Mike said. "He said that was good."

Mom nodded and bit at her bottom lip. "Maybe they could put you on a desk job."

"Maybe." Mike shrugged. "I don't know what they'll have me do."

"When do you leave?" Joel asked. His forehead furrowed, and he blinked faster than usual, the way he always did when he was trying not to cry.

"I go Monday morning for basic training."

"Gosh, Mike." Joel shook his head. "But today's Friday."

"I know." Mike couldn't bring himself to look at Joel. "The sooner I go, the sooner I get back."

"You'll do well, honey," Mom said, standing and reaching across the table to put her hand on his cheek. "I'm proud of you."

Under the table, Mike grabbed my hand and gave it a quick squeeze before letting it go. I was glad no one asked me to say anything. I wouldn't have been able to talk if they had. A rock had formed in my throat.

"Annie brought home some dessert," Mom said, lowering herself back into her chair. "Maybe now would be a good time for that."

I breathed in relief and stood to get the banket. It was nothing more than flaky crust wrapped around almond paste. Still, I knew it would help. From what I understood about life, there was nothing so bad that a little Dutch pastry couldn't remedy it.

●

I sat on my bed, Walt's letter resting on my lap, trying to remember the last time he'd given me so much as the time of day. All I could think of was when we were in junior high school and he'd made fun of my glasses in front of all his friends, calling me "four eyes." I recollected how broken my heart was and how I tried to cry secretly so he wouldn't see. It wasn't because the boys had laughed or because it was a zinger of an insult. I'd cried because it was Walt who had said it.

Up until then, I'd still considered him my friend even if at school he'd treated me like dirt.

I held the feather that Walt had folded into the letter up to my bedside lamp. It was mostly green with little shimmers of blue and purple. I wondered how something of such beauty could have escaped the world's notice. But Walt had noticed. And when he did, he had thought of me.

A hissing sound made me jump, and I dropped the feather onto the letter in my lap. Turning, I peeked out my window.

"Psst, Annie," Jocelyn called from the few feet that separated our houses. She was on the other side of her screened-in window, grinning at me. "Did I scare you?"

"No," I lied. "I was just reading."

"Oh, sorry to interrupt."

The first time I saw Jocelyn Falck was when she stepped out of her house and down her front porch for the first day of school. Her family had moved into their house the fall after we'd moved into ours. She had on a red plaid dress and the same kind of saddle shoes I was wearing. When she saw me in my yard, she smiled and waved. That was when I noticed that she had glasses too.

I knew right away that we'd be friends.

Ever since, we'd had nighttime talks through the screens, even sometimes in the winter. I'd never had a friend quite like her.

"How was your day?" she asked, pushing a lock of her dark hair behind her ear.

"All right," I answered. "Mike joined the Army."

Her eyes grew wide, and she let her mouth gape. "He did?"

I nodded. "He leaves on Monday."

"That's so soon."

"I know. I'll tell you about it later." I shrugged. "How was your day?"

"It was all right, I guess. Just a normal workday."

Jocelyn worked as a reporter writing articles for the *Fort Colson Chronicle*. It was a small newspaper operation. Mostly stories about local happenings with a few national stories sprinkled throughout.

"Anything exciting happen?" I asked.

"Nah. It was a slow news day." She smirked. "I wanted to write up something about the race riots in Florida, but the chief said it was too controversial. So, I interviewed a few fishermen who caught a salmon in Old Chip. So, really, I'm living my dreams of being a serious journalist."

"Fishing is serious business," I said.

"Don't I know it." She rolled her eyes. "Oh, and I guess he's hiring a second reporter."

"Huh. That's interesting."

"He said he was worried about me quitting to get married and have babies." She shook her head. "I don't even want to think about that right now."

"Well, I have a bit of news. Aside from Mike. You wanna hear it?"

"Of course I do," she answered, pushing up her wire-rimmed glasses.

"Remember Walt Vanderlaan?"

"Do you realize how many articles I was forced to write about him? Quarterback Walt, homecoming king Walt, vale-dictorian Walt." She sighed. "I only wish I could forget. What about him?"

"He sent me a letter," I said.

"Hold on," she said. "He did? What did he want?"

"I don't know."

"You mean you didn't read it?" She shook her head. "Annie!"

I slumped, leaning my elbow on the windowsill. "I read it. But it was strange. He sent me a feather."

"Excuse me? He sent you a feather? From Vietnam? Is that even legal?"

"I don't know. He said that he remembered how much I liked birds when we were little," I said. "It's a bit unsettling. Does that make sense?"

"Yes. He was a bully," she said. "But why would he write to you? You know he's engaged to Caroline."

We both rolled our eyes. The quarterback and the captain of the cheerleading squad. It was the All-American, gag-worthy love story. A story that, in my less proud moments, I found myself envying. Not that I would have ever admitted such a thing, not even to my closest friend.

"Do you think he wants you to write back?" Jocelyn asked.

I nodded. "He asked me to."

"Are you going to?"

"I don't know. Do you think I should?"

She shook her head as if she had no idea what I should do.

"I'm not going to," I said. "What would I have to say to him? I can't think of a single thing."

"Well, if you're okay with that, I am too." She looked at her wristwatch. "Gosh, I should go to sleep."

"Yeah, me too."

Before she shut off her light, she said my name again.

"Yeah?" I asked.

"Mike will be okay, don't you think?"

"I hope so."

"He's really a good guy." She smiled.

"I guess."

"No, really. He's always been good," she said.

"I'm not sure he ever had the choice not to be."

"I don't think that's true." She shook her head. "He could have chosen to be horrible. But he didn't."

I nodded, that lump forming in my throat again. She told me good night, and we gave each other the peace sign. She turned off her light, and I went back to looking at Walt's letter, laid flat across my thighs.

"I'm not writing back," I whispered, as if to make steady my resolve.

Folding the note and sliding it back into its envelope, the feather secured inside, I reached under my bed for the small cedar chest that held certain treasures I liked to keep for just myself.

Opening the lid, I pushed through the items with my finger. A few old coins that Frank had left behind. A postcard from Jocelyn when she'd visited Niagara Falls with her family. A picture of me and Mike sitting in a boat out in the middle of the lake with Grandpa Jacobson, fishing lines in the water.

I dropped the letter in and snapped the lid shut, as if I didn't want it to fall out and be lost forever. It wasn't the letter I wanted to keep or the feather even, but the memory. The memory of when Walt had still been good.

Across the hall I could hear Joel and Mike in the room they shared, their low voices nothing but a steady humming sound. I couldn't be sure, but I thought Mike was probably reassuring our baby brother that all would be well. No matter what happened, we would all be okay.

Mike was constantly reassuring one of us.

He had chosen to be good. He certainly had.

4

Mike picked me up from work in his pea-green, two-door Corvair. He'd worked two jobs the summer before to save up for that car, and the way he pampered it, everyone knew it was his most prized possession.

"Don't slam the door," he said as soon as I got in on the passenger's side.

"Golly, Mike," I said. "Exactly how strong do you think I am?"

He smirked and revved the engine, taking off as soon as I got settled in my seat.

The drive to our grandparents' house took us on a straight road full of hills. Mike knew every dip and bump and zipped along faster than I liked him to. There wasn't much for me to grab hold of, so I shoved my hands under my thighs and prayed we'd get there in one piece.

"I'm not scaring you, am I?" he asked, turning to look at me.

"Just keep your eyes on the road," I said through clenched teeth.

"Why do you get so scared?" He leaned his elbow out the

open window. "Nothing's going to happen. I'm in complete control."

"You don't know what's on the other side of a hill," I said. "There could be a fallen tree over the road or a deer. Or a person. Mike, you could hit a person!"

"Annie, you can't live your life afraid of what *might* happen."

"Who says I can't?"

"Don't duck and cover, pal." He glanced at me and grinned. "You remember that?"

"How could I forget?" I asked. "I hated those drills. They gave me nightmares."

A memory crossed my mind. Elementary school. The teacher telling us it was time for our duck and cover drill. We crawled under our desks, arms over our heads. This, we were told, would keep us safe if the nuclear bomb exploded.

"You know why they had us do that, don't you?" He slowed for the turn into Grandpa and Grandma's driveway. "It wasn't so we'd be safe. It was just so we wouldn't see what was coming."

●

Grandma Jacobson met us at the front door, giving both of us a kiss on the cheek as we came in. The floor of the entryway creaked under our feet in that comfortable way old houses have. The clock in the living room tick-ticked warmly as if saying hello.

"I didn't expect the two of you today," she said. "Not with this weather. I thought you'd be out swimming or something."

"And miss a visit with you?" Mike said.

"Oh, you." She swatted at him, teasing. "I didn't get around to making cookies."

"You don't have to do that for us," I said.

"Well, I know." She looked out the door. "Didn't Joel come?"

"He had to work."

"He got a job, did he?" Grandma sneezed and took tissues from her pocket. "At his age?"

"Just mowing lawns," Mike answered. "He's saving up for a guitar."

"Well, I wish your mother would let us know he needs money. We could help." She closed the door a little harder than she needed to. She'd never said the words exactly, but I knew she resented Mom. That she secretly believed she'd run Frank off. "You'll tell Joel I say 'hi.' Grandpa does too."

"Sure we will," Mike said. "Say, how is Grandpa doing today?"

"Same as usual," she answered. "He forgets things, you know."

Mike nodded his head. "Grandma, I have to tell you something."

"The draft got you?" she asked, looking up at him. "I knew it. As soon as I saw you pulling up, I knew."

"It would have." He licked his lips. "I enlisted. I leave on Monday for training."

"They'll send you, Michael," she said. "They'll make you go to Vietnam, you know."

"They might."

She nodded and cleared her throat. Her eyes were watery, the closest to crying I'd ever seen her. "Don't try to tell your grandfather. He won't understand."

"I know." Mike leaned his shoulder against the wall. "I just wanted to see him before I left."

She shrugged and looked in the direction of the living room.

"And you," Mike said.

"Well, you've seen me, then." She half-smiled and motioned for us to follow her. "Come on and see Grandpa."

Sunshine poured into the living room through the large windows. No matter how difficult caring for Grandpa was, Grandma kept her house tidy and free of dust. It seemed to be the one way she was able to maintain order in her life.

"Dear," she called as we entered the room. "You have some visitors."

My grandfather, Rockston Jacobson, sat in an easy chair clear to the other side of the room. He held a newspaper in his hand, folded up just so. He didn't seem to be reading it, just holding it. These days he always wanted one; they served almost as a security blanket for him.

"Who's that?" he asked, looking at us with dull, faraway eyes.

"It's Anne and Michael," Grandma answered, speaking louder and slower than she needed to. "Two of Frank's kids."

He looked between the two of us with no recognition. He shrugged and pulled the paper up in front of his face, a barrier to what confused him.

"Give him a few minutes," she told us.

We knew. It had been that way for Grandpa for a long time. It had started with small things, like a misplaced wallet or calling Grandma by the wrong name. Over time, the troubles deepened. He got lost and threw fits and had terrifying waking nightmares that were so very real to him. It seemed to get worse all the time. All that Dr. DeVries told Grandma was that there was no cure. No treatment. That it was just one more unpleasant part of getting old.

"Hi there," Mike said, pulling a footrest close to Grandpa's easy chair to sit on. "How are you feeling today?"

Grandpa lowered the newspaper an inch or two and looked over it at Mike's face. In a flash of recognition, he smiled, showing all of his teeth.

"My boy," he said. "I didn't know you were here. When did you get home? Your last letter didn't say anything about this. Mabel, why didn't you tell me Frank was home?"

"That's not Frank," Grandma half-yelled, shaking her head and crossing her arms. "That's Michael, Frank's son."

"You're lying," Grandpa said, pointing his finger at her, his face reddening. "Don't you think I'd know my own son if I saw him?"

"You're confused. That's Michael." She took a step forward. "Frank hasn't been home in years."

"She's trying to make a fool of me." He looked into Mike's eyes and reached for his hand. "I'm just glad you're here, son. No matter what she says."

"He won't listen to me," she said.

"It's all right," Mike said, holding Grandpa's hand. "Maybe it's better if we don't argue with him."

"I don't know about that."

"Your mother is trying to make me think I'm losing my mind," Grandpa said, glaring at her. "But I'm not."

"I know it, Pop," Mike said, using the name Frank had always used for Grandpa. "She means well."

"I'm not so sure about that." Grandpa hit the newspaper against his thigh. "Won't even let a man have a drink of brandy."

"Maybe she's saving it for something special," Mike said. "What do you think about that?"

"Then we should have it now." Grandpa nodded. "My son's come back home from war. I'd say that's cause for celebration."

"Sure is, Pop." Mike patted his hand.

"You do your old man a favor," Grandpa said, leaning his head closer to Mike's. "Go on out and get my bottle of brandy. I still keep it in the fallout shelter out back on that shelf. You know where, don't you?"

Mike cracked a smile. "I'm not certain I do, Pop."

"Of course you do." Grandpa reached out and knocked him gently on the shoulder. "Don't you remember I caught you down there sneaking a drink just last week?"

"That's right." Mike's voice was flat, like he was trying to hold back emotion. "You caught me all right, didn't you?"

"Did that happen?" I asked Grandma, whispering.

"When your father was seventeen," she answered. "I don't want to talk about it. It isn't a good memory."

She turned and left the room, headed for the kitchen. Mike lifted his head and watched her go.

"Listen, Pop," he said. "Let me see what I can do about that brandy. No promises, but I'll try. How does that sound?"

"Good, my boy." Grandpa rustled Mike's hair. "And while you're at it, get a haircut. You look like a doggone girl."

Mike smiled and got up from the footrest, headed toward the kitchen. I didn't believe he was thinking of giving Grandpa liquor. I thought he went to console Grandma.

"Can I sit with you?" I asked, taking Mike's spot.

"I guess you can," Grandpa answered, frowning. "I'm sorry, dear."

"What are you sorry for?"

"I don't remember you." His chin trembled. "I should know you, shouldn't I?"

"You don't have to feel bad."

"But I do." He cleared his throat. "It seems my mind isn't what it used to be."

"That's all right."

"He writes me every week, you know," he said.

"Who's that?"

"My son," he answered. "Frank. Have you met him?"

"Yes." I leaned toward him. "What does he say when he writes?"

It was Grandpa's favorite thing to talk about, the notes home from Frank. I knew he was telling me about nothing but an old bundle of letters that Frank had sent from Korea, letters that he'd read over and over. Still, I let him talk. Nothing could soothe him like bragging about his son.

I sat and listened to stories from letters that were nearly as old as I was. If I'd tried, I could have recited each in that stack by memory for all the times Grandpa had retold them to me in the last handful of years.

It made me feel guilty, how much I wanted to get back home.

5

Mike had insisted on mowing the lawn after church, even if it was the Sabbath and meant to be kept holy. He trimmed the hedges, swiped at the eaves for gunk, and checked the air in the tires on Mom's car. When I took him a glass of iced tea, I found him in the driveway, finishing up an oil change.

"Mom's not happy that you're doing all of this," I told him, setting the glass next to him. "She said the neighbors are going to talk."

"Well, they can say whatever they want." He wiped his hands on a rag before drinking half the tea in one go. "This is the only time I can do it."

"How much more are you planning on doing?"

"I just need to clean up." He lowered the hood of the car, letting it clunk into place. "I want to make things easier for Mom while I'm gone. I was thinking of going over to do Oma's yard next."

"She wouldn't let you. Not on a Sunday." I crossed my arms. "She'll get after you with her wooden spoon."

"That's true. I just don't want to leave things undone."

"You know Joel and I are sticking around, right?" I leaned up against the car, feeling the heat of the metal through my cotton shorts.

"I know."

He drank the rest of his tea. "I guess this just took my mind off things."

"Are you nervous?"

He shrugged.

"I would be." I took his empty glass from him. "It's all happening so fast."

"It's not that," he said. "I mean, I'm not looking forward to it or anything. But there's something else."

"What is it?"

"Well, I had a little talk with Grandma yesterday," he started. "You know, after she got sore at Grandpa and went into the kitchen?"

I told him I remembered.

"Well, we talked for a few minutes about me leaving." He scratched at his hairline. "Annie, she cried. I hated seeing her like that."

"She's worried about you." I shrugged. "She's probably afraid you'll come back shell-shocked like Frank did."

"Yeah. Maybe," he said. "What if I do?"

"You won't. You're not like him."

"I am." He nodded. "I'm a lot like him."

He opened his mouth to say something else but sighed instead. Licked his lips. Rubbed at his nose with the back of his hand, leaving a black smudge of oil there.

"Mike," I said, crossing my arms, "you're only like him in some ways. But you aren't him. You're different."

He smiled and breathed out his nose.

"I sure am going to miss you," he said. "But don't let it get to your head or anything."

Mom called us inside for little dishes of ice cream. Before we went in, Mike gave me his most earnest face, the one with lowered eyebrows and squinted eyes.

"You'll take care of Grandma, won't you?" he asked.

I nodded. "I'll take care of everybody."

"You promise?"

I did.

6

On most nights when Mom served boiled hot dogs on buns for dinner, we didn't sit at the dining room table. We'd fill our plates with dogs and baked beans and—if we were lucky—handfuls of chips and sit in front of the TV.

But that night, Mom had set the table and put out potato salad that she'd bought from Huisman's Market the day before. She'd even cut up a watermelon, serving the slices on one of her nice platters. She hummed while putting out the ketchup and mustard.

"Annie, will you call the boys for supper?" she said without looking up from her work.

I set my book down and walked to the foot of the stairs. "Boys! Supper!" I yelled.

"Well, that was ladylike," Mom said, shaking her head.

Mike and Joel ran down the stairs, shoving each other out of the way and smiling. So like puppies. Even at nearly twenty, Mike was still so much a little boy.

"No running in the house," Mom called after them. "You're going to break something."

Mom took her seat, as did I. But Mike just grabbed a hot dog and shook a good amount of ketchup on it.

"I'm going out with some of the fellas," he said before shoving at least half the hot dog into his mouth.

"Oh, I just thought . . ." Mom started.

"Can I go?" Joel interrupted her, grabbing a hot dog of his own.

"I guess so," Mike answered, shrugging. "A couple of guys are building a bonfire over at the old campgrounds."

"Is that all right, Mom?" Joel asked. "Can I?"

"No one will be drinking?" she asked. "There won't be girls there?"

"If there's any funny business, I'll bring Joel home. Promise."

Mom sighed and nodded, reaching for the dish of potato salad and serving herself a spoonful. "That's fine."

"Mike," I said, hoping to make him understand that it wasn't fine.

"Sorry," he said. "Just the guys this time, sis."

I tried to catch his eye, but he'd already turned his back on me, heading for the front door. "Come on, champ. Let's shake a leg."

"Keen," Joel said, putting his face close to his plate and scooping the rest of his baked beans into his mouth before picking up his dishes and silverware and taking them to the sink.

He didn't remember to rinse them.

The boys were halfway out the door before Mom called out for Mike to have Joel home by eleven.

"If you want to go, you can," she told me.

"He said it was just for the boys," I answered. "I'd rather stay in, anyway."

"You don't have to." She stabbed at a square potato chunk

54

with her fork. "You could see if Jocelyn wants to do something."

"Are you trying to get rid of me?"

She met my eye and smiled, shaking her head.

After we finished eating we cleaned up the dinner things, not saying too much as we did. It wasn't until I opened the fridge to put away the ketchup and mustard that I saw the cake on one of the shelves. It was round and layered, more than a little lopsided, as most of the cakes Mom made ended up being. It had homemade chocolate frosting spread thick over the top and the sides. I knew if I cut into it, I would have seen white cake. Mike's favorite.

"Mom," I said, holding the door open.

"Don't let all the cold air out," she said, standing at the sink. "It'll keep until tomorrow."

"Why didn't you tell him?" I asked.

She didn't answer but turned off the faucet and flicked the extra water off her hands. "His birthday's next week and we'll miss it. I just realized that this morning."

I shut the refrigerator and turned, leaning back against it. She dried her hands on an already damp hand towel. She wouldn't have grabbed a fresh one from the drawer, I knew it. Not at that time of day. Mornings were for fresh towels. She wouldn't have wanted to dirty another one when the one she'd used all day was good enough.

We poured ourselves tall glasses of iced tea and headed to the living room just in time to watch *The Ed Sullivan Show*. She sat in her chair, one leg tucked up under her. Every couple of minutes she'd sigh before going back to gnawing on her thumbnail. Her tea sat untouched, the sweat running down the glass onto the cork of her coaster.

"I suppose you don't remember when Frank was in Korea," she said in the middle of Spanky and Our Gang singing "Sunday Will Never Be the Same." "You were so small."

I told her I didn't remember, and she nodded.

"I'm glad." She didn't take her eyes from the television. "It was a hard time."

I didn't say anything back to her. I wouldn't have known what to say if I had. She rarely talked about Frank or his war.

"As afraid as I was then, I'm much more afraid now." She rubbed her forehead with the tips of her fingers.

"What are you afraid of?" I asked, just a whisper.

She turned from the TV and looked me straight in the eye. I couldn't read her expression, but I understood its meaning and I instantly felt stupid for having asked her.

"That isn't going to happen," I said with all the resolve I could muster.

Her eyes softened.

You can't live your life afraid of what might happen. That was what Mike had said. *Don't duck and cover.*

Mom turned back to the television to watch the rest of the show.

●

I was up reading on the living room couch when Mike, true to his word, returned Joel home at eleven o'clock sharp. The smell of campfire hung on their clothes and hair. Joel had a busted-up lip, and a bruise was starting to form under his swollen eye.

"Mike," I said, trying to keep my voice down so I wouldn't make Mom come out of her room. "What happened to him?"

Getting up, I went to Joel, touching his bruise and making him wince.

"It's nothing," Joel said, moving his head back and away from me. "Just a little shiner."

"Come on," I said, taking him by the hand and leading him to the kitchen. "We need to get some ice on that."

I shut the door that led to the hallway between Mom's room and the kitchen before getting a few ice cubes out of the freezer and wrapping them in a clean towel.

"Don't bleed on it," I warned Joel, handing it to him. "Mom would be furious."

He held it, just barely touching the skin over his cheekbone, and grimaced.

"What happened?" I turned on Mike. "You were supposed to be watching out for him."

He smirked into his half smile. "We were just playing a game of football on the beach, that's all. Joel was a wide receiver, and Adam tackled him."

"Adam Main?" I asked. "He's four heads taller than Joel."

"And our kid took it like a champ." Mike looked at our baby brother with eyes full of pride.

Joel smiled before sucking in a pained breath. "Gosh, it hurts to smile." He moved the ice down to his lip. "You think it'll scar?"

"I don't know," Mike answered. "Let me see it. Nah. It's not near deep enough."

"Rats."

"Well, I'm glad you boys had a good time," I said, leaning back into the counter and crossing my arms. "Did you know Mom made you a cake?"

"What for?"

"It's a birthday cake," I answered. "For you."

"Aw, Mike," Joel said. "We're going to miss your birthday."

"And she wanted to have it after supper."

"Why didn't she say anything?" Mike asked.

I shrugged. "You know how she is."

"She was upset." It wasn't a question. Mike knew enough. I nodded.

"She still up?" he asked.

"I'm not sure."

"I bet she is," he said. "She never sleeps when she's angry. Listen. I've got an idea to make this right."

Joel and I heard him out. True to form, Mike had a pretty good plan to smooth things over.

●

"You awake in there?" Mike asked through Mom's door. "Dear, sweet mother of mine?"

He waited another few seconds before she answered that she was.

"May we come in?"

"Who's 'we'?" she asked.

"Lyndon Baines and Ladybird Johnson and their pet dog Freckles," Mike answered. "Come on, pal. Let us in."

"Fine," she answered. "But don't call me 'pal.'"

Mike used one hand to open the door, the other to carry in a single rose he'd had Joel steal from the yard of a neighbor across the street. I followed behind him with the lopsided cake. Joel came last with a stack of plates and a fork for each of us.

"What are you kids doing?" she asked from where she sat on top of the covers, magazine open on her lap.

"We're having a birthday party for me," Mike said, handing her the rose. "Is that okay with you?"

"It's so late," she said, looking at the alarm clock on her bedside table. "We have to be up early to get you to the station."

"None of us are going to sleep tonight anyway." Mike winked at her. "We might as well have some cake with our insomnia."

She looked up at him out of the corner of her eye and shook her head, trying not to let herself smile too big. "You kids better not get any crumbs on my bedspread."

Pulling her legs to the side, bent at the knees, she made room for us on the bed. The mattress creaked a complaint under all of our weight. I served up oversized slices of the cake, which Mom said were too much but the boys declared just right.

"Don't tell Grandma," Mike said, a bite of cake shoved into his cheek. "You know how jealous she gets. But this is the best cake I've ever had."

"Don't talk with your mouth full." Mom shook her head and rolled her eyes, but still I could tell she was flattered even if she knew he wasn't telling the truth.

It wasn't until Mom was halfway finished eating her cake that she noticed Joel's face. When they told her what had happened, she sighed.

"That's what I get for having two boys."

But then she glanced down at the rose she'd put on her bedside table and smiled.

Hey, Annie.

Don't be too upset that we left without waking you up. This might not make a lot of sense to you, but I don't think I could have faced you without losing my cool. You wouldn't want to see your big brother crack up, would you? You can let me have it later.

I wanted to tell you something last night before bed, but I'm a yeller-bellied old dog.

Take a deep breath before you read on, all right? You might be angry at me and you might be upset. That's okay. Ready?

I found Frank.

Or at least I found a way to get ahold of him when we need to.

Remember yesterday how I told you that Grandma was crying? It wasn't because of me leaving for the Army. That didn't bother her at all, really. She said she worried that if something bad happened to me that Frank wouldn't find out right away. Then she asked me if I'd list him as a next of kin should I find out where he was.

I told her I'd do it in a heartbeat.

Annie, you have to promise that you won't be mad at her. Do you swear? She's known where he is all this time. She admitted that she lied when Mom asked her if she knew.

Please don't be angry at her. She did what she thought was right, as odd as that might seem to you and me. I guess he made her promise to keep it a secret. Right or wrong, she kept to her word.

Well, until yesterday, that is.

Promise me one more, will ya? If anything happens to me, you've got to let Frank know. I'll put his address at the bottom of this note. But only get ahold of him if you absolutely have to. We don't want to scare him off, do we?

Don't tell Mom, not yet at least. Got it? She'll blow a gasket if you do and storm whatever house or apartment Frank's holing up in and beat the snot out of him. Let's hold off on such a spectacle until absolutely necessary. Sound good?

Write me, will you? Mom's got the address, and I picked up a mess of stamps for you all. They're in the drawer by the telephone.

Oh. And be extra nice to Joel for a week or so. I think this is hardest on him.

I love you (I guess).

Mike

PS: I told Bernie to hire somebody in my place. He'll forget. You might want to remind him.

Where to reach Frank if need be:

Frank Jacobson
437 Magnolia St.
Bliss, MI

7

The morning had brought unexpected rain that hadn't let up by lunchtime. From inside the diner I couldn't even see across the street for the dense downpour. Thunder and lightning accompanied it, meaning any business we might have had was thin at best.

Mike had been gone six days and, as far as I knew, nobody had come in to inquire about the "help wanted" sign Bernie had hung in the window. That meant that, on top of taking orders, delivering food, and handling money, I also had to bus tables and scrub dishes. I really didn't mind the slower pace of that Saturday morning.

Bernie, however, was of a different mind.

We'd hardly served half a dozen at breakfast and only gone through two of the four pots of coffee I'd brewed. Saturdays were usually our busiest day. The empty booths had Bernie in a mood most foul.

"That costs, you know," Bernie said, watching as I poured the wasted coffee down the sink.

"I know," I said.

"That's ten cents a cup I won't be making." He went to wiping down the counter. "A dollar twenty each pot."

"We always make four pots," I mumbled.

"Not always," he grumbled. "You should have only made one at a time. What a waste."

"Take it out of my paycheck." It surprised me, the edge in my voice. Mom would have been proud of me for sticking up for myself, but it didn't seem right to me, speaking to an adult like that. I tried to apologize, but it just came out as a little squeak.

Bernie shook his head at me and went back into the kitchen, letting the door swing in-out-in-out-in behind him. I was certain he would have fired me on the spot if he'd had someone else working for him. As it was, he needed me to get through the lunch hour. If anyone came in, that was.

Putting the empty pots back near the coffeemaker, I went to the window, looking out into the rain. I hated how my hands shook, and I crossed my arms trying to still them. It bothered me how a little conflict like having made too much coffee could make me all kinds of jittery.

I tried to think of something else, something that could take my mind off being upset at Bernie.

At first, my brain wanted to worry over Frank's address that I'd hidden in the cedar box I kept stowed away under my bed. I'd gone to the library after my shift the day Mike left, trying to figure out where Bliss, Michigan, was. But it was, apparently, so small that it didn't even make it on the map.

The temptation to write to Frank overwhelmed me. It needled me when I tried to sleep, the address burning a hole in my little box. All there was to do was put it out of my mind completely.

So, I let my thoughts wander to Walt Vanderlaan. His second letter had arrived the day before. Lucky for me, I'd been the one to get the mail, so I didn't have to talk to Mom about it. I'd opened it up in my room with the door locked just in case.

I tried sending you one of the coins they use over here. But someone told me it wasn't allowed, he'd written. *Maybe they'll let me bring one back when my time here's through.*

I remember when we were kids. You had a coin collection, didn't you? he'd continued. *You had it on the bus with you one day, remember? I teased you about it and you made a face back at me for it. I think you even stuck your tongue out at me. You thought I was being mean. Really, it was because I liked you.*

How are you? Please write me a letter, he'd penned at the end of his brief note. *I'd like to hear from you. If you've got the time, that is.*

I tried to think about what I'd write to him, but my thoughts were interrupted by the diner door opening to let in five men dressed in fishing hats and vests with more pockets than were necessary. I was sure that if I caught a glimpse of their tackle boxes and fishing poles that I'd see they'd spent far more than they needed to at the bait-and-tackle shop down the road.

We didn't get too many people from out of town that came to Fort Colson. But when we did, they came to fish Old Chip in rented boats, leaving with trout or sunfish that, in their retelling, grew to salmon and bass.

The sound of rain pouring on the roof was rivaled by the deep voices of the men. They smelled of tobacco and the strong bite of aftershave and pomade. Even if we didn't get a lot of city people coming to town, I still could sniff them out.

"Looks like our table's open," one of the men said, winking at me. He pointed at table two. "We usually sit there."

"Go ahead. I'll be right with you," I told them.

"We don't need menus, honey," another said. "You just tell him back there that we're here. He knows what we want."

"All right," I said. "Coffee?"

"Sure thing."

I got a fresh pot of coffee brewing and went to the pass-through window between the dining room and the kitchen.

"There's a table of men here," I said. "They told me you'd know what they would want."

He looked around me at them and nodded. "Rare?"

"I don't know."

"Listen, these men come a couple of times every year. They order a lot and tip well," he said, meeting my eye. "Still, I want you to watch out for them."

"Why?"

"Just do."

He turned and got started on the steaks, and I carried the coffeepot to the table, reaching between the men to pour it.

"Now, where's the kid who usually takes care of us?" a man with slicked-back dusty-colored hair asked. "Mark, right?"

"Mike. He left for basic training last week." I held the pot in front of me.

"Drafted?"

"No. He enlisted."

"Well, either way I hope he gives them heck."

"My boy's over there," another of them said, squinting at me over his mug. "You believe that? I've got a kid old enough to be in the Army."

"I wouldn't have guessed," I said, lying.

"Now, what's your name, sweetheart?" the squinting man asked, his eyes flicking up and down my body so fast I wasn't sure if they really had.

"Annie," I answered, trying to hide how uncomfortable I felt.

"That's a pretty name."

"Thank you." I smiled.

"And that's a pretty smile."

"Your food should be out soon."

As I walked away, one of them called after me, "Oh, Don, you went and scared her off. Honey, he don't bite."

I looked over my shoulder and tried to laugh even if I didn't think it was funny. The man named Don followed me with his eyes the way I thought maybe a fox would watch a rabbit.

Waiting behind the counter, I was glad it didn't take long to cook a rare steak. Bernie took three of the plates to the table, leaving only two for me. With him there, the men were quieter, paid me less attention.

After giving them a little time to eat their food, I took the coffee around and refilled their cups. When I got to the squinting man, he looked up at me. I could see from his face that he'd been good looking at one time. Hints of it still lined his jaw and sparkled in his bright eyes. His wasn't an unkind face, but there was something about him that made me feel antsy, unsettled.

He put his meaty fingers around my wrist, the one not

holding the coffeepot, and he pulled me closer to him. He wrapped his arm around my waist.

"You're doing a good job," he said. "We like you. Don't we, boys?"

The men at the round table guffawed and nodded.

"You don't have to be so tense," Don said. "Lighten up. I swear we won't hurt you."

"Yes, sir," I answered, my voice shaking and wrist sore from how hard he'd held on to it.

"I wonder what you would look like without those glasses." He narrowed his eyes. "You ever go without them?"

I swallowed, not knowing what to say to him and trying to think of a way to make him let go of me. My mind had chosen the very worst time to go absolutely blank.

"Oh, never mind. How about you just get us some pie, huh?" He smirked at me while he moved his hand slightly along my lower back. "With a little ice cream too."

He let me go, and I took a step away from him. Just then I felt his hand tap my rear end and heard all the men at the table erupt with laughter.

My instinct was to turn and slap him across the face like Katharine Hepburn would have in a movie. Then I thought about slugging him in the nose the way Mike would have wanted me to. It occurred to me that I could give him an earful the way Mom would have done. But before I could do any of that, Bernie slammed through the kitchen door and stormed across the room, white blind rage in his eyes.

"Did you just touch her?" he asked, his voice a growl. "I'm talking to you."

The man named Don leaned back in his chair and jutted out his chin. "And what if I did?"

"Get out of my diner."

"Oh, come on." The man scowled and looked like a kid who'd gotten caught cheating on a test.

"I mean it." Bernie went around the table and hooked his hand in the man's bent elbow, pulling him to stand, sending the chair banging against the wall. "Get out."

"Listen here . . ." the man said in protest.

"You don't touch a lady like that."

"Who did I touch?"

"I'm not stupid and I'm not blind." Bernie pulled him to the door.

"You can't make me go out there," Don said. "It's raining."

"Tough." Bernie pushed the door open. "Don't come back."

The man tried to shove him off, but Bernie was at least a head taller and a good deal broader. He turned and looked at the men at the table.

"Did any of you stand up for her?"

Not a one of them said a word.

"No?" he asked. "Then you all go too. You aren't welcome here anymore."

He held the door for them until they'd all exited, their lunches half-eaten and the bill left unpaid. Shutting the door, Bernie locked it and turned the sign to "closed" before going back to the kitchen.

I didn't know what else to do, so I started bussing the table, carrying the dishes to the kitchen to scrape and wash them. There I found Bernie standing over the counter, his fingers curled around the edge. He breathed in and out through flared nostrils. His face was the brightest red I'd ever seen it.

"You okay?" he asked, his voice still gruff, his jaw still set.

I nodded, lifting the stack of plates onto the counter beside the sink.

"Some men . . ." he started, then bit at his lip. "Well, they don't respect women. They think they have power over them."

"I know." I shifted my weight and shoved my hands into the pockets of my apron, not wanting to talk to him about what had happened, I was so embarrassed.

"Don't let anybody treat you like that, all right?" He turned his face and caught my eyes. "You fight back."

"Okay."

"You have two brothers," he said. "I assume you know how to punch."

I nodded.

"Aim for the nose." He stood up straight and looked at the sink. "I'll do up those dishes. You can go home."

I reached behind me to untie my apron and couldn't seem to hold back the tears. Bernie cleared his throat before taking the hanky out of his jeans pocket.

"It's clean," he said, handing it to me.

"Thanks," I managed.

"What a day, huh?"

I nodded. "I'm sorry," I said, rubbing the soft cotton under my eyes.

"You didn't do anything wrong."

He turned and got started on the dishes, dumping the half-eaten steaks and piles of fries into the trash. I could almost see him calculating how much money he'd lost that day.

"I've got a kid coming to fill in for Mike," he said, his back to me. "He starts on Monday. I might need you to teach him the ropes."

"Okay."

"I'll see you at church tomorrow."

I grabbed my umbrella and stepped out the back door to the alley, grateful that the rain had eased up, even if only a little. Looking up at the clouds where the sun tried to break through, I thought about how nice it would be to see a rainbow.

Dear Walt,

Thank you for your letters. I apologize for being so late in writing back. I've been working a lot so far this summer. Also, Mike left for basic training a week ago.

It's a sorry excuse, I know, but I've been a bit busy.

Not much is new around Fort Colson, aside from Mike being gone.

I realized the other day that I never had the chance to congratulate you on your engagement to Caroline. You two make a nice couple and I wish you all the happiness possible.

You're on my prayer list, where you'll stay until you come home.

Sincerely,
Annie Jacobson

8

Quietly as I could, I got myself ready for work, waiting to put my shoes on until I was out the door so I wouldn't wake Mom or Joel. Banana in hand, book in the bend of my elbow, shoes dangling from fingers, I stepped out onto the front porch.

The air was crisp that morning in a way that would fade as the day wore on. The sky held the satiny color of blue that promised an explosion of vibrant hues in just a matter of minutes as the sun lifted up, breaking the darkness by inches.

Since I was small, I'd loved the still of morning. It was why I didn't mind taking the job at Bernie's. I could have time to myself first thing, without anyone interrupting. Early mornings were the best for solitary walks because nobody else in Fort Colson got up so early as I did. Except for Bernie, but he just lived in an apartment above the diner. There was no chance of running into him on the way to work.

Before stepping off the porch, I shoved my feet into my low-top sneakers that were still tied from the day before.

Mom hated that I wore those shoes. She hated even more that I'd stolen them from Joel when his feet had outgrown them in the winter. He'd only gotten to wear them once or twice.

With a lazy, in-no-hurry stride, I made my way down our front walk and onto the street, taking in the morning and glad for the sweater I'd grabbed on my way out of my bedroom.

Checking my watch, I saw that I had a few minutes to sit by Old Chip. I made my way down the dirt road that served as a public access to the lake and sat myself down on the rickety dock.

It was light enough for me to see the letter I'd been writing for the past few days. I would have been embarrassed to admit that I'd drafted more than one edition of the note, especially for as little as I'd written in it. Most of the drafts had ended up crumpled and tossed in my bedroom waste paper basket, hidden under tissues so that my mother wouldn't find and read them.

The last thing I needed was for her to know that I'd written to Walt.

For the slimmest of moments, I contemplated tossing the letter into the lake and watching it sink to the bottom. But I thought better of it, tightening my hold of it and standing up.

I'd already affixed a stamp to the upper right-hand corner of the envelope, and my Dutch heritage prevented me from even entertaining the thought of wasting it. I was committed. I left the dock, making my way to the main street of town. I dropped it into the mail slot of the post office just before I walked toward work.

I had more than a few twinges of regret throughout the morning.

●

Bernie had hired a high school boy who I didn't think had ever been made to wash dishes in all his life. When Bernie told him to get to scrubbing, the kid looked at the soapy water and the stack of breakfast dishes as if they might attack him should he get too close to them.

"He'll toughen up," Bernie whispered to me as we stood back and watched the kid pull a pair of yellow rubber gloves onto his hands.

"Let's hope," I said.

The kid winced when he put his hands into the hot water.

Bernie kept the "help wanted" sign close at hand just in case.

I spent most of the morning showing him how to scrub and wipe, rinse and dry. While we worked, I asked him questions, and he was more than happy to provide me with answers. His name was Larry Roberts and he lived in a neighborhood on the other side of Old Chip with his folks and three little sisters. His dad had been in Vietnam for about three months. A career Marine whose shoes Larry was eager to fill once he was old enough to enlist. Once he got talking, the words came tumbling from him, and I wondered if having three sisters in the house left little room for him to say much of anything.

In fact, by the time I left his side to prepare the dining room for the lunch rush, he was still chattering on about something or another.

I thought Larry was going to work out just fine. For the rest of the summer, at least.

●

I'd left Larry to the dishes after the lunch service was done and stood at the counter to wrap clean silverware in paper napkins for the next morning's breakfast crowd. Bernie had found himself in a good mood and let us turn the radio on. Not only that, but he'd allowed me to pick the station.

My back to the door, I hummed along with the Beatles about holding hands and feeling happy inside. I couldn't hardly help but let my head bob along with the music. Caught up with the song, I didn't hear the bell above the door as it jangled a welcome. I didn't realize anyone was standing at the counter, waiting for me, until he spoke.

"Excuse me, miss," he said.

I spun around, gasping and holding my hand to my chest.

"I'm sorry," he said. "I didn't mean to frighten you."

The man on the other side of the counter had dark skin, brown eyes behind a pair of Coke-bottle lenses, wide smile.

"It's all right," I said, reaching for the radio and turning down the volume. "I didn't hear you come in."

"Are you all right?"

"Sure." I breathed in deeply. "Can I get you anything?"

"Actually, I was wondering if it was too late to order lunch."

"Of course not." I looked at my wristwatch. "We're open for another hour or so."

"Great. Should I just find a seat?"

"Right. Yes. You can sit wherever you like."

"Thanks." He took the table closest to the coffeemaker and unrolled his silverware. "So, what's good here?"

"Everything," I said, stepping out from behind the counter and to the end of his table. "The special is an open-faced roast beef sandwich with either french fries or mashed potatoes."

"That sounds good." He looked around at the empty tables. "Is it always this quiet?"

"Only at two o'clock in the afternoon," I said. "Fries?"

"Sure," he answered.

I scribbled his order on my pad of paper. "Are you just in town for the day?"

"Well, it looks like I might be moving here," he answered. "I just took a job with the parks department."

"Congratulations, then," I said. I put out my hand. "I'm Annie."

"Hi there," he said, taking my hand. "I'm David Ward."

"It's nice to meet you."

"Likewise."

"I'll have him get this started for you." I went behind the counter and called through the window to let Bernie know we had an order.

While I waited, I hummed along again with the radio. Just not loudly enough for anybody to hear me.

●

David paid for his lunch, standing at the register waiting to hand me his money. It took a little persuading for the cash drawer to come out. My persuasion came in the form of shoving it with the meat of my hand more than a few times before it shot out, the coins jangling violently in the slots.

"I think this thing was made at the turn of the century," I said, trying to distract from my embarrassment.

"Maybe it's time for a new one," David said, waiting for me to make change.

"Oh, the boss will keep this one as long as he can still order parts for it," I said, dropping three quarters and a penny into his outstretched palm. "Dutch thrift."

"Dutch what?"

"You haven't been around many Dutch people, have you?"

"Not that I know of." He leaned his elbows on the counter.

"Well, you'll have to get used to us if you're moving into this town. Most of us are at least a little Dutch." I slammed the drawer shut again. "Dutch people are frugal."

"You mean cheap?"

"Don't let anybody hear you say that," I warned, half-smiling. "They just don't like spending money if they can help it."

He shrugged one shoulder. "Well, I think that makes a lot of sense."

"I suppose so." I grabbed a round, white mint from the little dish Bernie kept by the cash register and popped it into my mouth. "So, where are you from?"

"Lansing," he answered. "Have you ever been there?"

"Yes. Just once or twice."

"Let me guess, you went to see the Capitol?" He pushed up his glasses. They were black framed like the ones Buddy Holly had always worn.

"We went to the zoo too."

"Well, I grew up down the road from that zoo." He wrinkled the space between his eyebrows and shook his head. "I'll tell you, it's strange to wake up in the middle of the night to the roar of lions."

"I'll bet it is."

"How long have you lived here?"

"All my life," I answered.

"This might seem like a funny question, but are there any other black people around?"

"Um, maybe a few," I said, thinking. "Not very many, though."

"That's what I thought." He tossed the change up and down in the palm of his hand. "It's a whole different world from Lansing."

"Hopefully you'll like it here."

"I do so far." He handed me two of the quarters. "Nice to meet you, Annie. Maybe I'll see you around."

"I'm here every day but Sunday." I held up the coins. "Thanks."

"You're welcome."

I watched him walk out the door, hoping he might turn and look at me. When he did, I couldn't help but smile.

●

"Did you know that they hired someone new at the parks department?" I asked through my window. "He had lunch at the diner."

"I didn't know that," Jocelyn answered from her side of our screens. "What's he like?"

I leaned my chin on my hand. "Nice."

"Annie Jacobson!"

"What?"

"I know that face."

"So?" I narrowed my eyes at her but couldn't help but smile. "He's nice."

"Uh-huh. You already said that." She shook her head. "What does he look like?"

"Well, he wears glasses and has a friendly smile and kind eyes." I sighed. Then I lowered my voice to a whisper. "And he's black."

"He's what?" she asked.

"He's black." I shrugged.

"What would your mother think, though?"

"She doesn't have to think anything. I'm sure he didn't even notice me." I tilted my head. "I'm not getting my hopes up."

"Hope can be pretty nice sometimes, though."

"Maybe." I sat up straighter. "Anyway, I sent Walt a letter."

"Really?" she asked. "What did you say?"

"Nothing much. Just that I'm praying for him."

"Well, I think it's nice of you." She nodded. "Did you tell your mother about it?"

I shook my head. "And I'm not going to."

"That's probably for the best."

Of all the things that Mom had to worry about, I didn't want to be one of them. More because I didn't want her fussing over me and insisting on one of her sit-down talks. She'd see the letter as the cry of a lonely, lovesick girl in need of attention, even though nothing could have been further from the truth.

No matter how I protested, Mom would find a way to fret over me writing a handful of sentences to a boy eight thousand miles away.

I hoped she wouldn't hear about it.

For at least the tenth time that day I regretted dropping the letter in the mailbox.

Dear Mike,

Happy Birthday! I highly doubt that anyone sang to you or let you blow out candles. Bummer. But we're thinking of you here at home, wishing we could feed you more cake even if it's one Mom made (ha ha).

Mom said the reason we haven't heard from you was because you needed to focus on your training. I understand. But Joel's antsy to get a note. I guess he had a bad dream the other night. Something to do with you, but he wouldn't tell me anything else. He made me promise not to say anything to Mom about it.

If you have even a minute, could you please write him so he knows you're okay? I half wonder if he thinks you're already fighting the communists. Poor kiddo.

Take care of yourself, all right? And don't forget to write to Joel.

Love,
Annie

PS: Oma wants to know when she can send you cookies.

9

If Fort Colson legend was to be believed, the town started as an outpost for fur trappers before Michigan had even joined the union. Eventually, for reasons I never quite understood, Dutch immigrants settled the land. Following God's call to be fruitful and multiply, they brought forth upon the earth as many children as they could bear. It wasn't long before houses and shops and such popped up all along the shores of Chippewa Lake.

Right in the middle of the town they'd constructed a church. Over time it was leveled and rebuilt. Ours was a modest church with clear glass windows instead of stained and blocky wooden pews with no embellishment. But what we lacked in fancy, we made up for with heart.

The people of the First Christian Reformed Church of Fort Colson were rich in mercy and generous with their love.

It was the Sunday before the Fourth of July and all of the hymns listed on the register board were of a patriotic flavor. "God Bless America" and "The Battle Hymn of the Republic," closing with all four verses of "The Star-Spangled Banner."

The ever-present American flag was moved from behind the pulpit to right beside it.

When I looked through my bulletin, I saw that on the prayer card the secretary had included "Pray for our boys over there." In bold type was my brother's name. I dragged my fingertip over the letters, asking God for some way that Mike might be able to stay over here.

When I looked up from where we sat in the second row on the right-hand side of the sanctuary, I saw that Mrs. Vanderlaan held her prayer card up, reading it. When she noticed that I was looking at her, she flashed me a small smile, like she wasn't sure it was all right to.

I smiled back.

From the first time Walt had made fun of me, Mom had blamed Mrs. Vanderlaan. She'd called her on the telephone to ask her if she could keep her son in line. When Walt's mother had denied that her son would ever say such a thing, Mom had hung up on her, vowing to never speak to the woman again.

Mom's grudge didn't have to be mine.

●

"Gloria," Mrs. Vanderlaan said, approaching us in the narthex after the service. "Hi."

Mrs. Vanderlaan was of sweet face, soft features, hazel eyes. She dressed like they had money, always had. It was the way Mom had dressed before Frank left. I sometimes wondered if Mom resented the reminder of how her life had once been.

"Elizabeth," Mom said back to her.

"I saw Michael's name on the list." She held up the prayer card as if Mom wouldn't have seen it. "Was he drafted?"

"He enlisted," I answered. "In the Army."

"Good for him." Mrs. Vanderlaan kept her eyes on Mom. "Walter is in the Marines."

"Yes." Mom raised an eyebrow. "I read the article about him."

"Well, I'll pray for Michael." Mrs. Vanderlaan slipped the prayer card into her purse. "Do you need a service flag? Someone gave me an extra one, and I certainly don't need two of them hanging in my window. I'd be happy to let you have it."

"I have one," Mom said.

"Of course you do," Mrs. Vanderlaan said with not a hint of condescension, although I was sure Mom heard one. "Well, I'll be going now. Nice to see you."

Mom turned her eyes away, looking at a brick wall across the room.

"Nice to see you too, Mrs. Vanderlaan," I said.

As soon as she left, walking out the heavy wood door, Mom turned toward me and whispered, "You don't have to be nice to her."

"You don't have to be rude," I said back.

Mom pursed her lips in irritation and made her way to the door. I followed after her, thinking how exhausting it must be to hold so tightly to conflict.

10

Fourth of July morning was unseasonably cool. Opting for my navy-colored pedal pushers and pulling a red cardigan over my white T-shirt, I headed downstairs for the morning. An excitement swelled in my chest for the day. It was childish, I knew that. But I couldn't help but anticipate the crowds at the parade, the floats and later the fireworks.

I was glad that Bernie had decided to keep the diner closed for the day.

In the kitchen, Mom had a box on the table, its contents strewn around it. She was still in housecoat and rollers, the slippers she'd gotten for Christmas on her feet.

"It's cold out," she said, not looking up at me as I went to the cupboard for a mug. "You'll want a sweater."

"I'm already wearing one." I took down my favorite cup, a white one with an orange rooster crowing at a rising sun that had long ago worn off the ceramic. "Would you like some tea?"

"No," she answered. "Thank you, though."

"What are you looking for?" I asked, grabbing the kettle from the stove and putting it under the faucet.

"Oh, the old service flag. I've been looking for it since Sunday." She picked up a cubed jewelry box, considered it, then put it among the rest of the items. "You haven't seen it, have you?"

"No." I put the kettle on to boil and moved to stand next to her, looking into the box. "What is it?"

"It's just a cotton rectangle with a red border and blue star in the middle," she said. "We had it in the window when Frank was in Korea. It just lets everyone know that a family member is at war. I wanted to put it up for Michael."

"Are you sure you kept it?" I asked.

Years before while packing up the old house to move to the new one, Mom tossed nearly everything she found that reminded her of Frank. His shaving kit and Brylcreem. The underwear he'd left behind in his drawers and all of the records he'd enjoyed listening to. If anything was of value, she sold it. All other things went out to the curb for the trash collector to gather. She'd said it was so we'd have fewer things to move. But I knew that wasn't the whole reason.

"Maybe I'll just have to order a new one." One by one, she picked up what she'd unloaded, piling it back into the box. "I guess I didn't think ahead. Your water's boiling."

The kettle stopped its high-pitched whistle when I turned off the gas. I poured the water over my tea bag, the steam full of the scent of herbs and earth.

"I wish you'd known him before," she whispered.

"Who's that?" I asked.

"Frank." She shook her head. "I'm sure you hardly remember him."

"I do. Mostly the way he was after the war."

"I'm sorry about that."

She picked up the box, carting it back to her bedroom closet where she kept it hidden among the skirts of her wedding dress.

That dress was almost another casualty of what Mike sometimes called "Operation Frank Removal." But, all those years before, as she crumpled it in her arms to dump in the trash can, her face had changed, as if something inside had let loose. With just a hint of emotion, she had carried it right back to her room, smoothing the bodice and the train, fitting it back into its protective case.

From the kitchen, I could hear her wrestling with it once more as she fit the box back into the space where it would be cloaked by the skirt.

The Frank she'd worn that dress for hadn't come back from Korea. Instead, a different man returned. One haunted by explosions and death and the stink of war.

Blowing over the top of my tea, sending wisps of steam over the water, I prayed that Mike wouldn't have to go to Vietnam. And if he did, that he'd come home just the way he'd left.

●

If we climbed onto the roof of our house, we could see the fireworks light up the sky over Old Chip. Ours was a modest display. I was sure it was nothing compared to the one Grand Rapids or Lansing put on. Still, it was our celebration, and no amount of mosquitoes could keep us from it.

Joel and I reclined on the roof, our knees bent and heads resting just on the peak. Mom had opted to sit with Oma on the porch swing, the two of them chatting quietly, not as interested in the show as we were.

"You know who Jimi Hendrix is?" Joel asked, turning his head to look at me.

"I don't live under a rock," I answered.

"Do you know what the Monterey Pop Festival is?"

I sighed. "Yes, but I know you'll tell me anyway."

"It was in California. All the rock stars were there. You know what Jimi Hendrix did?"

"Nope."

"He lit his guitar on fire."

"Why would he do that?" I asked.

"I don't know." Joel smiled. "But it's pretty groovy, isn't it?"

"No. It's stupid."

"I bet he has a hundred guitars." He crossed his arms. "If I had a hundred guitars, I wouldn't think twice about setting one on fire."

"You don't even have one."

"Yeah, I know." He smacked a mosquito on his neck. "As soon as I save up enough to buy one, I'm getting a band together. Andy said he'd teach me how to play."

"That would be cool."

Purple sparks blasted across the sky, the sound of it echoing off the trees and houses.

"What do you think Mike's doing now?" Joel asked.

"I don't know," I answered. "Maybe the same thing as we are."

"I bet the Army's got better explosions than we do."

I smiled. "Probably."

Green blazed, then yellow and blue.

"Do you think he'll have to shoot anybody?" He rolled his head on the shingles, looking at me. "I mean in Vietnam."

When I shrugged, I felt the roughness of the roof scratch at my shoulders through my sweater. "He might."

"I wouldn't be able to live with myself."

"I guess you'd do what you had to in order to stay alive."

Orange bloomed, then red and white.

"Some guys go over there and just dig latrines all day," Joel said.

"Who told you that?"

"Pete."

"How would he know? He's what, twelve?"

"Maybe Mike'll do that," he said, ignoring my question. "Then he won't have to kill anybody."

We watched the last of the fireworks before climbing back down the ladder to the ground. Mom and Oma were heading inside for cups of hot tea. Joel went in for a cookie that Oma had promised earlier in the evening.

I stayed outside, sitting on the porch steps, pulling my cardigan close around me.

All the happenings of that day—the parade and fireworks and hot dogs and Fort Colson full of red-white-and-blue—were to celebrate independence. Independence won through fighting.

Every American war, including the Revolution, had required a Jacobson. Not all of them had made it home.

I was no hippie or flower child or anything like that. Not by a long shot. But I would have been happy if the war would just end.

As much as Uncle Sam thought he needed Mike, we needed him more.

Dear Mom, Annie, and Joel,

Well, I made it through the first two weeks here at basic training. You wouldn't recognize me if you saw me now. My hair is cut all the way down to the scalp (all my beautiful curls, swept into a pile in the corner of the barber's shop) and I've grown muscles where I never knew they existed before. I've done more sit-ups and push-ups over the last fourteen days than I have in all my life. I'm not even going to mention the pull-ups. Gosh, I'd like just one day when I don't have to run or jump or anything like that.

Between training and drills, we've been taught how to make a bed properly and that cleanliness is next to godliness. Mom, you'd be impressed by how tight I can pull a sheet over a bed now. You'd be surprised what a neatnik I can be with a drill sergeant breathing down my neck.

Don't get the idea that I'll keep this up at home, though.

We did some tests to figure out our jobs for the Army. Go figure, there's more than just shooting up the enemy. Who knew? Anyway, they say they want me to train as a medic. How about that? I guess it was a good thing I stuck with the Boy Scouts after all. Tell Mr. Riggs thanks for teaching me first aid in Scouts. I'm sure I'll put all he taught me to good use.

At the end of basic I'll be headed to Houston for Medic Training. I heard somebody say that some of the medics get stationed in Japan or someplace like that. Gosh, I'd sure hate to be sent somewhere like that and miss out on Vietnam altogether. That would be the pits.

Just joshing, Mom. I know you want me to avoid war if I can manage it. Believe me, I feel the same way.

I guess I better go. Lights out comes early here and, golly, am I ever ready for it when it comes. I've never been so tired in all my life. And hungry. They sure don't feed me so well as you do, Mom.

Joel, stop laughing about that. You'll hurt Mom's feelings.

I love you three. Annie, take care of Joel. Joel, take care of Mom. Mom, take care of Annie. All of you, take care of my car. That should do.

Mike

11

Twenty minutes from my front door was the sandy beach of Lake Michigan. Twenty-two minutes and I could have my toes in the cold water, hearing the rushing of the waves and the call of the seagulls soaring above my head. Twenty-five minutes and I'd ignore the shock of the frigid lake and run in up to my waist, my armpits, shoulders, and dive under the rush of water.

Bobbing up and down, I'd lose myself in the freedom of weightlessness.

I'd lose track of time, floating on my back and looking up into the endless blue sky above me.

The best of summers in Michigan were spontaneous trips west, to look out at the lake, never being able to see to the other side. Wisconsin seemed forever far away when squinting for it along the horizon.

The summer hadn't been hot enough to warm up the Big Lake. Still, Jocelyn and I had packed up our beach towels and a couple bottles of Coke. We wore our swimsuits under our clothes just in case we felt daring.

We hadn't left until after we both got out of work, but

summer days were long and our eighteen-year-old energy never fading. We rode in Mike's car, the radio turned up as loud as it could go to beat out the sound of air rushing through the windows. We sang along with Mama Cass and did our best to do the twist with Fats Domino. Our hair danced around our heads, wild in the wind, as we shimmied our shoulders and flubbed up the words to most of the songs that came on the radio.

Neither of us cared one little bit. No one was there to stare or to correct us.

The best part of having a kindred was knowing that it little mattered how silly I was. I would be loved regardless—liked, even—for being just the way I was.

●

When the sun was about to set, we made our way down the pier, sitting at the very end, letting the waves of the lake wet our bare feet and ankles. The sun seemed to melt into where the water met the sky. Orange and purple and pink and blue. The colors reflected in the rippling surface of the waves.

"Have you heard from Mike?" Jocelyn asked.

"Yeah," I answered. "He's doing pretty well, I guess."

"Good. Do you know if they're going to send him to Vietnam?"

I nodded. "I'm sure they will."

"Maybe it will end before he can go."

"Maybe."

I looked back to the water; the sun sank into it and glowed orange on the whitecaps. The waves were rough that day. Still, eager swimmers had risked the undertow.

You can't worry about something that might not happen.

•

We stayed to watch the Musical Fountain along the channel. Spouts of water shot in the air, backlit with colorful bulbs. Music played over loudspeakers, and the crowd that came in their cars or sat on blankets on the lawn oohed and ahhed as if it was the Fourth of July.

Jocelyn and I sat on the roof of Mike's car.

After the show was over, the people picked up their chairs and blankets, making their way to the parking lot and pulling away into the night toward their homes. We stayed, waiting for traffic to clear up. I was glad we'd thought ahead to bring a couple of blankets. The chilly evening had only grown colder.

"I got a letter in the mail this week too," Jocelyn said, keeping her eyes on the docked boats bobbing up and down in the channel. "Mine isn't from the Army, but it's still exciting."

"Oh yeah?" I pulled the blanket around me closer. "Where was it from?"

"Taylor University," she said. "In Indiana."

"Did they accept your application?"

She nodded and then turned toward me. "They did. And they offered me a scholarship."

Even with the evening so dark, I could still see the way her eyes lit up with the news.

"That's great," I said, feeling both that it was and that it wasn't. "For the fall?"

"Yes. But I don't know if I'm going." She talked fast, as if she'd prepared what she was going to say. "It's just so far away. It's a three-hour drive. Besides, what's the use of getting a degree just in time for me to get married and start having babies?"

"You don't even have a steady boyfriend yet."

"I know." She let her shoulders slump. "I guess I'm trying to talk myself out of being excited."

"Why?"

"Mother doesn't want me to go."

"What do you want?"

"Does it matter?" she asked. "Besides, I'm perfectly happy writing up stories about the water level of Old Chip and who asked whom to the homecoming dance."

"Really?" I asked.

"Well, no. But it's something to do for now."

"I think you should go," I said, hoping she'd hear the sincerity that added weight to each of the words. "It would be so good for you."

"But what about you?" she asked. "Don't you want to go to college?"

"I don't know. Maybe I can just take over the library when Mrs. Veenstra retires. I don't know that I have to go to college for that." I pulled the blanket up over my shoulders. "But if I can't have it for me, then I want it for you."

We went back to watching the sky and the way the stars mirrored dots across the rippled water.

12

The telephone rang in the middle of the eleven o'clock news and Mom reached it before anyone else, standing in the kitchen, the receiver to her ear, saying things like, "Uh-huh, okay, don't worry, we'll find him."

"Is it Grandpa?" Joel asked me.

"I think so," I answered.

"He's gone off again," Mom said, coming in and grabbing the keys to the station wagon. "Bring a flashlight."

We'd been told that it wasn't abnormal for someone in Grandpa's mental state to wander. Still, it was alarming whenever he did. Fort Colson wasn't a large town, but there were woods in which one could become lost and more than a few rivers or ponds to fall into.

The year before, he'd gotten all the way to the ice cream shop a mile and a half away from his house, throwing a fit because the girl behind the counter wouldn't give him a malt if he didn't have any money. Six months after that, he'd knocked on the door of an unsuspecting widow's house, asking for a glass of orange juice. He'd made it as far as the other side of town more than once. If I'd had to guess, he'd taken off at least half a dozen times.

And each time he'd been found within an hour of going missing.

But that night was dark and it would have been easy for him to get lost in the shadows, unseen by anyone who didn't know they should be looking for him.

"Your grandmother said the back door was wide open when she realized he was gone," Mom said, keeping her eyes moving from one side of the road to the other as she drove her station wagon, as if she might see Grandpa shuffling along on the shoulder.

Joel tapped his thigh with the flat of his hand. All the way down the country roads and around the sharp curves. *Tap, tap, tap.* Up the long drive to Main Street. *Tap. Tap. Tap.* Any normal day I would have sniped at him to stop.

The rhythmic slapping sound only added anxiety to worry.

We pulled into the driveway, and Mom threw the car into park, turning off the engine but leaving the key in the ignition in case we needed to leave fast.

Grandma stood on the porch, waiting for us. Her usually perfect posture was slumped and she held her arms crossed tight against her body. She didn't look at us but let her eyes swipe up and down the street, watching for him.

"No one's called," she said. "I didn't dare go looking for him by myself. It's too dark."

"That's okay, Gran," Joel said.

"I just went to the bathroom." She breathed in sharply. "I thought he was sleeping in his chair."

"We'll find him." Joel sighed. "Don't worry."

Mom climbed the porch steps. "Let's go inside." She put her arm around Grandma. "I'll make you a cup of tea."

Grandma didn't argue but followed behind her. Mom looked over her shoulder at me, giving me a sympathetic smile.

Joel and I went to the backyard. The garage door was open, hammers and screwdrivers pulled out of their chest and scattered across the workbench.

"The ax is gone," Joel said, looking out at the wooded area on the other side of the yard. "I bet he went out to chop wood."

"Let's go."

We ran to the tree line, the wide beam of Joel's flashlight leading the way. There was a well-worn path between the trees where we entered the woods. To the right was the clearing where Grandpa used to chop wood when he was well. Where Frank and Mike and Joel had, too, over the years.

"Look there." Joel pointed the beam to the chopping block. "He must've gotten tired of carrying it."

The ax lay, discarded, among last year's fallen leaves.

"Do you think he could have made it to the creek?" I asked.

"Gosh, I hope not."

The underbrush crunched beneath our feet as we ran the direction of the creek. It wasn't so deep that a full-grown man couldn't stand up in the middle and it wasn't so strong that it could drag him under. But with Grandpa's mind the way it was, I didn't trust that he had the sense to get out of it if he needed to.

God, don't let Grandpa be dead, I prayed. *I don't want Joel to see that.*

We made it to the edge of the creek, nothing but the nighttime noises of crackling tree limbs, scampering critters, and a stillness of dark around us. The sounds of Joel and my panting breath joined in, my own heartbeat pounding so hard in my head that I feared I'd miss a sound I needed to hear.

Joel knelt, looking in the soft mud of the shore for footprints, any sign that Grandpa had been that way. Then he pointed his flashlight up and down the creek. Nothing but the still water and the rocks we used when we were little to hop across to the other side.

"Should we split up?" I asked.

Joel shook his head. "I don't think that's a good idea." He stood, the knees of his jeans dirty. "Maybe he didn't come out here—"

I shushed him. "Did you hear that?"

We both quieted, not moving a muscle until we caught the sound. A weak, faint call off to the right of us.

"The tree house," Joel said, taking off ahead of me.

Nestled back in the woods was a tree house that Grandpa had built decades before. Frank had taken Mike on campouts there right after Korea. But not me. I'd never been allowed up there. The "Boys Only" sign had prohibited me.

But the tree house hadn't been used in a long time. Over the years it had fallen into disrepair. The only thing that spent any time there anymore might have been of the less-friendly variety. Opossums or raccoons, I imagined.

Dodging trees and jumping over fallen limbs, Joel and I made our way to the smaller clearing where the tree house was. We saw Grandpa right away, sitting cross-legged on the ground, his head hanging. He didn't move. But he gasped and cried.

"Somebody please help me," he whimpered, sounding the

way I imagined he might have when he was a little boy. "Is anybody there?"

He had on his pajamas. The faded red flannel ones he'd owned forever. And he had nothing on his feet, as if he'd forgotten the need of shoes when tromping through the woods.

We knew better than to rush up to him. Anything sudden could scare him, confusing him even more than I assumed he already felt. So, we walked slowly, evenly, with soft feet on the ground.

"Grandpa?" Joel called. "Are you hurt?"

Grandpa looked toward us, his eyes wild and mouth open from his sobbing.

"Who are you?" he asked.

"Rocky," I said. "Hey there, Rocky. We're friends."

"I don't remember you," he said, sobbing. "I can't find my way home."

"It's all right." I got close enough to kneel next to him. "We're going to help you out. Okay?"

He let me take his hand. It was so cold, clammy. I rubbed my hands against his skin, hoping to warm him up even if just a little.

"What happened?" I asked, trying to keep my voice calm.

"I don't know." His voice was thick, garbled.

"Are you hurt?"

He shook his head no, he frowned and sobbed.

"I just want to go home," he cried.

"Do you think you can walk?" Joel asked. "We know the way home."

"Help me up." Grandpa raised his arms, and between the two of us, we pulled him to his feet.

Walking was slow going, especially with his bare soles. He

had one arm resting across Joel's shoulders and put a good deal of weight on him. All along the way, he groaned, saying that it was taking too long.

"Are you sure we're going the right way?" he asked.

"We are," I told him. "I promise."

As soon as we got within sight of the house, he stopped, turning toward me.

"Gloria? Is it you?" Grandpa asked, squeezing my hand but believing that it belonged to my mother. "Gloria, I'm sorry."

"Why are you sorry?" I didn't correct him.

"Frank. He's gone. I'm afraid it was something I did."

"That wasn't your fault," I said, looking him in the eye. "He'll come back."

"What if he doesn't?" he asked.

"I don't know." I shook my head. "Let's just get you inside, okay? Maybe you can have a little hot chocolate. With marshmallows too? Would you like that?"

"And a cookie?"

"Maybe."

I put my hand on his cheek, feeling at least a few days of stubble there.

"Don't run away again," I said. "Please."

"I'll try not to."

13

It was past two in the morning when Mom got home from Grandma and Grandpa's house. She'd stayed behind, somehow managing to get Dr. DeVries to come check over Grandpa. He didn't usually do house calls, but for her, he made exceptions.

An hour earlier I'd driven the station wagon home, Joel snoozing in the passenger's seat. The good doctor had offered to drive Mom home. I thought it took some nerve, the way he looked at her in front of her husband's parents.

She stepped in through the back door and into the kitchen, kicking off her shoes as soon as she hit the linoleum and leaving them where they landed.

"What are you still doing up?" she asked, clunking her purse on the counter.

"I wanted to wait up for you," I answered.

"Don't you have to work in a few hours?"

I closed the book I was reading and put it on the table. "I'll be all right."

"You're still young." She sighed. "I, on the other hand, am far from it."

"How's Grandpa?"

She sighed again and dragged the step stool to the refrigerator, climbing on top and opening the cupboard. She reached all the way back for a dusty old coffee can that had been shoved into the far corner.

Ever since I could remember I knew that Mom kept a pack of cigarettes in that Folger's tin. For emergencies, she claimed, and I believed her. In all the years since Frank left, I'd only caught the smell of smoke on her breath three times.

"He'll be all right. Dr. DeVries thought it was best to take him to the hospital for observation. Just in case." She climbed back down and sat on the other side of the small, drop-leaf table. "He needed a few stitches in his foot. Otherwise, he's fine."

The pack of Lucky Strikes crinkled as she pulled them out. She took one, sticking the end between her lips and reaching into the bottom of the can for the book of matches she'd thrown in at some point. It took her more than a few attempts at lighting it before a flame burst from the end of the matchstick.

"I talked to your grandmother about what she needs to do next," she said, getting up for a saucer to catch her ashes. "She can't take care of him anymore."

She narrowed her eyes as she pulled on the cigarette and let out a little puff of smoke along with a cough.

"These sure are stale," she said, crushing the cigarette into the saucer.

"What else can she do?" I asked.

"She might have to find a place for him." She shook her head. "It's not safe for him there anymore. He's so big. I don't know how she's been getting him around that house.

He needs her to help him get to the bathroom. Sometimes he doesn't make it."

Crossing my arms, I leaned back in my chair, letting my shoulder blades push into the hard wood. It made me feel sick to my stomach just thinking about it.

"She doesn't need to be cleaning him up like that," Mom said.

"We can take turns helping her," I said. "I can make supper for them."

"He needs to be in a nursing home. I told your grandmother that, but I don't think she likes the idea too much." She got up and emptied the ashes and hardly smoked cigarette into the trash can. "I shouldn't have to make these decisions."

She didn't have to say anything for me to know that she meant that Frank should be the one to take care of his own parents. Frank and his sister, Rose.

"Should we get ahold of him?" I asked.

"Who?"

"Frank." I sat up straighter. "He should know about this."

"I wouldn't even know where to start looking for him." She drummed her fingertips on the countertop. "He could be in Siberia for all I know. All I care."

My knee bobbed up and down, my bare heel tapping the floor. Swallowing hard, I looked up to meet my mother's eyes.

"What?" she asked.

"What if there was a way to find him?"

"Does your grandmother know where he is? Did you talk to her about him?"

"No." I swallowed, regretting even bringing it up. I'd made a promise to Mike.

"Maybe I'll ask her."

"Did anyone call Aunt Rose?" I asked, hoping to change the subject.

Mom rolled her eyes. "I did. She said she can't come until tomorrow evening."

It was no surprise to me that Aunt Rose didn't get into her Lincoln or Cadillac or whatever rich women drove and come over from her enormous house in Grand Rapids to help Grandma when she was most needed.

I swallowed back the bitterness and wondered what my grandparents had done to deserve two ungrateful children.

"I'm sure your grandmother will get ahold of Frank eventually." She took another cigarette from the pack, holding it between her fingers, unlit. "If she even knows where he is."

"Are you upset?"

"About what?"

"I don't know. Just that I brought up Frank?"

She shook her head. "No. Honey, he's your father. No matter what he's done. Or not done."

"Do you think he'll ever come back?" As many times as that question had been on the tip of my tongue, I'd never asked it out loud before. "What would happen if he did?"

"I've asked myself that same thing for twelve years." She dropped the unlit cigarette into the can with the rest of the pack and stood, carrying it back to her hiding spot. "He wouldn't come here, you know. This has never been his house. He isn't welcome."

"Are you mad at him?"

She shrugged and wiped under her nose. "Not anymore, I don't think. I haven't had much time to be angry."

"You could be."

"But what good would that do me?" She padded her way to the door that led in the direction of her bedroom. "I can't let something that happened twelve years ago unravel all I have to hold together today. Wait to talk to your grandmother about this until Monday, all right?"

I nodded.

"With your aunt Rose on her way here, she'll have plenty to handle."

She told me good night and went to her room.

After flipping the kitchen light off, I took the stairs to my room. Checking the clock, I saw that I needed to be up for work in three hours. I couldn't decide if it would be better to sleep that little or just stay up.

The way my mind was spinning, I didn't think I'd be able to sleep even if I tried.

Instead of lying down, I grabbed one of the books Frank had left behind, a survivor of the purge Mom had done twelve years before. Between the pages was the postcard he'd sent us just after he'd gone. I touched the letters as if I might be able to feel them carved into the paper.

I didn't feel anything, so I shut the book and put it back on the shelf where it could stay and collect dust for all I cared.

I lay awake in my bed until my alarm went off.

14

For several years after Frank left, Grandpa would stop by our house on a Saturday morning for a cup of coffee with Mom. He'd play catch with Mike in the backyard and let Joel sit on his lap, reading to him from a book he'd brought from home. He would meet me at the kitchen table, drinking water from my miniature-sized tea set, always sticking his pinky finger up in the air.

Before he'd leave, he'd hand something to Mom, which she'd always try to refuse. It wasn't until later that I realized it was money to put toward the mortgage or to buy a week's worth of groceries. When I'd asked him about it, he'd made me promise to keep it a secret from Grandma.

"She wouldn't understand," he'd said.

He came less frequently as we got older and Mom's job started paying better. But, still, when he came, he'd hand her a little money.

"Let me help," he'd say. "Please."

It wasn't until the day when he'd gone to the old house, the one that backed up to the lake, insisting on visiting his grandchildren, that we knew something had gone wrong with him.

That was when Grandma took his car keys, insisting that he go nowhere without her.

After that he'd slipped quickly, his mind dropping some memories and holding dearly to others. His hair thinned, and his body too. And nearly all the time he had a look of fear and detachment behind his eyes.

But that fear was gone, dissolved, when we went to see him in the hospital.

It was a Tuesday and I'd taken Joel along with me. Mom had given us a few dollars to pick up a bouquet for his room. Not as much for him as for Grandma.

Grandpa lay in his bed, his head resting on his pillow, his hair sticking up and dull looking as if it could use a good wash. The room held the smell of medicine and antiseptic. Sterile yet sick.

In a chair pulled up to the bed, Grandma sat, a magazine on her lap but her eyes fixed on the wall over Grandpa's bed. She looked so small and frail, as if she'd shrunk in the few days since I'd last seen her. I feared if she stood that she'd crumble.

"Grandma," I whispered, not wanting to break the silence and frighten her. "Hi."

"Oh, kids," she said. "Come in. Rose, do you see who came?"

Aunt Rose was sitting, straight as a pin, to Grandpa's right-hand side. When she saw us, she jolted up, letting go of his hand and coming around the end of the bed.

"Look at you two," she said, extending her arms toward us. Giving us each a stiff hug, she pecked our cheeks with no softness of lips. "I'm glad you came."

"How was your drive over?" Joel asked, rubbing at the spot where she'd hit him with her lips.

"Oh, you know. Traffic was miserable." She used a hand to fluff the bottom of her dark hair. "But you didn't come to hear about my trip. Dad, did you see who's visiting?"

"Who's that?" he asked.

"Francis's kids," she yelled. "Well, two of them at least."

Joel and I stepped forward when Aunt Rose pulled at our arms. Grandpa looked from Joel to me and back again. He smiled, his eyes watery.

"Well, hello," he said, his voice thick and gravelly. "I don't remember you, but I'm glad you're here."

"Hi, Grandpa," Joel said, moving to the bedside and taking his hand. "How are you feeling?"

"Not good. Not good." Grandpa looked up into Joel's face. "My, do you look like Frank. Is this him?"

"No, honey," Grandma answered. "This is Joel. Frank's son."

"He looks like him, doesn't he?" Then he looked at me. "And you, who are you?"

"Annie," I answered.

"Come sit by me, Annie." He patted the edge of his bed, where my aunt had been.

"Frank wrote me," he said.

"Rockston," Grandma said.

"He sends me a letter every week," Grandpa went on.

"Now, he does not," she said. "You'll just upset the children, saying things like that."

I met eyes with her. She didn't hold mine longer than a moment.

"Can you read?" Grandpa asked Joel.

"Yes, sir."

"Good for you." He smiled and clapped his hands together. "Will you read me a story?"

Joel moved to sit on the other side of Grandpa's bed, reading to him from a *Time* magazine Grandma had on the bedside table. When he'd finished one article, Grandpa asked for another. He beamed at Joel the whole time.

It wasn't long, though, before he was tired and wanted to sleep. Joel gave him a hug, and Grandpa patted his cheek.

"You'll be a good boy, won't you?" Grandpa asked.

Joel nodded, saying he would try.

Then I went to hug him. Grandpa turned his face, planting five kisses on my cheek. Then he put his hands on my shoulders, pushing me away so he could look into my eyes.

"Do you know why I kissed you five times?" he asked.

"Why?"

"Because I forgot how to count."

Even though tears prickled in the corners of my eyes, I couldn't help but smile.

"I love you, Grandpa," I said.

"I love you, Annie."

"You remembered my name."

"And I remembered to love you."

Joel and I left the hospital, the corridor seeming so long as we walked toward the exit.

For the rest of that day, I felt the prickle of his stubble on my cheek.

Fort Knox, Kentucky

Dear All,

   Sorry to hear about Grandpa. I wish I could be there
to help out. I bet he's madder than a wasp about having to stay at the hospital. How's Grandma managing? I
wrote to her, but she didn't write back. I know she probably doesn't have time right now.

   I asked the chaplain here to pray for Grandpa. He said
he would. He seems like a real nice guy. You'll be glad to
know that I haven't missed church on a Sunday. He's an
okay preacher. Nothing like home, but that's all right. I
guess they have church over in Nam too. I know Oma will
be happy about that. You too, Mom, I'm sure.

   I've got some good news and bad news. I'll start with
the good. Uncle Sam decided that he does, indeed, need me
as a medic. The bad? He tagged eight more weeks on to
my training. After basic is done, I'll be hopping on a plane
to Texas to learn how to save lives.

   Joel, I know you were hoping I'd be back in time for
your birthday. But, I'm sorry that I've got to miss this
one, pal. Fourteen is a big one, isn't it? Tell you what.
My gift to you is letting you drive the Corvair around
the cemetery a few times. That way you won't be able to
kill anybody. Make sure somebody takes a picture of you
behind the wheel. I'll bet you'll look plenty tough driving it.

I gotta run. A few fellas are putting together a touch football game here after chow. See, they aren't running us too hard.

I miss you. Joel, you too.

Mike

15

Detroit was on fire. Just one more race riot for the summer. Buffalo, Newark, Minneapolis. And then Detroit. Even in the black and white of our television screen, I could see the hot flames licking up the sides of buildings and houses. Plumes of smoke filled the sky like clouds. Police wearing helmets and carrying shields marched through the streets while black residents ran or fought back.

We watched all evening, Mom shaking her head most of the time. Joel fell asleep on the sofa about eleven. I sat on the floor, legs bent and knees tucked up under my chin. It was near midnight when a gray bar spanned across the screen followed by the face of the president.

Johnson called the riots "extreme disorder in Detroit, Michigan." From what I saw, I would have thought the words "war zone" were more apt.

A war zone less than a three-hours' drive from our front door. It simply did not seem possible.

"No one is going to win this," Mom said, standing to turn the television off.

She looked at Joel and smiled. He looked snug as a bug.

Since he was a baby, he could always sleep anywhere, a skill I had never learned.

"We can let him sleep there tonight," she said. "I'd hate to wake him."

●

On that Thursday afternoon, the rain came in lazy showers, and a pair of retired local men drank coffee and grumbled amongst themselves about the weather being no good for fishing. They'd not ordered food but asked for endless warm-ups on their coffee. Bernie rolled his eyes and shook his head.

"They're going to bankrupt me," he muttered.

I offered to water down the coffee. To that he'd made a hissing sound. But the corner of his mouth had twitched and I knew he was trying not to laugh.

David came in, as always, for a late lunch, sitting in the booth closest to the coffeemaker like he did every time he came. While he waited for me he read one of the papers that Bernie set out for customers. He had it opened to the comics.

"My favorite is Charlie Brown," I said, pulling the order pad out of my apron pocket.

"I'm a sucker for Marmaduke," he said, smiling up at me. "I had a big dog like him when I was a kid."

"I would have figured you for a Batman reader."

"He's all right." He folded the paper. "But he never made me laugh. Now, Marmaduke. That dog gets me every time."

"What was your dog's name?"

"Baby," he answered. "My little sister named him."

"I like that name."

"That's because you didn't have to chase him whenever he ran away," he said. "Come back, Baby! Be a good boy, Baby."

I smiled, imagining it. "What can I get you?"

"The special is fine, please," he answered. "And a glass of milk?"

"Sure," I said, leaving him to his comics to put his order in.

While I waited for Bernie to serve up his plate of baked chicken and mashed potatoes with a side of green beans, I gave the table of men their bills, collecting their empty coffee cups. They grumbled their thanks before going on in their conversation.

"You hear about these riots over in Detroit?" one of the men said. "You hear about them?"

"Sure I did. Couldn't hardly not," the other said. "It's all they wanna talk about on the news."

"Awful mess, don't you think?"

"Can't even imagine."

"What do you think they're trying to accomplish? We already got one war on our hands. All these riots. They trying to start a second Civil War?"

The second man crossed his arms and shrugged.

"What do the blacks want anyhow? They can get jobs, they've got places to live, they get protected by the police. Heck, they got the vote. What do they want?"

"Don't know."

"It's all those marches, got them riled." He shook his head. "With that Martin King. He makes them think they've got it worse off than the rest of us. I don't buy it."

The men both paused in their conversation, staying quiet the way men have of doing with one another. I looked at David; he kept his eyes on the paper as if he didn't hear a word they said. The way he was able to turn the other cheek astounded me.

"Order up," Bernie called through the window between the kitchen and the dining area.

I carried it over to David.

"I'll get your milk in a minute," I said.

"Thanks." He gave me a quick smile before turning his face back to look at the food and the paper.

When I turned, I noticed that one of the men was looking at David out of the corner of his eye. It wasn't a friendly look, not one that I would have wanted trained on me.

"All they're doing is burning their own town," the one with the stink-eye said. "I say we just let them do it. Be less trouble for us if they'd just leave."

"That's an awful thing to say," I muttered, hoping it was loud enough for him to hear it.

It was and he turned his unfriendly eye on me. Turning my back on him, I went to pour David's glass of milk.

The men got out of their seats, dropping a few coins on the table. Without looking, I knew it would only be enough to cover the cups of coffee. They were never the kind to leave a tip anyway.

"Thank you," David said when I brought his glass of milk. Then he looked straight into my eyes. "I don't let them get to me. It's just talk."

"Well, they don't have to be mean," I said. "I'll let you get to your lunch."

When he was finished, I brought him his bill and the last doughnut out of the bakery case, wrapped in a napkin. "On the house," I said.

"You don't have to do that." He grinned and pulled out his billfold. "But I'll take it anyway."

Sliding out of his seat, he followed me to the counter,

doughnut in hand. I told him his total, and he handed me his money.

"I have a question for you," he said.

"All right?"

"Did you know there are loons in Chippewa Lake?"

"They come every year. Maybe not the same ones, but it doesn't matter to us."

"I've been hearing them lately."

"Kind of spooky, huh?"

"You got that right." He put his wallet into his back pocket. "But a beautiful kind of spooky. I don't know that I've ever heard anything like it."

"You'll get used to them."

"Hm. I hope I don't." He held up the doughnut. "Thanks for this."

"You're welcome."

"Have a good day, Annie."

"You too."

I took my time setting the fresh place mats on the tables along with the place settings for the next morning. Then I wiped the lunch special off the chalkboard and wrote in the breakfast deal. Two fried eggs, two pancakes, and two sausage links.

Bernie liked to have a new Bible verse on the board for each day. He said it let customers know what kind of establishment they'd come to. Never had he elaborated on that thought, and I'd not asked him to. But he kept a stack of index cards under the counter for me to copy in chalk on the blackboard.

Iron sharpeneth iron, I wrote. *So a man sharpeneth the countenance of his friend.*

Just when I finished writing it, the bell over the door dinged, letting me know we had another customer. Of course, right before we were supposed to close for the day.

"I'll be right with you," I called over my shoulder, climbing down the step stool. "Go ahead and sit anywhere you'd like."

"It's me."

I turned and looked to see Mom standing in the doorway. When she stepped closer, she was hesitant.

"I'm sorry, honey," she said. "I have some bad news."

Slowly, as if I was dreaming, I stepped around the counter.

"It's your grandpa," she said.

"Is he . . ." I couldn't bear to finish the sentence.

She nodded. "He went in his sleep just a little while ago. Just like a light turning off. It didn't hurt at all."

"How do you know that?"

"I just do."

I covered my face with my hands and cried. It was all I could do.

16

Grandma didn't want to go home. She asked us to take her to our house where at least she didn't have to look at an empty chair that should have held Grandpa. Mom had gone to pick her up, having taken the rest of the day off of work.

I'd gone home early too. Bernie had let me know that he didn't need my help, that he and Larry would make do for a few days. From him, that was as good as a sympathy card.

The moment Oma heard, she rushed over, taking her place in our kitchen, making it smell of baking bread and sausages and butter.

Grandma stepped into our house, letting her eyes scan the living room and breathing in the good smells of food. Joel went right to her, pulling her into a long hug. She patted his back as if she wanted him to let go, but he didn't. Finally, she let her hands be still on his back when she realized he was crying.

"That's all right," she whispered to him. "That's all right."

We stayed at home all day, welcoming half of the town as they came to offer their sympathies to Grandma. She sat in a rocking chair, looking shrunken and glossy eyed. No matter what someone said to her, she could only muster two words.

"Thank you."

After a while they stopped coming. I didn't know if it was the rain that kept them away, but I was glad. Grandma's eyes were heavy, her skin looking pale. I wondered when she'd last slept a full night.

"We have to write the obituary," she said, crossing her arms. "It's been so long since I've written one . . ."

"We can ask Jocelyn to help," I offered. "She writes them all the time."

"All right," Grandma said. "She'll know what needs to be in there."

"She will."

"When did Rose say she'd be here?" She shook her head. "I know she's upset that she has to come back again so soon."

"She'll just have to be all right with it," Mom muttered. "It isn't that far."

"What about Frank?" I asked. "Shouldn't we let him know?"

Grandma narrowed her eyes at me and tightened her lips into a pucker. "You call your father by his first name?"

I lowered my eyes to the floor.

"I suppose you don't think he's been much of a father to you," she said. "Maybe he hasn't been."

Mom cleared her throat, setting her jaw as if she was struggling to keep in a burst of temper. At least I knew it wasn't me she was angry with. I was glad, though, that she worked at defusing her dynamite even if just for the sake of a woman who'd been recently widowed.

"I'm sorry," I whispered.

"You don't need to apologize to me." She folded her hands

in her lap, using her feet to rock the chair. It creaked into the quiet room. "I have his address. We should write to him. We should ask him to come home."

Mom stood up fast and walked to the kitchen, her spine rigid. Her voice carried to the living room in hisses and hard-edged tones. I thought if Oma wasn't there, we also would have been treated to the clanging of pots and pans and the slamming of cupboard doors.

"Do you think he'll want to come?" Joel asked.

"He promised he would." The skin of Grandma's forehead gathered in the middle and she looked at her shoes. "If something like this happened, he'd come back if I wanted him to."

"Will you ask him to come home?" he asked.

Joel, the son who hardly remembered Frank, held no bitterness toward him. He inched to the edge of his chair as if in excitement.

Grandma nodded. "Hand me my purse."

I brought it to her, the weight of it more than I'd anticipated. It was classic black with a gold-colored clasp. It smelled of the violet mints she always kept in the little pocket sewn into the lining next to an embroidered hanky and a tiny pair of scissors. She took the purse from me, pulling it open and taking out her wallet that was of the same color.

From the space behind where she kept her driver's license, she removed a little piece of paper that had been folded once. She handed it to me.

"I wish I had a telephone number for him," she said. "But this is what he gave me."

I held that paper, feeling the softness of it from years in Grandma's wallet. I thought about telling her that I already had the address, that she should keep it stowed away in her wallet.

"Thank you," I said instead.

I didn't want her to think that Mike had betrayed her.

She'd already lost so much.

To whom it may concern:

I'm attempting to reach Frank Jacobson. If this is not the correct address for him, please write back or call 1-231-555-6986 to let us know as much.

If, however, this is where he may be reached, please let him know that his father, Rockston Jacobson, passed away and that his mother has requested that he come home. To that end, we've delayed the funeral until August 2 at eleven in the morning to be held at First United Methodist Church in Fort Colson, Michigan.

Frank knows the location.

Thank you,
Anne Jacobson

PS: I can be reached most mornings and afternoons at Bernie's Diner on Main Street in Fort Colson.

17

It had rained most of the week. I hadn't minded at all. Between Grandpa's funeral arrangements and the news out of Detroit, the gloomy skies represented well my downtrodden spirit.

Frank hadn't come and he hadn't called. Every time the telephone rang, I jumped, answering it with my heart pounding so fast it made me breathless.

"The letter might not have gotten to him yet," Joel said, sitting on the couch.

"I sent the letter on Friday," I said. "He should've called when he got it."

"It's only Sunday. Be patient, Annie."

Mom reached for the TV, turning the volume up. She hushed us. "I'm trying to watch the news."

More footage of the Detroit riots moved across the screen. Police, wielding shotguns, walked up and down the sidewalk, passing storefronts with busted-out windows. Crowds lined the streets, examining the destruction as if in shock.

The anchorman delivered the report of a white woman

shot and killed as she stood looking out her hotel window and of a little black girl, only four years old, who suffered the same from the weapons of the National Guard in Detroit.

It didn't make sense to me. Not even a little. It seemed like the world was just too hard, too dark. I bit the inside of my cheek, trying not to cry.

"Their poor mothers," Mom whispered.

●

He walked through the door of the diner at five minutes until closing time and came directly to where I stood refilling salt shakers at the counter. I knew him instantly. He hadn't changed much at all. Just a little gray peppered his hair and more lines creased his face. But the eyes, they were the same. Dark and brooding.

The last I'd seen him, his eyes had been like that. He had come to tuck me into bed and listen to me say my prayers like he did some nights. When he'd lowered his face to kiss my forehead, I saw that his eyes held all the sadness in the world.

Those were the eyes that met mine that Monday afternoon.

When I noticed that my hands were trembling, I shoved them into my apron pocket. Swallowing, I willed myself to be steady, to be calm. Of all the times I'd imagined him coming back, I'd never thought I'd feel so nervous, so emotional.

"Hi, Frank," I whispered, not ready or willing to use the name Dad.

He nodded as if to say that he knew he didn't deserve more. "Anne," he said.

"I still go by Annie."

"Okay." He looked straight, his hands at his sides. His right he held in a fist. To calm the trembling, I imagined.

I felt at a loss as to what to say. Turning, I saw Bernie peek out through the pass-through window, checking to see if I was okay. I nodded at him to say I was.

"Do you want some coffee?" I asked. "I can make new, but you'll have to pay for it."

"Just whatever you have on hand," he said. "I don't mind old."

"Why don't you go have a seat."

He picked the table closest to the window, taking the chair that put his back against the wall.

I made my way to the coffeemaker, holding the air in my lungs a good ten seconds before letting it back out. *Mike should be here*, I thought. *He'd know what to do.*

What I imagined Mike would do was take the cup of coffee to Frank and ask him how he'd been all those years. He'd have some charming way to ease the tension, to iron out the wrinkles that had formed after years of estrangement before giving him the third degree to find out why he'd left and where he'd been.

Behind me I heard the sloshing of Larry's dishwashing and the radio Bernie had on a station that only played classical music. Pouring the last of the coffee into a mug, I allowed the complexity of wanting Frank to leave and hoping he'd stay wash over me.

Both anger and relief burbled inside of me, as if they grumbled different songs.

"Annie," Bernie called out to me through the pass-through. "He going to want anything from the grill?"

Turning, I shook my head. "I didn't ask yet."

"Well, find out, would ya? I want to clean this thing if I can."

"It's Frank," I whispered. The two words were out before I realized it.

"It's who?" He lowered his eyebrows and squinted. Lifting a hand to wipe at a line of sweat on his forehead, he looked in the direction of our sole customer. "Frank? As in your father?"

I nodded.

"You're sure?" he asked.

He didn't wait for me to finish. He moved from the pass-through to the kitchen door, pushing it open and joining me behind the counter.

"You want me to make him leave?" He crossed his arms, looking at Frank.

"No," I said, overeager. "I need him."

Trying to pretend I hadn't said those last words, I took the cup to Frank's table, not bothering to grab a pitcher of cream or a cube of sugar. He'd want it black.

I didn't know much about him, but of that I was sure.

"When did you get here?" I asked, putting the cup in front of him. "Into town, I mean."

"Just now." He looked at the coffee as if it were from an alien planet. "This was my first stop."

"Are you going to order food?" My voice was more clipped than usual. It surprised me how much I sounded like my mother. "Bernie wants to shut down the grill."

"I'm not hungry." He lifted the cup to his lips, taking a sip. "You have time to talk?"

"My shift isn't over until quarter after three."

He sighed and nodded.

"I'm sure you're in a hurry to get out of town, but we all have lives to live," I said, barely over a whisper. I looked at my wristwatch. "If you want to talk, you'll have to wait twenty minutes. You think you can manage that?"

He looked at me with a half grin, one that reminded me of Mike. "You sure are like your mother."

I pushed up my glasses, feeling the heat of my cheeks with my fingertips.

"That's a compliment," he said. "I can wait here. Unless you need to clean the table."

"You can stay," I said. "Just as long as you order something to eat. The special is meat loaf."

He grimaced. "How about a piece of pie."

"All right." I jotted a note. "Ice cream?"

"Sure."

"I'll have that out to you in a few minutes," I said as if talking to any customer who had walked in off the street. "Anything else?"

"Nope."

I turned away from him, leaving his table.

"Annie," he said.

I looked at him over my shoulder.

"You look like your mother."

I'd heard that my whole life from just about every single person who lived in Fort Colson. Never before had it made me feel anything. It was just something people said. But then Frank said it, and I thought it was a roundabout way of telling me that he thought I was pretty.

I'd waited my whole life for my father to say something like that to me.

I was sure to stuff away that warm feeling, trying to ignore how good it was.

I couldn't afford to let him break my heart again.

●

Bernie agreed to let me punch out early, before the cleaning routine at the end of the shift. Larry said he didn't mind covering my tasks. He didn't have anything else to do and could use the extra half hour's pay.

"If I were you, I'd tell him to take a hike," Bernie whispered. "You want me to tell him? I don't mind."

"No." I hung my apron up on the peg behind the kitchen door. "I need to talk to him."

"All right. But if you change your mind, I'll be around," he said. "Get yourself a glass of Coke. You can talk to him right here if you want. When you're done, just lock the door behind you."

"Thank you."

"And I mean it. If you want me to kick him to the curb, I'm more than happy to."

"I hope that won't be necessary," I said, pushing my way through the swinging door and into the dining area.

Frank read a paperback at his table. I had a flash of memory cross my mind of when he used to sit in his recliner, the one Mom had sold to a neighbor for three dollars after he'd left. In the evenings of his good days, he'd read something out loud to Mike and me while Mom cleaned up after supper. He liked reading Kipling the most.

I still had his Kipling book on the shelf in my bedroom. I'd never opened it on my own, fearing the stories wouldn't be nearly as good as I'd remembered from when he read them to me.

"I'm done," I said, putting my glass of pop on the table and pulling out the chair across from him. "Bernie said we could talk here. Unless you wanted to go somewhere else."

He put his finger up to tell me to wait just a minute before dog-earing the page and shutting the book. I tried not to let that annoy me. He'd been gone for twelve years and he couldn't put his book down before finishing a sentence. I clenched my jaw to keep from saying anything about it.

"What are you reading?" I asked instead.

He turned the book so I could see the cover. "Some Steinbeck," he answered. "He travels around the country with his dog."

"Is it any good?"

"It's Steinbeck."

I bobbed the straw up and down in my glass, trying to decide if he meant that the book was good or bad.

"Aren't you going to eat something?" he asked, folding his hands on the table.

"I already had lunch."

"You been working here long?"

I shook my head. "Just a month or so. Since graduation."

"Are you planning to go to college?"

"I don't think so." I sipped my Coke, hoping it would settle the nerves that had taken over my stomach. "It's too expensive."

"I imagine Michael would be halfway through by now."

"He's at basic training."

He shook his head. "Army?"

"Yes."

"Somebody should have told him to enlist in the Navy," he muttered, grimacing.

"Why?"

"Because they won't send them." His voice was deeper than I remembered it, full of more gravel. He sounded a lot like Grandpa, and when I realized that, it stung. "They always send the Army. Always."

"How would we have known?" I asked, surprised by the calm of my voice.

He held his empty mug with both hands, spinning it around and around, keeping his eyes on it. I turned in my chair, my legs off the side of it, and looked out the window. Larry came in from the kitchen with the crate of glasses he'd just washed. I hoped he wouldn't look over at Frank and me.

"Your mom still lives in the house?" Frank asked.

I knew he meant the one that backed up to the lake. I shook my head.

"We had to sell it after you left," I said.

He let out a sigh that had a low rumble to it. I prepared to pounce on his words if he had anything to say about that. But he didn't.

"We live on Lewis," I said. "Not too far from Oma."

"You still live at home?"

I nodded.

"I thought you might have been married by now."

"I'm just eighteen."

"Plenty of girls your age are married."

I shook my head. "No qualified candidates have presented themselves so far."

His lips rose in his half smile. "It's good to be picky, I suppose."

"Where have you been?" I turned toward him.

He crossed his arms and kept his eyes on the table between us.

"Well—" he started. "The loons come this year?"

"They come every year."

"I'd like to see them while I'm in town."

"I'm sure you will." The sun coming through the diner

window warmed me, making me sleepy. "Are you going to tell me where you've been?"

"I traveled for a while," he said. "I made it out west for a few years. The weather didn't suit me, though, so I came back to Michigan."

"To Bliss?"

He nodded. "Somewhere in between Detroit and Toledo."

"Do you have a job?"

"I do." He didn't elaborate.

"Doing?"

"I own a car shop," he said. "We fix them up and sell them cheap."

"Anything else I should know?"

"I've got a dog. He's out in the truck if you want to see him."

"No thank you."

He rubbed at his nose with the backside of his forefinger and turned his attention to a spot on the floor where a dot of light jolted and jerked around, reflecting off something. I wasn't in the mood to figure out what it was.

"It would have been nice to know you were still alive," I said. "You could have written at least a few times. At Christmas or our birthdays."

"Maybe I could have."

"Why did you make Grandma keep it a secret?" I leaned forward on the table. "Why would you do that?"

He didn't answer me. Instead, he thrummed his fingertips on the cover of the Steinbeck book.

"How's your mother?" he asked after a few minutes.

"Fine," I answered. "She works for Dr. DeVries."

"I'm sure he loves that," he mumbled, crossing his arms.

"Well, she had to get some kind of job after you left." I tried to keep my voice calm but failed miserably. "How else were we supposed to survive?"

He cleared his throat again.

"It was hard for us, you know." I pushed up my glasses, hoping they'd hide how watery my eyes had gotten. "It was especially hard for her."

"Not nearly as hard as if I'd stayed," he said, raising his head and squinting up at me.

"I'm not sure that's true."

As a little girl I'd entertained daydreams of when Frank would come back. We'd be having supper at the table and he'd come right through the front door. Mom would welcome him straightaway and all would be as it was.

But in my imagination, Frank didn't have heavy bags under his eyes and age spots on his forehead. Somehow I hadn't factored in that he would have aged at all. In my mind, he'd been stuck in his early thirties.

And in my imagination he'd smiled, glad to see us, eager to make all right again. The man sitting across the table from me didn't seem capable of gladness.

"Your mother won't like that I'm here." He clasped his hands together on the tabletop.

"Does it matter?" I asked.

"She won't want to see me."

"Probably not." I shrugged. "You can't blame her, can you?"

"Fair enough."

I bit my lower lip, raking my teeth over it before letting it go. "Have you met anyone?"

"What do you mean?" He frowned at me.

"Have you seen anyone," I said. "Since you left?"

"I haven't taken up with another woman, if that's what you're wondering."

I sighed and my shoulders relaxed. Looking into his eyes I saw earnestness there. I couldn't help but believe him.

"I've never been unfaithful to your mother. Not in that way, at least. I haven't even made a single friend," he said. "Can you believe that?"

"You aren't exactly friendly."

That half smile again.

"I'm staying for the week," he said. "I'll be over at the campground. I've got a trailer."

"Why won't you stay at Grandma's house?"

"Too many memories," he answered. "But if you need me, you can find me there."

"Will you help her?" I asked. "She needs someone to make funeral arrangements."

"I'll do my best."

"What should I tell Mom?"

"Whatever you want."

"What if she does want to see you?"

"That would surprise me." He stood, taking his wallet from his back pocket and digging out a few bills.

"You haven't asked about Joel," I said, an edge to my voice. "Remember, your youngest child?"

"Of course I do." He swallowed hard. "How old is he now? Eleven? Twelve?"

"He's turning fourteen next week."

"Have I been gone that long?"

"Yeah. You have."

I stood, going toward the exit. He followed me, stepping to the side when I opened the door.

"I suppose I should have been a gentleman," he said, squinting at the bright day.

"What do you mean?"

"I should have opened the door for you."

"It's all right," I said. "I can manage."

He looked at me before walking out to the sidewalk behind me.

"You aren't one of those feminists, are you?"

"Would it matter if I was?"

For that I'd earned a full smile.

"You sure are like your mother," he said.

That time, I took it as a compliment.

●

I didn't tell Mom that night that Frank was in Fort Colson. She was already worn out by the time she got home from work. She heated up frozen dinners for us in the oven and told Joel and me we'd eat in the living room.

She didn't even have the energy to set the table.

Joel set up TV tables and Mom took her place in her chair, curling her legs up under her. There she fell asleep before her dinner had even had the chance to cool off.

Joel and I watched more coverage of the riots in Detroit. The reporter interviewed a white woman wearing a headband to hold back wilted hair from her head. She stared at the camera as if she couldn't believe what was happening.

"It sounded like we was in Vietnam, all the shooting and such," she said. "I got down on the floor and prayed none of them bullets would hit me. I thought I was going to die. I think I'll have nightmares the rest of my life over this."

I thought of Frank alone at the campgrounds.

I wondered if he still had nightmares.

●

"He just showed up at the diner?" Jocelyn asked, whispering into the space between our windows. "He didn't call first or anything?"

I shook my head. It had felt good to spill the beans to somebody. Whenever I had a secret to tell, I went to Jocelyn first.

"Unbelievable." She shook her head, her eyes wide. "What did your mom say?"

"She doesn't know yet."

"You're kidding me." She let her mouth hang open. "You know she's going to slap him. I sort of hope I'm there to see it."

"Yeah, she might."

Then Jocelyn tilted her head and made her sympathetic face. "Do you think he's here to stay for a while?"

"I'm not sure," I answered. "He said he'd be here for a week. I don't know if he'll extend his stay or not."

"Do you want him to?"

I didn't answer right away. Shrugging, I looked at the roof that peaked above her head.

"It's okay if you don't know what you want," she said. "It makes perfect sense. It's all positively confusing."

There were few people in the world who had the privilege of seeing me cry. Jocelyn was one. And on that night, I didn't hold back. Not even a little.

"Are you going to be okay?" she asked.

I nodded.

Eventually I would.

Fort Knox, Kentucky

Dear Mom, Annie, and Joel,

Thanks for calling me about Grandpa. I know I was awful quiet on the phone, Mom. That was because I was trying not to cry in front of my drill sergeant. He's been calling me a ninny ever since the day I got off the bus, and I didn't think he needed another excuse for the nickname.

I asked if I could get leave to come home for the funeral. No such luck. I can only go if it's an immediate family member, so unless we can trick them into thinking Grandpa was my big brother, I'm stuck here.

I know I shouldn't tell jokes at a time like this, but it's the only way I can keep from boo-hooing in front of all my buddies.

Gosh, I'm heartbroken over not being there with you all. I'll bet Grandma's not taking it so well. She's been doing everything for him for so long. And I'm not just talking about when he was sick. Tell her I'm sorry, will you? And, Joel, give her the best hug you've got for me.

I'll be thinking about you all day on Wednesday. And I'll even think about Frank if he decides to show up. I hope he does the right thing and comes home. It would do Grandma's heart good, don't you think?

Write me again soon, will you? I miss everybody back home something awful, especially when I think about how I'm missing out on something so important.

I sure do hate being so far from you all.

Love,
Mike

18

Mom was up. Not only was she awake, she was upset. I could smell the cigarette smoke from my room. In my mind there was only one reason for her to be smoking, especially at five o'clock on a Tuesday morning.

She'd found out about Frank.

I got myself dressed and wasn't careful to be quiet going down the stairs. I wanted her to know I was coming. The only thing worse than Mom being upset about something was if she thought I was trying to sneak out the door.

She stood at the sink, looking out the window, a smoldering cigarette between her fingers. She'd bought a fresh pack since the last time.

"You know, when my window is open I can hear everything you and Jocelyn say." She put the cigarette to her lips and breathed in.

"I meant to tell you." I sighed. "Sorry."

"Don't be. I'm sure you were surprised by him." She blew the smoke out toward the open window. "Is he going to help your grandmother?"

"He said he would."

"He's said a lot of things." She said it under her breath and rolled her eyes.

"Are you mad at me?"

Turning on the tap, she soaked her half-smoked cigarette before dropping it into the sink. "No."

It was a clipped no. An unconvincing no.

"I have to get ready for work," I said, heading toward the bathroom.

"Did you tell Joel?" she asked.

"Not yet."

"Do you think he remembers him?" she asked. "Do you know?"

"I don't know how he would."

"You're probably right. He was so small."

"He asks me about Frank sometimes."

"Why don't you take your brother to meet him," she said. "After work today, maybe."

"Do you want me to tell Frank anything for you?"

She shook her head. "I can't think of a single thing I have to say to him."

She turned toward me and crossed her arms. That was when I noticed she wasn't wearing her wedding ring. When she caught me looking, she held her hand up.

"I don't want him to get any ideas," she said.

●

Joel and I rode our bikes out to the campground where Frank had said he was staying. I'd thought about driving, but it seemed like a waste of a sunny day and a bit of gas. We took our time, the afternoon warmer than it had been in a week. Once we got to the dirt road leading to the entrance of the park, we rode side by side.

"What's he like?" Joel asked.

"I don't know," I answered, pushing a stray hair away from my face. "Pleasant, I guess."

"Pleasant?" He laughed. "I'm not sure I ever imagined him being pleasant."

"Well, it's probably not the right word. I mean, he isn't horrible, really. But he isn't all that friendly."

"You aren't really making me feel good about this."

"All right," I said, sighing. "He's really smart. He reads a lot. When he thinks something's funny, he smiles like Mike but doesn't laugh. In fact, he's a lot like Mike."

"Except for the friendly part."

"Right."

We took the turn into the park. Bright blue flicker of a jay swooped between tree branches. Somewhere a squirrel chitter-chattered his disapproval of something, perhaps the bird.

"I'm nervous," Joel said.

"You don't need to be," I said.

"What if he doesn't like me?"

"How could anyone not like you?"

He shrugged. "I'm sure it's possible."

We pedaled down the road that led to the campsites. Only a couple of them were occupied. One site housed a pup tent and the other a small camper beside a rust-red pickup truck. A square of wood with the number 44 etched into it was nailed to the peeling trunk of a birch tree.

"I think that's it," I said.

We parked our bikes and knocked on the door of the camper, and an old hound dog bayed from where he lay next to a tree.

"Simmer down, Shadow," Frank said, coming from around the backside of the camper, holding a tin kettle with steam ribboning out of the spout. "Don't worry about him. He's all bark and no bite. He's too lazy to start a fight."

He was wearing a white undershirt and the slacks he'd worn the day before. He hadn't slicked his hair back, and it hung over his forehead.

Joel stood beside me, his eyes not leaving Frank's face. His lips parted, and I couldn't tell if he was trying to say something or not.

"Is that Joel?" Frank asked, setting the kettle on a fold-up table and putting his hands into his pockets. "My gosh, how you've grown."

Joel pushed his shoulders back and tried to stand as tall as he could.

"I thought he should meet you," I said. "Before the funeral."

Frank took two steps toward us and put out his hand for Joel to take. Disappointment dulled my brother's smile. But only for a moment. He did shake hands, but I wondered if he'd expected Frank to show a little more affection. I wondered if he'd wanted a hug.

"You drink coffee?" Frank asked, letting go of Joel's hand. "I just heated up some."

"You don't have to make us anything," I answered. "We can't stay long."

"I'd like some," Joel said, stepping on top of my words. "If it isn't too much trouble."

"All I have is what's left over from this morning. I hope that's okay." Frank crossed his arms. "How do you take it?"

"However you do."

"Black?"

"Sure, thanks."

Never in his life had Joel so much as taken a sip of coffee. He was in for a big surprise.

Frank stepped inside his camper and rustled around for something. A cupboard slammed and a silverware drawer clattered. Joel and I stood beside each other, trying to see through the narrow door at what he might have been struggling against.

After a few minutes, he returned, holding two camp cups by their handles. Tipping the kettle, he filled the cups, handing one to Joel. It looked more like sludge than liquid and I wondered if he'd made it thick on purpose.

"I hope it's not too strong for you," he said.

"It should be fine," Joel said. "Thanks."

"Your mother know I'm in town?" Frank asked, sipping his coffee and letting out a subtle "ah."

I nodded in answer.

"She doesn't care to see me, does she?"

"No."

"I guess I don't blame her." He took a good-sized drink, looking over the rim of his cup at Joel. "It's not too hot."

Joel tipped his cup, taking a bigger drink than he should have. He held it in his mouth, his cheeks puffing out and his eyes starting to water.

"Just swallow it," I whispered. "You won't taste it anymore."

He forced it down before hacking and spitting, his face red.

"It'll put hair on your chest," Frank said, grinning. "Takes some getting used to, I guess."

Joel nodded, trying to hide the grimace he could hardly

conceal on his face. He didn't finish the coffee but looked around to see where he could dump it when Frank wasn't looking.

"You don't have to drink that mud." Frank reached for the cup. "Even I don't care for it. I had better when I was in the Marines. Come on. I'll get you a bottle of Coke. I think I saw a machine out by the restrooms."

"That's okay," I said.

"It'll only take a minute," Frank said. "You want one?"

"No thanks. I'll just stay here."

Frank handed me his empty cup and Joel's that was still mostly full. I wondered if he expected me to wash them. As they walked away, Frank called the old hound to come with them and I stepped up into the camper. I'd decided I'd just put the cups on the counter or in the sink, if the camper even had something like that.

The ceiling wasn't high enough for me to stand to full height, so I stooped. On one side of the camper was a small cot, with barely room for one, covered with a pea green, wooly blanket and a yellowed and misshapen pillow. The contents of the camper were sparse. A suitcase that seemed to function as a dresser, a hot plate, and a few provisions were what I could see without digging through things or opening the two cupboards. I set the cups on a tiny table pushed up against one of the walls.

Out of the corner of my eye I saw a photo taped on the wall just above the pillow. It was a small square with scalloped edges. Moving toward it and bending down, I saw that it was of Mike, Joel, and me, sitting on the dock that used to be ours, each with our legs dangling over the edge. Mike's feet were in the water, mine skimming the surface.

But Joel's chubby legs jutted out straight in front of him. We all wore our happiest smiles. Mom stood in the water beside us, her hands on Joel's waist. She was in the middle of saying something.

Sitting on the edge of the cot, I couldn't seem to take my eyes off the picture. I wanted to take in every detail. The baseball cap sitting sideways on Mike's head. My pinstriped swimsuit that I remembered having been so proud of. The way Joel reached toward the camera with one of his little hands.

Every single thing about that picture said that we'd been happy once. At least in that moment.

I'd become so drawn in, I didn't hear the creak of the camper when someone came in and stood beside me.

"She was worried that Joel would fall in the water," Frank said, pointing at the photo. "Your mother was."

I stood quickly, stepping back from the picture, leaning into the wall of the camper, hoping he wouldn't be angry at my intrusion. If he was, it didn't show.

"I told her he'd learn how to swim real quick if he did." He shook his head. "She told me I was wrong. Well, in her way."

"She likes being right," I said.

"That she does." He shrugged. "Nobody likes being wrong, though, do they?"

I told him I was sure nobody did.

"She's a good mother," he said. "I knew that from the time Mike was born."

"She's strong, that's for sure."

"Strongest person I ever met. Man or woman."

He cleared his throat and went back outside, the camper jostling up and down as he exited. I gave that picture one last look. The crinkling, dried-out old tape that held it in place bore testimony to how long he'd had it there.

When I followed him down the camper steps, I breathed in the fresh air, feeling lighter somehow than I had in a week.

19

Mom had picked up a new black dress for me from the department store in town. It was simple. Just a shift dress with capped sleeves. She'd lamented its lack of shape and how the hemline skimmed the top of my knee, worried that it might offend someone.

"It was all I could find in a pinch," she'd said.

I pulled on a baby blue knit cardigan, hoping that Mom wouldn't think it was too casual for a funeral. It wasn't warm enough to go without. Slipping my feet into my black flats, I went downstairs.

Joel had on a suit that had been Mike's at least three years before. Mom had him standing on a chair in the kitchen as she pinned up the hem of the slacks.

"You should have tried these on yesterday," she said, straight pins held between her lips. "Annie? What time is it?"

"Nine," I answered. "We've got time."

"Well, at least I can do a quick job of it." She stood and swatted at Joel. "Get down and take those off so I can stitch them real fast."

He hopped down, shaking the whole kitchen as he did. Then up to his room he went to change out of the slacks.

"Are you going with us?" I asked, starting the water for a cup of tea.

"I don't know," she answered, sitting at the table. "Do you think I should?"

"It's up to you." I reached into the cupboard for a mug. "It might be nice for Grandma."

Mom nodded and sighed. "Joel said he liked meeting your father."

"I guess so."

"He said he thinks he's changed. As if he'd know." She picked up a spool of black thread from the table. Then she lowered her voice. "Do you think Joel expects Frank and me to get back together?"

"No," I said, dropping a tea bag into my mug. "No. He wouldn't think that."

I said those words, but in my mind I was sure he held out hope.

"Do you think Frank wants to see me?"

"He might," I answered. "If you end up going to the funeral, he will whether he likes it or not."

"How did he look?"

"Older."

"Has he put on any weight?"

"I think he's skinnier." I turned off the heat under the kettle.

Joel thundered down the steps with his pants in hand, a pair of shorts on with his dress shirt, tie, and jacket. Mom rushed with the slacks to her bedroom. The whirr of her sewing machine started up soon after.

He stood just outside her bedroom, watching her work,

and I thought about telling him not to get his hopes up too high about Frank sticking around.

No matter how I thought of it, I knew Joel would end up disappointed.

●

We'd arrived at the church an hour before the funeral, joining Grandma in welcoming everyone who came to pay their respects. Frank hadn't shown up yet even though he'd promised Grandma he'd be early. Mom said she didn't care if he came at all. Still, every time someone new came in, she looked up from where we stood in the narthex.

"He'll be here," I told her. "Even Aunt Rose isn't here yet."

She nodded and tried to smile at me but tapped a finger on the tip of her chin the way she did when she was nervous. It didn't help when Aunt Rose finally did arrive and sashayed across the room toward us. She wore a black suit, very much like the one Jackie had worn to President Kennedy's funeral. But at least Aunt Rose only wore a veil that covered half her face.

It looked perfect on her, of course. I wondered how long she'd waited to wear it.

"Gloria," she said to Mom in the way that snooty women had. "I'm surprised to see you here."

"Rose." Mom didn't turn toward her. "You look well."

"I am." Aunt Rose sighed. "Aside from the terrible mess in Grand Rapids. I'm sure you've heard that we had riots of our own. I could see the smoke clouds from my front door. It's quite troubling."

"I'm sure." Mom flicked an imaginary speck off the sleeve of her dress. "I'm sorry about your father. He was a good man."

"Thank you." Aunt Rose pretended to see someone across the room. "Excuse me."

After she left, Mom grumbled, "I hate her."

"That's not very nice," Joel said.

"I dislike her greatly." Mom looked at him out of the corner of her eyes. "Is that better?"

"Annie," Grandma said, coming to me and taking my hand. "There's someone who wants to meet you. An old neighbor of ours. She remembers when you were small."

I followed behind her to the other side of the room, leaving Mom and Joel by themselves.

The church was full of hushed whispers except for the loud talking of Grandma's old neighbor who absolutely could not believe how much I'd grown. She told me more than a few times how she'd given me butter rum candies whenever I came to visit.

Even though I told her that I remembered, I didn't.

The old neighbor had me cornered, Grandma having abandoned me to greet another old friend. I was sure that I'd have a butter rum Lifesaver forced upon me at any moment. I could only hope that it wasn't from a roll that had been in her handbag for overlong, with lint stuck to the candy.

I was just about to excuse myself when Frank finally came through the doors.

He had on a three-piece suit, black, with a gray tie. His hair was styled with pomade and he'd shaved. Though the gray in his hair looked haggard the day before, now it made him look distinguished.

If someone had told me that he was the brother of Gregory Peck, I would have believed it, cleaned up the way he was.

The whole narthex silenced, save for the woman in front

of me. But I blocked out her voice. All eyes were on Frank. Surely they'd heard one way or the other that he'd returned to Fort Colson. But seeing him was still something to behold.

Even with all that attention, he looked only at my mother. And she blinked at him, not smiling or showing any sign of recognition.

"Excuse me, please," I said, moving away from Mrs. Butter-Rum-Candy and making my way to where Mom and Joel stood.

Frank made it there just about the same time I did.

"Hi, Glo," Frank said.

"I'll be sitting in the family row," she told him.

He nodded, putting out his arm for her. She didn't take it but walked right on by him. Not knowing what to do but also not wanting all the town to talk, I slipped my hand into his crooked elbow. He reached up with his right hand, enclosing my fingers in his. It might have been instinct or a moment of thoughtless movement. Still, it almost felt familiar to me.

"She needs time," I whispered.

But then I felt foolish for saying it.

She wouldn't get time. None of us would. I reminded myself that Frank wouldn't allow for that. I was sure he'd pull his camper out of the park as soon as he could change out of that nice suit of his. His promise of a week was nothing more than words. I just knew it.

Forgiveness would take time.

Time I doubted he'd be willing to make.

●

I wasn't sure who decided such things, but throughout the funeral Grandpa's casket stood open behind the minister.

From where I sat, all I could see was the tip of his pale nose peeking beyond the edge of the coffin.

"I'm not going to look at him," I whispered to Joel during the close of the service.

"You don't have to." He gave me a smile, but his eyes were sad.

"Are you going to?"

Frank cleared his throat from where he sat on the other side of Joel. Mom put her hand on mine and gave me the hairy eyeball, what Mike always called the "church scold." I turned my face to look straight forward but avoided the casket.

I stood when the minister lifted his hands and made an attempt to sing the words of the closing hymn. The best I could do was mouth them. Even then, I was certain the rock would dislodge itself from where it had settled in my throat and I'd collapse from the release of grief.

Shutting my mouth, I clamped my emotions, resolved to hold them off until I was alone in my room. At the long, drawn-out amen, an usher came, directing our row to exit. But instead of retreating toward the back of the sanctuary, he pointed us toward the casket.

Mom put her hand on the small of my back, pushing me. "You'll regret it later if you don't," she whispered into my ear.

I let her guide me, but only because I didn't want to make a scene.

Frank stepped to the casket first, putting his fingers on the silky white fabric that hung over the side. His expression didn't change as he looked at Grandpa's face. I wondered if he felt any regret. I wondered if he wished he'd had one last chance to visit him.

He bent the knuckles of his fingers, knocking on the silk

twice before stepping aside to let Joel and Mom have their turn. I stayed back a step or two, hoping I'd be able to pass by without having to look in. I didn't know what it was that made me want to rush out. It wasn't fear. I knew that much to be true.

"Annie," Mom said, reaching for me and cupping her hand around my elbow, pulling me forward.

I felt all the eyes of the sanctuary on me as I stood at the head of the casket. Shutting my lids, I breathed in as deeply as I could, taking in the sickly fragrant aroma of the floral arrangements mixed with whatever chemicals they'd used in their embalming of my grandfather.

Steeling myself, I opened my eyes, seeing his face for the first time since we'd last visited him. He looked so natural, so like himself. I'd heard that before and, from the other funerals I'd been to, I'd never thought it was so. All the other dead people I'd seen had a waxy, artificial look about them.

But my grandpa, lying in his casket with his hair parted the way he preferred, his tie knotted perfectly, the color on his cheek so naturally painted, he could have been sleeping.

A memory rushed into my mind. Some afternoon when we drove out to visit. Before Frank had left. Sun streaming through flossy sheers. Grandpa on his back on top of the quilt Grandma spread across their bed. My squeaky, little girl voice calling for him, telling him to wake up. His exaggerated snores rumbling from his nose and mouth. A twitch of a smile played at the corner of his lips. Tiny hand shaking old man's shoulder. His smile cracked wide, his eyes opening.

"You all right?" Joel whispered.

I couldn't answer. All I could do was cover my face with my hands. That was when I felt arms thicker than Joel's around me. The smells of Old Spice and Brylcreem overpowered the flowers, and I knew it was Frank. I patted his back, hoping that would be enough to get him to let me go. It was.

Breaking away, I pushed through a side door that led to a stairway. I rushed down the steps to a fellowship hall, where a few ladies worked getting the luncheon put together. Before they could see me, I snuck behind a burnt orange colored curtain pulled across a stage. I sat on the ancient, threadbare carpet. In one corner was a manger and right behind it, a tomb painted on particle board, no doubt props for Sunday school plays.

O, death, where is your victory? O, death, where is your sting?

The victory was upstairs in the casket. The sting was in my chest.

I heard footsteps on the stairs. The curtain rustled, letting a little light into the stage area. Mom ducked in and sat on the floor beside me.

"Well, this is a good place to hide," she said.

"I don't want to go to the graveside." I wiped at my eyes under my glasses.

"Neither do I." She pulled a hanky from her handbag, reaching over and dabbing at my cheek. "But your grandmother needs us there. Do you think Frank's going to offer her any kind of comfort? Or Aunt Rose?"

I laughed, a tear falling off the tip of my nose.

"I just wish Mike could have come home."

"I know," she said. "Me too."

We sat there just long enough to be sure that most of the mourners were out of the sanctuary. Then, out we went to join the procession of cars that snaked its way through town and to the cemetery, Grandpa in the hearse that led the way.

•

Frank hitched a ride back with us to the church, where his pickup was still parked. Mom drove, he was in the passenger's seat, and Joel and I sat in the back. Frank kept sneaking peeks at Mom, who kept her face straight, her eyes on the road.

"Mom, what's for supper?" Joel asked, leaning forward and resting his chest against the back of the front seat. "Maybe you could come over, Dad."

Hearing Joel use that name for Frank made a shiver jolt up my spine and caused my stomach to lurch. I resisted the urge to elbow him in the ribs.

The name hadn't escaped Mom's attention either. Her shoulders tensed and she gripped the steering wheel a little tighter.

"Not tonight, son," Frank answered, looking at Joel over his shoulder. "I've got a few things I need to do in town."

Joel nodded, but I knew from the way he leaned back in his seat that he was disappointed.

Mom's eyes flicked into the rearview mirror, glancing at him. If she had a soft spot for anyone, it was Joel.

"Friday is Joel's birthday," she said. "Why don't you join us for dinner then. Unless you have something else planned."

"I can be there," Frank answered.

"Bring Grandma," I said. "She shouldn't be alone."

Mom nodded. "The more the merrier."

Joel smiled the rest of the evening.

Dear Annie,

Thanks for writing back to me. I don't receive many letters from home, believe it or not. It was nice to have my name shouted out at mail call for once. Caroline isn't one to write much. If you see her around, could you let her know I'd like a letter from her?

When you write back, would you tell me about the books you're reading? Maybe even tell me what you think of the world, politics, this war, ANYTHING.

I miss intellectual conversations. The guys I'm stationed with aren't exactly the smartest around.

Yours,
Walt

Dear Walt,

To be honest, I don't see Caroline very much. Even if I do, I don't know that she'd listen to me, but I'm willing to try. If nothing else, I could have my oma write to you. She loves nothing more than sending letters.

Today was my grandfather's funeral and I'm not too keen to write much more. It's been an exhausting day.

Sincerely,
Annie

PS: I'm currently reading The Outsiders. It's about the conflict between poor greasers and rich kids in the same town. It's pretty good.

20

There were three meals Mom made well. Two more that were edible. And a host of dishes that she could render poisonous just by thinking of them. Of those recipes, meat loaf was her best.

Still, that wasn't saying much.

She'd come home early from work that afternoon, making sure that everything was just right. When I'd offered to help, she'd given me a list and sent me to the grocery store.

"Don't take too long," she'd said. "I'm going to need you to make the potatoes."

By the time I got home from the store, the house was tidied, dusted, floors swept and windows cleaned. Mom made short work of unpacking the groceries and dumping the ground beef into a bowl.

"Get started on those taters," she said, cracking an egg into the meat.

I tried not to see the bits of shell that fell into the mix.

She measured oats and salt and pepper while I peeled potatoes. She mixed with her hands while I chopped. She fit the mess into bread loaf pans and I filled the pot with water and put them on the stove. While I was glad it hadn't gotten too hot that day, it was humid, making the kitchen feel awfully close.

Steam fogged up my glasses, making them slip down my nose. "I wish I didn't have to wear these things," I muttered.

"Don't complain," she said from behind me. "They make you look smart."

"Thanks, I guess."

"A man doesn't underestimate a woman he thinks is smarter than he is." She washed her hands in the sink, working the soap into a rich lather. "But then again, most men would never admit that a woman was smarter than they are."

"'Men seldom make passes at girls who wear glasses,'" I said.

"Don't use Dorothy Parker against me." She looked at me out of the corner of her eye. "You aren't the only one who reads around here."

"I know that."

She set her timer and I knew I'd need to check on the meat loaf when she wasn't looking. Mom had a habit of over-estimating how long something needed to cook and I didn't want to end up eating charred bricks that evening.

"After supper, we'll let Joel open his presents," she said. "I can't wait for him to see what I got him."

"Tell me," I said, intrigued by the smile in her voice.

She cupped her hands around my ear and whispered, "I had Opa's guitar fixed and restrung for him."

"You did?" I turned to her, pushing up my glasses again. "He'll be so surprised."

"I even asked the man at the music store to polish it." She sighed. "It looks brand new."

It wasn't often that Mom talked to me like we were a couple of girlfriends. When she did, it was like looking behind the curtain at a softer-edged, more fun version of her. The Gloria she'd been before life reshuffled the deck and gave her a worse hand of cards.

"Bernie said that you have a new regular at the diner," Mom said, pouring a splash more of milk into the potatoes.

I stopped mashing. "Oh, that's David."

"Oh." She made a short humming sound through her nose. "Where is he from?"

"Lansing."

"Huh."

I went back to work, trying to figure out what Mom was getting at.

"Does he have a family?" Mom asked.

She watched my face, scrutinizing it.

"I'm sure he does."

"I mean, is he married?"

"No," I answered. "He's only a few years older than me."

"Bernie seems to think the man comes to see you."

"I think he just wants lunch."

"Hm."

When I chanced a glance at her again, I couldn't help but blush.

●

Frank arrived just when Mom told him to and stood on the other side of the screen door with a cardboard carrier full of Pepsi bottles and a package of Oreo cookies. It seemed strange, him standing on the porch of that house. I couldn't decide if he belonged or didn't.

I pushed the door open for him, holding it until he walked past me and into the living room. Looking around, he handed me the cookies and one of the bottles of pop.

"Nice house," he said.

"Thanks." I nodded for him to follow me into the dining room. "Didn't Grandma want to come?"

"She said she wasn't up for it." He shrugged. "I wasn't going to force her."

"That's fine." I looked out the door. "Joel went to get Oma."

"Oh, good." He bit at his lip.

The screen door swung open, Joel holding it for Oma to walk through. She acknowledged Frank with a nod of the head and went directly for a seat at the dining room table. Never in my life had I witnessed her give anyone a sour look before that.

"Hey, Dad," Joel said, oblivious to the tension. "I'm glad you came."

"Happy birthday, son." Frank clapped Joel on the back, relieved to have at least one person excited to see him.

Mom stood in the kitchen doorway, one of the meat loaf tins held between her oven-mitted hands. She hadn't changed from her pedal pushers and everyday blouse, hadn't bothered to put on lipstick. There was no set of pearls at her neck and her hair was falling loose out of her rubber band. Still, Frank looked at her as if she was the most beautiful person he'd ever seen.

"Gloria," he said.

"Have a seat." She put the meat loaf on a trivet with a thud. Then she turned and went back into the kitchen.

Frank looked at the chairs set around the table as if he

didn't know what they were. Oma turned her face from him as if to say that he'd better not even think of sitting next to her.

"Not that one," I whispered when he put his hand on the back of where Mike always sat. Then I pointed at my seat.

By the time we were all settled, Mom came back with the mashed potatoes.

"Joel, go ahead and say grace," she said, pulling her chair out and sitting down.

"Lord," Joel started, "thank you for this food and for the hands that prepared it. Be with Mike and thank you for having Dad come home. In Jesus's name, amen."

"Amen," Oma repeated, putting her napkin in her lap.

"Thanks, son," Frank said, his voice deep and quiet.

Mom reached over the table, serving up slices of the meat loaf right out of the tin, grease dripping off the bottom of each. When she dropped a chunk of it on Frank's plate, she looked up at him, almost daring him to say something.

"Any ketchup?" he asked, unfolding his napkin and placing it on his knee.

"I'll get it." I jumped up from my chair and retreated to the kitchen, pulling open the refrigerator, all the bottles in the door clanging together. I grabbed the Heinz, giving it a gentle shake as I walked back into the dining room. "Here you go."

"Thank you," he said, twisting off the cap. He held it over his meat loaf and slapped the bottom.

"Hit the 57 on the bottle," I said, taking my seat. "It comes out better that way."

"Who told you that?" Joel asked.

"Bernie. It works every time."

"Just use a knife." Mom closed her eyes and breathed in through her nose as if all her patience was tried.

"I know how to get ketchup out of a bottle, thank you."
He shook it and a blob of red hit, splat, on top of the meat.

Joel took the bottle next, whacking it just like Frank. Mom
pinched the bridge of her nose between thumb and forefinger. I served myself a spoonful of potatoes and passed the
dish to Oma on my right.

"Have you heard when Mike will get back from basic?"
Frank asked, cutting his meat loaf into a dozen square bites.

"They're sending him to medic school," I answered.
"Somewhere in Texas."

"Fort Sam Houston," Mom added.

Frank shook his head in a way that made me think he
disapproved.

"What?" Mom asked. "You think he should have done
something different?"

"No," he answered. "It'll be fine."

His tone was less than convincing.

Clinking forks and knives on dishes, Joel's sipping of Pepsi
and the ice knocking against the glass, and Mom's occasional
sighs were the only sounds for longer than was comfortable.
I spun the gears in my brain, trying to think of something to
talk about. Nothing. I had nothing.

"You know how I went over to Andy's house yesterday?"
Joel said, shoving a forkful of potatoes into his mouth.

"Who's Andy?" Frank asked. "Is he the kid who used to
live next door to us?"

"That's Walt Vanderlaan," I answered.

Mom cleared her throat. "Andy Ferris," she answered.
"You wouldn't know him, Frank."

"Well," Joel went on. "He let me try out his guitar. He
taught me a couple things on it."

Mom glanced at me, pushing her lips closed so she wouldn't give away her secret. I could tell she was pleased with herself.

"He told me I was pretty okay at it." Joel shrugged.

"Well," Frank said, "how about I give you your present now."

"You didn't have to get him anything," Mom said before scooping a bite of potatoes with her fork.

"Sure I did."

"He can wait until we're finished eating," I said.

Frank's eyes sparkled and his mouth was held in the widest smile I'd seen on him. "I'd like for him to have it now. Go on out to my truck. It's lying on the front seat."

Mom pretended not to notice when Joel hopped up from his chair, bounding for the door. She looked down at her dinner, pushing the creamed corn around on her plate.

The front door creaked open and shut, Joel's footsteps sounded on the living room floor. He stood in the entryway with a look of utter shock on his face. In his hand he held the neck of a shined-up, sapphire-colored electric guitar.

"You aren't joshing me, are you?" he said.

"I'm not." Frank grinned at Joel. "That's for you."

"To keep?"

"If you want."

"Thank you." Joel's voice cracked, but he didn't seem embarrassed by it. He was just that excited. "It's beautiful."

"I'm glad you like it."

My mouth hung open, and my eyes went right for Mom's. But she kept her eyes lowered.

"I love it." Joel's smile was wider than I'd ever seen it.

"Go ahead, show us what your friend taught you," Frank said, pushing his chair back a few inches.

"Come finish your supper." Mom still hadn't looked up from her plate, at least not that I could tell. "You can play with it later."

Joel shot a look at me, and I widened my eyes, hoping that he'd know that meant he better do what she said. Her tone might have been pleasant and even, but I knew her temper wasn't. From where I sat, I watched him turn and place the guitar as gently as possible on the couch in the living room.

"Thanks, Dad," Joel said, returning to his seat.

Mom flinched at the word.

"It's a Gibson," Frank said. "Les Paul Custom, the man who sold it to me said. They don't make those anymore. That one sat on the display for a year and then went right into the box. Never played. Just like brand new."

"How do you have money for something like that?" Mom asked, putting her fork down on her plate.

"Mom—" I started.

"A guitar that nice must have been pretty expensive."

"I don't want to say how much I paid," Frank said, tossing his napkin on his hardly touched plate of food. "But my boy's worth it."

"Your boy." Mom crossed her arms.

"Fourteen is a big year."

"And the last you saw him was before he'd even turned two years old." Mom cocked an eyebrow. "Were all the birthdays in between less of a big deal?"

"Gloria," Oma said.

But she didn't hear her. Or she didn't listen, which was more likely. "Twelve years, Frank. Twelve."

He didn't look at her but instead lifted the napkin to examine the remaining meat loaf, frowning at the sight of it.

"You didn't send us a dime," she said. "But you come home for two days and spend a hundred dollars on a guitar."

"Actually, I'm sure it was more like two hundred," Joel said.

"That's not going to help," I whispered to him.

"It was a gift." Frank dropped the napkin again and looked up at her, his eyes hard and narrowed. "That's all."

"A two-hundred-dollar gift." Mom put a hand to her forehead. "Do you know how many mortgage payments I could have made with a two-hundred-dollar gift so that your children had a roof over their heads? Or how many bags of groceries to feed them? Goodness, two hundred dollars would have come in handy when Michael's appendix burst when he was thirteen or when Joel broke his arm falling off the slide at school."

"Mom, please," I said.

"If I'd known, I could have sent a check," Frank said.

"If you'd known?" Mom pushed back her chair and shifted to the edge of it, her hands on the table, palms down. "If you'd *known*? How could you have possibly known?"

She waited for him to answer, tilting her chin down and opening her eyes wider.

"Oh, that's right." She stood. "You never called. You never wrote. You stayed away. You couldn't have known."

Oma murmured something in Dutch, but Mom waved her off.

"No, Mother," she said. "I will not calm down."

I folded my hands in my lap and breathed through my mouth, wishing the windows weren't open so wide and hoping that none of the neighbors were listening too closely. If only the rain hadn't stopped.

"If you'd wanted to know so badly," Mom said, her voice icy, "all you had to do was ask."

She took up the pan with only half a meat loaf left in it and turned to go into the kitchen.

"Gloria," he said. "You know it wasn't easy for me."

"You could have called anytime," she said.

"And get scolded like this?" Frank crossed his arms and wrinkled his nose. "No thanks."

Not missing a beat, Mom turned, her hand digging out the remaining meat loaf, which she threw with a pitcher's precision right at Frank's head. If he hadn't ducked, it would have smacked him right in the face. Instead, it hit the wall, sliding down the plaster and leaving a greasy yellow trail behind it.

Without another word, Mom walked into the kitchen.

"She hasn't changed one bit," Frank said under his breath. In his eye was a spark, not of anger, but of something else that seemed akin to awe.

When Mom slammed the door to her bedroom, it shook the whole house.

●

Frank stayed to help Joel clear the table while I took a sponge to the wall, working out the grease stain as much as I could. Oma had gone to Mom's room, knocking softly on the door until she was let in. We didn't speak, but if we did, it was in whispers as if we didn't want to wake a sleeping dragon.

It was less than half an hour later when Mom and Oma came out of the room, the fury passed. Mom bundled the tablecloth, the last thing Frank and Joel had to do, and took it to the laundry room. Milk carton in one hand, she pulled five glasses from the cupboard and carried them into the dining room.

"You brought cookies?" she asked, her voice even, without a trace of fierceness. It had all been spent.

"Yes," Frank answered, wiping his hands on a dishcloth.

"Put them on a plate," Mom called to him.

The sound of crinkling plastic and tearing paper followed by the plinking of cookies hitting dish came from the kitchen.

"Leave that." Mom nodded at the mess on the wall, most of it gone. "I'll finish later."

We sat at the table, the plate of Oreos in the middle, glasses of milk in front of each of us. When Frank reached for a cookie, I saw how his right hand shook. Just like it had when I was a little girl.

He still hadn't outrun Korea.

Mom noticed too.

Without a word, she took his glass of milk and moved it to his left side.

●

Mom made me promise that I would never tell Joel about Opa's guitar. I told her that she could give it to him at Christmas or for another birthday in a few years.

"Maybe," she'd said.

She wrapped it in an old blanket and stowed it on the shelf in her closet right above her wedding dress.

"Maybe," she'd said again before sliding the closet door closed.

Dear Joel,

Happy Birthday, little brother! Fourteen years old. Gosh and golly and holy smokes! I'll bet you're a good two inches taller, now that you've gotten so old. I expect you to write back and tell me all about your day. What did you get? Did Mom make you something "delicious" for dinner? Did you take the Corvair for a spin in the graveyard?

Whatever happened, I hope it was a great day for you, bud.

I tried picking out a good card for you from the px here on base but no dice. They were all sappy, kissy-face ones for fellows to send home to their girls. I didn't think you'd want something like that.

By the way, if you don't know what a px is, don't feel dumb. At first I didn't and had to have somebody explain it to me. It's what they call our little store down here. Postal Exchange. Although, all they like doing is exchanging cash from my check for a bottle of Coke or a Hershey's bar.

Anyway, I'm doing fine here. Just waiting for graduation. Tell Mom that she doesn't need to come down for it. Truly. I guess a lot of the guys' parents don't. Would you tell her it isn't a big deal? It's not like I'm getting a PhD or anything. Although, if I were, I might not be in this mess.

Tell her I'll be headed right to Texas from here. No stop

*in Fort Colson for me until after my medic training. I
wish I could, though. I miss you all something awful.*

*Could you do me a favor? Could you ask Oma to make
me a couple of cookies and send them to Texas when she
gets a chance? I'll give you a buck when I get home if you
do.*

Happy Birthday, Tiger. You're the greatest.

Your favorite brother,

Mike

*PS: Mom and Annie, don't be too sore that I didn't write
to you this time. The kid only turns fourteen once. He
deserved his own letter. Oh, and Mom, if Frank's still
around, try to control your temper. I know he deserves
your anger, but it won't help anybody. Annie, if Mom does
something crazy (like whack him on the head with a rolling pin), I want to hear every little detail. My money's on
her.*

Love you all.

21

Overhead, a woodpecker hammered into a tree. Looking up, I squinted against the sun, trying to see the bird. No luck. Countless leaf-laden branches spread from a multitude of ancient trees. Trees that I imagined had taken seed a hundred years before anyone who looked like me had put foot on Michigan soil.

Breathing in the musty smell of damp earth and the floral aroma of trees, I shut my eyes and listened. Birds chirped back and forth to each other, filling the woods with their song. Standing in the middle of the trail, I allowed a memory to grab hold of me.

Frank on one of his better days so long ago, walking with me along the tree line, not too far from our old house. He stopped, lowered to one knee, and put a finger to his lips to let me know I should be quiet.

"Do you hear that?" he whispered. "The trees are singing."

"But I don't hear them," I'd said.

"Ah. Listen closer."

I'd watched his face, trying to tune my ear to the song of the trees. With every bird twitter or chatter, each call or screech, he put up his pointer finger as if to say, "There and there and there."

"Those aren't trees," I'd said, giggling. "They're birds."

"You don't say." He'd scrunched his face up tight. "I could have sworn."

"Daddy. You're silly."

"You know what I read in my Bible the other day?" he asked. "Something about the trees singing when God is nearby."

"Does that count for birds too?"

"Why not."

"I hear birds all the time," I'd said.

Frank had narrowed his eyes and made a humming sound. When he stood up, he'd taken my hand.

●

I continued on the trail that I knew would eventually lead to Frank's campsite, ambling along with no hurry to my steps. As I did, I rehearsed in my head what I'd say to him and worked up the nerve to ask him to stay.

He'd been to dinner every night since Friday and I thought that, surely, he'd come that night again. And in the last two evenings Mom hadn't whipped anything at his head. In fact, the night before she'd even smiled at a joke Frank had told.

I didn't hold out hope for him to rejoin our family. But I also didn't want him to go away.

It surprised me to happen upon a family coming the other way down the trail. A mother and father led four kids of various heights. Each child looked all around them as if they didn't want to miss anything. Sky-tall trees and flittering, twittering birds. Undergrowth so thick they couldn't see the ground beneath. Wildflowers of purple, blue, and yellow.

I couldn't help but smile at their wonder. Warmth filled me as the smallest among them repeated "Lookathat" as they passed by me.

I could still hear them when I stepped off the trail and into the camping area. Frank's truck was gone, which wasn't much of a surprise. What caught me off guard was that the camper was gone too. The fire pit had no smolder left to heat up a pot of too-strong coffee, and the ground had nothing but a trace of tire track. The old hound didn't bellow a greeting.

Nothing remained of Frank.

Turning around twice, I thought maybe I'd come to the wrong site. That I'd exited the trail in error. But I saw the peeling birch with the number 44 nailed to its trunk. It was the right spot.

I kicked the old barrel trash can that stood to one side of the site; it clanged hollow. Even that had been emptied of any trace of Frank.

●

It wasn't far from the campground to our house on Lewis Street. At most it was two miles. Still, the dejection sitting heavily in my heart made it feel like no matter how many steps I took, I got no closer to home.

When I heard the rumble of an engine, I stepped to the side of the dirt road to let the car pass, hoping it wouldn't kick up gravel at me. But as soon as the old yellow Buick passed me, the driver stepped on the brakes.

Walking to the passenger's side window I saw that David sat inside, his radio playing the Beach Boys. I sighed. I could have sworn he'd have better taste than that.

"Hi there," he called out the rolled-down window before

reaching for the volume knob on the radio and turning it down. "Do you need a ride somewhere?"

"No." I shook my head. "Actually, maybe. If it isn't any trouble."

"It's no trouble at all." He leaned across the bucket seat and pulled the door latch. "Come on in."

Just before stepping down into the car, I thought how Mom would never approve of me taking a ride from a man I hardly knew. Especially a man who looked like David.

But I needed a ride, and David hadn't given me any reason not to trust him. Besides, Bernie seemed to like him, which was quite an accomplishment.

"Which way were you headed?" David asked. Then he saw my face. "Are you all right?"

"I'm fine." I wiped under my eyes, bumping my glasses and making them go crooked. "I was going home. Do you know where Lewis Street is?"

"I think so," he said. "You might have to help me."

"Okay."

He put the car into drive. "Did you read Marmaduke today?"

●

He drove at a nice speed—not too fast or slow—down the country roads toward town. The song on the radio had changed from "Good Vibrations" to "I Was Made to Love Her." David tapped his fingers on the steering wheel, keeping time with Stevie Wonder's smooth-as-silk voice.

Every few minutes he'd breathe in deeply of the air coming in through the windows.

"Summer smells good, doesn't it?" I asked, instantly wondering if it had made me sound like an oddball.

"Yeah," he said, nodding his head at me and smiling. "You noticed too, huh?"

I grinned at him and thought how nice it was to be understood.

"So, what were you doing out this way?" I asked, folding my hands in my lap.

"Just getting the lay of the land." He licked his lips. "Did you know that Al Capone had a hideout around here?"

"Who told you that?"

"Bernie Jager." He glanced at me. "Shouldn't I trust him?"

"Not about mobsters," I said. "This town has all kinds of legends and closet-dwelling skeletons. More of them are imagined than not."

"I guess he was making up that bit about Bonnie and Clyde too, then?"

"Probably."

He slowed for a squirrel crossing the road.

"How do you like living out here?"

"It's nice. Lots of wild spaces," he answered. "Growing up in the city, I didn't get too many chances to spend time outside. I mean, I'd play in my backyard or walk to the park, but that's not the same as being in the woods. My father would drive me over to a nature center in town. It was another world there, and he'd have to drag me, kicking and spitting, back to the car when it was time to go home."

We reached the place in the road where the pavement met the dirt and where the sounds of Fort Colson started. It wasn't quite as loud as the city, but not nearly as peaceful as the park. We were less than a block away from my street. Part of me wished we had longer to go.

"My mother was relieved when I got the job here," he said. "She was afraid I'd end up living in a cave somewhere."

"Although living in a cave doesn't sound half bad some-times."

"So true." He chuckled. "How about you?"

"Hm?"

"What did you want to be when you were a little kid?"

"Oh, I don't know." I rubbed a spot behind my ear. "For a while I wanted to be a nurse. Then a dancer. More than anything, though, I wanted to be a librarian."

"A librarian?"

"Is that bad?" I asked.

"No. I think it's great." He pointed at the street sign. "I turn left here?"

I nodded.

"Now, how does one become a librarian?" He steered the car down the road. "College?"

"Maybe," I answered. "But I don't know if that's going to happen for me."

"That's all right," he said. "You're smart enough already. I see you reading those thick books at the diner. If there's anyone in this town who could work her way around a library, it's you."

He pulled onto my street and when I told him which was my house, he parked in front of it. We both got out. He stood by his door, and I walked toward the lawn.

"Thanks for the ride," I said.

"You're welcome." He smiled.

"You didn't ask what I was doing out there by myself."

"It didn't seem like my business."

"I guess I'm just used to everyone around here making everything their business."

"Must be the way in a small town like this, huh?"

"Yup." Out of the corner of my eye, I saw one of my neighbors watching us, not bothering to be a subtle spy in the least. "I should go."

He looked around me, seeing the neighbor lady stand with hands on her hips. Just then, out from behind her skirts peeked her son, Roger. He couldn't have been more than four years old. When she marched to where her lawn met the street, Roger came right along behind her, holding tightly to the fabric of her dress.

"Annie?" she called, squinting at me from across the street.

"Oh, hi, Mrs. Chapman," I said, lacing my words with syrupy sweetness.

Roger stood, staring at David with big, round eyes.

"Are you all right?" Mrs. Chapman asked, glancing at David.

"Yes, I'm fine," I said. "David was giving me a ride home."

"Why?"

"Just to be nice."

"Are you sure you're okay?" She spoke through a fake smile, looking again at David. Then she said quietly, "He's not bothering you, is he?"

"No, he's not. He's my friend."

"Mama," Roger said, pointing. "Look at his skin."

"It's brown, isn't it?" David said to Roger. "Say, do you like going to the park?"

Roger nodded.

"What's your favorite thing to do there?"

"Splash in the puddles," Roger answered.

"Hey, me too." David grinned. "Did you know that my job is to work at the park? I get paid to splash in puddles now."

Roger's eyes grew even larger.

"Do you think that sounds like a fun job?" David asked.

"Yes, sir," Roger answered, stepping out all the way from behind his mother. "I like catching worms."

"All right." Mrs. Chapman put her hand on Roger's shoulder as if she feared he might dash across the street. "If you're sure you're okay, Annie."

"He's a good person," I said.

Mrs. Chapman took Roger's hand, turning from us and going to her porch. I had no doubt she was going to let my mother know all about this. I'd done nothing wrong, but I already felt defensive.

"Nice to meet you," David called after them. "You too, buddy."

"Bye," Roger said, looking over his shoulder and waving.

"Have a good day, champ."

The Chapmans' door slammed behind them. If I'd had to bet, it would have been that she locked her door for the very first time since moving into that house.

"I'm sorry," I said.

"Don't be." He shook his head. "Happens all the time."

"That doesn't make it okay."

"I know."

"You were nice about it."

"I've had to learn how to react," he said. "If I get mad, they might call the police. If I ignore them, they yell louder. Some days it's easier than others. But my father made sure to teach me the importance of turning the other cheek."

"You're a better person than I am."

"I don't think that's true." He smiled at me. "Thing is, I might not be able to change the minds of people like Mrs. Chapman. But that little boy? I might have a chance."

"I think I'd just get mad."

"I do. Believe me, I do."

He watched me walk to the porch and climb the steps. I waved at him before opening the screen door. From inside, I heard the tinging of Joel's unplugged guitar.

With a twinge of regret, I knew I'd have to tell him that Frank was gone.

I looked over my shoulder one last time to see David still watching me.

"Thank you," I said.

"Anytime."

•

Joel went for a walk by himself after I told him the news about Frank. Probably to the campsite to make sure I was telling him the truth. By the time Mom came home from work, a bag of groceries in her arms, he still wasn't back.

"Well," she said when I told her. "We knew Frank wouldn't stay around long, didn't we?"

I followed her to the kitchen to help her put away the things she'd picked up from the market. Among the usual items of onion, flour, and orange juice was a paper-wrapped package from the butcher and a bottle of beer.

Never in my life had I known Mom to buy alcohol.

"It was for Frank," she said, taking it from me and reaching for the bottle opener. She popped the top and turned it over into the sink. The skunky smell of it filled the kitchen as it fizzed its way down the drain. "Why don't you run over and ask if Oma wants to have supper with us."

I told her I would.

"Annie? Have you ever cooked steak before?"

"No," I answered.

She sighed.

Dear Frank,

You should have let us know that you were leaving. Even a note would have been nice. It's just good manners, you know? Saying "good-bye."

Joel's heart is broken. I thought you should know that. If you want to do the right thing, at least write to him and tell him that you'll see him again sometime.

Unless you plan on staying away. In that case, it's probably best if you just leave him alone.

We liked having you here, you know. You might not believe me, but I was glad you came.

I'd missed you.

Annie

Fort Knox, Kentucky

All,

I don't have much time to write today. Sorry. I have to pack all my gear and tie up loose ends here before I head out for the great state of Texas.

Sorry about Frank leaving. Or is it congratulations for Frank leaving? I'm not sure. Maybe it's a little of both, huh? Either way, I'm sure you're all feeling a little worn down by his visit.

Mom, I hope the meat loaf didn't stain the wall too badly. If it did, I'll see if I can fix it when I get home in October.

Gosh, doesn't that seem forever away? October. Hopefully it will zip by like nothing. All the fun I have in medic training should make the time fly, don't you think?

No?

Me either.

Anyway, it would be too long, even if it was only a day. I miss you all. Joel, I expect you to learn a few good licks on that new guitar of yours by the time I get back. I have no doubt you will, you smarty-pants, you.

> *Love,*
> *Mike*

22

I'd wrangled Mom's ironing board up the stairs and to my room, unfolding it in the corner by my one electrical outlet. Plugging in the iron, I contemplated what Jocelyn wanted me to do.

"Are you sure about this?" I asked, hoping she would tell me she wasn't. "What if I burn all your hair off?"

"You won't." She smiled at me.

"How do you know?"

"Well, I don't. But I trust you anyway."

"You shouldn't." I set the iron on the board. "You don't want to be bald, do you?"

"Of course I don't." She grabbed my pillow. "That's why I'm not doing it myself. Just use a pillowcase. That should help, right?"

I raised my shoulders and took the case she'd pulled off my pillow.

She tilted her head so that her long, dark hair lay flat on the ironing board. I put the smooth fabric of the pillowcase on top of it before lowering the iron to it, moving it slowly the way she'd told me to.

Every summer, on the third Friday of August, Fort Colson held a beach bash on the shore of Old Chip. Someone would play records while the more daring kids danced. We'd grill hot dogs and roast marshmallows and sit around a bonfire telling stories.

It was our way of trying to hold on to a summer that was all too quickly dashing away from us.

"Tell me again why you want your hair done," I said, still running the iron over the pillowcase.

"I don't know. Just to see what it's like."

"Should I do my hair too?"

"If you want."

"Let's see how yours turns out first."

"Have you gotten another letter from Walt?" she asked.

"No. It's been a long time since I heard from him," I answered, lifting the pillowcase to see perfectly flattened hair under it and glad that it was still attached to her head and not burned off. "Honestly, it wouldn't break my heart if he didn't write again."

"Hm. That's interesting."

"What is?" I took up another handful of hair, smoothing it out on the ironing board.

"Oh," she said. "I figured you knew already."

"Knew about what?"

"Haven't you heard?" She fingered the smooth section of hair I'd just finished. "Caroline sent him a 'Dear John' letter."

"No." A sinking feeling pulled at the space behind my sternum. If I'd had to assign a name to it, I would have called it pity. It wasn't the first time I'd ever felt sorry for Walt, but it had been years. When I took in a breath, it was gone. Just like that.

"I'm sorry. I thought you would have heard by now." She sat up, her half-smooth hair hanging against the side of her face. "It's actually the talk of the town."

"Do you know why she dumped him?"

"All I know is that her parents came to the paper last week to cancel the wedding announcement they'd already paid for."

"Poor Walt. I'm sure he did something to deserve it, though," I said. "Put your head down. Let me finish or you'll look like Cousin Itt."

●

Mom pulled Jocelyn and me aside before we left the house. She spoke in low tones with her arms crossed, her face as serious as it got. It was the same talk she'd given us a hundred times over. Still, she delivered it with the utmost intensity.

"There might be drinking at this party, girls," she said. "There might even be drugging. If there is, you come right back here. Understand?"

We both nodded.

"If by chance you drink something you shouldn't and you can't get yourselves home, use the pay phone and call me." She pursed her lips and handed each of us a dime. "I'll come get you. No questions asked."

We both nodded again.

"And if a boy tries to get you to go off with him alone, you're to say 'no.'" She put her fists on her hips. "There's only one thing a boy wants, being by himself with a girl, and ladies, it isn't to hold your hand."

"What's that?" I asked, smirking at her. "What do they want?"

"Oh, you know." Mom swatted a hand at me. "I just don't want anything bad to happen to you."

"It's just the Beach Bash, Mom," I said. "The hardest drink there will be cream soda."

"There probably won't even be that many boys," Jocelyn said. "And I think they all go to church."

"You think that makes a difference?" Mom crossed her arms again. "Listen to me, girls. Boys who go to church are not immune to, well, desire."

"I promise," I said. "If a boy finds himself overwhelmed with desire for me and tries to get me drunk and drugged up so that he can kiss me, I will sock him in the nose."

"You aren't funny." Mom rolled her eyes and shook her head.

"Sure I am." I gave her an exaggerated wink. "See you in a few hours."

Mom gave me the hairy eyeball, but I knew she was holding back a laugh. "Have fun. Just not too much."

●

For all the fears Mom held that I'd give in to the dangers and temptations of my generation—free love, acid trips, and war protests—the riskiest activity in which I engaged was participating in a potato sack race in the sand.

The party hadn't attracted too many people. But enough had come so that we had fun. It was the kind of gathering I much preferred. After the sun went down, a few of us bundled in blankets and beach towels and sat in old camp chairs, our sneakered feet propped up on the bricks of the fire pit.

Conversation turned, as I'd expected it would, to Walt and Caroline. Not much happened in Fort Colson, especially not the joining of the two most popular kids in town. But when that union was smashed, it was double the news.

"Oh, she sent that letter a month ago. I guess she told someone that she didn't want to go to Michigan State having a boyfriend," one girl in the circle said. "She wanted to keep her options open."

"It seems pretty hard of her," a boy piped in. "Letting him down while he's at war."

"I heard that he's been writing to other girls," someone else said. "I wouldn't like that either."

I peeked at Jocelyn, knowing she wouldn't have told anyone. She'd kept all my secrets up until then; I knew she wouldn't betray my trust over something small like that.

"Maybe they just weren't a good match," Jocelyn said. "Better to realize it now than after getting married."

The girls in the round nodded their heads and the boys crossed their arms and we all looked into the fire for a while, not saying anything. Then, from the other side of the pit, a girl a year behind me in school sat up straight and cleared her throat.

"If I were her, I'd be afraid to have a boyfriend over there," she said. "Can you imagine if he got killed? Wouldn't that be awful for her?"

"How about we go for a walk?" Jocelyn whispered into my ear, grabbing my hand and pulling me away from the bonfire.

As soon as we were away from the glow of the flames, I felt the chill of the evening. I pushed the buttons through the holes of my jacket, trying to trap at least a little warmth.

The sounds of the fireside gossip faded the closer we got to the public access dock. Jocelyn pointed out a couple who were kissing under a tree.

"You'd think they'd need to come up for air," she said, giggling. "Or at least try to hide a little better."

We walked to the end of the dock and sat. The wood slats were wide enough that we could sit cross-legged and face each other without fear of falling off the side.

"Do you think Caroline knew that Walt was writing to me?" I asked.

"Who knows," she answered. "Either way, you can't blame yourself for their breakup. I won't allow it."

"They were just friendly letters. Nothing else."

"I believe you."

The water of Old Chip was calm that night, as it was most of the time. Every minute or so, we'd hear a *plip* and *plop* of a fish surfacing or the *sploosh* of a duck landing on top of the lake. The loons were quiet, most likely shy because of the music and laughter from the shore.

"Annie?" Jocelyn said. "I need to tell you something."

"Yeah?"

She gathered her silky hair in her hands, pulling it over the front of one of her shoulders. She sighed and met my eyes.

"I decided that I should go to college after all," she said. "It took her a while, but my mother finally agreed that it was a good opportunity."

"It is," I said, taking her hand. "You are too talented to write another article for the *Chronicle*."

"Actually, I still have a few to write." She rolled her eyes. "Next week is the tractor pull out at the fairgrounds."

"You'll miss the simple and quaint stories you write here, won't you?"

"Maybe a little, if I'm completely honest." She folded her hands in her lap. "I just wish you could come with me."

"I do too."

"You'll write to me, won't you?"

"Of course I will," I said.

We didn't stay at the end of the dock much longer. Someone had turned up the radio, and the sound of horns blasted from the speakers along with Aretha Franklin's no-nonsense voice. A bunch of girls left the fire, squealing and running to the makeshift dance floor in the sand to sing along, spelling out R-E-S-P-E-C-T at the top of their lungs.

Jocelyn and I jumped up, dashing down the dock to join them. None of us could dance to save our lives. And most of us couldn't carry a tune in a bucket. But it was summer and we were young and for just a minute or two we could forget about all the madness in the world.

Dear Annie,

I haven't written in a long time, I guess. We've had lots of missions to go on and we haven't been back to base in so long I got lost going to the mess hall. War isn't for sissies, I can tell you that.

You've probably heard by now—I'm sure the whole town knows—but Caroline called it off with me. I got her letter a while back, but it's taken me a week or so to really understand what happened.

Are you sure you never see her? Does she come to the diner sometimes? Has she been with another guy? It would kill me if she has, but I've got to know.

Write back soon, please.

Walt

Walt,

I was sorry to hear about you and Caroline. But, if I were you, I'd focus on getting back home in one piece. You can't let yourself be distracted right now, especially since you've only got a few months left to go.

Caroline hasn't been around much this summer. Sorry. I don't think she comes to my side of the lake very much, really. If she did, I doubt that she'd want to talk to me about something as personal as her decision to break up with you. I would try, though, for your sake.

I know this must be so hard for you. But it will be okay in time. I promise. You'll have no trouble finding another girl. I'm sure there will be a dozen to choose from once you get home.

You just have to make sure you survive until then.

Take care, Walt.

Annie

23

One Sunday out of every month, Mom and Oma helped out in the church nursery. They'd rock babies while their parents sat in the service, cooing to them or feeding them a bottle of milk. It seemed there were never more than five babies at a time; still, Mom liked me to lend a hand every once in a while.

"So you have some practice," she'd say, winking at me. "Not that I'm rushing you."

That morning three came to the nursery. One for each of us. Oma had the Martinezes' two-month-old, Donna. Mom sat on the floor, rolling a ball to an eighteen-month-old named Sammy. I had little Joanne, who had chosen that day to be a bit fussy.

"Take her for a little walk," Mom said. "She might like a change of scenery."

As I stepped out of the nursery, I could hear Oma singing a Dutch lullaby to Donna.

"*Slaap, kindje, slaap*," she sang.

I smiled, humming along to the tune of the song I knew as well as any hymn, the words as well as a Psalm. Oma would have thought it sacrilege to compare a lullaby to Scripture. But when I was little, I heard the song—*sleep, baby, sleep*—imagining it in the voice of God singing to a little shepherd boy—*outside there is a sheep*—who would one day become the king of Israel.

The shepherd guards him day and night—the song of a Lord promising care and gentleness and rest—*sleep, baby, sleep.*

Joanne and I bobbed our way around the narthex, looking at the pictures of missionaries displayed on the bulletin board and the stack of gold-plated offering trays. It only took a few minutes before she rested her head into my neck and fell asleep.

I turned to go back to the nursery to see if she'd let me put her in a crib when I saw David walk in. He had on a short-sleeve dress shirt and a black tie. Quite a change from his everyday clothes. He looked from me to the baby, narrowing his eyes and cocking his head to the side.

"Is she . . . ?" he started, his voice just above a whisper.

"Not mine," I said. "I'm helping in the nursery today."

He formed his lips into an "oh" and nodded.

"You're just a little late."

He looked at his watch. "I got a call about a fawn who got herself trapped in somebody's yard. I had to rescue the poor damsel."

"I guess that's a good excuse."

"Well, I guess I should catch the tail end of the sermon," he said, pointing at the sanctuary.

"Right." I nodded. "I hope it's a good one."

When I turned back toward the nursery, I saw both Mom and Oma looking out at me, two sets of blue eyes open wide.

"You know him?" Mom asked when I neared the door.

"He's the regular at the diner," I answered, handing Joanne to Oma. "The one Bernie told you about."

"Him?" Mom shifted her head to try and see him.

"He's nice," I said.

"I should think so," Oma whispered, carrying the baby to the corner and lowering Joanne into one of the cribs.

Mom leaned into the doorjamb and crossed her arms. "Is he the one who drove you home that day?" she asked. "Mrs. Chapman called me at work about that, you know."

"I was upset . . ." I started. "About Frank."

"You don't have to explain it to me." She rubbed her lips together. "It would be very difficult, you know."

"What would be?"

"If the two of you—"

"Gosh, Mom," I interrupted her. "There is no two of us."

"Okay. If you say so." She turned and went back to Sammy where he sat stacking blocks. "What's his name?"

"David."

"All I'm going to say is this—and then I'll be quiet about it because I'm sure you don't want me to interfere—guard your heart, honey."

I felt numb, not knowing what to say or even what she meant by that.

Oma's clear voice took up the lullaby again.

Sleep, baby, sleep.

24

August was nearly spent before we knew it. Most of the people in Fort Colson tried to hold on tightly to the last days of summer even if it wasn't terribly warm and Old Chip had already gone too cold for swimming. The sun set earlier every night, it seemed, reminding us that, soon enough, autumn would come to usher us into winter.

I wasn't ready for summer to be done.

Joel and I took turns checking in on Grandma Jacobson, taking her cans of soup or fixings for sandwiches, sitting with her to make sure she'd eat. Each time I went, I hoped she'd have gotten a letter or phone call from Frank. Whenever I asked, she denied that she had.

The problem was, I wasn't sure if I should believe her or not.

It was a Thursday and I used Mike's car to drive to her house. Bernie had wrapped up a burger in tin foil for me to take to her. I didn't knock on the door, instead I opted to let myself in. It seemed better than making her get up to answer it.

I found her in the living room, where she sat in Grandpa's

chair, staring out the window. She'd left a full cup of tea on the side table at her elbow. It had gone cold.

"Would you like me to make you a fresh cup?" I asked.

She shook her head. "I can't keep anything down," she said.

"How long has that been going on?"

"Don't worry about me." She waved me off as if it wasn't important. "I'll be all right."

"But if you're sick, we should call the doctor."

"I'm not sick in that way."

Sighing, she turned her face from me. Instead of pushing her to say more, I took her cold cup of tea into the kitchen and washed what few dishes she had used in the days since I'd last been there.

On the small table that stood flush against the kitchen wall was a box of old photographs. A layer of dust had settled on the top, which lay removed and discarded on the other side of the table. A few photos lay fanned out and face up. Gathering them in my hands, I recognized the young man in the first picture—tall and thin and grinning—as my grandfather. The beautiful woman on his arm was my grandma. In each picture they stood as close together as they could get. In a few, she held a baby that was either Frank or Aunt Rose, I couldn't always tell. I flipped through a stack of them before I heard her shuffle in and stand beside me.

"I got those out last night," she said. "I haven't been sleeping, and it seemed like something to occupy my time."

"I don't think I've ever seen these before." I looked at another. "Is this Grandpa?"

"He was handsome, wasn't he?"

She had a hanky held tightly in her hand, raised to her

chin. I couldn't be sure, but I thought she might have been wearing the same housedress she'd had on the last time I'd visited. The sour smell of her told me she most likely was. Her typically set-perfect hair was flat in the back and dingy looking, as if it hadn't been touched since the funeral.

"You miss him?" I asked.

"Of course I do." She said it as if I was stupid for asking it. "I've missed him for years, though, haven't I?"

I nodded, putting the stack of pictures down and turning to face her.

"It would have been better if he'd died five years ago," she said. "He suffered so."

"Grandma, don't say that." I swallowed hard, trying to push down the heaviness that threatened to erupt out of me. "You don't mean it."

"Maybe not. I don't know. But, Annie, there are some things worse than dying." Her dark eyes filled with tears, and she made to leave the room. "Lock the door when you leave. I won't have you barging in here again. An old woman deserves a little dignity."

"Have you heard from my father?" I asked.

She stopped, her shoulders tensing. "No," she said. "He hasn't contacted me. But I'm sure he's back in the same place he's been for twelve years."

"Why did he leave?"

"How would I know?"

She left me in the kitchen, alone with a box full of memories that stung me to riffle through.

I did as she asked.

I locked the door behind me.

Everybody,

Remember in my last letter how I said medic training wasn't near as bad as basic training? Well, I hate to admit that I was wrong. But I was. And how.

This week we learned how to give shots and start IVs. Guess who we practiced on. Each other. I have more needle holes in me than a pin cushion. I don't mind telling you that I am sore! My partner blew my vein at least three times. I've never had an uglier bruise in my whole life.

I tried getting sympathy from one of the nurses here. But she said an angry bruise didn't warrant a date off-base. Strike out for Mikey. I never did have much luck with the ladies.

Sorry, Joel. I'm afraid the lack of wooing skills is hereditary. You can thank Frank for that.

We're on to splints and fixing dislocated shoulders next. Let's just hope we don't have to put a shoulder out of socket to learn how it feels. Now that I think of it, that might be a way to convince her to let me buy her a bottle of Coke.

They show us a lot of films here as part of our training. Just not the kind you'd want to eat popcorn while watching. I think they're trying to get us ready for what's coming, but they're scaring me half to death. I guess I'm in the right place if eventually I get scared all the way to death. I'd bet these guys would love a little real-life opportunity to try out what they're learning.

Don't worry, Mom. The worst that's happened so far is me getting sick in a garbage can.

One of the guys I met here said he's been at Fort Sam for three months and hasn't gotten his orders yet. He's working in the hospital they've got on base. He said if I'm lucky, maybe they won't send me to Vietnam after all. Wouldn't that be something?

Would you all do me a big favor when you think of it? Go see Grandma a little more. Would you? She sent me a letter and I could tell she's lonely. I know she's not always the nicest, especially to you, Annie. But just pop your head in for a minute here or there. You're all she's got right now. We all know that Aunt Rose isn't making any extra trips from Grand Rapids, don't we?

Write back soon and tell me how it's going. Joel, I bet you start school soon, huh? Eighth grade, right? Can't believe how fast this summer went by.

Love,
Mike

25

My alarm clanged a full hour earlier than it needed to. As fast as I could, I turned it off for fear of waking Joel or Mom. Looking out the window I saw that Jocelyn's bedroom light was already on, and I wondered how long she'd been up.

For all I knew, she might not have slept at all. If I'd been her, I wouldn't have been able to the night before leaving for college.

Mrs. Falck let me in after I tapped on her kitchen door. She was wearing a pale pink bathrobe and slippers and had rollers in her hair.

"She's upstairs," she told me. "Just getting the last few things in order. You can go on up."

"Thank you," I said.

"I'm making coffee. Would you like a cup?"

"Oh yes, please."

"I'll bring it to you," she said. "Now, go on."

I climbed the steps, not needing to guide myself to the room that was Jocelyn's. I knew the way as if I were going to my own bedroom. Her door was open a crack, and I pushed it to find her sitting in the middle of the room, half the books from her shelf on the floor, encircling her.

"What are you doing?" I asked.

"How will I ever decide which ones to take?" She wiped under her eye. "I don't want to leave any of them."

"Do you even have room in your dormitory for them?" I stepped carefully over a row of books, joining her in the circle.

"I don't know. Most likely not."

"You'll probably get more books for your classes, don't you think?"

"Oh, you're right." She frowned. "But what am I going to do with all of these?"

"You can leave them here, can't you?"

"But they'll be lonely."

Had Jocelyn said that to anyone else, they might have questioned her sanity. Or laughed at her. Or told her to stop being so sentimental. But I understood exactly what she'd meant. Any true reader would. Within the pages of each book in the ring around us was a friend, fictional or not. The March sisters and Miss Maude, Charlotte and Wilbur, Jem and Scout, Cosette and Anne Shirley.

To leave the books behind would be to depart from a good friend.

"I can take care of them for you," I said.

"I know I'm just being silly."

"You aren't." I picked up a copy of *A Tree Grows in Brooklyn.* "Can I help you put these back on the shelf?"

It was short work, putting the books where they belonged, and Jocelyn only cried once. I'd determined that I wouldn't cry. Not when we carried her few crates to the trunk of her father's Ford or when I hugged her good-bye. I wouldn't break as they drove away, leaving me in their front yard to wave until they were out of sight.

Instead, I cried all the way on my walk to work, glad for the dark morning.

●

The lunch special was spaghetti and meatballs with a side of garlic toast and boiled broccoli. It was the first time David opted for something other than what was written on the chalkboard.

"You don't like spaghetti?" I asked.

"Is that strange?" He grinned.

"A little bit."

He leaned his chin on his fist, raising his eyebrows at me and smiling.

"What would you like instead?" I asked, looking down at my order pad and feeling strangely flushed.

"Do you think Bernie could make me a grilled cheese?" he asked.

"I think he could." I jotted it down. "Anything else?"

"Some chips and some of that broccoli, please. And a glass of milk too."

"Sure thing."

When I got to the pass-through window, I noticed Bernie looking out at me, a big goofy grin on his face.

"What?" I said, handing him the order slip.

"Nothing." He shook his head and laughed. "Nothing at all."

"Bernie . . ."

"Grilled cheese coming right up." He turned for the grill, still shaking his head and laughing.

An elderly couple from church came in for a pastry and cups of coffee. They asked me how Oma was and about whether or not Grandma Jacobson was all right.

"We're praying for Michael," the woman said, patting my arm. "We pray for him every day."

"Thank you," I said. "Don't stop, please."

When Bernie called out that the grilled cheese was up, I excused myself and went to get the plate. But instead of one, there were two.

"Take a break," Bernie said. "You haven't had your lunch yet."

"But I . . ."

"Take a break or I'll fire you." He smirked. "Go have lunch with him."

"With who?"

"Him." He nodded in the direction of David.

I couldn't think of anything to say, so I tittered and picked up the plates.

"Don't drop them," Bernie called after me. "Oh, and you're welcome."

I took the sandwiches to David's table, putting one of them in front of him. "I don't know how to say this," I started. "But my boss told me I have to eat lunch with you or else I'm fired."

"We wouldn't want you to lose your job, would we?" David asked, leaning forward, hands on his thighs.

"Not over something like that."

"Well, do you want to have lunch with me?"

"Only if it's okay with you."

"I cannot think of anything I would be more okay with." He motioned to the seat opposite him. "Please eat lunch with me, Annie."

I put the plate down before sliding into the booth.

Dear Annie,

Of all the people I write to, you're the only one who writes back every time. It makes me think maybe everybody else hates me. Everybody but you.

Thanks for sending me letters.

Do you remember when we were kids and I told everybody to stop being your friend because your dad left? Mike punched me in the face for it. Did you know that? He broke my nose. It's been a little crooked ever since.

Well, anyway, I'm sorry I said mean things about you. I'm even more sorry I said them to you. Being out here and seeing what I do makes you think about things. I've been thinking a lot about the ways I've been a bad person. I guess I'm not good enough to have anybody write me letters after all.

For all the mean things I said or did, I feel worse about having done them to you. You never deserved it and I'm sorry.

Forgive me? Please.

Your friend (I hope),
Walt

Dear Walt,

I wish I could say that I don't remember you ever being mean to me. But that wouldn't be true. Although I do remember, I don't hold it against you. Golly, it really did hurt at the time. I can and have forgiven you, though.

You aren't a bad person. Not really. You're just somebody who did the wrong thing a few times (or more than that). We've all fallen short. The mean things you did? They aren't what makes you who you are. As my oma would say, who you are is God's child. That's all.

Sorry for the sermon. I hope you didn't mind it too much.

Mike is, without a doubt, sorry about your crooked nose. That's a drag. I never noticed, though.

> Your friend (why not?),
> Annie

26

For nearly two weeks my visits with Grandma Jacobson consisted of me bringing food that I knew she wouldn't eat and asking her questions about how she was that I knew she wouldn't answer. In fact, she rarely said more than "hi" and "good-bye" to me.

"Take your oma with you," Bernie had said after I told him about it. "They've been through the same kind of loss. Your oma will know how to help."

So, the next time it was my turn to drive out to Grandma's house, I took Oma along. She'd brought with her a pot of homemade soup and a loaf of fresh-baked bread. Grandma was too polite to tell her that she wasn't going to eat. She even let us wipe the dust off the dining room table and set it with her pretty plates and bowls. When I brought out the linen napkins, she didn't put up the slightest fight.

It had ended up being a stroke of genius, bringing Oma along.

"Would you like me to say the blessing?" Oma asked, reaching for our hands on either side of her.

I took hers and watched as Grandma contemplated it.

After hesitating, she gave in, just letting Oma have the tips of her fingers. But she didn't reach for my hand. I tried not to take it personally.

"Dear God," Oma began, her eyes closed tight. "We come to Thee to thank Thee for Thy many blessings and to ask for Thy forgiveness for our many sins."

I lifted one eyelid to look at Grandma, whose forehead wrinkled at the last sentence. Her Methodist roots had often been at odds with Oma's Reformed background.

"Remind us of our errors," Oma continued. "And remind us that, without Thee, we are but dust. We can do no good thing apart from Thee. In the name of Jesus Christ, amen."

"Amen," Grandma repeated, her eyes on the napkin she was busy spreading on her lap.

Oma served Grandma, ladling the steaming soup into her bowl and cutting off a chunk of bread to go with it. I passed the butter to Grandma, and she took a good-sized pat.

Her veiny hands still possessed their gentle grace, and she held her knife properly as she smoothed the butter onto the bread. She'd always been a lady. Even in grief, she still was.

"This is good," she said after swallowing a spoonful of soup. "Thank you."

"I'm glad you like it." Oma blew over her bowl, sending steam rising in a beam of light. "It's one my mother made often. We call it *erwtensoep*."

"How interesting." Grandma took another bite. "My mother made it too. She called it split pea with ham."

Both ladies smiled, Oma with a sparkle in her eye. "Perhaps our mothers had the same recipe book. Ours must have been the Dutch translation."

"Maybe." Grandma was still smiling when she bit into her bread.

"When did Great-Grandma come from England?" I asked.

"Right before the turn of the century," Grandma said. She turned to Oma. "She and my father eloped."

"They did?" I put my spoon down. "I didn't know that."

"You never asked before." Grandma blinked at me. "They were young. Sixteen or seventeen, if memory serves. She found herself in a family way. You know what that means, don't you?"

She raised her eyebrows at me, and I nodded.

"I'm glad. I'd hate to be the one to have to tell you about all that." She shrugged. "Her father threatened to kill them both. From what I've heard, he wasn't a kind and understanding man."

"I should say not," Oma said.

"The two of them stole money from their respective parents and bought tickets to America." Grandma lifted her hands as if to say what-can-you-do before taking a drink from her water glass. "Of course, that baby was my elder brother Alfred. I was born within wedlock."

"Did they ever speak to their parents again?" I asked, putting my hands in my lap.

"Why would they have?" Grandma shook her head. "They had a new life. There was no use going back to a family that didn't want them."

We finished our soup and bread, Oma and Grandma sharing stories about the different meals their mothers prepared. I couldn't follow their conversation, my mind wandered too much for that. All I could think of was my great-grandparents sneaking off together and boarding a boat to put an ocean's distance between them and their families.

Grandma hadn't said anything about what her grandmother had been like. I wondered if she'd been as mean as her husband or if she felt powerless to resist him. On a normal day, I might have asked Grandma about it. But Grandma hadn't had a normal day in too long.

There was one thing I learned from the story, though.

Ours was a history of running away.

●

Stacking the bowls and plates, I cleared the table and insisted that I could do the dishes by myself. Neither lady argued and I was glad. It seemed Grandma enjoyed visiting with Oma. I guessed it was just what she'd needed.

It didn't take long to wash and dry the dishes and wipe down the counters, so I took a rag to the windowsills and the hutch, the crystal glasses and the shelf of cookbooks. My last chore was to bundle the trash and take it to the garbage can in the garage.

Outside, I listened to the neighbor kids playing in the yard next door to Grandma's house. One of them was counting "One-Mississippi-Two-Mississippi." Hide and go seek, I was sure. Trash in hand, I opened the garage door and stepped inside to lift the lid off the garbage can.

The small windows let in just a few squares of orange sunlight. It was enough, though, for me to see Grandpa's tools still laid out the way he'd left them on the night he'd last wandered off.

Letting go of the trash, I stepped in farther, lifting my hand as if I could catch the dust motes as they danced in the beams of sunshine. Breathing in the smell of gasoline fumes and rubbery tires, I remembered being small, barely able to see over the workbench.

Grandpa had lifted me to sit beside his screwdrivers and wrenches and drill bits, warning me not to get them mixed up.

"You don't want to confuse me, do you?" he'd asked, a sparkle in his eyes.

I'd giggled in a way that only he could conjure out of me.

"What are you doing?" I'd asked him.

"Mikey and I are going to change the oil," he'd answered. "That all right with you?"

I'd nodded and watched the two of them lie on their backs and shimmy up under the car's engine. He'd told Mike different names for the parts of the car, but I hadn't been listening. I'd just sat on the workbench, watching the two of them. All I could see was their legs, knees bent into peaks.

Before I left the garage I arranged his tools in the way he would have liked them, trying with all of my might to remember where they should have gone. Wishing that he was there to tell me if I was right.

I didn't have it right. I knew I didn't. So, I stepped out of the garage, shutting the door behind me. The kid next door was still counting, and I wondered how many times he'd lost track.

●

Grandma's voice was more hushed than usual from the other side of the kitchen door. I pushed it open and saw that she and Oma still sat at the dining room table.

"I don't know that I have much choice," Grandma said.

"Of course you do," Oma answered. "You must make the decision for yourself."

"It's no good, me living here alone." Grandma shifted in her seat. "I'm not sleeping well. This old place makes too many noises at night. And, darn it all, I'm lonely."

"Would you feel welcome at your daughter's house?"

I eased the door closed again, still listening.

"I suppose so." Grandma's voice was higher than usual, more uncertain, I thought. "Rose has always been good to me in her way."

"Do you want to be with her?" Oma asked. "Do you think that can bring you joy?"

"I think I do."

Leaning back against the kitchen wall, I tried to imagine Grandma gone too. All I could think of, though, was that the hole was just getting wider and deeper.

"I'll miss the kids, though," Grandma went on. "Gloria has done a good job with them."

"She certainly has."

"I want to thank you for being a good grandmother to them. I couldn't always be, I don't think. Especially not when Rocky was sick."

"You did your best, Mabel."

They were quiet for longer than a minute, and I pushed the door open so I could see them again. Grandma had her face in her hands, her shoulders shaking from silent mourning. Oma had her hand resting on Grandma's shoulder.

"We built this life," Grandma managed to say between gulping breaths. "It took us so many years. And now it's all gone."

"No," Oma said. "No. It is not gone. It remains. Believe me, I know. It is not gone."

Grandma lowered her hands and looked into Oma's eyes.

"And if you do go," Oma went on, "all will be well. They have many who care for them here. So many who have watched them grow and who love them. And you can love them from wherever you go. That will never change."

"How will I tell them?" Grandma asked. "They've needed us for so long. How can I tell them I'm leaving? Especially after Frank . . ."

She didn't finish.

"You are not responsible for what Frank has or has not done for them." Oma glanced at the door and nodded, letting me know I should come in. "They will understand if you need to go. They will want what is best for you."

I knelt next to Grandma's chair and she put her hands on my face, using a thumb to wipe a tear off my cheek.

"Your aunt Rose has invited me to live with her in Grand Rapids," she said.

"It's all right, Grandma," I answered. "We'll be okay."

"Are you sure?"

I wasn't. But I told her I was anyway.

Fort Sam
Texas

Dear Y'all (as they'd say down in these here parts),

You know, a fella lives his whole life without much excitement. Then he goes off and joins the Army and his family has all kinds of switch-ups and changes without him. I can't believe Grandma's moving away. That will be hard for her, I'm sure.

Send her my love, will you? Please. And tell her how much I miss her.

Tell her that I promise I'll come to see her at Aunt Rose's while I'm home.

Speaking of which, I'll be home October 10 for a whole week of fun. Mom, buy some extra groceries. Joel, clean the room. Annie, dust off your camera. We'll want to preserve all the memories we can before I ship out for at least a year of adventure in the far-off land of Vietnam.

That's right, folks. I got my orders. I guess I didn't hit the stay-at-home jackpot after all.

Sorry this is a short one. There's not too much to say. I'll see you soon.

Love,
Mike

Dear Mike,

Sorry I didn't write you back before. It's been busy, getting Grandma's house ready to sell and all. She's being a bit crabby about the whole thing, which makes matters much worse. She did, though, ask me to tell you that she looks forward to seeing you in a few weeks.

Just a few more weeks! We're all jazzed for you to come home.

Mom wanted me to ask if you would like us to at least try to have Frank come see you. No promises that he will or that he'll even call or write us back. But it's worth the try, right? Or not right? You let me know what you want.

Either way is fine by all of us.

Joel told me to write that he's in a real rock 'n' roll band with a few guys from school. They're all right for a bunch of eighth graders. Mom is looking for a place for them to practice that isn't our living room. So far, no luck.

If we are all still able to hear by the time you get home, it will be a miracle of the highest order.

Love you, brother.

Annie

PS: We're all praying that Uncle Sam realizes that he doesn't really need you in Vietnam after all. Oma keeps insisting on praying for God's will. Let's just hope that God's will and the Army's agree with letting you stay in America. Wouldn't that be something?

27

Aunt Rose had arranged everything for Grandma's move. She'd hired a cleaning lady to scrub every surface of the house, to oil all the woodwork, to tidy all the rooms. A real-estate man to show it to buyers. A moving company to pack everything and load it all onto a truck. She'd thought of everything.

Everything except for how Grandma would feel about the better part of her life being handled by strangers.

"It's all under control, Mother," she'd say in her clipped and icy voice whenever Grandma asked where such and such a thing had gotten off to. "Trust me."

From the way Grandma glared at her, I didn't think she was so inclined.

It didn't take long for a new family to buy the house. By the third week of September, Grandma was leaving with promises of trips to come and see us, provided we agreed to drive over to Grand Rapids once in a while to visit her.

I knew, for all the promises we made on both sides, we still wouldn't see much of Grandma.

•

Mom had gone to bed and Joel was watching Herman's Hermits on *The Smothers Brothers Comedy Hour*. I sat on the porch swing, reading with my flashlight glowing on the page, an afghan over my lap.

I lifted my eyes from the book when I heard the tremolo of a loon coming from the direction of Old Chip. It was a faint call, dampened by the trees and houses between the lake and my front porch. Right in the middle of "Green Street Green" the television turned off.

The screen door squeaked open and Joel came out, lowering himself to sit on the top step of the porch. He reached his arms around his knees, lacing his fingers together.

"You didn't want to listen to the Hermits anymore?" I asked.

"Nah. I wasn't diggin' it," he answered. "They're a little mellow for my taste."

"They aren't the kind to play guitar with their teeth, are they?"

"Not even close." He pushed up his glasses. "The loons are noisy tonight, huh?"

"Yup."

"When I was a kid, Mike convinced me that there was a ghost in the lake." He shook his head. "I believed him for a long time."

"He's just a big bully."

"Why do you think God made their voices sound so sad?"

"I don't know." I stood, holding the afghan around my waist. "Scoot over so I can sit by you."

"I'm sure there's some kind of scientific answer." He moved to one side, letting me have room. "Will you share the blanket with me? Please?"

"Oh, all right, if I have to."

We sat close, the blanket covering our legs. We listened to the loons for a few minutes, and I wondered if anyone else in the town was out doing the same as we were.

"Can I tell you something?" he asked.

"Of course."

"I'm kind of sad that we can't go over to Grandma and Grandpa's house anymore."

I nodded. "Me too, buddy."

"Do you think she'll be happy?"

"I don't know," I said. "Aunt Rose is kind of snooty."

"She isn't all that bad."

I nudged him with my elbow and snorted. "She's horrible. Sometimes I wish I understood why she and Frank both turned out to be so selfish."

Joel's jaw tensed.

"I'm sorry," I said. "I shouldn't have said that."

"It's kind of true, I guess." He cleared his throat. "I thought that if I was good enough, I might be able to make him stay."

The loons' calls faded, seeming to recede to farther away on the lake.

"After he left the first time, I was sure it was my fault," I whispered. "But it wasn't. It took me a long time to figure that out. Frank left because he decided to. End of story."

"What if he never comes back?" he asked.

"We'll be okay. We were okay for a long time without him before. Nothing has changed."

"But before we had Mike." His eyes met mine. "And now we don't."

"For now," I said. "In the meantime we'll just have to be strong together. Okay?"

The loon song had gone quiet. Still, I knew they were there.

Fort Sam Houston
Texas

Dear Mom, Annie, and Joel,

It sure was a hot one here for September. I think it got up to eighty-five degrees. I complained about it to one of the doctors here who laughed right in my face. See, he got back from Vietnam a few months ago. He said I don't know the definition of the word "hot" yet.

Oh boy. I guess I'm in for it.

Just a week and a day and I'll be home. I sure wish I was coming home to stay instead of just for a week. It's going to be hard to leave you all, knowing I won't see you for a whole year.

Mom, I know you're going to cry when I go. If you want to know a secret, I probably will too. But if any of you tell a soul, I swear I won't bring back any souvenirs once my tour of duty is done.

Joel, you've got one week to get all your stuff off my bed. Especially your stuffed puppy dog. I don't want that stinky, raggedy thing on my pillow.

Annie, you're going to need to drink some coffee when I'm there. I'll expect some late-night chats with you. I've missed those.

See you soon.

Love,
Mike

28

It was less than half an hour, the news special. Less than half an hour of clicking and whirring film footage of tanks, explosions, guns. And boys wearing helmets, ducking and running or reclining against sandbags.

Two of them sat in a trench, shirtless, talking into the interviewer's microphone. They were of smooth face, the kind that hadn't yet seen the need for a razor all that much. One wore his hat at the back of his dark, curly hair.

"You can't be safe. You can be lucky. That's it," he said.

"He could be Michael," Mom whispered from her chair where she leaned forward as if to get closer to the screen. "Don't you think he looks a bit like him?"

I didn't answer her, afraid to miss something that the boy had to say. But the camera cut away, showing a man in glasses, tying his boot laces, telling the microphone about getting scared by the stuff the enemy kept throwing at them. Tying his boots, talking about war, and feeling lucky to be alive afterward.

Watching, hardly blinking, I bit at the inside of my cheek.

Breathing shallow, I took in the images of war in black and white.

This is real. This is real. This is real, I thought.

The front door opened, Joel stepped inside, home from church youth group. "Whatcha watching?" he asked.

Mom shushed him, waving him off.

"It's some place in Vietnam," I answered, making room for him to sit by me on the couch. "Con Thien, they said."

Explosions. Soldiers lay on their stomachs, tapped their fingers, waiting out the weapons aimed right at them. Then quiet. Bandaging of wounds, calls for something called a "medevac." Powdering of feet, cleaning of weapons, writing of letters.

"Hey, who you writing to?" one boy asked.

"Grandmom," the other answered.

Smoking and sleeping and joking around. Sitting in tall grass and walking along muddy tank tracks.

"You gotta just look to God," a soldier said. "When I get scared, it's about the only thing I can do."

Planes flew through the clouds, letting loose hundreds upon hundreds of bombs. They fell, the cylinders, in graceful form, pirouettes dropping through the clouds. But when they hit the ground, fire burst upward.

I covered my mouth, hoping Mom hadn't heard my gasp. That was someone's death.

"Golly," whispered Joel.

Mike Wallace narrated, but his words held no meaning for me. It was just a sharp undertone to the pictures that moved on the screen.

Two soldiers struggled to heft something onto the back of a Jeep marked with the American Red Cross. They lifted, rolled, and shoved it. It wasn't until I saw the arm, dangling and lifeless, that I realized what it was.

I hardly made it to the bathroom to get sick. Afterward, I stayed there, my cheek leaning against the cool plaster of the wall, hoping to wait it out so I wouldn't see anything else from that special report.

When I shut my eyes, all I could see was that arm.

A song from that morning's church service echoed in my head.

Oh God, our help in ages past, our hope for years to come.

I breathed in through my nose and out my mouth. Eyes still closed. My mind couldn't let go of the image. The struggle, the arm, the cross on the Jeep.

"He could be Michael." Mom's words in my mind.

Oh God, our help.

"He could be Michael."

Oh God.

Mike. That could be Mike.

Help.

29

Mom had spent the weekend buzzing about, busying herself with all manner of things to prepare for Mike's arrival on Tuesday. She'd cleaned the house, filled the refrigerator with all of Mike's favorite foods, had her hair done, and worried over how best to keep him entertained for his week of leave.

She'd found plenty of jobs for Joel and me to do as well. When she'd insisted that Joel clean out the gutters, he'd told her that he was sure Mike wouldn't think to look there. That had only earned him a dirty look and the additional task of weeding around the sidewalk.

I was glad when Monday came and I could go to work to get some rest.

On my break after the breakfast rush, I sat on my stool behind the counter and cracked open a book I'd brought from home. It was worn, my copy of *The Grapes of Wrath*, the binding held together with strips of masking tape. The margins were full of my scrawling notes, black pen had underlined certain passages, and the corners of pages were dogeared.

I couldn't say how many times I'd read the story. But with each reading, it so consumed me I forgot myself, swearing that I could feel the grit of a dust storm in the air.

So engrossed was I in the story, I didn't hear the bell over the door or the customer coming into the diner. I didn't even know he was there until he was just on the other side of the counter, clearing his throat.

"What's a guy gotta do to get a cup of coffee around here?" he asked.

I knew before I even looked up. Mike.

Dropping the book, not caring that the fall broke loose a few pages, I ran to the other side of the counter and threw my arms around his neck. He steadied himself so he didn't fall over, laughing the whole time.

"You aren't supposed to get here until tomorrow," I said, stepping away from him.

"Well, I guess I better leave, then." He made for the door, and I grabbed his arm. "I caught an early bus. You think Mom'll be surprised?"

"I think she'll have a heart attack," I answered.

"What's all that noise out there?" Bernie grumped, pushing his way through the swinging door from the kitchen, rubbing his hands on a dishrag and looking at Mike.

Mike was in his dress uniform, looking taller and broader than I'd ever seen him. His hair was short, buzzed into a flattop. If I hadn't known better, I might have thought he'd aged at least two years in the months he was gone.

"Look at you," Bernie said, tossing the rag onto the counter and rushing toward Mike, hand extended. "They sure did make a man out of you, didn't they?"

"Despite my resisting, I guess they did." Mike shook Bernie's hand, looking up into his face the way a son would a father. "Annie been doing an okay job for you?"

"I guess she has." Bernie nodded at Mike. "I hear they trained you to be a medic."

"Yes, sir," Mike answered. "I just hope I don't have to put all I learned into practice over in Vietnam."

"You never know," Bernie said, crossing his arms. "You might get lucky."

●

We hid Mike in the laundry room. Joel and I had already set the table with Mom's best dishes, and we had chop suey from the Chinese restaurant in the oven, keeping warm. We stood side by side in the dining room, waiting for Mom to get home, as excited as we'd ever been as little kids with a present for her.

She finally stepped through the front door at five twenty, kicking off her kitten heels and tossing her purse onto the couch. Then she saw the two of us grinning like fools.

"What?" she said, her no-nonsense tone thick. Then she sniffed. "What are you cooking?"

"Nothing," I said.

"Did you two get into trouble?" Crossing her arms, she stood, flat on her feet. "Whose window did you break, Joel? What is that smell?"

"Chinese food," Joel answered.

She stepped past us into the dining room. "There are four places set," she said. "Don't you dare tell me that Frank's back."

Joel and I turned to watch her rush into the kitchen. The laundry room door opened slowly and Mike stepped out.

The woman who had somehow come to expect anything life could toss at her was, at last, caught off guard.

That day, Mike managed to surprise her. First, she gasped then screamed. Then she ran at him, her arms spread wide to grab hold of him. Then she put her hands on his face, having to reach higher than she had before, making me wonder if they'd put him on some kind of stretching machine.

She cried. Gloria Anne Jacobson cried.

"But you aren't coming until tomorrow," she said before covering her mouth. "Did you lie?"

"No, I caught an earlier bus," he said. "Come on. Let's eat before your chop suey gets cold."

"We got egg rolls too," Joel said. "And some soup."

"I don't think she cares," I said, patting his shoulder. "She's got what she wanted. The food is really just for you."

"Really?" he asked, his eyes lighting up.

"Well, you do have to share."

I pulled the food out of the oven, placing the containers on trivets in the middle of the dining room table. Mom insisted on lighting her special tapered candles and turning off the overhead light.

"We may as well be fancy," she said.

Mike said the prayer and we passed the rice and noodles and chop suey around, helping ourselves. Mom even agreed to try using chopsticks, failing miserably and laughing all the while.

"So, Mom, did you really throw a whole meat loaf at Frank's head?" Mike asked before sucking a noodle in through his puckered lips.

"Not a whole meat loaf," Mom corrected.

"Only half," I said, taking a sip of water.

"At Frank's head?" Mike grinned at me.

"Well, not at his head." Mom pointed at him. "I'll remind you that I am a lady."

"Yes, at his head," I said. "You would have gotten him, too, if he hadn't ducked."

"And just because he bought Joel a secondhand guitar?" Mike asked.

"Not just any guitar," Joel said. "A Les Paul."

"Well, then. Maybe you should have thrown the whole meat loaf." Mike winked at Mom.

"Anyway, we are not going to spend this entire evening discussing my temper tantrum. And we are certainly not going to talk about Frank," Mom said. "We are going to celebrate Michael being home for a whole week."

"A whole week and a day," I said, raising my glass.

"Yeah." Mike nodded and smiled, but it wasn't his real smile. And his eyes seemed to focus on nothing in particular.

As far as I could tell, neither Mom or Joel noticed it. The look on Mike's face was passing, fleeting. Then he was back to himself again.

But I couldn't seem to shake the heavy feeling in myself.

Dear Friend Annie,

I'm thinking of you this week while Mike's home. I hope you have all the good times in the world and that the week feels a lot longer than seven days. Don't worry about writing back to me while he's there. I wouldn't want to take a moment's attention away from him.

After he leaves, though, I want to hear everything!

I wanted to send you an article I had printed in the university newspaper. Can you believe it? I'm published somewhere other than Fort Colson! My column appeared on the back page, but at least it's something! I clipped it for you. I hope you like it.

I'm well here at Taylor. A bit lonely even with people around all the time. My roommate is nice, but she likes to stay up late and talk when all I want to do is sleep. Oh well. At least she isn't mean.

Oh, when you think about it, let me know if there's anything new with David. I really think he likes you. How could he not?

Write back soon,
Jocelyn

30

Bernie had given me Wednesday off, insisting that I spend the day with Mike. He'd even threatened to fire me if I dared to come in that morning.

"I'll manage by myself," he'd grumbled. "Ran the place for ten years before I hired anybody else. Somehow I'll make do without you for one day."

So, first thing Wednesday morning, Mike and I headed east on the highway, toward Grand Rapids, to visit Grandma at Aunt Rose's house.

Mike drove his Corvair through the rain until we got half-way there and found bright skies and soft-looking clouds. His shoulders relaxed once he had wheels on drier pavement, and he eased up his grip on the steering wheel.

"Joel grew over the summer, don't you think?" he said, glancing at me. "He's nearly as tall as me."

"I think his voice got deeper too." I crossed my legs and angled my body so I was half facing him. "And he almost has to shave every other week or so."

"Our baby's getting to be a man, I guess."

I chuckled. "I wouldn't go that far."

"I asked him what he thought of Frank."

"Huh."

"He said he was underwhelmed."

"He said that?" I asked. "Underwhelmed?"

"I swear, that's the word he used." Mike shook his head before changing lanes to pass a slow-moving station wagon.

"Well, he was sufficiently impressed by Frank at first." I used my forefinger to push up my glasses. "Joel was sure he'd come to stay."

"Poor kid."

"Yeah."

"Sure wish I could've been here," he said. "I'd have liked to see Frank again. Just, you know, see what he's like."

"He's a bit moody."

"Huh. I guess that doesn't surprise me so much at all."

"Me either. He was kind of quiet sometimes too." I shrugged. "Quiet like Henry Fonda."

"You think Henry Fonda's quiet?" Mike smirked at me. "I think he's grumpy."

"Well, just quiet and intense and—" I took a second to think. "And sullen. But kind of easygoing. And sometimes he wasn't quiet. He was almost charming."

"Sounds complicated."

"Maybe." I watched a field of wheat speed by on the other side of the window. "Maybe that's why I can't seem to figure him out. Like I said, he's moody."

"He wrote to me," Mike said. "Did you know that?"

I told him I didn't.

"He asked if I'd list him as my secondary kin." He licked his lips.

"What does that mean?"

"That if something happens to me while I'm over there, he'll get notified."

"Nothing's going to happen to you," I said.

"We don't know that, do we?"

I didn't answer him. He was right. We didn't know. And it was that not knowing that made my stomach lurch.

You can't worry about something that might not happen.

It seemed like years since he'd said that to me.

"Anyway," Mike went on, "I listed him. So, if anything happens, you won't have to worry about getting ahold of him. He'll know as soon as you do."

We didn't say anything for at least three miles, just the humming of the Corvair's engine filling the silence.

"You'll let Mom know, right?" he asked. "Not now. Just, if something happens. You'll let her know that Frank'll find out too?"

"Of course."

I didn't know if I was carsick, but I cracked the window, needing a little fresh air.

31

Aunt Rose lived in a beautiful and expansive two-story house in a pristine suburb of Grand Rapids. All the lawns were trimmed and edged perfectly; the autumn leaves seemed to have been removed from the premises the moment they fell. Shiny cars were parked in the driveways, and every porch had set out the welcome mat.

It was as if there was a book of rules that instructed on how all things must look. Everything was just so. Perfect.

"It's like Camazotz," I whispered.

"What?" Mike asked.

"It's from *A Wrinkle in Time*," I answered. "Don't tell me you haven't read it."

"Sorry, pal."

"You have to read it."

"If you say so," he said.

"Anyway, Camazotz is this planet where everything is perfectly and terrifyingly the same. All the people there are controlled by an evil called The Dark Thing that has a stranglehold on everyone, forcing them to conform."

"Speaking of which," Mike said, turning into a driveway. "We're here."

As if on cue, or as if she'd been waiting, Aunt Rose opened wide the front door as soon as Mike cut the engine. She wore her hair in a perfect bouffant and her lips were perfectly red and spread in a wide and less-than-convincing smile.

"You found it," she said, her smile not fading but looking increasingly like it pained her to hold it. "I'm so glad."

"Uncle Eliot gave us great directions," Mike said, shutting his car door.

"Perfect," she said. "Come in. Please come in."

She welcomed us inside with such urgency I thought she was afraid the neighbors might see us and judge her unfit for having such country-bumpkin family.

"Mother is in her room," she said, shutting the gleaming white door behind us. "That's where she likes to spend much of her time. I'll get her and we can all have tea."

If it was possible for someone to glide up the steps, Aunt Rose had found a way. Watching her walk in her pumps, I imagined she'd been the kind of girl to practice gliding with a textbook balanced on top of her head.

I was glad that God had been wise enough to allow me to be my mother's daughter instead of Aunt Rose's. I simply was not created for such poise and grace. Although, had I belonged to her, Aunt Rose would have found a way to mold me into such a creature even if I resisted with all my strength.

I felt a bit strangled just thinking about it.

"Are we supposed to wait here?" Mike whispered. "Or should we go sit down?"

"I don't know," I answered. "We should probably wait."

"This house is huge. How does she clean it?"

"I'm sure she pays someone."

"You think Uncle Eliot makes that much money?" Mike asked.

"I wouldn't know."

The entryway, what I was sure Aunt Rose called a "foyer" with a flawlessly smooshy French accent, was as big as my bedroom and full of antiques that probably cost more than Mike's car. Everything about her, from her ever-present string of pearls to the Oriental rug on her immaculately waxed wood floors, spoke of wealth.

I thought I understood why Uncle Eliot missed out on most of our family gatherings. He had to have been constantly working to afford Aunt Rose's expensive taste.

Aunt Rose glided back down the stairs, her fingertips barely skimming the surface of the ornately carved wooden banister. Grandma followed behind her, taking the steps with great care and with a firm grip of the handrail.

I was surprised that Aunt Rose didn't scold her for getting fingerprint smudges on the polished mahogany. Or whatever kind of wood it was made of.

"Look at you," Grandma said, her eyes on Mike while she made it down the last few steps. "You look so like your father."

I stepped out of her way so she could walk across the foyer to be near him. Looking up at him, she beamed. He was her favorite. Always had been. I liked to pretend that it didn't bother me. That it little mattered. I wasn't sure that I had anyone fooled.

"How are you, Grandma?" he asked, leaning down to give her a kiss on the cheek. "You holding up?"

"I suppose," she answered. "Rose takes good care of me."

"I bet she does." Mike raised his eyes to look around. "This is quite the place."

"Oh, it's nothing special," Aunt Rose said, fingering the pearls at her neck. "I'll get the tea ready. Mother, you can have them sit in the parlor."

Aunt Rose swooshed away toward what I imagined was the kitchen.

"This place is cold," Grandma said, taking Mike's arm and nodding to a room toward her right. "Always cold. I need an afghan on me all the time."

"Have you asked her to turn up the heat?" I asked, following behind them.

"As if she listens to a word I say." She pointed at a wing-backed chair. "I'll sit there."

She eased herself into the chair, seeming more stiff and weak than I'd seen her before. It was as if the past few months since Grandpa died had aged her rapidly. She told me to hand her the off-white blanket that had been draped across the back of a rocking chair.

"Just put it over my legs," she told me, flapping her hand in the space beside her head.

"Annie," Aunt Rose called to me from wherever it was she'd gone to make tea. "Would you mind giving me a hand?"

Mike took the afghan and nodded at me. "Better you than me," he said, winking.

Back in the foyer, I followed the hallway to a brightly lit room full of chrome appliances and avocado-green laminate countertops. Aunt Rose stood at the counter, her back to me, pouring steaming hot water into a fine china teapot.

Her spine was perfectly straight, but with one shoulder

slightly lower than the other and her head tipped to the side. With the top of her right foot, she rubbed at the back of her left calf. She looked altogether normal and I didn't know what to think of that.

"Aunt Rose?" I asked, my voice soft as if it felt timid in such a large room. "Did you need me?"

She finished filling the pot and fit the lid on top with a clinking of china on china. Then she turned, a smaller, much more believable smile on her face.

"She isn't happy here," she said, hardly moving her lips. "I've tried everything to make her happy."

Her eyebrow flicked up and down, and I wondered if she knew she was doing it.

"Maybe she still misses Grandpa," I said, putting my hands into the pockets of my jeans. "I don't think she'd be happy anywhere right now."

"I thought I was doing the right thing by bringing her here."

"It was nice of you to invite her to live with you."

"All she does is criticize me." She blinked a half dozen times fast, her false eyelashes flittering. "All my life, I've never done anything good enough."

"I'm sure she doesn't mean anything by it."

"And then there's Frank." She was going to keep going, I could tell. "He runs off without a trace. Not just once. Twice. And you'd think he hung the stars. Ever the perfect son."

"Do you want me to carry something?" I asked, hoping she'd just stop talking.

"There are cookies on the counter over there," she said. "Did I make a mistake? By having her move here?"

"No." I picked up the fancy dish with an assortment of

cookies placed just so. "But it might take time for you two to work things out."

"She stays in her room all day."

"She likes to go shopping," I said. "She didn't get to do much of it when Grandpa was sick. Maybe she'd like to go with you."

"So she can complain about how much money I spend?"

"I don't know," I said. "It was just an idea."

I took the cookies with me back down the hall and toward the sound of Mike telling a story and Grandma giggling.

I knew that if I turned around I'd see a sour-faced Aunt Rose following behind me, tea service in hand.

It wasn't enough for her to resent Frank, she needed to resent Mike too.

●

Grandma took us up to her room. It was a good size with space enough for all she'd brought with her from her old house. She had her bed, dresser, vanity, and a nice sitting area.

"I have something I want to show you," she said, crossing to the vanity and picking up an ancient-looking metal box. "Sit down."

Mike and I took the settee, and Grandma sat on the edge of a matching armchair. She put the box on the coffee table between us. Its hinges rasped as she lifted the lid. Inside was a mess of papers and odds and ends. Pushing aside a few things with her fingers, Grandma grasped what looked like an old coin on a chain.

"Your great-grandfather Jacobson wore this in WWI. And my nephew Tobias wore it in WWII," she said, holding it in the palm of her hand. "And your father wore it in Korea. They each made it home in one piece. Now, I don't know that I believe in lucky charms, exactly, but if I did, I'd think this was a pretty successful one."

She handed it to Mike. He felt of the metal, flipping it one way and then another to see what was on each side.

"Saint Michael," Grandma said. "The patron saint of soldiers."

"I didn't know we were Catholic," Mike said, handing it to me.

I felt of the pendant with the pad of my thumb, feeling the image of a warrior holding a sword and ready for battle.

"We aren't," Grandma said. "Never were, as far as I know. But your great-grandfather figured it couldn't hurt to wear it."

I made to hand it back to her and she shook her head. "It's for Michael," she said. "To wear when he goes to war. It's tradition."

Mike pulled the chain over his head, letting the pendant rest on the outside of his T-shirt. "Thanks, Grandma."

"I'm going to tell you the same thing I said to your father," she said. "You bring that medallion home. Whatever it takes, you bring it home so I can put it back into my box."

"I'll do my best, Grandma."

"Jacobson men always come home." As soon as she said it, she put a hand to her heart and frowned.

Mike stood up and knelt down beside her. "Don't be worried about me. I'm going to be all right."

She took the hand that was on her heart and patted the Saint Michael medallion on his chest.

"I know that can't protect you," she said, her voice raspy. "It's just metal."

But by the way she kept her hand on it, I thought maybe she did put a better part of her hope in the pendant. As if it held some sort of ~~magical~~ power.

If only it was true.

If only.

32

It rained nearly every day that Mike was home. The skies cast a gloom over all things and the red-orange-brown of autumn leaves hung from the fingertips of trees, drenched and sad.

Still, there was sunshine and laughter and good feelings inside our house while Mike was there. Every evening Mom ordered takeout if Oma hadn't made something to bring over. We sat at the table, sharing stories that we'd told a hundred times over. But then they were fresh, new. Joel's homework went undone. I lacked sleep. The mail stacked up, envelopes stayed sealed.

"We'll get to that later," Mom said about nearly everything that needed to be done. "Let's not worry about that right now."

And whenever someone brought up Mike going to Vietnam, she'd say the same thing.

Time was shorter than we wanted it to be. The days fell into each other, ending before we were ready for them to. Before we knew it, Mike would have to go.

I felt on the edge of panic whenever I remembered it.

•

It had to have been after two in the morning. Something had jostled me from sleep. Thinking it was from my dream, I shut my eyes, trying to settle back into my deep slumber. But then I heard it again, a thunking sound. A scratching, rustling thud from above me.

When I heard the laughter, I groped around on my bedside table for my glasses. Sitting up, I pushed aside the curtain over my window, flipped the lock, and pushed up the pane. Sure enough, I heard Joel and Mike, their deep voices coming from the roof.

"Shhhh," one of them hissed. "Don't wake up Mom."

"All right." Then another bout of laughter.

Their voices had the same tone and, just from listening to them, I couldn't tell which was which.

"Oh man," one of them said. "It's wet."

"Don't worry," the other said. "Your rear end'll dry out eventually. Just lay back and look at the stars."

Dipping my head, I tried to see if the clouds had cleared enough for the stars to poke their way through. All I managed to accomplish, though, was bumping my head against the window frame.

"You think they've got the same stars in Vietnam?" That was Joel. It was exactly the kind of question he was apt to ask. "You know, because it's all the way on the other side of the world."

"Don't know," Mike answered. "I'll let you know as soon as I figure it out."

"I should've asked Dad what stars he saw in Korea."

"He wouldn't have wanted to talk about it, pal."

"You're probably right." Joel's voice was tinted with disappointment. "You think he'll ever come back home?"

"I don't know," Mike said. "The thing is, Frank never got over the war. I think being here just reminded him of another thing it stole from him. Thing is, it's probably better if you don't wait around for him. You know? You could spend your whole life hoping he'll come around, but he most likely won't. I'm not sure he can. It took me a long time to realize that. He's not a dad. He's just Frank."

"I don't understand what you mean."

"You don't have to." Mike cleared his throat. "You just have to choose to be a better man than he is."

"He's not so bad, I guess."

"Well, you're the one who saw him. You and Annie, who might as well stop snooping on us and get herself up here."

"I'm not snooping," I said.

"Sure." Mike hung over the roof, his face a foot from my window. "Bring some towels. It's wet up here."

●

Mom had a stack of rejected rag towels that she kept on a shelf in the laundry room. Most of them were a wedding gift from Aunt Rose. Long before that night they'd been a bright, egg yolk yellow, and Mom hated them at first sight. Partly because she didn't like yellow. Mostly because they'd come from Aunt Rose.

I grabbed the stack of them, trying to be as quiet as I could so as not to wake Mom, and stepped out the back door.

Mike and Joel had set the ladder against the edge of the roof, and as soon as I started to climb, towels hugged close to my body with one arm, Joel's face popped up over the edge, a smile spread from ear to ear.

"Hi," he whispered.

"Hello," I whispered back. "You boys are nuts."

He shrugged. "Probably."

When I got to the top of the ladder, he helped me up. I didn't protest, even though I could have managed fine without him. Mom had told me years ago that I needed to allow the boys to be gentlemanly to me so they'd have practice for how to treat a lady.

Because of this, I hardly had to open a door for myself when they were around, and they always made sure to pull out a chair for me. For growing up without their father, my brothers had turned into really great young men.

I handed each of them one of the ugly yellow towels, and we spread them across the shingles as if it was the beach. On our backs, knees bent, feet flat, we lay side by side, looking up at the stars.

It had cleared up after all.

"Remember that time I told Mom I was running away?" Joel asked.

"Yeah. How dare she make you eat your Brussels sprouts." Mike turned his head toward Joel.

"They smell funny." Joel pulled a face. "And they taste worse."

I didn't tell him it was because Mom typically boiled them to mush.

"Anyway," Joel went on, "I couldn't figure out where to go."

"Remember how you packed your stuffed puppy dog?" I asked. "What was its name?"

"Willow," he answered. "Anyway, I packed Willow in my pillowcase—"

"And nothing else, if I recall," Mike interrupted.

"I was five."

"Six," I corrected him. "You were in first grade."

"How do you know?"

"Because you wrote your own runaway letter."

Better than Frank did, I thought.

"Anyway," Joel said, exasperated. "I didn't know where to go, so I climbed up here."

"Remember whose idea it was?" Mike asked. "It was mine. I told you Mom would never find you up here, especially if I put the ladder away."

Joel chuckled and nodded. "I started crying because I was tired and cold and I couldn't get down."

"Yeah. You ran away for a whole ten minutes. Such a prodigal son."

"I remember being so mad at you," I said. "Mom served Brussels sprouts every night that week to teach you a lesson."

"The house smelled like moldy socks." Joel shuddered.

"Did you notice that Mom never ate them?" Mike said.

"You think they'll make you eat them in Vietnam?" Joel asked.

"Gosh, I hope not." Mike rolled his head so he was looking straight up again. "Although they're a heck of a lot better than the C-rations they'll give us when we're off base."

"See, Mike," Joel said. "Mom was just getting you ready for the Army."

"Who knew?"

Crossing my arms, I shivered, feeling the goose bumps rising under my sleeves. I was glad I'd thought to grab my jacket, but I could have kicked myself for not bringing out a blanket too.

"I wish I didn't have to go," Mike said, his voice so quiet.

I wondered if he'd meant to say it out loud. "I wish I could stay here with you kids and Mom. I wish I still had my job at Bernie's and that I could maybe take a couple of classes at college or something. I wish the whole ███ war was just over already."

Neither Joel or I said anything to him. It wouldn't have seemed right, whatever we could think of to say. But we all knew that President Johnson had no plans to bring our boys home. Not yet, at least. And we'd all heard on the news how the bigwigs in Washington DC had said there was no use in talking peace with North Vietnam.

The war would go on.

And on.

And on some more.

And for it to go on, they required our boys—our Mike—to leave us.

"It's only a year," Joel said, his voice quiet and flat. "You'll be back before we even start missing you."

"Sure wish that was true, pal," Mike said.

We stayed there on the roof until we were all too cold to stand it anymore.

Dear Annie,

Thank you for the invitation. I'd like to come see Michael before he goes, but only if he wants me to. And I wouldn't want to impose on your mother. I'm sure she's less than pleased with me.

I'm sorry for the way I left. I needed to get back to work and I'm awful at good-byes.

But you're smart and I guess you've realized that.

I'll be there Sunday.

Only if it's okay.

Frank

Dear Frank,

Mom said it was okay if you came. But on one condition. That you promise not to leave again without letting us know. You don't have to say "good-bye." Just tell us that you're going.

Mike wants to see you. Joel does too.

And I might miss you too. Just a little.

Annie

33

The church ladies had lost no time in organizing an after-service potluck in Mike's honor. All during the sermon, they checked their wristwatches as if they were anxious about the pastor going even a minute longer than usual. The aromas of creamy casseroles and sweet ham and fresh-baked rolls mingled and filled the sanctuary.

The pastor's sermon ended right on time. If not a few minutes earlier.

We held back, letting the ladies get to the fellowship hall ahead of us to put all the food on the long tables. Mom thought they'd want Mike to make a bit of an entrance so they could make a fuss and clap for him.

"They like doing that sort of thing," she said.

"They shouldn't have gone to all this trouble," Mike said, standing stiff and straight in his dress uniform. Mom had convinced him to wear it to church.

"Everyone wants to see you before you go." I nudged him with my shoulder. "Besides, I think Mrs. Kaiser made French silk pie just for you."

"I'll be too nervous to eat it." He sighed and furrowed his brow. "I don't like all this attention."

"They're going to miss you," Mom said. "They wanted to give you a good send-off."

"I don't know what I'll say to all of them. I'd rather just go home and be with you."

"Michael. These people have known you your entire life. They've prayed for you and sent you birthday cards with dollar bills in them and taken care of you during the worst days." Mom widened her eyes the way she did when she wanted to make sure we understood that she was serious. "You will go to this potluck and you will eat a bite from every single one of the casseroles on that table and you will compliment each of the cooks."

"Gosh, Mom," he said. "All right. I didn't mean . . ."

"Son, these little old ladies might not look very big to you." She blinked fast. "But they promised to pray every day for you. And I'm going to need them to pray so hard so that you come home in one piece."

He nodded, swallowing.

"Don't take them for granted." She put her hand on his shoulder. "Don't go a day without thanking God that he put them in our lives. All right?"

"Yeah. You're right." He excused himself and went into the restroom just outside the sanctuary doors.

When he came out, his tie was straightened, his shoulders pulled back, and he wore his most winning smile. He offered his arm to Mom and led her into the fellowship hall.

I followed behind them, watching our mother's backbone straighten as they walked through the doors.

•

By the end of the potluck Mike and Joel were seated at a table to the far corner of the room, surrounded by the elder men of the congregation. They'd long since shed their suit coats, loosened their ties, and rolled up their shirtsleeves.

I stood at the buffet, collecting casserole pans and serving spoons to carry into the kitchen, where some of the church ladies were washing dishes in sinks, sudsy with detergent. Lingering there, I tried to hear what the men said in their low voices.

"Probably telling all their old war stories," Mom said, standing beside me, her arms crossed. "Or at least the ones that made them out to be heroes."

I couldn't see Mike's face, his back was turned toward me. But Joel's was in clear sight. He stared, mouth agape, at the man who was speaking and his eyes were wide behind his glasses.

"He's going to have nightmares tonight," I said, shaking my head.

"Maybe." She picked up a stack of dirty plates. "Come on. Let's leave the men to their talk."

She turned and went back into the kitchen.

I stayed, watching them for a moment more. The one telling the story clapped his hands for emphasis, and Joel flinched before breaking into a smile, his eyes brightening.

At the far end of the table sat Bernie, leaned back in his chair. He kept his eyes on Mike as if he was trying to read something from his face. When he caught me watching him, he gave me a nod and the kind of frown-smile he used when passing someone along the street.

The whole group of men erupted in laughter at however

the storyteller's tale had ended. I hoisted my load of casserole dishes and headed into the kitchen, where the chattering of women's voices bubbled as much as the dish soap.

Two women parted, making room for me to rinse as they washed and dried.

Warmth bloomed inside my chest, something between gratitude and belonging.

●

By the time we had the kitchen cleaned up, most of the men had moved outside to the church lawn. One of them had a new car and several stood around it, the hood propped up with the engine running, rumbling into the Sunday afternoon quiet.

Mike wasn't in that group. He and Bernie stood off to the side of the church, their backs to me. Bernie had his hand resting on Mike's shoulder.

"Mom wants to go home," Joel said, coming up from behind me.

"Go ahead," I answered. "I'll wait for Mike."

"Cool," he said. "Later."

Standing alone on the sidewalk, I tried tuning my ears to hear what Mike and Bernie were talking about, but the Cadillac only grew louder as its owner revved it to the delight of the men standing around with hands on hips or arms crossed.

Those men of shed jackets and gray hair had once been young, sent to fight in a war far bigger than they. They'd gone and returned to get married and hold down jobs, to build houses and buy cars. They raised kids who got married and had children of their own.

Mike had every chance they'd had to come back. It was the hope I held on to for dear life.

"Were you waiting for me?" Mike asked, walking toward me.

"Nah." I nodded at the half circle of men around the Caddy. "I'm just admiring that fine piece of American engineering."

Mike rolled his eyes. "Mom's probably getting impatient. We should make our way home."

"So, what did Bernie have to say?"

He started walking and put his hands in his pants pockets. "Nothing much."

We left the churchyard and traveled along the road that would lead us to Lewis Street. I didn't believe him. Bernie never said anything unless it had meaning. He was the kind who weighed his words before using them, making sure that they'd count for something before he let them out.

"Just man stuff," Mike said after a few yards of walking. "He told me he'd check in on you three while I'm gone."

"We'll be okay," I said. "We'll manage."

"I know." He let out a big, thick sigh. "I'll just feel better if I know he's keeping an eye on you."

Bernie Jager played the part of a grumpy man to a T. Had since I knew him. Mom said it was because he'd put his whole life into running the diner and hadn't taken the time to get married and have a family.

That may well have been true.

But underneath that crusty attitude and gruff grimace was a tenderhearted man who had made it his business to take Mike and me under his wing. And he'd taught us more about what a godly man was than any sermon could have.

He hadn't wasted his life. He'd spent a good amount of it on us.

34

Mom had once told me about the day Frank came home from the Korean War. Mike and I had been playing in the yard over at our old house. She'd said that Mike got all full of dirt that day, as was usual. But that I'd managed to find even more of it, making my white-blonde hair a muddy shade of brown.

It little mattered, though. Mom's solution to dirty kids was to send us into the lake to rinse off before supper. Sometimes she even brought out a bar of soap and gave us our bath right there among the minnows and the seaweed.

"Frank came around the corner," she'd said. "I didn't even know he was coming home that day."

She'd told me how she dropped the spade she'd been using to dig holes for her violet plants. She'd run to him, gardening gloves still on.

"When Michael saw us kissing, he cried," she'd said. "He didn't know Frank. Didn't remember him."

The way she told the story, it had taken Mike a full week to stop eyeballing Frank as if he were an intruder. And a whole month before he'd speak to him.

I thought of that story when Mike and I turned the corner at Lewis and Pine and I saw Frank's rust-red–colored truck parked in front of our house.

"Whose truck is that?" Mike asked.

"Frank's." I glanced at his face. "He said he'd come."

"I know." Mike grinned. "I guess I didn't believe him."

He ran the last few yards home, hopping up the porch steps and pulling the screen door open so hard, I worried he'd pull it right off its hinges.

I hung back, taking my time, wanting to give them a chance to meet. I imagined that Frank looked up at Mike's face, his brows knit and his eyes brooding the way they did. He'd have taken Mike's hand and told him how smart he looked in that uniform. Mike would pull his shoulders back, standing as tall and at attention as he could.

Unfortunately, that wasn't what happened. Not at all.

When I got to the front door, I saw the two of them sitting in the living room. Mike on the couch, Frank in the easy chair. Mike was looking at Frank as if he were an exhibit in a museum. Frank inspected his hands folded in his lap.

Neither of them looked up when I walked in, not even when I cleared my throat. I headed toward the kitchen, where I heard Mom fussing with something. Joel was there, too, sitting at the table with a glass of milk.

"I don't know what either of them expected," Mom said when I joined her at the counter. "Cut of the same fabric, those two."

"What happened?" I asked.

"As soon as they shook hands Frank asked why Michael didn't join the Navy." She rolled her eyes. "And Michael refused to say anything."

"Oh boy."

"I moved Mom's good vase from the mantel just in case they get into a fight," Joel said.

"They won't," I said. "Will they?"

She lifted both of her hands, palms up, and shrugged. "Who knows with those two."

I peeked around the corner to see them still in their seats, not speaking or moving so much as an inch.

"Hey, Joel. You feel up to playing a song on your guitar?" I asked. "You know a few, don't you?"

"I guess so." He smirked. "Why?"

"Come on." I tugged on his arm. "We've got to do something about that."

"All right."

Joel brought his Les Paul down from his room, insisting that we didn't need to plug it into the amp.

"They'll still be able to hear it well enough," he said, walking toward the living room.

As soon as he entered, both Mike and Frank lit up. There was something about Joel that was special to the two of them. Another thing they had in common.

"I asked Joel if he'd like to play a little for you," I said.

"Sure, bud," Mike said.

Frank sat up straighter, watching Joel sling the guitar strap around his neck and shoulders. He didn't take his eyes off him while he played what he called riffs from a few different songs he'd heard on the radio. His was a stuttering "House of the Rising Sun" and a tentative "Purple Haze," but with time and practice he'd get better.

Mom stood in the doorway to the dining room, a cup of hot tea in hand. She looked back and forth between her sons and husband.

Had I been a stranger just happening by our house, I'd have looked through the window and thought what a nice family we had, all in one place and paying all of our attention to the youngest among us.

It almost felt normal.

●

We all stayed up well past our bedtimes. Mom popped some corn and I made hot chocolate. Mike had changed out of his dress uniform and sat more comfortably on the floor in jeans and T-shirt, his back resting against the couch.

Frank didn't say a whole lot. He sat in the easy chair, bowl of popcorn in his lap, listening to the three of us kids tell story after story. The day Joel passed out after I convinced him to yank out his first tooth. Or the time when Mike told me that he was going to put rollers in my hair but instead used burrs. And the story of how, one spring Joel had sold all his baseball cards to buy Mom a necklace for Mother's Day.

Most of the stories earned half a smile from Frank. Still, his eyes remained far away, detached, and brooding.

Mom watched his face through the telling of each story, her eyes narrowed, scrutinizing. I was sure that if I could have heard her thoughts, they all would have been directed at him.

You missed so much.

You missed everything.

35

Mike had borrowed Bernie's old fishing boat with the plans of staying out on Old Chip all day while Joel was at school and Mom and I were at work. It was his last day in Fort Colson for a year. He planned to catch and release every single fish in the lake. At least that was what he told Mom.

"It'll do him some good," Bernie told me when I got to work.

"He could have come here. He could have asked Mom to take the day off," I said.

"Nope." Bernie shook his head. "He needed some time by himself."

"I don't understand."

"Oh well."

I left the kitchen, starting the first pots of coffee for the day. Outside, the sun still hadn't risen and all I could think about was Mike's boat in the water, oars dipping below the surface.

It made me feel lonely.

•

The day had never sloughed off the gloom of dark clouds and I wondered if it would rain. I went the long way home, the way that took me along the shore of the lake, hoping that I'd see Mike and that I could talk him into coming with me.

What I didn't expect was for him to call out my name, yelling for me to "hold on."

He rowed in to shore, which didn't take too long. There was no current to push against his oars. Once he got close to where I was, he didn't get out. Instead, he gave me his goofy grin.

"Get in," he said.

Any other day I might have argued, resisted, told him he was off his rocker. I might have pointed at the laden clouds and asked if he noticed how chilly it was. I'd have told him we might freeze to death should we capsize.

But this was no ordinary day. So, without a question, I climbed into the boat.

The rubber soles of my sneakers clonked against the aluminum bottom, and the water on either side of the boat sloshed, making a sound that was as familiar to me as my own voice. Sitting, I felt of the damp wood of the seat, knowing that my pants would be wet by the time the ride was over.

Mike rowed us all the way to the middle of the lake. When I looked to the south of us, I could see the house we'd lived in before and the Vanderlaans' next door. To the north was the old campgrounds. West was a beach, and east the public access. And all the spaces in between were wild with reeds and cattails.

"See them?" Mike whispered, nodding his head toward the cove carved out of the shore to the north of us.

Sitting as still as I could, afraid to scare them off, I watched the loons with their chick. They regarded us but weren't spooked because Mike had made sure to keep a respectful distance.

"It won't be long," he said. "They migrate soon, don't you think?"

"Probably by the end of the month," I answered. "If not, then at the beginning of November."

"You'll miss them, won't you?"

I nodded.

Soundlessly, the loons moved back into the cove, keeping their eyes on us. They were shy, and I couldn't blame them. But what they lost in being shy, they made up for with their evening songs.

"Can you believe I'm leaving tomorrow?" Mike asked.

I shook my head. "You know Mom forbade this conversation, right?"

"She's not here," he said. "And I need to talk about it."

Swallowing, I wished I'd brought a cup of coffee with me or some hot tea to take off the chill.

"You know why they let us have these weeks before we go to Vietnam, right?" He leaned his elbows on his knees.

"No," I answered, not interested in venturing a guess.

"So we can see our family one more time," he said. "In case we don't come home."

"You're coming home."

"I hope you're right."

"Everybody at church is praying for you, Mike," I said. "They started as soon as you went to training. And I know they'll keep praying."

"Prayer is good. But it can't make me bulletproof." He

looked up at me, his face serious. "Things happen. People die."

"I don't want to think about it."

"Come on, sis." He shook his head. "Don't duck and cover now. I need you to think about what to do if I end up in a body bag."

"God won't let that happen to you," I said, my voice sounding like it came from a little girl. "He wouldn't do that to us."

"He might." He grabbed my hand. "Annie, it's happening every day over there. It could happen to me."

Had I not worried about hypothermia, I would have climbed right out of that boat. I would have gladly submerged in the water, letting it fill my ears so I wouldn't have to hear him talk anymore.

"I shouldn't be saying all this to you," he said. "It'll just worry you."

I didn't bother telling him that I was worried already.

But I was sure he knew it.

36

Of all the things in the world that Mom had in plenteous supply, it was opinions. She held to them stringently, never wavering from them even if they were proved to be wrong. One such strongly adhered to opinion was that, under no circumstances, should Christmas decorations be put up before Thanksgiving. And, if she'd had her druthers, never before December first.

"It's indecent," she'd said. "Decorating for Christmas in the fall is tacky."

When Joel had reminded her that winter didn't officially begin until December twenty-first, she'd told him to go jump in the lake.

So, when Mike and I made our way home to find the aluminum Christmas tree set up in the front window on that evening in the middle of October, we were both struck with disbelief.

"My goodness," Mike said, shaking his head. "She just can't help but outdo herself, can she?"

Stepping into the house was like a dream. Bing Crosby

crooned carols from the record player, and on the floor beside the tree, the rotating color wheel sent blue, green, and red beams of light into the silvery boughs, making them glow. Mom had even hung Mike's stocking over the fireplace, where yellow and orange flames made the logs crackle.

The aroma of a pot roast came from the kitchen, rich and inviting. Mom's card table was set up in the corner of the living room, covered with windmill cookies and chocolates, no doubt made that very day by Oma.

Frank stood by the cookies, hands behind his back like a little boy who's been told not to touch. Joel and Mom were in the dining room, setting the table. Bernie and Oma sat on the couch.

"Did you know about this?" Mike asked me.

"I had no idea," I answered.

"You two never could keep a secret from each other," Mom said, coming in from the dining room. Her smile was brilliant, wide. "Merry Christmas in October."

"You didn't have to go to all this trouble just for me," he said.

"If it makes you feel better, it's more for me than you." Mom winked at him. "We got you a present. Why don't you go ahead and open it."

Mike sat down on the floor by the tree, reaching for the single present that lay there. Carefully, just the way Mom had taught us, he peeled away the tape, unfolding the wrapping paper and trying not to rip it.

"Just tear into it," Frank said.

"But she'll want to use this paper again," Mike said. Then he grinned up at Mom. "Waste not want not."

"Oh, for goodness' sake, I don't care about thrift today." She sighed. "Just open it already."

For the first time in his life, Mike shredded the paper, laughing as if it was the most fun he would ever have.

But as soon as he saw the box inside, he stopped, his mouth opened wide.

"This is too expensive," he whispered, holding the camera box.

It was a Canon and looked like a million dollars. Mike held it in careful hands, as if dropping it would be the end of the world.

"We all threw in a couple of bucks," Bernie said. "It wasn't too bad."

"Will you send some of your photographs home to us?" Oma asked. "We want to see what you see."

"Only if you promise to send me cookies sometimes," Mike said.

"Of course, *mijn schatje.*"

Mike lost no time loading the camera with a roll of film that came in the box. "Let's get a picture of us," he said.

"I'll take it," said Frank.

"No." Mike shook his head. "I want you to be in it."

Frank's half smile pulled up one corner of his mouth and the brooding left his eyes, if only for a minute.

"Annie," Mom said. "See if Mr. Falck will take it."

I ran out the door and down the porch steps. But before I left our yard to enter the Falcks', I looked through the picture window. Mom was directing everyone where to stand, her voice carrying through the front door that I'd left ajar. She arranged them in the space between the Christmas tree and the fireplace, men in the back, Oma in front of Bernie, Mom beside her. Mike, of course, in the dead center.

"And Annie can stand in front of Frank," she said. "This is going to be a beautiful picture."

From where I stood, looking in from the outside, it already was.

37

I said good-bye to Mike in the space between our bedroom doors. He had on his dress uniform and his pack was slung over his shoulder.

"Don't you want me to come to the airport?" I asked. "Bernie said he'd give me the time off."

"You've already taken so much time for me." Mike shook his head. "It's all right. Mom and Frank decided to take me."

"I don't mind, really."

He scratched behind his ear, looking away from me. "Annie, it's just . . ."

I moved my head so my eyes were in his line of vision. "It's just what?"

"It's already going to be hard for me to get on that plane." He shifted his eyes to the ceiling. "If you and Joel are there, it'll be that much harder."

"I don't understand."

"I'll want to stay. If you two are there, I won't be able to leave."

"Mike . . ."

"You all made my leave so good," he said. "Too good."

I leaned back against the doorjamb.

"I have so much to say," I whispered. "I just don't know how."

"Write to me," he whispered back. "All the time, okay?"

He put his pack down on the floor and reached for me, wrapping his arms all the way around me. "You'll be okay," he said.

"So will you," I told him.

He let go of me far too soon and picked up his bag, walking down the steps, and only looking back at me once.

Then he was gone.

•

Bernie didn't say a single word about me showing up late. And he didn't get after me for wearing a pair of bell-bottom jeans instead of the slacks he required. But after I dropped my second plate, making it shatter across the kitchen floor, he pulled me aside and stooped so his face was level with mine.

"Get your mind off him," he said, his voice gruff. "Just stop thinking about him."

"I can't." I felt myself breaking and I breathed in deeply.

"Okay, then." He pushed his shoulders back and crossed his arms. "Tell me what you're thinking about."

"My brother."

"I'm not dumb, Annie." He rolled his eyes. "What are you thinking about him?"

I stammered, trying to figure out what he wanted me to say. "I'm worried about him."

"All right." He nodded. "What else."

"I'm scared."

"Of what?"

"That something will happen to him." I shoved my hands into my back pockets and blinked quickly, hoping that would discourage my tears.

"Don't tell me generalizations. Be specific," he said. "What are you afraid will happen?"

I couldn't say the words. They were stuck. I started and stopped more than a couple of times before my breath became shallow and I could no longer deny the crying.

"I'm afraid," I started. "I'm afraid that he'll get killed."

I shook, certain that I would fall down right there on the kitchen floor among the shards of the dish I'd broken. But Bernie put his thick, strong hands on my arms—his grip more gentle than I'd expected—holding me still.

"I'm afraid of that too," he said, all the harshness out of his voice. "Because it might happen. But it might not. We can't know."

"What will we do if it does?" I cried.

"I don't know." He shook his head. "We can't plan for it. What we have to do is keep going. We have to live today and then tomorrow and then the next day. And if something happens to him, we'll live that day too. Can we do that?"

I shook my head. "I don't know how."

"The same way you've lived all the other days up until now."

He told me to go to the restroom and put a cold washcloth on my forehead.

I let the water run in the sink to get good and cold and took off my glasses so I could wipe them clean on the bottom of my shirt.

When I looked up in the mirror I saw my reflection, blurry

from tears and not having my glasses on. Squinting, I got a clearer view. I moved my face from one side to the other, tipping my chin this way and that.

It was like being face-to-face with my mother. My jawline and the slope of my nose. Cheekbones, eye shape, fullness of lip.

She'd been a year younger than I was when she first met Frank and only one year older when they got married. A handful of years later and they had Mike and me. Then Frank had gone to Korea.

Live today and then tomorrow and then the next day . . . the same way you've lived all the other days.

Don't duck and cover. Keep your eyes open.

I put on my glasses and smoothed my hair. Turning off the faucet, I took one last look in the mirror.

I made sure to turn out the light behind me.

38

Very rarely did Joel come to Bernie's Diner. Partly, it was because he never had any spare money. He spent every penny, nickel, and dime on comic books and movies. Another reason was because Bernie would try to put him to work washing dishes or cleaning windows.

Joel wasn't afraid of work, exactly. But he didn't like the exacting standards Bernie Jager adhered to.

But the day Mike left, he'd stood at the counter after school let out, eating a piece of pie and sipping a glass of milk that I'd paid for, waiting for me to have half a minute to talk to him.

"Annie," he said, shoving a mouthful of crust into his cheek. "Remember *Parent Trap*?"

"Yup," I answered, trying to count the money from the cash register but losing my place and having to start all over again.

"Remember how they tricked their parents into having dinner together?" He grinned. "And it ended up being romantic, with candles and music. And then their parents fell in love with each other again."

"I remember," I said. "And, no, we aren't doing that to Mom and Frank."

"Come on."

"Joel, it would never work."

"Why not?"

"They've seen the movie."

"Mom has," Joel said. "But are you sure about Frank?"

I wrote down my total and tapped the stack of bills on the counter, making them even. "We are not going to trick our parents into getting back together."

Ever since he was small, Joel had a pout that could melt me into doing just about anything he wanted me to. So, I turned my back on him and stuffed the cash into an envelope for Bernie to put in the safe.

"Come on, Annie," he said, making his voice sound younger. "Please."

"Nope."

"He'll leave soon, you know that, right?"

"I know," I said.

"This is our chance."

Sighing, I turned back toward him. "We can't trick him into staying. And we can't force Mom to take him back."

Slumping, he leaned his elbows on the counter. "I just want to know what it's like to have a normal family for once."

"Then you're going to have to find another family that will let you join them," I said. "Pal, we're anything but normal."

"You sound like Mike."

"I'll take that as a compliment." I took his empty plate and glass. "If you wait half a minute, I'll walk home with you."

I did up Joel's dishes, thinking about how easy it had been for the mother and father in *The Parent Trap*. All it had taken was remembering how good it had been before. Kiss, second wedding, happily ever after.

Putting the dishes in the drainer to dry overnight, I wished it was that simple, putting a family back together. But then again, I wondered if I'd even want Frank to live in our house again, to upset the rhythm of our life.

I hung up my apron and grabbed my jacket.

●

Frank didn't come for supper that night. I thought for sure that he'd pulled up stakes again and went back to Bliss. Mom had me warm up three frozen dinners in the oven and we ate off of TV trays in the living room, watching the news.

The Christmas tree was still up, looking stark and gray without the colorful lights shining at it.

I wondered how long it would take to fly from Michigan to Vietnam. If they'd fly straight over the Pacific Ocean or if they'd swoop up over Canada and Russia. Did they stop somewhere to refuel the plane? How many boys were with him? Had he made any friends?

As I chewed a rubbery square of turkey, my stomach turned. I spit the meat out into my napkin, deciding that I couldn't eat one more bite of it.

Joel's head perked up. "Frank's coming," he said.

"How do you know?" I asked.

"I can hear his truck."

Neither Mom or I questioned him. Since he was little, Joel had an uncanny ability to recognize a vehicle by its rumble or growl or whine.

Sure enough, around the corner came the dull headlights of Frank's truck. He parked in front of the house and cut the engine. Joel and I watched him from behind Mom's flossy sheers as he sat a moment longer. I half feared that he'd give up, start the engine again, and drive away.

But he didn't. He got out, slammed the door shut, and made his way up the walk.

Mom didn't turn off the television or stop eating the mashed potatoes from her dinner.

Joel let Frank in without waiting for him to knock. Frank had on a red flannel shirt and a well-worn pair of jeans. He glanced at Mom.

"Did you have supper?" Joel asked.

"I'm all right," Frank answered. "I can't stay long."

"Close the door," Mom said, not looking away from the TV. "I don't pay good money to heat the outdoors."

Frank and Joel moved, doing as she'd asked. The program went to a commercial break, and I pushed out my TV tray to turn it off. Mom gave me a dirty look but didn't say anything.

"I'm leaving tomorrow," Frank said, not meeting eyes with any of us. "First thing in the morning. I have to get back to work."

Joel's smile fell.

"Sorry, son. I wish I could stay."

Joel nodded. "You'll come see us again?"

"I will," Frank said. "I promise."

●

Frank stayed until Mom told Joel it was time for him to get to bed. The two of them shook hands, Joel no longer having any hope for a hug.

"I'll walk you out," I said, grabbing a sweater off the end of the couch and pushing my arms through the sleeves.

I followed him onto the porch, pulling the cardigan tighter around me. The air was crisp, the way an October evening should be.

"He wanted a hug," I said after shutting the door behind me.

"You think so?" Frank asked.

"He wants to know you." I turned toward him. "And he wants you to know him."

"Did he say that?"

"Not in those words, but yes."

"I figured I'd missed my chance."

"Not with him, you haven't."

We walked down the porch steps and along the path toward his truck. He put his hand on the top edge of the tailgate as if holding on for dear life.

"Do you ever wish you hadn't left?" I asked. "I mean that first time."

"Every day." He turned and looked into the truck bed as if he might find something there. "But I couldn't have been a fit father to you kids."

"Sometimes I wonder if an unfit father would have been better than no father."

He rubbed a hand along his jawline and furrowed his brow. "I asked your mother if she wanted me to give her a divorce."

I swallowed, regretting that I ate even one bite of that frozen dinner.

"Why did you ask her that?"

"In case she wanted to get remarried." He shrugged. "Some other man could give her the kind of good life she deserves."

"What did she say?" I leaned my hip into the back of the truck, looking up into his face.

"She said she has to think about it," he said. "I told her she could have as much time as she needs."

"Do you really want a divorce?" I lowered my voice when I said the last word, it felt wrong coming from my mouth, like a cuss word.

He cleared his throat. "Not if she doesn't want one."

He let go of the truck and crossed his arms.

"Will you come and visit again?" I nudged up my glasses with my knuckles. "You won't be a stranger again, will you?"

He shook his head.

"Well, I'd better get going. It's a long drive." He turned toward me, looking me full in the face. "Do you want me to hug you?"

Without answering him, I took a step forward, lifting my arms and putting them around his neck. He put his hands between my shoulder blades. It was only a second, but it didn't matter.

I thought about how a normal father wouldn't have had to ask. That a normal daughter wouldn't have felt awkward in his arms. That the usual thing for a girl to say to her dad was how she loved him. It would have been ordinary for him to say it back.

It was a bitter pill to swallow, knowing that I couldn't have an ordinary life with Frank.

I'd long given up that hope.

Frank,

Why did you tell Annie that you asked if I wanted a divorce? Doesn't she have enough to worry her with Michael being away? She's not your friend and she's not your confidante. She's your daughter. You would do well to remember that.

As to your question of divorce, I still have no answer to give you. You're just going to have to wait.

Gloria

Dear Gloria,

I didn't realize I'd upset Annie. That wasn't my intention. I shouldn't have told her, I know that now.

Take all the time you need. I'm in no hurry.

Sincerely,
Frank

39

October had gotten cold all of a sudden. Every time someone opened the door, walking into Bernie's, a chill came
along with them, making me shiver even as I rushed around
delivering plates of eggs and bacon and refilling cups of coffee. I almost looked forward to submerging my hands into
the hot dishwater.

The door opened as I carried a stack of used dishes to the
kitchen. Turning to bump the door open with my rear end,
I saw that it was Walt's mother, Mrs. Vanderlaan, her winter
coat gathered together in her hand at her neck as if she hadn't
thought to button it up.

Shoulders slumped forward, she found a seat at one of the
far tables, her back toward the window. When I brought the
coffeepot, filling her cup, I saw that her face was drawn, her
eyes wet. She'd lit a cigarette and smoked it as if desperate,
her fingers trembling. I'd never seen her smoke before. Of all
the people in town that I least expected to light up, it was her.

"Mrs. Vanderlaan, are you all right?" I asked.

"Don't tell my husband. Please," she said. "Vince would
kill me if he knew I was smoking."

"All right," I answered. "Would you like a little breakfast? Bernie still has pancakes going."

She shook her head, staring off into nothing. "Just the coffee. I don't need any cream."

"Is everything okay?"

She shook her head and pulled on her cigarette again, holding the smoke while she talked.

"I just couldn't stay home. Not while *they* are in the neighborhood." She let the smoke out before dropping the cigarette into the ashtray. "I saw the car coming down the road and I was sure it was going to pull into our driveway."

"Who?" I asked.

"The men who come to bring bad news about our boys." She used the knuckle of her thumb to wipe under her eye. "You know that they send men to give bad news if something happens to the boys over there."

"Is it Walt?" I asked, my voice sounding far away from my body, as if it came from someone else altogether.

She shook her head. "They went to the house across the street. Do you know the Robertses? They moved in just a few years ago."

I put the coffeepot down, feeling light-headed. "I know Larry."

"His father was killed in Vietnam. Alan. Alan Roberts." She shook her head. "They came to their house first thing this morning. I was sure they'd come for me. I was just sure."

"Oh no." The two smallest of words came out, riding on my sigh, holding very little meaning. And yet, all the meaning I could muster. "Oh no."

"I was so relieved when they didn't come to my house."

She looked up at me. "I didn't think to be horrified for that family. All I could feel was relief."

I nodded, not knowing that there was anything I could or should say to her.

"What kind of a monster thinks that way?" She opened her purse and fished out her pack of cigarettes, lighting another one and pulling on it as if it would keep her alive.

I walked from her table, hardly noticing that I still carried the half-full pot of coffee, its weight feeling like nothing to me. All over, I'd become numb. Numb except for the sick feeling in my stomach.

Putting the pot back on the warmer, I pushed my way into the kitchen, rubbing the palms of my tingling hands on my apron, feeling nothing, but hearing the whisper of skin on soft cotton. Bernie's low, growly voice sounded far away, underwater, even.

"Annie?" he said. "We've got customers, you know."

"What?" I asked, turning. "Oh yeah. Sorry."

"You sick?"

"No. It's just . . ."

I didn't finish. To speak the words would give the truth more reality than I could handle.

To say that Larry's father was killed in Vietnam was to admit to myself that it really happened. Not just to his dad or to some kid who lived across the country.

It could happen to my brother.

It could happen to Mike.

Stepping back out of the kitchen, I swallowed against the bile and begged God to spare my brother.

●

Water boiled in Mom's stockpot, waiting for her to drop in the box of dried spaghetti. It bubbled and hissed, but she seemed to have forgotten all about it. The telephone receiver to her ear, she bit on her thumbnail and said, "Uh-huh . . . Oh heavens . . . How awful . . . Yes," to whoever was on the other line.

When she caught sight of me, she pointed at the pot and covered the mouthpiece. "Could you do that?" she whispered.

I was glad to have something to do, hoping I'd hear more from her end of the conversation without her thinking I was eavesdropping.

"How old are the little girls?" she asked then paused, listening. "Oh, they're so little. And three of them? Plus the boy?"

I assumed she was talking about Larry and his younger sisters. How would such small kids be able to understand, I wondered. It couldn't be possible. It was just too horrible.

"Oh, bless their hearts."

Turning, I saw her in profile as she ran a finger under her eye and blew a sigh out between her lips.

"You take care, Elizabeth, all right? I know you've had an incredible shock." She swallowed. "Let me know if they need anything. Do you promise?"

I popped the top off the Ragu bottle and poured it into a saucepan, setting it on one of the back burners.

"All right, you too," Mom said. "Buh-bye."

She hung up the phone and clasped the clip-on earring back on her lobe. "Heat up both jars, if you would," she said. "Joel has a friend coming for supper."

"Who?" I asked.

"His friend Andy. You know, the tall one. They have a test to study for." She looked into the pan. "Should we add anything to that sauce? Some peppers or carrots?"

"No," I said. "This is fine."

"Are you sure?"

"They're boys. They won't want it fancy."

"I've got meatballs in the oven." She crossed her arms. "Don't worry, I didn't make them. I got them premade from Huisman's."

"I wasn't worried."

"Uh-huh." She covered a yawn with her hand. "I'm sorry. It's been a long day."

"Was that Mrs. Vanderlaan on the phone?" I stirred the noodles as they softened in the water. "Are you suddenly on speaking terms again?"

"Don't be smart."

"I wasn't trying to be," I said. "I'm sorry."

"You worked with the boy, didn't you?"

I told her that I had.

"Do you know if they go to church?" She touched her temple as if she had a headache coming on. "Mrs. Vanderlaan seemed to think they don't."

"I don't know."

"They'll need a place to hold the funeral. Maybe they can have it at ours." She nodded. "And Oma could arrange for the luncheon."

"I think that would be nice."

"Mrs. Vanderlaan told me that Mrs. Roberts fainted when the men came this morning." She opened the cupboard and counted out plates. "I can't blame her. They knocked on the door before the kids had even had breakfast. Those little girls had to hear about their father that way. It just breaks my heart."

"How awful."

"It would be the worst thing for you and Joel to hear news like that."

"Don't talk like that," I said. "I don't want to think about it."

I put the lid on the saucepan harder than I'd meant to. It made a slamming sound and the pot clattered against the grate. Without any sense of control, I'd started crying. A heaving, messy, bending-at-the-waist kind of cry.

"Honey," Mom said, grabbing my shoulders and pulling me upright. "Annie, it's all right."

"I'm just scared for him." I leaned against her, knowing she was strong enough to keep me from falling. "I don't want anything to happen to him."

"I know. I know." She rubbed circles on my back with the palm of her hand. "He'll be fine. He's special. Nothing's going to happen to him."

But they were all special. Every single one that went over there. All the ones who wouldn't come home. They were special to somebody.

Dear Annie,

Your visit with Mike sounds like it was absolutely perfect in every way! I'm proud of your mom for thinking up Christmas in October, especially considering her aversion to seasonal decorations. Please tell her that I say, "Bravo, Mrs. Jacobson!" What a wonderful idea.

I'm sure you're missing him and I know that you're worried about him. To be honest, I would be too. But I know that no matter what happens, God sees your fears and he knows your heart. At the very same time he has his eye on Mike's every move, no matter what he's doing over there.

I stumbled upon a quote that I think might help. It happened in the library when I borrowed a book for one of my history assignments. In the front cover, someone had written in pen. (Pen! Can you believe someone would do such a thing?) At first I was aghast (see previous parenthetical). But when I read the words three or four times over, I was glad for the defacement of library property.

"All shall be well, and all shall be well, and all manner of things shall be well."

I don't understand why, but those words brought peace to my heart.

I asked the librarian what she knew of the quote (because we are well aware that librarians are knowledgeable about all things). She told me that a mystic from the fourteenth century wrote it. And, get this, it was a woman! Her name was Julian.

Anyway, Annie my dear. When you become afraid or worried or even just tired, think of our friend Julian's words.

"All manner of things shall be well."

I love you,
Jocelyn

40

For all the attention the hippies got on the news and television programs, I'd only seen a handful of them in real life. The fact was, they mostly kept to the big cities and university campuses. They weren't too interested in our small town, not really.

The few times they had made their way to our neck of the woods, they were met with suspicion and sideways glances. Most of the adults in town believed the hippies had come to indoctrinate the youth of Fort Colson to put flowers in their hair and dance, stoned and scantily clad, to psychedelic music that was sure to melt our brains and common sense completely away.

The fact was, when they did come to stay at the campground or to take a swim in Old Chip, they mostly kept to themselves. I thought that was due to the tepid welcome they received. Mom, though, was of the opinion that it was so they could engage in their "drugging" without anybody getting in their way.

In the weeks after Mike left, most every news report had some kind of story about the hippies. In fourteen days I'd seen more of them on the TV screen than I had in the first seven years of the decade. They marched in Washington DC more than once, in New York City, in San Francisco. They even protested in Wisconsin. They held signs touting "Free Love" and "Peace." They burned their draft cards and pushed back against police.

The clips of them on the news were soon followed by a report on Vietnam, including how many American boys had been killed that day. The contrast was stark, jarring. I couldn't tell which riled Mom more, the daily death count or the hippies.

Most nights, they showed film footage from the war. Mom would lean forward, closer to the screen. She never said so, but I knew she was hoping to catch a glimpse of Mike. It was a long shot, her seeing him. But I was quite certain there were mothers all across the country doing the very same thing.

All I could think of, though, was how it might be for Larry. How he felt about the daily reported death count now that his father was among the numbered. And what he thought of the protests. I hoped it didn't make him wonder if his father's death had been nothing but a waste.

I could think of nothing worse.

●

Joel looked like an oversized kid, sitting Indian style on the floor in front of the television, watching the Charlie Brown Halloween special. His loud laughter had drawn me into the room to see him there.

Stepping around the end table, I lowered down to sit beside him even if the floor was hard and cold.

"Poor Charlie Brown," he said, shaking his head. "All he got for trick-or-treat was a lousy old rock."

He pushed up his glasses, never taking his eyes off the screen.

In four years he'd have to register for the draft. The boy who still laughed at Charlie Brown and shook his head at the injustice of Lucy bullying him. A child who would try to talk Mom into letting him trick-or-treat just one more year. He wanted to dress up as John Lennon since he already had the right kind of glasses.

I wasn't the kind of person to take the side of the hippies. There was no war protest in my veins. But I did hope, as they did, that soon we'd have peace in Vietnam, that all our boys would be able to come back home.

And that no more of them would have to go.

I rested my head on Joel's shoulder.

I couldn't bear the possibility of him having to go to war.

Dear Mom, Annie, and Joel,

Well, I made it all right. It sure was a long flight over. I thought we'd circled the earth at least three times. When I asked the stewardess, she just laughed and told me I was silly. I didn't have the heart to tell her I wasn't joking.

I never did find out the real answer.

It sure is hot here and humid. It's like walking through a steam cloud all the time. No matter what I do, I can't seem to get comfortable. From what I understand, winter starts soon and everything will dry out and cool off. Although the guy who told me that is from Florida, so I'm not sure he understands what cool really means to a Michigan boy.

It didn't take long for me to be put right in the middle of the action. They've got me on what we call a "dust-off." That's just a Huey helicopter that goes into the middle of the fighting to pick up wounded guys to take back to base where the hospital is.

The night before I went on my first medevac mission (like an ambulance in the sky) I was so scared I hardly slept at all. Then, before I hopped on the dust-off, I couldn't keep my breakfast down. Talk about embarrassing!

Our first call was to go get a kid who cut his leg with a machete. It wasn't all that bad, really. I just applied pressure to the wound for the whole chopper ride. He'll be fine after his stitches heal and he gets all his shots.

He was pretty upset when he found out that wasn't his ticket back home. I think I would have been too.

I already miss you all. Write to me as much as you can. And tell Oma that she can start baking whenever she's so inclined. I've already promised my buddies that I'd share with them, but only if they promise to send her thank-you notes.

Love,
Mike

Dear Mike,

    While you've been basking in the heat we've been freezing our noses off. I fully expect it to snow any day now.

    Not too much going on here. Just the normal, everyday, quiet life of our sleepy town. You might want to know, though, that Fort Colson High beat Borculo High at our homecoming game. I, of course, know nothing of football, but I was informed that it was "a heck of a game" by Bernie. I'll have to take his word for it.

    Don't worry, cookies should be coming soon. Oma and I baked the day after you left. She shipped them in old coffee cans. You've got two on their way. We made the kind with the peanuts on top and some molasses cookies (I used Grandma Jacobson's recipe). We hope you like them!

    Let me know if you have any special requests. Oma and I are happy to keep sending them. She's so worried that you're not going to get enough to eat over there. So, cookies to the rescue!

    Praying for you all the time.

                  Love,
                  Annie

41

They buried Larry's father, Alan Roberts, on the morning of Halloween. A breeze wove through us as we stood at the graveside, apart from the family who had wooden folding chairs under a black canopy. The dark clouds threatened rain, and I was glad that Mom had thought to bring an umbrella.

Larry sat to the left of his mother, head hung. I imagined he was either crying or trying hard not to. His little sisters—two standing on either side of their mother, the third on her lap—cried without reservation. They wept and wailed so that I could hardly hear the words of the minister.

It was all right. I didn't need to know what he was saying. I was just glad no one tried to hush the girls. Mrs. Roberts reached her arms around all three, holding them tightly, the only way she could, holding them as close as she could manage.

Mom stood beside me, hanky folded in her hand and held to her lips. She kept her eyes on the girls. Every once in a while she'd shake her head ever so slightly.

"And the words that Jesus said to Martha I now share with you." The minister held up a hand as if in blessing over the family. "He said, 'I am the resurrection, and the life: he that believeth in me, though he were dead, yet shall he live.'"

It seemed odd to me, his quoting from the story of Jesus raising Lazarus from the dead at a funeral. There would be no calling of Alan Roberts's name. He would not come forth from the grave. And, even though I knew in my heart that Jesus meant for the resurrection to be into a heavenly life, it still struck me as cruel. It almost seemed to be a tease.

Jesus raised this one man. But he isn't going to raise your father. Not today. Not this side of heaven.

My faith in that moment felt less akin to Martha and more to her sister Mary who had wept at Jesus's feet.

If you had been here, my brother would not have died.

I held my hands in tight fists, my eyes on the three little girls, on their mother, on Larry. And I struggled, knowing that God could have spared the life of their father, of her husband, and knowing that he'd chosen not to.

But then, out of the corner of my eye, I caught the sight of a tiny brown sparrow, perched on a gravestone nearby. It shook the rainwater from its feathers before taking back off to flight.

My fists relaxed, but the tightness in my chest didn't relent.

I wished I could watch that bird and come upon some sort of transforming revelation about the goodness of God even in the midst of sorrow. But I couldn't. Not hearing the cries of those little girls, not watching the way Larry's shoulders shook.

So, instead, I gritted my teeth and tried to remember the words of Jocelyn's latest letter, even if I wasn't so sure I believed them.

All manner of things shall be well.

●

I'd come upstairs from the church fellowship hall, looking for a few spare folding chairs to take down to the funeral luncheon. That was when I saw Larry sitting on the steps outside. Everybody else was inside eating cold cut sandwiches and potato salad. But Larry was alone, staring off toward Old Chip.

The chairs could wait.

Crossing my arms around myself against the chill, I stepped out and sat beside him. The concrete was cold beneath me and sent a shiver up my spine.

What I knew from having brothers was that if a boy didn't want to talk, no amount of prompting would persuade him. I'd learned that it was better to be quiet and let them start on their own.

So, I kept my mouth shut and waited.

After a couple of minutes, he spoke.

"It's cold out here," he said.

"A little bit," I answered.

He reached into his pocket and pulled out a pack of Juicy Fruit, offering it to me first. I took a slice, thanking him, and unwrapped it. He nodded, not looking at me.

He folded his stick of gum before popping it in his mouth, sucking on it for a second or two before chewing.

"Do they have anything good down there?" he asked. "Cake or anything?"

I nodded. "A couple of the ladies made sheet cake. All different flavors."

"Hm."

"I could get you a piece. I'd bring it out here for you if you didn't want to go inside."

"Nah." He tucked the gum into his cheek. "I don't feel much like eating."

"That's all right."

"Did you get a sandwich or something?" He wiped under his nose.

I shook my head. "I'm not hungry either."

Resting my elbows against my thighs, I watched a flock of Canada geese flying in an uneven V shape. It always made me sad, seeing the geese rehearse their leaving. Winter would come soon and I never seemed ready.

"Why do people keep telling me they're sorry?" Larry asked.

"I don't know." I tilted my chin so I could watch the flock glide through the sky over our heads. "Maybe they don't know what else to say."

"How am I supposed to answer them? Am I supposed to say it's okay?"

"You don't have to say anything." I swallowed. "They'll understand."

"Nobody laughs around me now." He turned his face, looking at me for the first time since I sat down. "Everybody's being so serious."

"Well, maybe because they don't want to seem disrespectful."

"You know what my dad always said?" he asked. "He said, 'You can make it through anything if you find a way to laugh.'"

I smiled at him. Licked my lips. The sweetness of the gum was starting to fade, still I chewed it, rubbery against my teeth.

"Knock, knock," I said.

He smirked. "Who's there?"

"Owl say."

"Owl say who?"

"Yes, they do."

"That was bad," Larry said, shaking his head but chuckling. "You know any more?"

I told him every joke I could think of until people started to leave the luncheon. They quieted their voices as they walked past us down the steps.

"I should see how my mother's doing," he said, standing and rubbing his hands on the thighs of his slacks. "Thanks."

I knew he meant for the jokes. I nodded and smiled at him.

He went inside, but I stayed seated on the steps.

I'd never gotten the chairs Mom had asked for.

Hi, All!

I've been hearing from some of the fellas here that there've been a bunch of protests back in The World. That's what they call America around here. And they call Vietnam "In Country." Don't know why, exactly.

Anyway, they said there's a bunch of hippies and such protesting the war. I read in the Stars and Stripes (the newspaper we get every day) that some of them even had flags from North Vietnam they were waving.

In case anybody was confused, North Vietnam happens to be the folks we're fighting against. Them and the Viet Cong. And neither is all that friendly when you get down to it.

If anybody in Fort Colson is protesting, you tell them to knock it off, would you? For me and all the other guys in country. It's just making our hard job that much more difficult. You know how hard it is to be fighting for a bunch of people who are against you?

Besides, the NVA (North Vietnamese Army, in case you didn't know) keeps saying that our own country is against us. That's not exactly good for morale.

Sorry that I'm so grumpy. I haven't slept very well since I got here. It's not good for my temperament.

Other than that, I'm in one piece and eating three squares a day. Those squares happen to taste like cardboard covered in tasteless gravy sometimes. Other times it's cardboard covered in gravy that has a flavor to it. Too bad that flavor happens to be stinky socks.

> *Anyway, I love all of you.*
> *Mike*

42

Bernie had set up a television on one of the tables in the diner, and all our breakfast regulars gathered around, silent, watching NASA's launch of Saturn V. I stood on a chair to see over their heads, holding my breath as soon as the twenty-second countdown started.

David rushed in, grabbing a chair and standing on it, right beside me.

"Good morning," he said.

"You made it just in time." I smiled.

The screen looked like it was on fire when the injectors went off, and everyone in the diner cheered as Walter Cronkite yelled out about the "terrible roar" of the launch. I held my hands folded together and over my heart.

David stood, unmoving and unblinking, not taking his eyes off the television, his mouth open in an awestruck grin.

Climbing down the chair, I couldn't help but feel a measure of disbelief. How could such a thing be possible? I still couldn't grasp it even after so many other launches. I pushed open the door of the diner and stepped outside. It was cold and I'd left my jacket inside, so I wrapped my arms around my waist.

David had followed me, offering me his jacket.

"It's all right," I said. "I have to go back inside soon."

"No matter how many times I watch those launches, I'm always amazed," he said.

"It makes me feel small."

"Yeah." He nodded. "Do you really believe they'll be able to send a man to the moon?"

"I don't know. It seems too wonderful."

"Yeah."

Staring at the sky, I wondered what it might feel like, blasting off so far and so fast away from earth. I couldn't imagine it.

"Well, I better go," David said, uncrossing his arms and checking his watch. "But if all goes as planned, I'll see you at lunch."

"See you then." I watched him walk toward his office. He looked back once before opening the door and going inside.

For the first time in so long, anything seemed possible.

●

Just about ten o'clock Bernie locked the door and turned the sign to "closed." When I asked him what he was doing, he just told me we needed to have a talk, pulling out a chair at one of the tables near the counter.

I took the seat across from him, worried that I was going to get in trouble for something. Worried that he couldn't balance the books and that he'd have to close down the restaurant. Concerned that maybe something had happened that I didn't even want to allow my imagination to picture.

"Annie," he said, clearing his throat. "I got the mail a little bit ago. I didn't look at the name on the front. I just opened it."

"Okay," I said.

"It was a letter for you." He patted his shirt pocket. "From Mike."

"He sent it here?"

Bernie nodded. "He did."

"Why would he do that?"

"Some things are too hard to write to your own mother." He took it from his pocket. It had been folded in half, still in the envelope. "I only read a little of it before I realized it wasn't for me."

"That's all right." I reached for it.

He held it just an inch from my fingertips. "Go someplace alone to read it. And don't let your mother see it."

"Is it bad?"

"It's not good."

"Is he . . ."

"In one piece? Yes." He put the air mail envelope in my hand. "You can read it in the office if you want. I won't disturb you."

"I'll just stay here," I said. My legs felt as if they'd turned to jelly, and I didn't want to try to walk on them.

I waited until Bernie had gone into the kitchen and the door had stopped swinging before I looked at the envelope. He had used a straight edge to open it, his pocket knife, I would have guessed. The slice at the top was clean and crisp.

I put the letter on the table in front of me, smoothing it across the cold, flat top.

I took in a deep breath before I read.

Hey, Pal,

I have no idea what day it is. All I know is that it's night because it's dark and that means I can't go out on missions anymore until the morning.

Gosh, I wish this night could go on until I can come home. My chest gets tight whenever I think about morning.

They still have me on the dust-off, picking up wounded guys, sometimes two or three at a time, and bringing them to base. Then we turn around and go back out. Over and over. All day long. Sometimes we've got to land in a hot LZ (that means a lively and terrifying landing zone with shots going off all around us).

We had to get this one kid today, gosh he looked young. He looked younger than me, even. I could've sworn he was no older than Joel. He was injured in his stomach and was bleeding so bad. I couldn't stop it no matter what I did. Even with my training at Fort Sam, I didn't know somebody had so much blood in them.

He asked me if he was going to make it.

He asked me that, Annie.

I didn't know what to say, so I lied and told him he'd be just fine. He made me promise him and I did.

The kid was dead before we made it back to base. There was nothing I could do for him.

I've never seen somebody die before. It was awful. One minute he was there and the next he was gone. The glisten faded from his eyes. He was just dead.

At the end of our runs I had to clean all the blood out of the chopper. I don't want to tell you too much about that, I don't want you to have that picture in your mind. Just know that it's the least pleasant job I have to do.

I didn't get halfway done when I lost it. Never in my whole life have I cried like that. I was just glad that nobody was around to see it. It was the first time I've ever thought I very well could lose my mind.

It scared me. A whole lot.

Tomorrow I have to do it all over again and I don't believe I have the stomach for it.

Pray for me, Annie. Please. Pray every day. Pray all day long. I need to know you'll do that for me.

I'll never make it out of here if you don't.

I love you.

Mike

PS: You can't ever let Mom or Joel see this. Burn it, eat it, throw it in the lake, but don't let them read it. And promise you'll never tell them about this, either. They don't need to know.

Dear Mike,

Don't be angry. But Bernie read the letter you wrote to me. He opened the envelope, not knowing that it was for me until he'd already seen enough to know what happened.

He told me that I should write you back. When I asked him what I should say, he told me "Anything that might get his mind off it."

When I asked him if that was what he'd want me to do, he shook his head and said, "That's what Mike would want, though."

So, here goes. Consider this your five minutes of distraction from your current reality.

We had our first freezing rain of the winter on Sunday. The loons hadn't left yet. You better believe they took off for warmer climates directly afterward. I already miss them.

Not as much as I miss you though, I guess.

Joel has gotten pretty decent on his guitar, and his rock and roll band isn't half bad. They've even come up with a name. They call themselves the Bus Drivers. Mom thinks they've lost their minds. But the kids are certain that they're the next big thing.

Wouldn't it be something if our baby brother became a rock star?

Mom tried a new recipe a few days ago. It had something to do with pork chops, sliced apples, and garlic. To make a long story a whole lot shorter, the fire department *came and we never did find out if the recipe was any good. Mom sure has a knack, doesn't she?*

Next week we're going to Aunt Rose's mansion for Thanksgiving dinner. Frank's going to meet us there. Even Mom is going and Oma too. Thank goodness Aunt Rose insists that we don't bring anything but ourselves. I don't know that Mom's stove top could take any more abuse for a while.

You remember Walt Vanderlaan, don't you? I guess he's coming home from Vietnam next week. The church is holding a dessert reception for him. You know who organized that?

You'll never guess.

It was Mom.

Apparently she and Mrs. Vanderlaan are back on speaking terms. When I told her that it was nice of her, she told me it was something she'd want someone to put together for you. It's still nice, if you ask me.

How am I, you ask? Fine. There's nothing new for me. I'm just working at Bernie's. That's about it.

Take care of yourself, will you? And try not to carry the whole world on your shoulders. That's an impossible thing to ask of you, I realize that. But try.

You can't save everyone. But I know you can save some.

I'm proud of you.

Annie

43

Three long tables were covered in every kind of dessert imaginable. Trays of cookies, all varieties and shapes. Sheet cakes and layered cakes and cupcakes, all with different colored frosting. Pies with fancy lattice tops and perfectly pinched crusts. Chocolates molded by hand and filled with creams of many flavors.

Along the far wall of the church fellowship hall was a hand-painted banner. *Welcome Home, US Marine Vanderlaan!*

Nearly the whole town had come to give Walt the welcome worthy of a war hero. They milled around, chatting with each other as we waited for the Vanderlaans to arrive.

"Annie," Mom said, putting her hand on my shoulder. "Could you get another stack of coffee cups from the kitchen, please?"

"Sure," I answered. "This will be some party."

"It certainly will be. Do you think we'll have enough dessert?"

"I think we'll be fine." I shook my head. "Let me get those cups for you."

I wove through the masses toward the kitchen, amazed

by how many people had come for Walt. Sure, he'd been popular. But popular didn't always mean the same thing as well-liked. Either way, I was glad that so many had come. It would have been horrible if the crowd had been thin.

Once I made it out of the fellowship hall and into the doorway of the kitchen, I breathed easier. It wasn't usual for me to feel claustrophobic. But that mashing up of people had done it.

That was when I saw someone coming down the steps from the corner of my eye. Walt stepped off the last stair, his lanky arms hanging rigidly at his sides. The brass buttons of his uniform jacket caught the light, standing out against the dark fabric. Reaching up, he removed the white hat, holding it by its black bill. His white-blond hair was cut so short I could see the pink of his scalp.

"Annie?" he said.

"Hi," I answered, smoothing the burnt orange fabric of my A-line dress.

"You look nice." His voice wasn't nearly as loud as I'd remembered it. It lacked his usual bravado. Instead, he was tentative, almost shy. "I like your dress."

"Thank you."

"My parents are still in the car," he said. "They're arguing. Typical, huh?"

"I'm sorry."

"They told me to come in without them." He looked down at his hat. "It seems odd, walking in by myself."

"No one would even notice," I said. "All they care about is seeing you."

He shrugged. "Some way for a boy to come home from war, huh?"

"I can walk in with you," I said. "If you'd like."

"Just like kindergarten." He reached up and scratched the back of his head. "You remember that, don't you?"

I shook my head.

"It was Mike's and my first day of school." He swallowed. "You and your mom were there to see him to his classroom. My mother told me to walk with you. She didn't want to come in."

"I think I remember now."

"Mike ran into the school like he owned the place," he said. "I was scared."

"And I told you that I'd go with you."

"You held my hand." He put his hand out to me, stepping forward. "Just like kindergarten?"

"Sure."

His hand was warm and rough with calluses. He squeezed mine just as we walked into the crowd.

He only let go after I squeezed it back.

●

Mom got after me for keeping my window open to talk to Jocelyn.

"It's too cold for that nonsense," she said, standing in my bedroom door.

"But she just got home from college," I said from where I sat on my bed. "I have so much to tell her."

"Then just have her come over here. And keep that window shut, for goodness' sake."

So, Jocelyn had come and sat at the foot of the bed while I sat at the head. It was late and we both wore our nighties. Jocelyn's coat hung on my doorknob.

"Now, tell me again how he convinced you to hold his

hand," she said, hugging my old teddy bear to her chest. "I'm so sorry I missed all of it."

"Why do you want to hear about that?" I asked.

"Because it's romantic."

"Not really." I grimaced.

"Come on, Annie. Just humor me, would ya?"

"Oh, all right," I said, resting my head against the wall. "He reminded me of when we were little."

"Uh-huh." She sounded skeptical. "You didn't feel anything when you took his hand, did you?"

"Just that his palm was rough."

"That's not what I mean," she said. "I mean, was there an electric charge or anything? Like in the movies?"

"Not that I remember. Should there have been?"

"I'm not sure." She scrunched her lips to one side of her face. "You said he seemed different?"

I nodded. "Not so arrogant."

"Hm. Maybe the drill sergeants beat it out of him." She shrugged. "You just never know how being at war can change a man."

"He asked if he could take me to the movies or something," I said, hoping the cool wall would keep the blush from burning in my cheeks. "I told him he could."

"Annie Jacobson."

"What? I told him we'd go just as friends."

"I don't know what to say to you." She leaned forward. "Will this be your first date?"

"It won't be a date," I answered. "Besides, what about when I had lunch with David at the diner?"

"Do you want that to count?" she asked. "Because it counts if you want it to."

I nodded my head.

"Then this is your second date."

"Jocie, it's just as friends."

"Yeah, that's what you said." She put both hands on her cheeks. "Oh, what will you wear?"

"I don't have the slightest clue," I said. "Golly, I should have said no."

"Just because you don't know what to wear?" She laughed. "Don't worry. You could wear a flour sack and look beautiful. Besides, you know that boys don't care what a woman wears, right?"

"That's not it." I shook my head. "He's going to get the wrong idea about me."

"Hold on," she said. "This is about David, isn't it? You really *do* like him."

I nodded, rubbing at my temples with the meat of my hands. "I just wish it was different. Mom would have a stroke."

"The world's changing, Annie. Every day." She put her fingertips on my knee, so gently I hardly felt them. "Maybe this will change too. Who knows?"

"I guess anything is possible, right?" I cleared my throat. "I'm not going to count this with Walt as a date."

"Then it isn't a date." She nodded decisively. "It's just a movie."

"Exactly." I sighed. "Now, I want to hear about you. How was college? Tell me every single thing."

We stayed up until far too late in the night. I knew I'd be beat when my alarm went off in the morning, but I just did not care. I had my dearest friend home for a few days.

I felt like one lost in the desert who had just found a spring of fresh water.

Dear Family,

Happy Thanksgiving to all! I hope you have a good trip to Auntie Rose's house. Give her a stiff, obligatory hug for me, will you? And give Grandma a kiss on the cheek. As for Frank, maybe a firm handshake will do, compliments of old Mikey.

Gosh, I sure am going to miss eating myself silly with all of you and sitting down to watch the game. But don't you worry about me. I've heard that on base we'll have a turkey with all the fixings. If we're lucky, Uncle Sam might even spring for a slice of pumpkin pie.

Let's just hope Charlie gives us a break for the day. He doesn't like letting up, but maybe if we ask nicely, he'll stop shooting at our boys for a few hours.

That doesn't seem like too much to ask, do you think? Say, I'm thankful for you.

All my love,
Mike

44

Frank's rusty truck stood out like a sore thumb against the pristinely kept yard and the bright, white siding of Aunt Rose's house. I imagined her nose wrinkling when she saw it parked there. I couldn't help but smile at the thought of it.

Mom pulled our station wagon into the driveway. "Leave it to Rose to live in a house like this."

"*Weggegooid geld*," Oma said, turning from her seat in the front of the car to wink at me before opening her door.

"What did she say?" Joel asked.

"That this"—Mom nodded at the house—"is a waste of money."

"This much house for only a few people?" Oma said. "I'm right, you know."

"Can you imagine how much it costs to heat this place?" Mom shook her head.

The four of us stood on the porch, and Mom let Joel push the doorbell. Aunt Rose opened it before it stopped chiming.

"Happy Thanksgiving," she said, pulling the door wide and holding it as we all filed inside. "Welcome."

"Thank you for having us," Mom said, submitting herself to the air kiss Aunt Rose smooched next to her face. "Your house is lovely."

"How nice of you to say." Aunt Rose touched her cheek to mine and make a *mwah* sound close to my ear. "I'm sorry to say that Eliot had to go out of town on business despite my feelings. He sends his regards."

Joel and I met eyes. My brothers and I had hardly seen Uncle Eliot more than a couple of times. Mike had Joel convinced for years that Uncle Eliot wasn't real and that Aunt Rose made all her money working as an assassin during World War II. From the look on Joel's face, I thought he still half believed it.

"Frank is in the drawing room," Aunt Rose said. "First door on the left."

"What's a drawing room?" Joel whispered to me.

"Just a fancy living room, I guess," I answered.

"Huh. Rich people are strange."

I shushed him. "You know she's right behind us, don't you?"

He grimaced and covered his mouth with his hand. "Do you think she heard me?"

"For your sake, I hope not."

Frank stood at a window in the drawing room, a mug in his hand with the tail of a tea bag dangling from the lip. He turned toward us, giving Mom his half grin.

"Happy Thanksgiving," he said, lifting his mug in a toast.

"I'm glad to see you dressed up," Mom said.

"Oh, this old thing?" He rubbed the front of his well-worn flannel shirt and grinned.

"I asked him to wear something with a collar," Aunt Rose

said, crossing her arms. "I suppose I should have been more specific."

"Where's Grandma?" Joel asked, his eyes darting across the room.

"In the kitchen." Aunt Rose sighed. "She insisted on doing all the cooking."

"I'd like to say hello to her," Oma said. "If I may."

"Of course. Just this way."

Aunt Rose led Oma out of the room, turning and looking at Mom as if she wasn't sure what to make of her. I was glad that Mom hadn't seemed to notice.

Joel crossed the room, taking Frank's hand. "How ya doing, Dad?"

"Swell," Frank answered. "Isn't that what you hip cats say these days."

Joel's mouth spread in a wide smile. "Right on."

"You're still playing that guitar, aren't you?"

"Sure am."

"He's getting pretty good," I said. "I should know, I hear him practice every single day."

"Well, anybody could play it if they wanted to." Joel put his hands in his pockets.

"I couldn't," I said.

"You could. I'll teach you."

Frank's eyes went from Joel to me, observing the back and forth of our conversation as if it was the most interesting thing he'd ever seen.

You could have had this every day, I wanted to say to him. *You don't know what you gave up.*

But from the look in his eyes, the longing I read there, I thought he knew exactly what he'd lost.

•

Grandma looked healthier than I'd seen her in years. She stood without a stoop and smiled wide enough to show her teeth. As she moved around the kitchen there was more life to her steps and she hummed every once in a while. I thought she'd even put on a few pounds. She hadn't gotten plump, not nearly. But she looked as if she'd been eating better, which was an improvement over the last time I'd visited with Mike.

It was the grandmother I remembered from before Grandpa had gotten sick.

She busied herself, basting the turkey and filling the kitchen with the rich smells of stuffing and sweet potatoes, buttered mashed potatoes and yeast rolls. Oma whisked flour into turkey drippings for gravy while Mom cut a mincemeat pie. Aunt Rose and I filled relish trays with olives and pickles and radishes cut to look like flowers.

"Mother," Aunt Rose said. "Have you told them what you've done?"

"Oh, they don't care about that," Grandma said, her glasses fogged up from the steamy oven.

"I do," I said.

"Well, if you must know, I've joined a Dorcas Society. Rose made me," she told us. "We meet on Tuesday mornings to sew and then we have lunch together someplace in town. It's something to do, I guess."

"Don't let her fool you. She loves it," Aunt Rose said. "It was a moment of genius on Eliot's part, really. He saw the announcement in the church bulletin and knew it would be a good thing for Mother."

"What do you sew?" I asked.

"Oh, some ladies make quilts and others knit sweaters," Grandma said. "I've been working on making little dresses for girls. Then we send all of it to the needy."

"How nice," Mom said, moving on to cutting up a pumpkin pie. "And you've made friends?"

"I suppose you could say I have," she answered. "There's this one named Edith who comes and takes me to see a movie every once in a while. We have a good time."

"She's doing well here," I whispered to my aunt. "This is a good place for her."

"I'm trying," Aunt Rose said, not looking up from the block of cheese she'd started slicing.

"You're doing a good job," I said.

She met my eyes. I didn't think I'd ever before seen a more sincere expression on her face. Her lips trembled and she pulled them together as if to still them.

"Thank you," she whispered.

●

Grandma insisted that Frank carve the turkey, which he did with a surprisingly steady hand. He doled out the meat, light or dark. We passed seemingly endless dishes of all varieties, filling our plates with all things delicious and traditional. No matter how much food everyone took, there still was more. More than we ever could have eaten in one sitting.

"Son," Grandma said. "Bless the food, would you?"

He nodded, taking my hand on his right and Grandma's on his left. The tremor was slight, hardly noticeable. But when I curled my fingers around his hand, it nearly stopped altogether.

His prayer was simple and full of thanks. And he asked God to watch over the ones who weren't with us that day, especially Mike. It surprised me how true his voice sounded, how humbled and yet how confident. For twelve years I'd thought that when Frank walked away from us, he'd left God behind too.

I wondered if I'd been wrong all that time.

●

November days always ended early. Mom was anxious to get on the road before it got too dark. Aunt Rose wrapped up leftovers for us to take home including a whole extra pie that Joel declared would be his breakfast the next morning.

Frank walked us out to the car. He shook Joel's hand, even going as far as putting his left hand on his shoulder. And when Joel pulled him into a hug, he didn't make a face. Instead, he put an arm around his neck, giving one back.

"You'll come to our house for Christmas, won't you?" Joel asked.

"If I'm invited," Frank said, slapping him on the back. "You'll be taller than me by then, I bet."

"Bye, Frank," I said, giving him a hug of my own. "See you soon."

"Take care of them," he whispered. "Will you?"

"I always do."

When he let go of me he looked me right in the eye. I expected him to say something, but he just smiled. That said much more to me than any words could have.

We all climbed in the car, except for Mom. She stayed out, talking to Frank.

"What do you think she's saying to him?" Joel asked.

"I have no idea," I answered.

"Whatever it is, he's smiling," Oma said.

"I knew it," Joel whispered to me, nodding. "*Something's* happening."

For the first time in twelve years, I hoped. For Frank.

Dear Mike,

Thanksgiving was nice. Aunt Rose even laughed at one of Joel's stories! And not her robot laugh, either. A real one that made her eyes water. Can you believe it? Her face didn't crack, even. Really, she behaved herself and so did Mom.

Grandma is doing better than you could ever imagine. She pretended to be curmudgeonly, but I could tell it was an act. You should write and ask her what she's been up to. She has friends, Mike. Grandma has buddies. It truly is the best we could have wished for.

I guess that's what I'm most thankful for this year.

Well, I really could have used my big brother around today. A little advice could have helped me a whole lot. Why, you ask?

Walt Vanderlaan is taking me out tomorrow night. I think we're going to catch a movie and maybe have some dinner afterward. When he first mentioned it a week ago, I didn't think it was a date. I pictured it as old friends getting reacquainted. But then he called today and the way he asked me over the phone, the formality of it all, I think he wants it to be one.

Should I have said no? Should I have asked if Joel could come along? Am I doing the right thing by going? What if he tries to kiss me? Should I knock his lights out?

Okay, I know how you'd answer those last two.

I'm sweaty and shaky and nauseous just thinking

about it. How am I supposed to eat if I feel like upchucking whenever I think about it? Can you believe I even thought about calling Frank to ask him?

No, I haven't told Mom yet. She'll blow her lid. This will be worse than when you told her about you joining the Army.

Maybe I'll talk to Bernie. Strike that. That is a horrible idea.

Anyway, I'll write you to let you know how it goes. Thank goodness Jocelyn is still home on Thanksgiving break. At least I have one voice of reason still around.

Go ahead. Laugh at me. I know you want to.

Miss you,
Annie

45

Have you completely lost your mind?" Mom slammed the cupboard shut. "You do remember how awful he was to you, don't you?"

"That was before," I said, moving out of her way when she reached for the canister of sugar. "He's different now. Besides, it isn't a date."

"Do I need to make a list of the names he called you? Or the times you came home crying about how mean he'd been?"

"No, I remember them well enough, thank you."

"You aren't going on this date," she said, pointing at me.

"I already told you it isn't a date."

"Does he know that?"

"Well, I'm not sure."

She dug her ring of measuring spoons from the drawer. "What does a boy like him want with a girl like you?"

It felt like a slap to my face. "What do you mean by that?"

Mom closed her eyes and breathed through her nose. Her voice softened and lowered in tone. "Not what you think."

The numbness started in my toes and my fingers, spreading inch by inch so fast it took my breath away.

"You aren't like Caroline Mann," Mom said. "Before you jump to conclusions, I need you to listen to me. Can you do that?"

I nodded.

"You care about more than the kind of clothes you wear or how you do your makeup. For goodness' sake, you don't even own any makeup that I know of. You know that your worth isn't in what we've saved up in our bank account." Mom stepped toward me, putting her hands on my shoulders. "There's depth to you. The soul inside you is startlingly beautiful. And I wonder how a boy who could love a girl like Caroline would ever be good enough for a girl like you."

"Mom . . ."

"You can go on that date with him. Or whatever you're calling it," she said. "But don't let him make you forget who you are."

●

Jocelyn had ironed my hair as straight as a board. When I saw it in the mirror, I hardly knew it was really mine. It fell around my shoulders, soft and sleek. But our attempts to draw on eyeliner failed miserably.

I decided it would be best if I didn't wear any makeup at all, especially if I didn't want Walt to get the wrong idea.

Joel answered the door when Walt knocked, standing as tall as he could, his chest puffed out like he was trying to be bigger.

I came out of the dining room just as he was about to give Walt the third degree, I was sure of it.

"See you later, Joelie," I said, reaching up and ruffling his hair.

"Hey, quit it," he said.

"Don't wait up," Walt said, putting an arm around my shoulders.

I tried to remember to breathe.

●

The movie theater in Fort Colson only showed two shows at a time. That night they had either *The Jungle Book* or *Cool Hand Luke*. Without asking which I'd rather see, Walt bought two tickets to the Paul Newman flick.

"I didn't think you'd want to see the cartoon," he said, holding the door for me to step inside. "You want any popcorn?"

I shook my head. "No thanks."

"You aren't afraid of getting fat, are you?" He looked at my waistline.

"No," I answered, putting a hand on my stomach. "I'm just not hungry."

"Good." He ordered a bucket of popcorn with extra butter. "Caroline was always worried about getting fat like her mother."

I raised my eyebrows and looked away from him, glad that soon the movie would start and he couldn't talk about her anymore. Since he'd picked me up, all he seemed to want to talk about was Caroline this and Caroline that. How she was always looking at herself in the mirror or how she complained about going to the movies all the time. We were only ten minutes into our evening and I was already wondering when I could ask him to take me home.

"At least let me get you something to drink," Walt said, nudging me with his elbow.

Had he been one of my brothers I would have socked him in the arm. I hated being nudged. Instead, I told him I'd like a Dr Pepper and pushed up my glasses.

●

Blue, tan, green, and red. The whole movie flickered on the screen in muted colors the way I imagined they were in the South. Fist fights and egg eating and slow conversations drew my attention away from the buttery smell of Walt's popcorn and the munching sounds of him eating it by the handful.

At the very end, the crack of a gunshot made me jump and cover my mouth with my hand. Warm tears rolled down my cheeks, and I was glad I'd decided to forgo the makeup.

It was a rough-edged movie and somehow so beautiful. By the time the credits rolled up the screen, I felt like all the air had been knocked out of me and that I'd been refilled by something with just a little grit to it.

"Ready?" Walt said, sounding bored. Popcorn fell from his lap when he stood up. "You wanna get some burgers or something?"

"Sure," I said, wondering if he'd seen the same movie I had for how casually he was able to go on with the evening. "Did you like the movie?"

"It was all right, I guess."

He didn't bother asking me what I had thought of it.

I decided I was going to order the biggest burger on the menu, wherever we ended up going. And that I would eat every single one of my french fries dipped in ketchup. And if he said one more word about Caroline Mann, I would order a shake to go with it.

If I was feeling especially annoyed, I determined to dump that shake in his lap.

Just like your mother, Frank would have said.

He would have been right.

●

Walt walked me to the front door after driving me home, hands in the pockets of his letterman jacket. The front of his pants were not soaked in milkshake and I was glad he'd behaved himself. I stood on the first step and turned toward him.

"I had a good time," he said.

I nodded.

"Listen, I don't know how to do this." He breathed in through his mouth. "Caroline really threw me for a loop, you know."

"I'm sure she did."

He rubbed at the back of his still-short hair. "Gosh, here I am with you and you're beautiful and all I can talk about is her. What's wrong with me?"

"Do you want me to come up with a list?" I smirked.

"I don't know that my ego could take it." He grabbed one of my hands. "You're funny. I mean that in a good way."

"Thanks?"

He moved closer to me. I blinked and then felt something warm and wet touch the corner of my mouth. I pulled my head back and looked at his puckered-up lips and closed eyes. Then he smiled and opened his eyes.

"Why did you do that?" I asked. "Was that a kiss?"

"I thought you wanted me to," he said. "Didn't you like it?"

"No. I mean, it was all right," I lied. "But you don't have to do it again."

"I don't?"

"I thought we were just going to be friends." I hesitated, trying to find the right words. "You're a swell guy and all, but you're like a brother to me."

"Oh," he said. "All right, I guess."

"Did I hurt your feelings?"

He shook his head. "Nah. I'd better get home."

"Thanks for the movie and dinner."

"Sure thing," he said, walking to his car. "I'll see you around, I guess."

I put my fingertips to my lips, hoping he wouldn't look back to see me wiping away the first kiss I ever had.

It was nothing like I'd always hoped it would be.

46

No set of rules in our home was more strict and fiercely kept than Mom's table rules. We were to always chew with our mouths closed and to never speak while we had food stuffed in our cheeks. We weren't to reach across the table for something, and when we asked for it to be passed, we were to remember our pleases and thank-yous.

And, no matter what, we didn't take telephone calls during supper. The next-door neighbor's house could be burning to the ground and we wouldn't get up to use the phone. Not until we were finished eating and had put our dishes in the sink.

So, when the phone rang not once, twice, or three times, but four during our Monday evening dinner, Mom was more than a little miffed. She stood and walked to the kitchen, pulling off her right clip-on earring before answering.

"Jacobson residence," she said in a voice that could have turned boiling water to ice. "No, she may not come to the phone right now. It's the dinner hour."

She listened for a moment before going on. "Is this some sort of emergency, Walter? No? Then you may call back in thirty minutes. Not a moment sooner. Do you understand? And I won't have you calling over and over until someone answers. That's just bad manners."

Mom sighed and listened again. "I accept your apology. Good-bye."

The receiver clicked into place and Mom came back to her seat.

"I'm sorry," I said, putting my fork on the edge of my plate.

"Did you tell him to call four times in a row?"

"No."

"And did you ask him to call during dinner?"

I shook my head.

"Then you have nothing to apologize for." She picked up her fork.

"Why's he calling you?" Joel asked.

"Beats me," I said.

●

Thirty minutes—exactly—passed and Walt called again. That time I answered before anyone else had the chance.

"Annie?" Walt said. "I've been trying to get ahold of you all day. No one ever answered."

"I was at work," I told him.

"Right." He cleared his throat. "Hey, I wanted to ask if I could see you again."

"Walt, I . . ."

"Tomorrow night? I can pick you up."

"I . . ."

"Six o'clock."

I pulled in a breath so that I could tell him I couldn't. My mind spun, trying to find an excuse to say no.

"Annie? Are you still there?"

"Yes," I answered. "I have to go. I'll see you tomorrow."

●

Annie? Are you still there?

I sat in my bedroom, those words echoing in my mind, stirring a memory that had laid still and quiet for so long.

"Annie? Are you still there?"

It wasn't in the voice of the twenty-year-old Walt. The voice in my memory was higher, from a Walt before puberty hit. Before we moved to the other side of Old Chip.

"Annie? Are you still there?"

It was early evening, just after dusk took the shine off the day. The shed was dark already, the small windows didn't let in much light.

"I'm here," I'd answered.

"You aren't going away, are you?" His voice had trembled, and I reached out, taking his hand.

"If I do, I promise to come back."

"Please don't leave me alone."

For all of Frank's bad days, he'd never hit us more than a spank on the behind or a slap on the back of the hand, neither of which ever hurt all that much. He had never blackened our eyes or bloodied our lips like Walt's father had done to him. And he'd never roared at us so loudly that the neighbors had to close their windows.

The memory passed, but its after-image had burned into my closed eyelids. And with it, Walt's small, young boy voice.

Please don't leave me alone.

47

I hung up my apron on the hook, all my jobs done for the day. Larry had come in after school to wash the windows, mop the floors, and scrub down the restrooms. He came most days, working a couple hours doing odd jobs around the diner. I knew Bernie had found plenty of what he called "make-work" for the boy, hoping to help their family in the best way he could think of.

As a result, the diner had never been so clean or smelled so fresh.

"I'll see you in the morning," I said to Bernie, headed for the back door.

"Hold up," he called to me from the office. "Come have a seat in here for a minute."

"Are you going to fire me or something?" I asked, standing in the doorway of the office.

"Nope," he answered, pulling a deck of cards from the middle drawer of his desk. "Not today, at least."

"Well, that's a relief," I said, laying the sarcasm on thick.

He pointed at the extra chair he had in the room. "Sit down."

The cards were old and didn't make a crisp sound when

he shuffled them. It was more of a whisper. He tapped them against the desktop after each shuffle, paying close attention so he wouldn't lose control of them, sending them flying across the room.

He dealt us each ten cards. "Gin rummy," he said. "Every time you put down a set you say why you think being around Walt Vanderlaan is a good idea. Every time I do, I say why I disagree."

"But I . . ." I began.

"You go first."

I drew a card, adding it to my hand and discarding the two of diamonds. He picked up my two, putting the heart and club beside it and laying it on the table in front of him.

"He's full of himself," Bernie said before discarding a five of spades.

I drew off the pile, completing a run of clubs. "He's smart."

We drew, discarded, laid down cards, and gave our reasons.

Bernie had plenty. Walt didn't go to church with his parents. He hadn't found a job. He'd always caused trouble for his folks. Before he'd gone into the service he'd had a reputation for drinking too much. And on and on.

I couldn't find nearly as many. He'd held the door for me at the movie theater and paid for my ticket. He thought I was funny. He said I was beautiful.

"Ha," he said, going out with a set of threes. He rubbed his chin as if really trying to come up with a good one. He looked me straight in the eye and smirked. "David's a better man."

I couldn't disagree with him. Not in the slightest.

Bernie picked up the cards, putting them back in their tidy stack and returning them to the desk drawer.

"I know what you're trying to do," I said. "But I don't think you understand."

"I don't, huh?" He frowned and made a *hm* sound.

"I don't feel anything for Walt other than friendship," I said, putting my hands in my lap. "And I'm not even sure he's all that good of a friend."

"Did you tell him that?"

"I tried."

"He wouldn't listen, would he?"

I shook my head.

"You don't owe him anything," Bernie said, lowering his voice and resting his forearms on the table.

"Are you trying to be a father figure to me?"

"I'm your cousin, that would be impossible."

"My third cousin," I said.

"You're splitting hairs."

I stood and went to the door but turned before I left.

"You'd be a good father, you know." I shrugged. "Maybe you should fit that into your schedule."

"Yeah, yeah." He swatted a hand at me. "I've got enough trouble trying to keep an eye on you."

"See you tomorrow."

"Yup."

I left out the back door and walked down the alley toward the main street in town, thinking of one reason I shouldn't be around Walt that Bernie hadn't mentioned.

He didn't want to be with me, necessarily.

He just didn't want to be alone.

48

We sat in a booth at the Big Boy just outside of Fort Colson. Walt's southern fried chicken went mostly untouched, the white gravy on top congealed and unappetizing.

"Do you ever hear from Mike?" Walt asked, pushing his plate to the end of the table for the waitress to remove.

"He writes often," I said, finishing off the last spoonful of my soup. "Weren't you hungry?"

He shook his head.

"Are you eating at all?" I remembered Frank on his bad days, unable to stomach anything.

"You sound like my mother." He crossed his arms and stared at the paper place mat in front of him.

"Sorry."

I leaned back into the soft cushion of the booth, staring out the window next to us. A family climbed out of a station wagon. Two parents and a handful of kids, all wearing what I assumed to be their Sunday best even though it was a Tuesday. The smallest two girls held their father's hand as they walked across the parking lot to the door of the restaurant.

"Does he ever say anything about what it's like for him in country?" Walt asked.

"Who, Mike?" I turned back to him. "Yeah."

"He's a medic, right?"

I nodded.

"Those guys see everything." Walt rubbed at his eyes. "Our first medic got hit with some shrapnel. Lobbed his arm clean off. But he got to come home. We called that the 'million dollar wound.'"

The family I'd seen out the window followed a man in a tie to the large, round table less than two feet from where Walt and I sat. One of the little girls smiled at me before sitting and pulling her chair in.

"The next medic didn't wear the red cross badge. Said it made him a moving target. You ought to tell Mike that," Walt said. "Medics and officers are the ones those animals kill off first. They get paid extra for picking them off. They know if the medic's dead, the rest of us are toast."

He finished by describing in detail what he would have done if he'd ever caught somebody from the North Vietnamese army or the Viet Cong. His graphic description was peppered with words I didn't know but could tell were filthy. It turned my stomach, picturing what he described and the way his eyes hardened, the pupils dilated.

The father at the other table turned his head and glanced at us.

"Walt," I said, leaning forward and nodding my head toward the family.

"Sorry," he said, then turned toward the father and raised his voice. "I'm sorry. I didn't realize . . ."

The man put up his hand as if to say it was all right.

"Do you want to go?" I asked.

"I didn't mean . . ." he started, regret heavy in his voice. "I shouldn't have said all that. I forget myself sometimes."

"It's all right," I said, looking back at the little girl and smiling at her again. "Let's go, okay?"

I stood and took Walt's hand, making sure he came with me. He turned back toward the family as we walked away.

"I'm sorry, sir," he said.

"Don't worry about it, son," the man said, his voice deep and warm. "I understand."

The little girl waved at me before turning her attention to the menu on the table in front of her.

●

Walt didn't say anything while he drove me home. He just kept switching through the radio stations, not stopping long enough to even hear what song played on each. When he pulled up in front of my house, he turned the knob, killing the volume.

"Do you hate me?" he asked, keeping his face straight, his eyes looking out into the dark on the other side of the windshield.

"No," I answered. "Why would you ask that?"

He sniffled. "I don't know."

I wasn't sure if he wanted me to get out of the car or not. The engine still ran and the headlights beamed on into the night, so I thought he was waiting for me to leave. But as soon as I put my hand on the door, he asked me to stay.

"Don't go yet," he said, turning toward me. "I don't want to be alone."

"Are you afraid?"

"I'm not sure." He took my left hand, looking at it as if he'd never seen anything like it before. "Do you remember that ring I gave you when we were little?"

"You got it out of a Cracker Jack box, didn't you?"

He shook his head. "I bought it at the five-and-dime." He smiled. "Well, my mother paid for it. She said it was sweet that I wanted to give it to you."

"It had a green plastic stone."

"Do you still have it?"

"Yes." In my mind's eye I could see it in my little cedar box that I kept under my bed. "I outgrew it."

He smiled. "I really meant it when I said I wanted to marry you."

"It's probably a good thing four-year-olds aren't allowed to make such decisions."

"Maybe."

He turned back, facing forward, still holding on to my hand. Out of the corner of my eye, I saw the curtains in our living room part and Mom's face appear between them. I waved at her, hoping she'd see that we weren't in Walt's car, necking for all the neighborhood to see.

She pulled them closed again.

"Annie, I . . ."

"Walt . . ."

We said each other's names at the same time, both facing each other simultaneously.

"Go ahead," I said.

He licked his lips. "When I was a kid I had a night-light. It was this blue plastic mouse that sat on my bedside table."

"I had a Raggedy Ann one," I said.

"There was this little switch on mine that I could flick on

whenever I had a bad dream or got scared in the middle of the night. It was never really bright, but it calmed me down. Just knowing it was there always helped." He drew in a breath. "I put that thing up in a box in my closet a long time ago."

He bit at his bottom lip and squeezed my hand.

"I had to get it out the other night," he whispered.

"Did you have a nightmare?" I held his hand tighter. "I won't think less of you if you did."

"We had to do things over there. My father said it's just the way war is." He shook his head. "The dreams can't last forever, can they?"

"I hope not."

He pinched the bridge of his nose between thumb and forefinger. "Sometimes it was them or us. If I didn't do something, they would have killed us." He looked up at me. "You know."

"You did what you had to," I said.

"It helped to think they weren't human. To forget that they had family that loved them or a girl they wanted to marry." He stared straight ahead. "If I could just pretend they were animals—if I could actually believe it—I could shoot at them and not feel anything about it. Just like hunting."

"Walt . . ."

"I hate how easy it got toward the end." He reached into his jacket pocket, pulling out a pack of cigarettes, lighting one and drawing deeply of it. "Who ended up being the animal after all?"

"You aren't an animal."

"There's at least a few men in a shallow grave in Vietnam that would beg to differ."

"What choice did you have?" I asked. "Let them kill you?"

"That's about it."

He stopped talking, finishing his cigarette and smashing it into the ashtray and lighting another.

"You're not there anymore," I said. "You're here now. All you had to do over there, that's not who you are."

"Then who am I?"

"You're my friend."

He blew a lungful of smoke up into the ceiling. "Listen, I better go. Your mom's standing on the porch."

Sighing, I saw that he was right. I opened the car door and put one foot on the pavement.

"Take care of yourself, okay?" I said.

"Yeah."

He drove away as soon as I shut the door.

Somehow I knew he wouldn't call the next day.

Frank,

I hope all's well in Bliss and that you're selling loads of cars. It's funny, you know, when I was a kid and I'd imagine what you were doing with your time, the last thing I would have thought was that you were selling cars.

I'd always had you pegged as a police officer or a delivery man. It's funny how a boy's brain works.

I've been seeing lots of action over here in Nam. More than I'd expected, as a matter of fact. It's downright brutal. But I'm sure you can imagine how it is.

The other day there was a kid that stepped on a booby trap in the jungle and got his legs blown off. When we got to him, I was sure he was a goner. But he surprised all of us and held on.

They rushed him into the hospital once we landed and I went to wash up. The kid's blood was all over my hands.

It scared me, what was going through my mind. I envied the kid. Actually felt jealous. Because whatever happened to him, if he lived or died, he'd get to leave Vietnam.

Scrubbing the soap on my hands I saw they were shaking and I thought of the tremors you had in your right hand. For the first time I felt that I understood you.

And for the first time, I wasn't mad at you for leaving us.

I understand now.

Mike

Mike,

Business is going fine. I sold a cherry red Bel Air a couple days ago to a boy who just got home from Vietnam. Gave him a good deal too. When I said my son was over there, he told me to wish you luck.

I've tried to stay away from the news reports about Vietnam. Brings back more memories of my own war that I'd rather not recall. But it comes as no surprise to me that it's as gory as you say. War comes out of a dark part of the human soul, son. It's shocking what men have created in order to destroy each other.

When I was in Korea and my thoughts threatened to overtake me I'd try to remember what my duty was. To keep my buddies alive, to keep myself from getting killed, and to beat the communists. Not necessarily in that order.

I didn't do most things right in my life. But I did survive that war and I pray you'll survive yours.

I'm proud of you, son.
Frank

49

By some ~~magic~~ unknown to me, Joel was able to get away with a multitude of things that Mike and I never could have even dreamed up without Mom getting after us. So, I was unsurprised when, after coming home from work to a house full of boys, Mom didn't throw a~~n unholy~~ fit over Joel wanting them all to stay for supper.

She'd just written up a list and asked me to run to the grocery store.

"Get some of that macaroni and cheese dinner," she said. "And some cans of tuna fish to mix into it."

"Mom, hot dogs." I nodded. "Trust me."

"Don't boys like tuna?"

"Not all of them." I scratched out the fish on the list. "But they all like hot dogs."

"Get some Kool-Aid too." She crossed her arms. "Unless boys suddenly dislike that too."

I smirked at her and grabbed the keys for Mike's car off the hook, glad to be leaving the certain odor that had overtaken our house with the occupation of the four teenaged boys.

Huisman's Market was just a few minutes away, right on

the highway that led to Mackinaw City two-hundred-some miles to the north and all the way down to Indiana and beyond in the south. Had I ventured out that way on a long summer day, I might have felt a tug to pick a direction and drive on until I got to the end of the road, wherever that may be.

But it was the close of November and the already-dark evening made me not want to linger. Pulling into the half-full parking lot of the store made me feel lonely. Blue, even. I wanted to get back home, even if the boys were loud and stinky.

I pushed my cart toward where I knew the boxed macaroni dinners were, wondering if two would be enough to feed the ravenous horde back at home. I decided to buy four. Mom could always put one or two of them in the pantry for later if she wanted.

Consulting my list, I saw that Mom had written that I should only get one box.

I rubbed at my eye under my glasses and sighed before grabbing four anyway. I would have thought that if raising Mike had taught her anything, it was that boys had hollow legs.

"Everything all right?"

David stood beside me, his arms full of groceries. So full, in fact, that I was sure he'd drop all of it at any moment. A glass jar of pickles was nestled precariously between his elbow and side.

"Yes," I said. "Would you like a cart?"

"Oh, I just came in for a few things," he said. Then, looking at his load, "Maybe I could use one."

"Just share mine."

"You're sure?"

"Of course," I answered, noticing the way the man behind the deli counter watched us. "Here, I'll help you."

We put his items in the cart, and David pushed them all to one side. "So we don't get our food mixed up."

I took inventory of his things. A package of bologna lunch meat, cheese slices, a bag of chips, loaf of bread, and a box of Little Debbies. And the jar of pickles, safe from being dropped and smashed on the floor.

"Do you have other things to get?" I asked.

"Not that I know of," he answered.

"Is that your dinner?"

He shrugged. "I hate to admit this to you, but I don't know how to cook. That's why I eat at the diner every day."

"Funny," I said. "I thought it was just so you could enjoy Bernie's charming personality."

I let David push the cart and I nodded in the direction of the aisle where I believed they shelved the Kool-Aid.

"My mother is afraid I'm going to starve to death over here," he said. "I'm her only son and she's waiting for me to get married so she can stop worrying about what I'm eating."

"What if you marry someone who isn't a good cook?"

"I believe she'd faint." He chuckled. "Then she'd insist on moving in and taking over the kitchen."

I picked out a packet of cherry punch and dropped it into the cart.

"Why don't you come over to our house for supper?" I asked. "We already have my brother's friends over. You might as well join us."

"Are you sure?"

"Of course." I pointed him toward the meat department. "If you don't mind boxed macaroni and cheese."

"I don't mind at all."

"Oh, and which do you like better, hot dogs or tuna?"

He pulled a face. "Hot dogs. Any old day."

"That's what I thought."

•

David followed me in his Buick. All the way home I felt anxious, antsy. I couldn't believe I'd asked someone to dinner without checking with Mom first. That was something that only Joel could have pulled off.

But, more than that, I'd asked a black man. And one Mom didn't know. One she hadn't even met, as far as I knew.

I wasn't sure if even Joel could have gotten away with that.

50

Mom was in the kitchen, the water for the pasta already boiling on the stove top in the biggest pot we had. She stood at the sink, peeling carrots.

"That took you long enough," she said, not looking up at me. "Did you buy the whole store?"

I slid the two paper bags of groceries onto the counter.

"Oh, I just ran into somebody," I said.

"Who's that?"

"A friend of mine." I glanced over my shoulder toward the living room, where I'd told David he could have a seat. "Don't be mad, okay. But I invited him to dinner."

"You did what? Him? Who's him?" She lifted her face. "Annie."

"I thought since we already had company, it wouldn't matter." I pulled the macaroni out of the bag, tearing open the tops and dumping the noodles into the water. "The house is clean at least."

She sighed. "What's one more? Who is it? Please tell me it isn't Walt."

"Good news. It's not," I answered. "Do you remember David?"

"The David I still haven't met officially?" She put a freshly peeled carrot on her chopping block. "Him?"

I nodded.

"Well, at least you didn't bring Walt home. I don't think I could endure a meal with that boy." She smoothed her apron and glanced around me toward the living room. "You're sure he won't expect something fancier?"

"He can't cook," I answered. "I think he'll be happy with anything."

"Well, I guess I should get the leaf for the table."

Stirring the pasta, I blew out a sigh of relief.

●

Mom did her best to observe David without being too obvious. From the way she smiled at his stories or offered him another helping of macaroni and cheese, I thought he was winning her favor little by little.

As for Joel and his mop-top–headed friends, they scarfed their food, earning Mom's cautions about choking to death on hot dogs. Once they'd polished off all that we'd offered by way of dinner, they scrambled their way upstairs, claiming that they had a song to write.

"They started a band," I told David.

"How about that," he said. "Are they any good?"

"They're loud, that's for sure," Mom said. "John Tyler— the one with the dark hair—he likes to think he's the next Elvis Presley."

"I think I heard them say that they're what would happen if Jimi Hendrix played a gig with the Rolling Stones," I added. "And with a little of the Beatles mixed in for good measure."

"Huh. Sounds outta sight." David wiped his lips with his

napkin. "Thanks for supper, Mrs. Jacobson. It was nice to have a home-cooked meal."

"Oh, I wouldn't call this home-cooked," she said. "But you're welcome just the same."

"At least it was nice to have a little company for a change." He folded his napkin and tucked it under the edge of his plate. "It gets lonely always eating in front of the TV in my apartment."

"Well, we would be happy to have you come again." She nodded. "Next time I'll have my mother bring a dessert."

"That would be nice."

From upstairs we heard a loud crashing sound and an uproarious round of laughter. Mom's eyes grew wide and she bared her teeth. "I'd better see what that was."

David and I sat across the table from each other, alone in the room and hearing Mom's voice as she got after the boys for whatever they'd managed to break upstairs.

I sighed. "Boys, huh?"

"It wasn't too long ago that I was just like them," he said.

"I can't imagine that."

"I was as wild as a pastor's kid can get away with being."

"Your dad's a pastor?" I asked. "I didn't know that."

"Yup. My father was a preacher all of his life." David nodded. "Passed away a couple of years ago."

"I'm sorry to hear that."

"Thank you." He rubbed his forehead. "It was a hard time. That's another reason my mother was upset about me moving all the way over here."

"Do you see her very often?" I asked.

"I try to get over there a couple of times a month." He grinned. "I have a little niece who lives down the street from her, so I don't stay away too long. That little girl is so fun."

"How old is she?"

"Just turned three." He reached into his back pocket for his wallet. "Her name's Naomi."

He opened the wallet, handing it to me so I could see a little black and white photo of a sweet girl. She had her hair in braids tied off with ribbons, and her face was stretched into the sweetest smile I'd ever seen. Held tight in her chubby arms was a little stuffed kitty that looked as if it had seen better days.

It looked well loved.

"She's beautiful," I whispered.

"She gets it from her Uncle Davie," he said, taking the wallet back. "If I can ever talk my family into coming out here, I'll make sure you meet her."

"I would like that very much."

"No doubt they'd be interested in meeting this Annie Jacobson I've told them about."

"You've told them about me?" The room seemed to rise in temperature at least a hundred degrees.

"Of course I have." He grinned. "You were my first friend here in Fort Colson."

Friend, I told myself. *Just a friend.*

It was a title I could be happy with.

●

After David left, Mom had driven all of Joel's friends back to their respective homes, and when she returned, she came into the kitchen, shaking her head.

"Those boys have watched more than their fair share of John Wayne movies," she said.

"What do you mean?" I pulled the plug from the sink to let out the dirty dishwater.

"Oh, they were sitting in the back of the station wagon, talking about growing up to be war heroes or some such ridiculousness."

"Don't all boys dream of that?"

"I don't know." She grabbed a couple of clean glasses and put them up in the cupboard. "But I let it be known that war isn't glamorous like they've seen in the movies. There's nothing glorious about dying in battle."

"I'm glad you were there to set them straight."

"If nothing else, at least I can do that." She leaned against the counter and crossed her arms. "I was glad to meet David."

"You were?"

"For what it's worth, I think Mike would approve." She sighed. "As for Frank . . ."

"We're just friends," I said, interrupting.

"That's a fine thing to be." She swatted her hand at the drainer where the dishes sat. "Leave those. I'll put them away in the morning. You should get some sleep."

I told her good night and gave her a kiss on the cheek before going up to my room. She smiled and looked at me as if she was trying to take in every detail of my face, my hair, my everything. It was the way she'd looked at me when I was little and sang my first solo at church or when I'd learned how to ride a bike on my own. When I came in second place at the school spelling bee and the day I graduated from high school.

If I read it right, it was of love and pride and maybe a little bit of mourning. As if she knew that each step I took was a step away from needing her so much.

It both warmed my heart and broke it at the same time.

Hi, All-Of-You!

Well, believe it or not, I have sustained my very first war wound. Some Neanderthal (me) slammed my fingers in the door of one of our transport vehicles. Don't worry. None of them are broken—my fingers or the vehicles. They're just sore and look like something Dr. Frankenstein might have sewn onto his monster.

I asked if this could get me sent home. No dice. And it didn't earn me a Purple Heart, either. But I will get a week or two off from taking rides on the dust-off. Instead, I'm stuck on base, rolling gauze and divvying out malaria pills. Believe you me, I don't mind this dull and uneventful work at all. It sure beats getting shot at.

I bet by the time you get this you'll be getting ready for Sinterklaas Day. I sure will miss taking part in that. There's just something about hanging some tinsel on a light pole that gets me into the spirit of Christmas.

Do me a favor, will you? Have somebody take a picture of you with whatever tree they put up in town this year. Please? And make sure Oma's in it too. She always makes any picture prettier.

I love you all,
Mike

PS: Mom, don't let Annie spend another minute with that Walt Vanderlaan character, all right? He's bad news. Joel, if he comes around again, I give you permission to give him a right uppercut to the eye. Remember how I taught you.

51

The fifth day of December was marked on all calendars in Fort Colson as Sinterklaas Day. School kids had the day off, most businesses stayed closed, and the sheriff's department shut down the main street from first thing in the morning until near midnight.

It was a day of hanging wreaths and tinsel and strings of electric lights. Banners were stretched across the road between telephone poles with greetings of "Merry Christmas" and "*Fijne feestdagen!* Fort Colson Wishes You Joy for the Holidays."

In the front yard of the church was set up wooden cutouts of the Nativity. Mary in her blue and pristine white, Joseph in his red and dull brown. The shepherds to one side with black-nosed sheep ~~and the Wise Men to the other with their gilded gifts in hand~~. *Wise men were not there!*

At the center of it all sat a flat manger, hand-painted straw curled soft over the edges. And resting there, swaddled in pure and clean cloths, was a blond-headed baby Jesus, eyes already a startling shade of blue and looking up to the heavens.

Every few years the Nativity got a new paint job to keep it looking fresh. That year the artist had given Jesus rosy cheeks and perfectly shaped pink lips, the corners pulled up in a smile.

●

Bernie had kept the diner open late to serve hot drinks and doughnuts to whoever wandered in. While he was constitutionally opposed to decorating, he had no problem making a little money from a day like that.

Customers had come in steadily throughout the day, bundled in hats and scarves and mittens, as the weather had proven to be colder than expected. Cups of coffee and tea and hot chocolate steamed up at them, and they sipped as they sat at a booth or table, keeping warm inside.

I couldn't hear the jangling of the bell on the door for the din that filled the diner. But I wouldn't have been able to miss when the door opened, letting Mr. and Mrs. Vanderlaan in, followed by Walt holding hands with Caroline Mann.

"I'll take care of them," Bernie told me, reaching out for the coffeepot.

"No, I don't mind," I answered, stepping around him and making my way to the table they'd picked by the big window.

Walt had his arm draped over Caroline's shoulders and he slumped beside her as if wishing he could hide from me. His parents sat across from them, stiff and not touching.

"Coffee?" I asked.

They all turned over the cups in front of them, watching me pour.

"Annie," Mrs. Vanderlaan said, "I believe you know Caroline."

"Yes," I answered, looking up. "It's been a while."

"I've been away at college," Caroline said. I'd forgotten the high pitch of her voice, how like a little girl's it was. "I'm home for the weekend to see my Wally."

"Isn't that nice." I rested the coffeepot on the end of the table. "Would anyone like doughnuts?"

"Oh, not me," Caroline squeaked. "I wouldn't dare."

I glanced at Walt, who rolled his eyes. "You're skinny enough."

"Let her be, son," Mr. Vanderlaan said. "Just two. The ladies won't have any."

Mrs. Vanderlaan stared ahead, not saying anything.

"Would you like one?" I asked her. "I have it on good authority that doughnuts are as healthy as an apple on Sinterklaas Day."

"Well, then," she said. "In that case, how can I resist?"

"Caroline?" Walt said. "Come on. Be a sport and eat a doughnut."

"Oh, all right," she said.

"Four doughnuts coming up," I said.

It was only as I turned to walk away that I saw the glint of a diamond ring on Caroline's left hand.

●

Walt brought the check to the cash register, sliding it across the countertop toward me. He didn't lift his eyes to meet mine.

"So, you're back with Caroline?" I asked, punching the numbers into the register. "When did that happen?"

"Yeah. I went out to see her at MSU." He pulled a few bills from his wallet. "I guess she changed her mind about me."

"I noticed that she's wearing her engagement ring."

"Listen, Annie," he said, talking fast. "I'm sorry. I shouldn't have gotten your hopes up about something happening between you and me."

"You didn't." I took his money and made change. "I just want to know if you're happy. With her. With yourself. With life. I want you to be okay."

It was then that he looked up at me, wearing his old cocky smile. "I guess I'll be all right. She makes me happy. She really does."

●

Just a little after five o'clock, the sun set and the pinprick glow of rainbow-colored Christmas tree lights showed up against the dark of evening. Main Street was abuzz with people lining the sidewalks and waiting for the start of the parade.

Bernie had left me to lock up the diner, and as soon as I turned the key in the door, I tried to catch sight of Mom and Oma. They'd promised to save me a spot. But all I could see were stocking-capped heads and clusters of families that didn't belong to me.

That was when I saw David making his way to me, lifting a hand in a wave to get my attention. "Over here," he called.

"Hi," I said when he got closer.

"Hi."

"What do you think of all this?" I asked.

"I think it's great." He tilted his head back. "Now if only it would snow, it would be perfect."

"Too bad we don't get to order the weather, huh?"

"Indeed." He took my hand. "Your mom and grandmother are over this way."

I followed behind him, his hand holding mine.

Dear Annie,

There are days around here when there isn't much to do but twiddle our thumbs. You might think I'd like days like that, but I don't. I hate them. I'm always on edge and I can't seem to relax because I never know when the shoe is going to drop.

I never know when the calm is going to erupt into chaos and I want to be ready for when it does.

What a fatalistic view of life, huh?

Anyway, back to all I've been thinking about.

I've been thinking about Mom and how strong she's always been. Do you think she'll crack if something were to happen to me? Do you think she'd be all right? I'm not saying that I'm the most important person to her, but I am her child. Her firstborn. What will happen to her if I don't get to come back home?

And Joel. He's just a kid. I'm not going to pretend that I don't know how much he looks up to me. What's going to happen to him? Who's going to step in and be a big brother to him?

Don't feel left out, pal. I've been thinking about you too. I don't want to think about you having to go through losing me. I know that sounds like I'm stuck on myself, but hear me out. It kills me to think of you suffering or grieving over me. It makes me all kinds of antsy just thinking about how lonely you'd be.

I'm starting to pray that somehow I'm able to outlast all of you so you won't have to live through losing me.

But, I'm telling you. I don't think that's going to happen. I really don't. Not with how close I am every day to it all coming to an end. Every single day I have at least one second where I think I'm not making it home. And sometimes I'm so tired I think how it might not be so bad for it all to be over.

I sound like a loon, don't I? I'm telling you, being over here, it isn't too hard to lose your mind. It's a strange thing, but I think I understand a little why Frank came back from Korea the way he did.

The things we see, Annie, they're enough to make anybody go a little nutty. We weren't made for this. I can't believe that God created us for all this death and destruction. War wasn't his idea. I'll bet he hates it more than I do, even.

I hope I'm not scaring you. Gosh, I hope I'm not.

Write back, would you? I sure could use something to make me smile right now. If nothing good's happening in The World, just make something up. For me. Can I count on you for that?

I miss you.

Mike

Dear Mike,

First off, you didn't scare me too badly. But you did make me want to pray even more that you come back in one piece. Both in your body and in your soul. Although, if you do come back haunted like Frank was, we'll work it out together, all right? You won't need to run off like he did.

Please promise that you won't do that. Okay?

Now, I present to you a much-needed distraction. (Imagine movie introduction music here.)

I'm sending you the promised family picture from Sinterklaas Day. Everybody's there. Even Sinterklaas himself in his red suit and bushy white beard. Can you take a guess who drew the short straw and had to wear the costume this year?

That's right. Bernie Jager, the old Scrooge. He grumbled about it for a week, but he played the part well. So well, in fact, that some have said he should dress up like old Saint Nicholas every year. Wouldn't that be something?

By the way, you don't have to worry about Walt coming around and bothering me, at least I don't think so. His wedding to Caroline is back on. For now, that is. I'm happy for them. I really am.

And Mom's happy that he isn't calling a hundred times a day anymore. All without Joel having to throw a punch. We all win.

Despite what everybody around here seems to think, I

never held a candle for him. If nothing else, being around him reminded me that I deserve someone who will like (or even love) me the way I am.

Maybe when you get back you can meet my friend David. The one I told you about. I think you'd like him. Golly, you might even want to go fishing with him. I haven't told anyone but Jocelyn this, but if there's a candle to be held, it's for him.

Don't you tease me about it, though. I'm an adult woman now, and blushing doesn't become a lady.

Big brother, no matter what happens, I believe with all my heart that you'll make it back home. In fact, I need you to.

Love you,
Annie

52

Oma and I worked in her small kitchen; cookies filled every countertop space, table, chair, and so forth in various stages of baking. Round and thin *stroopwafels* with caramel filling and thick, candied *bastognekoeken*. Braided sweet Dutch pretzels and sugar cookies waiting to be frosted.

Some of my fondest memories of childhood were of standing on a step stool at her counter, stirring away at the ingredients in her robin's egg colored mixing bowl with a heavy wooden spoon. As I got older, Oma asked me to read the recipes to her, although I knew she had them memorized. Half of the Dutch words I'd learned were related to baking.

She never lost her patience with me when I mixed too hard and sent a dusting of flour onto the floor, and she didn't get after me for tasting a pinch of the dough.

"A good baker always tastes," she'd say, dipping into the bowl herself and placing the crumble on her tongue. "Just right."

I no longer found the step stool necessary and I had no need to double-check the cookbook. My pronunciation of the Dutch words had become more comfortable to me as I moved my mouth around them. Being in the kitchen with Oma had become as natural to me as breathing or putting one foot in front of the other.

That day, with all our Christmas baking to do, we moved at an easy pace. No rushing, not hurrying, just enjoying our time. Usually we waited until the week before Christmas, but that year we wanted to get it done early so we could send some to Mike.

"I have a little bird that comes to visit me in the afternoons on the tree outside the window," Oma said. "Nuthatch is what it's called."

"They're cute little fellows, aren't they?" I said.

"Oh, so cute." She twisted off the top of the jar of cinnamon. "He climbs up and down the tree and cranes his neck to see if I have a treat for him in the feeder. Oh, I love to see him come."

I worked a rolling pin over a lump of dough to be cut into molasses cookies, sprinkling a pinch of flour over it every few rolls to keep it from sticking.

"I haven't told you much of Pieter, have I?" she asked.

"No," I answered.

Oma didn't speak of her family very often. And she especially didn't bring up *Oom* Pieter, her younger brother. Mom had told me that it was just too hard for Oma. There was simply too much grief in the stories. When we looked through the old photo albums she'd brought from the Netherlands, she'd point to the people and tell me their names and little else.

Mostly, what I knew of Uncle Pieter was that he was tall with a strong jawline. He was less than a year younger than

Oma and two years older than their younger sister. That was all that Oma offered usually.

But the way that she drew in a good breath and nodded, I knew that she was working up to talk about him. I didn't push but instead waited for her to begin.

"When your opa and I came to America, Pieter was still in university in Amsterdam, studying to be a teacher. He'd wanted to be a teacher since we were small." She smiled. "Always had to teach someone something, even if it was just the lambs my father raised."

I left my dough, sufficiently flattened on the counter, and watched her as she told her story. The lines on the outside corners of her eyes deepened, and I knew she was glad to remember her brother.

"And he did just that," she went on. "He taught in the little schoolhouse in our village. Even after the Germans came, he continued to teach."

"You mean the Nazis?" I asked.

"*Ja.* From his letters, he tried to keep on like normal for the sake of the children. I imagine they were frightened. It was a terrifying time. Many of their fathers were taken away to work for the Germans. Several of their classmates were removed to the camps. These were the Jewish children, of course. The children and their families." She rested her hands on the edge of the counter. "Pieter joined the resistance. My mother wrote about this to me years ago and I seem to have forgotten all he did to resist the Germans. But he was caught. Arrested. Mama seemed to believe it was one of their neighbors who informed against him."

"That's horrible."

"It was. It was there, in the prison, that he was killed." She released a sigh. "That winter was the worst I've had. I could do nothing for them. Here I was, the world between them and me, and I could do nothing."

"I'm sorry."

"It was a dark winter and gray. Your mother was about your age then, I believe, just married to your father. I would stand here in this kitchen." She pointed her finger at the small window in front of her. "And I would look out into the gloomy days, praying. Mostly I asked God where he had gone. 'Where are you?' I'd call to him. Many days, he gave no answer."

I hardly dared to breathe, her voice had grown so soft, and I worried that I might miss a word. Leaning forward, I waited for her to go on.

"In those days I didn't keep a feeder for the birds," she said. "Your opa thought it a waste, paying money for seeds that a bird could forage in the woods for free. I suppose he had a good argument. But the birds didn't visit as often then because I offered them nothing."

She glanced my way and smiled.

"One day, as I prayed and cried, a cardinal came to rest in the branches of my tree there." She nodded at the maple in her backyard. "His red stood out against the gray, so vivid. Behind him, through the clouds shone a sliver of sunshine. Just for a moment, it bled through."

Back to mixing, she smiled again.

"*Achter de wolken schijnt de zon*," she said. "Behind the clouds the sun is shining. If only we have eyes to see it."

She used her fingers to separate clumps of dough, rolling them into balls between the palms of her hands.

———————◆———————

Dear Frank,

   This is your official invitation to join us for Christmas. Believe it or not, it was Mom who reminded me to invite you. She even beat Joel to the punch. So, will you come? If you wanted, you could even show up on the Friday before and spend the whole weekend. It would be nice to have you here.

   Please say yes.

                    Annie

———————◆———————

Dear Annie,

   I'll see you on Friday. I'll bring dessert.

                    Frank

53

Joel paced through the living room, taking peeks out the front window every time he heard a car drive by. His face was drawn in a sullen expression and I thought he looked more like Frank in that moment than ever before.

"Sit down, honey," Mom said, looking up from the book she was reading. "You're making me nervous."

He did as she asked, dropping onto the couch. "Why isn't he here yet? He said he'd be here."

"It's only seven o'clock," I said. "Give him just a little more time, okay?"

"But he said he'd be here for dinner."

"No. He said he'd bring dessert. He probably had to work all day."

Mom shook her head, rolled her eyes, and went back to reading.

She wanted to seem as if she wasn't waiting with bated breath. But her freshly set hair and newly lipsticked mouth didn't escape my notice.

Joel could hardly help himself, he turned from his seat on

the couch and looked out the window again, slumping back around and sighing.

"Maybe the roads are bad," I said. "Give him a little time."

But part of me held a niggling fear that he'd decided not to come.

●

Frank's knock on the door came at half past eight and Joel popped right up from his spot on the couch to answer it. He threw open the door and stepped to one side so Frank could come in.

"The roads were a bit slick," Frank said, standing in the middle of the doorway. "I'm sorry. I didn't pick up a dessert after all."

"That's all right," I said, standing. "I'm glad you made it."

"You know what, though." Frank put a finger to his temple. "I brought somebody with me who had a little something on hand."

He stepped to one side, making room for Grandma, a covered pie tin in her hand.

"I thought you'd never get to it, Francis. I nearly froze to death out there," she said, handing the plate to Joel and then patting him on the cheek. "Look how you've grown."

"I even shaved this morning," Joel said, feeling his jawline.

"Good for you." Grandma laughed and turned toward me. "Annie. Pretty as ever."

"Thanks." I pushed my hair behind my ear, not knowing what else to say.

Compliments from Grandma typically didn't come in my direction.

"And, Gloria. So nice to see you again," Grandma went on. "I hope you don't mind an old lady showing up unannounced."

"Of course not," Mom said, her voice tense. She closed her book and put it on the end table beside her. "You're always welcome."

"Especially when you bring dessert," Joel said.

Mom stood and walked in the direction of the dining room. "Should I get out plates?"

"I'll help," I said, following her. Once we got into the kitchen, I whispered, "What's wrong?"

"I don't like surprises," she said, not bothering to talk softly. "He knows that."

"It wasn't a surprise meant for you." I grabbed a stack of napkins. "Did you see how happy Joel is?"

"I hate it when you're right." She rolled her eyes. "I mean, I strongly dislike it."

●

Grandma served slices of treacle tart and Mom brewed coffee for Frank and me. Joel declined, even though Frank tried to talk him into giving it another try. We got out a deck of cards and played a few rounds of bridge well into the evening. Joel and Grandma played as a team, taking nearly all the tricks there were to be had.

When Grandma started yawning, she asked Frank to take her to the hotel.

"Nonsense," Mom said, tensing. "You can have my bed. There's no need for you to go to a hotel."

"That's kind of you," Grandma said. "But Rose put me up for the weekend at the new Lakeview Grand Inn."

"How nice." Mom's shoulders relaxed.

"It's my Christmas present." Grandma pushed her chair out from the table and stood. "I think Rose was feeling bad about going away on vacation and leaving me behind."

"Well, you'll have to tell me what it's like," Mom said, gathering the cards into a pile. "It sure got a nice article in the *Chronicle* a few months ago."

"Why don't you come drop her off with me?" Frank said. "You could look around a little."

"Aren't you staying there too?" I asked.

"Rose doesn't like me that much." He smirked. "I was just going to get a bed at the motel here in town. Glo, I could bring you back after you see Mother's room."

"I wouldn't want to impose." Mom touched her strand of look-alike pearls. "It would be out of your way to drive me home."

"Only a few miles," Frank said.

"Joel, Annie, did you want to come?" Mom asked.

Joel put a fist to his mouth and faked the most exaggerated yawn I'd ever seen.

"I'm beat," he said. "Excuse me. But I'd better stay home."

"Well, that's too bad." Mom raised an eyebrow at him. "And Annie has to work tomorrow, don't you?"

"Yes. I should probably get to bed." I gave Mom my sweetest smile. "Maybe I'll go see it tomorrow."

"All right." Mom shook her head.

"I'll get the truck warmed up," Frank said, grabbing his coat off the back of Mom's easy chair.

"And I should powder my nose before going out into the cold," Grandma said, headed to the bathroom.

Once alone with us, Mom lowered her voice and put her face close to ours.

"Listen, you two," she said. "I've seen *Parent Trap*. It's not going to work."

I thought the goofy grin on Joel's face would never fade.

54

Mike had once discovered that if he lay flat on the landing between his bedroom and mine, he would be unseen by anyone looking up the stairs. But, if he stayed right there, he could hear nearly any conversation being had in the kitchen, the living room, and sometimes even the dining room.

Not that anything too exciting ever happened in the house that Mike hadn't either instigated or participated in. But he'd said it was good to know just in case.

And, as any good big brother would, he'd told Joel about it too.

That was why I was unsurprised when I stepped out of my room and nearly tripped over my little brother, spread out in front of my bedroom door.

"Unless you hadn't noticed, they aren't back yet," I said, stepping over him.

"I want to be ready when they get here," he said, sitting up. "Come on, be a spy with me."

"Not a chance." I went down two steps. "Mom would tan your hide if she knew you were going to eavesdrop."

"How would she find out?"

"You aren't exactly quiet."

"I can be if I need to," he said.

"Uh-huh." I went all the way to the bottom of the steps and to the bathroom, grabbing my toothbrush.

Just then I heard the rumble of Frank's truck and Joel hissing, "That's them." Without even thinking about what I was doing, I clambered up the steps, hitting the deck beside Joel and shushing him, trying not to giggle.

The front door opened and closed, a single pair of shoes clipped across the living room floor. The rumble of Frank's truck sounded again and I could almost feel Joel's disappointment. He got up from the floor and went to his bedroom, shutting the door behind him.

"You might as well come down," Mom called up the stairs. "I know you're there."

"Sorry," I said, popping my head up and looking down at her.

"Oh, I expected your brother." She took off her earrings. "I was thinking of having some tea. Would you like some?"

We sat at the kitchen table, tea bags of chamomile floating in our steaming cups. Mom had changed out of her dress and wore her housecoat and slippers. The bright red had been washed off her lips and the false pearls unclasped from her neck and, I assumed, tucked back into the jewelry box on her dresser.

"Was the hotel nice?" I asked.

"It wasn't as grand as I'd expected." She sighed. "If anything, it's grossly overpriced."

"That's too bad."

"I'm sure it will be booked through the summer, though."

She bobbed her tea bag up and down in her cup. "Do you think Joel still hopes Frank and I will get back together?"

"I believe you know the answer to that," I said, fishing my bag out of the cup with a spoon and twisting the string around it to squeeze out all the water. "Of course he does."

"That's what I thought." She picked up her cup, blowing into it before taking a sip. "There was a time when I would have taken Frank back. It would have been hard, but I was determined I could have made it work out."

"But you wouldn't anymore?"

"Well, I didn't say that." She sighed. "Never say never. Right?"

"Do you still love him?" I asked.

Putting her cup down, she raised a hand to her lips and looked to her right. "That's a hard question to answer, honey. If you'd asked me six months ago I might have said no without hesitating. Now I'm not sure how to feel about him."

"Do you think he loves you still?"

"I have no doubt."

"What if Frank wanted to come home?"

"I don't know that he would," she said. "But if he did, it would take me a long time to make up my mind. What if I couldn't be a good wife to him? Sometimes I think I've been alone so long that I couldn't be with anybody. I've grown too headstrong over the years."

"You weren't always headstrong?" I grinned at her.

"I told him tonight that I don't want that divorce. Not for now, at least." She put up her hands. "That's not to say he's coming back."

"Are you going to talk to Joel about this?"

"I wouldn't know what to tell him," she answered. "I don't

want him to get his hopes up and I don't want to break his heart."

"Mike would know," I said. "He always knows what to say."

"Goodness, I miss him."

"Me too."

We sipped our tea until our cups were empty and then we turned off the lights and went our separate ways. At the top of the stairs, I put an ear to Joel's door, trying to hear if he was still awake or not. All I could hear was a light, airy snore.

All he wanted was a normal family.

It seemed such a small thing to want.

And such a difficult thing to have.

Greetings,

~~Ho-Ho-Ho!~~ *Merry Christmas, Family!*

I tried to send this out in time for you to get it right before Christmas. Did it work? Or am I late? Golly, I hope I got the timing right.

This week the guys in my hooch (just a funny word that means the shack we have the pleasure of calling home-sweet-home) got ahold of some red streamers and hung them up around our bunks. They had a little Christmas tree somebody brought with them from home, just about a foot tall, that they put in the corner with the smallest ornaments you've ever seen all over it.

It almost feels festive. We sure could use some snow to really put it over the top. I've been told that it never snows here. Too bad. These folks don't know what they're missing.

I didn't get around to shopping for all of your presents. Don't worry, I'll bring a few things back with me when I come home next year. Joel, I asked if I could bring home a monkey for you. My commanding officer wasn't amused.

But what I did was get a picture of me holding a monkey to send to you. Joel, you're going to have to share with everybody, though. Can you do that, pal? We can't have you bogarting the image of my good looks.

Well, I hope you all have a wonderful Christmas. Eat all the cookies you can (I hope some are coming my way too!), sing a few carols, play in the snow, and take pic-

tures of every single moment and send a few of them my way.

Love,
Mike

PS: My fingers are all healed up now. Rats! Looks like I'll be back on the dust-off in the next few days. Well, the busy work was fun while it lasted!

55

It was still dark when I woke up. The house quiet. Squinting at my alarm clock I saw that it was just five thirty in the morning. I tried closing my eyes and going back to sleep, but it was no use. After sitting up and putting on my glasses, I pushed open my curtains.

The snow fell in clumps on the other side of my window. The clusters dropped lazily, as if they had all the time in the world to reach the ground.

Trying not to make a sound, I bundled myself in a sweater and extra socks, pulling my hair into a messy ponytail, and tiptoed down the stairs. Coat and boots, hat and mittens. I closed the door behind me as softly as I could.

Most of the people in my neighborhood had left their Christmas trees lit all night as if in an effort to guide Santa to their homes. I walked on as-of-yet undisturbed snow, the bulbs glowing bright in my periphery.

Before long, I stood on the sidewalk in front of the church. Using my mittened hand, I brushed off the dusting of snow that had gathered on the painted plywood. Last of all, I wiped off the cutout of Jesus, tracing the perfect pink smile with my finger, the wooly yarn of my mitten scratching against it.

The little Lord Jesus no crying he makes.

Standing upright, I wondered if that was true, that Jesus hadn't cried.

But my thoughts were interrupted by the sound of a car coming down the road. I turned to see a yellow Buick pulling up next to me, its brakes squeaking in the quiet of the morning.

David waved at me from the driver's seat and made an attempt at rolling down his window. Finding it stuck, probably frozen shut, he opened his car door instead.

"Merry Christmas," he said.

"Merry Christmas." I put my hands in the pockets of my coat. "Where are you headed?"

"Lansing." He stood, keeping his engine running. "I want to get there before my niece wakes up."

"That's sweet."

"What are you doing? It's pretty early to be up on your day off, isn't it?"

"I couldn't sleep." I lifted one shoulder in a shrug. "It seemed like a nice morning for a walk."

He rested his forearm on the top of his car door and looked at the Nativity. "And this is where you ended up, huh?"

"It seemed appropriate."

"Right on," he said, nodding and looking my way. "Can I give you a ride home?"

"I think I'll stay here for a few more minutes," I answered. "Thanks, though."

"Anytime." He put a foot into his car but then turned back toward me. Lifting one hand, he rubbed at his head. "I guess, uh, there's a New Year's Eve party. Over at the American Legion next Sunday. I didn't know if you were planning on going or not, but I wondered if you'd like to, maybe, go with me."

"Really?"

"Unless you already were going with somebody else."

I shook my head. "You're the only one to ask."

"Oh." He smiled and laughed. "Would you like to go with me?"

"Sure. Yes. I'd like that." My voice went up at least an octave. I was glad that David was too polite to mention it. "Thanks for asking."

"Thanks for saying yes." He nodded. "I like being around you, Annie."

"Me too," I said. "Around you, I mean. Not around me. I'm around me all the time."

He laughed again. "I dig it."

Sitting down into his car, he looked up at me before closing his door.

"Merry Christmas, Annie."

"Merry Christmas, David," I said.

Somehow I managed to make my way home without remembering a single step I took. All I could think about was David's smile and the light and swelling feeling in my chest.

Recorded on a reel-to-reel on December 25, 1967

Frank: *Did you push the button?*

Joel: *I think so. It's turning.*

Frank: *Good. Just talk into the microphone.*

Joel: *All right. (pause) Hey, Mike! Merry Christmas! Dad got us a reel-to-reel so we can record messages to you. Isn't that swell? We just finished opening presents here at the house and, let me tell you, Mom outdid herself. She gave me Opa's old guitar. So now I have two.*

Gloria: *Joel, let Annie say something.*

Joel: *Oh, all right.*

Annie: *Hi, Mike. Merry Christmas. I hope that you got the care package that Oma and I sent you. It was all I could do to hide the cookies so Joel wouldn't eat them.*

Joel: *There were cookies?*

Annie: *She wanted me to tell you that she didn't forget to send some Wilhelmina mints. She knows how you like them.*

Oma: *Tell him I sent three packages of them.*

Annie: *I'm sure you heard that. (pause) I guess Oma would like to have a turn.*

Oma: *I don't need to. I wouldn't know what to say.*

Gloria: *Just say "hello" to Michael. He'll be glad to hear your voice.*

Oma: *Oh, fine then. Hello, Mike. Merry Christmas. (pause) Is that enough?*

Gloria: *I guess so. (pause) Michael, hi. It's your mother. We miss you and wish you could be here with us today, son. It isn't the same without you. But we're so proud of you for serving our country over there in Vietnam. We're looking forward to seeing you when you come home. And we'll plan on having you here with us next year. We love you.*

Frank: *My turn? (pause) Hello, son. It's your father. Frank Jacobson. Like your mother said, we're sure proud of you. Stay safe. Oh. And Merry Christmas.*

Joel: *Grandma? Do you want a turn?*

Grandma: *Hello?*

Joel: *He isn't going to talk back to you. It's not a telephone.*

Grandma: *Oh, I know that. Michael, I want to make sure you're still wearing that medallion. I didn't see it on you in the picture you sent. Happy Christmas from your grandma. (pause) I'm done now. Do I have to do anything?*

Joel: *I'll take it. I guess that's all of us. Bernie was supposed to come, but he has the flu. Poor guy, huh? Anyway, Mom said she'd get this in the*

*mail to you tomorrow. So, I guess by the time
you get it, it'll be 1968. Merry Christmas and
Happy New Year, big brother. We all like you
sort of a little.*

Frank: *Just push that button to turn it off.*

(click)

56

I rode along with Frank and Grandma to the hotel, where I
found that Mom had been correct. It was neither grand nor
worth the cost of the stay. Grandma, though, didn't mind in
the least. I thought she thoroughly enjoyed spending Aunt
Rose's money.

Frank had kept the truck running, waiting for me to catch
a quick look at the inn. I was glad when I climbed into the
passenger's seat and it was still warm.

"Ready?" he asked once I closed the door.

"Sure," I answered.

He pulled away from the hotel, turning left to head back
to Lewis Street.

"Has Mike been writing to you?" I asked.

"Yup. Every couple of weeks or so," he answered. "Is that
all right?"

"Of course." I pulled off one of my mittens to pick at a
ragged nail. "Does he ever tell you what's going on?"

"Well, I guess he does."

"I mean, does he tell you the bad things?"

Frank nodded. "He has a couple of times."

"Me too."

"Do they scare you?"

"A little."

He pulled onto the main highway. "He asked me not to tell your mother about them."

"He told me that too."

"You haven't told her, have you?"

"I wouldn't. Joel either."

"That's good."

After a few minutes he turned off onto a side street, taking the back way home.

"I don't know what to do," I said.

"About what?"

"The letters." I put my mitten back on. "What am I supposed to do?"

"Well, I imagine you write back to him."

"Yes."

"That's about all there is to do," he said.

He slowed down, driving through a neighborhood a few blocks from home. My memory perked up, reminding me of how he'd take me for long rides to see the lights when I was little. How he'd point at them, not wanting me to miss a single one.

But in those days, I'd be nestled up under his arm to keep warm, not all the way to the other side of the bench seat.

I caught his eye and he gave me a half smile. "It's all going to be okay."

"Do you promise?" I asked.

"Nope," he said. "But I sure hope I'm right."

He pulled the truck into our driveway, not cutting the engine.

"Thanks," I said.

"That's all right." He nodded. "Your grandmother and I have to leave in the morning. We'll stop over before we go."

"I'll be at work early."

"Then I guess we'll have some breakfast at the diner." He grinned at me.

That grin. It was the one that I remembered from his good days when I was a child. When he smiled at me that way it made me feel safe and it reminded me that no matter how many bad days he had, he loved me.

For the first time in twelve years, I felt the overwhelming urge to tell him that I loved him. Instead, I chewed on the inside of my cheek, afraid that he might not be able to say it back to me. So I reached across the divide between us, giving him a quick peck on the cheek.

I opened my door. "Merry Christmas, Dad."

He waited for me to get inside and shut the door before he pulled away.

Cedar Falls, Iowa

Dear Annie,

Why, oh why do I have to be in Iowa while you're there preparing for a real, actual, bona fide date with David? Visiting family here is all right, but I want to be there with you. I want to play the part of wallflower at the New Year's Eve party. I promise I would look away if he tried to kiss you at midnight.

Do you think he'll want a kiss? Would you give him one? Do you think it would be better than when Walt kissed you?

I do not understand why calling long distance has to cost so much money. But my grandmother would be none too pleased if I left her with a hefty telephone bill just so you could answer my kissing questions.

Oh goodness. Did I just write that?

Anyway, I don't know that you'll get this letter before the party. Just know that I'm dying to know how it goes. We'll be home on the second, and then I take a bus back to college a few days after that.

Can we go somewhere for pie and french fries? I just want to sit across from you and listen to you talk for hours.

Your friend,
Jocelyn

57

My Christmas present from Mom was a mod trapeze dress in purple, blue, and gray paisley. When I'd tried it on the next day, I thought she'd have to return it for a bigger size. But when she saw me in it, she'd clapped her hands and declared it perfect, even if it was halfway up my thigh.

"You'll wear tights with it," she'd said. "It will be fine."

"Are you sure?" I'd asked.

"Of course." She'd motioned with her finger that she wanted me to twirl around. "That's how all the girls wear them these days."

"But I don't have any place to wear it." I spun for her. "It wouldn't pass at church."

"Well, you can wear it to the party," she'd said. "Now, let's figure out what we're going to do with your hair."

All week she paged through magazines, trying to decide how she would do my hair and what kind of makeup she'd need to best make the blue of my eyes stand out from behind my glasses. The way she went on, I feared I'd end up with Raquel Welch's enormous hair, Twiggy's buggy eyes, and perfectly drawn-on *I Love Lucy* lips.

"I don't want to look like I'm wearing a costume," I told her. "I want him to actually recognize me."

"Of course he will," Mom said. "You have to trust me."

"Just please don't give me a bouffant."

She sighed and shook her head. "So picky."

●

After making me wear cucumbers on my eyes for half an hour, sit under a hot dryer with rollers in my hair, and absolutely suffocating me with at least a can's worth of hairspray, Mom declared me nearly ready for the party.

"Now we just need to do your makeup," she said. "Sit here."

She pulled the kitchen step stool so it was under the ceiling light.

"Don't make it very heavy, please," I said, sitting.

"Oh, shush." She opened her case of rouge, lipstick, mascara, and such. "Take off your glasses and shut your eyes."

"I don't know why I let you talk me into this." I put my glasses on the counter and tilted my face toward her, eyes closed. "I thought men didn't care about makeup."

"They don't," she said. "But if I do this right, he won't even know you're wearing any. Now stop fluttering your eyelids so I can get it even."

Relieved that she wouldn't go over the top, I relaxed. "Is it silly that I'm nervous?"

"Not at all." She was so close to me I could feel her breath on my face when she talked. "He's a nice young man."

"You really think so?"

"I do." She dabbed at the outside corner of my eye with her soft fingertip. "It would be a lie if I said I wasn't worried about you being with him, though."

"Why?" I opened my one eye that she wasn't currently working on.

"Well, sweetie, it would be so difficult, him being black and you white. Even now with how some things have changed." She looked in my open eye. "You aren't making this easy for me, you know."

"Sorry." I shut my eye.

"When I was your age, there was a couple that got married." She went back to brushing on eye shadow. "She was black and he was white. They had a few kids together and it was very hard on those children."

"That was the forties, Mom."

"You do know that wasn't so long ago, don't you?" she asked. "I always worried about those children. I worried that they didn't know what they were. If they were black or white."

"I'm just going to a party with David," I said. "It doesn't mean we're going to get married."

"I know that. And I want you to have a wonderful time." She sighed. "I just want your life to be easy."

I opened both of my eyes to see her digging through her makeup case, her lips pushed together tightly.

"Who said that life was supposed to be easy?" I asked.

"Well, then, I want your life to be easier than mine has been."

"Mom, so far my life has been pretty great," I said. "Mostly because you worked hard to make sure it was."

"I really am a fantastic mother." She winked at me. "I like David. He's sweet to you and he's got nice manners. And if I had to choose between him and Walt . . ."

"Mom, no," I interrupted. "You know that was nothing."

"Oh, all right." She shook her head. "Just close your eyes so I can finish up."

I didn't argue with her and I tried to keep my face as still as possible so she could finish up. The powdery smell of the blush and the pasty texture of the lipstick made me think of the times when she'd let me play at her vanity when I was little.

"It's so nice to have a daughter," Mom said, as if reading the memory from my mind. "I always wanted a little girl. Did you know that?"

"No," I answered.

"I can't imagine God giving me a better one than you." She touched my cheek with her cool hand. "Now, don't you dare cry. You'll put streaks in your foundation."

58

The dance hall was full near to bursting with all the people of Fort Colson. Even as cold as it was outside, inside it was so warm and I worried I'd sweat through the underarms of my dress. But once the hired band started playing, I forgot all about that.

It had taken very little convincing for David to get me to dance with him. The lights were kept low and the floor was so crowded, I was certain no one was watching my sorry efforts at doing the twist or the swim.

But then the electric keyboard started a new song with a slow melody. I knew right away which song it was. "Never My Love." A tune that earned more than a few eye rolls when Mom had heard it on the radio.

All of the dancers around us either paired up, moving close to each other, or left the floor for glasses of punch or to stand along the wall, wishing they had someone to dance with. David put out his hands and grinned at me.

"Can I have this dance?" he asked.

I nodded, putting my hands into his, feeling his fingers closing over them. He lifted my left to his shoulder before putting his right hand on the small of my back. My stomach flipped and fluttered, making me feel somewhere between excited and ill. Whatever it was, I hoped the song would last a long time.

"Have I told you how pretty you look tonight?" he asked.

"A few times," I answered.

"I hope you don't get sick of hearing it."

"How could I?"

The singer didn't have the smooth voice I'd expected for the song. He lent a harder edge to the lyrics, but it little mattered. They could have played any song for all I cared in that moment. All of the band started in on the "duh-buh-duh" part of the song and David joined in, off-key and making me laugh.

"You can't sing," I said.

"That surprises you?"

"It's a nice surprise."

"How's that?" he asked.

"I'm just glad that you aren't perfect."

"Not even close."

When the song ended, we let go of one another, clapping along with everyone else. I hoped for another slow song and that David would want to dance to that one too. But no luck.

"Thank you," the bandleader said. "Now it's time for us to take five. But don't worry, we asked a brand-new band to play a song or two to fill in for us. It's their debut here in Fort Colson. Join me in welcoming the Bus Drivers!"

"That's Joel's band," I said, looking up at David with eyes wide. "That's my brother's band."

Sure enough, Joel took the stage, his Les Paul hanging around his neck and a big, silly grin on his face. The other boys joined him. John and Andy taking the microphones, Chris sitting at the drum kit. They wore their best suits, even if they didn't match and the slacks were a few inches shorter than they'd been just a few months earlier.

Once set, Andy counted to four and Joel started on his guitar.

"Oh no," I said, covering my mouth with my hands. "Why did they choose this song?"

Mom was no fan of the Rolling Stones and especially not of that song. When Joel had asked her why, she'd just said that she was little interested in "those British boys' pursuit of satisfaction" and that it was "no surprise they couldn't get a girl when they insisted on going on and on about it."

The silly smile was gone from Joel's face as he played, replaced instead by an expression of intensity, concentration. He looked grown up, and I thought it was good Mom hadn't come and yet wished she could have seen him.

John and Andy sang into their microphones, their melody and harmony less rough-edged than Mick Jagger and Keith Richards. Chris hit the drums so hard, I feared they'd tip over.

They were good. As good as a bunch of fourteen-year-old boys could be. And when they finished, they took a bow, a spark in each of their eyes as if they had just realized that they'd gotten away with it.

The only thing that would have made it more perfect was if Mike had been there to hear it.

●

At ten seconds before midnight we counted down, all of us yelling at the top of our lungs. 1968 was so close, I could feel it. It seemed as if in just a few moments the whole world could change for the better, that only good things lay around the corner for us.

"...Five...Four...Three...Two...One..." we yelled. "Happy New Year!"

The regular band played "Auld Lang Syne" and the couples all around us shared kisses. I tried not to turn toward David, not wanting him to think he had to kiss me and unsure if I would survive something like that in front of half the town.

That was when he took my hand in his and lifted it to his lips.

It took me what felt like a whole minute to breathe again.

Dear Annie,

Hey, pal. I've been writing you some real doozies lately, haven't I? If I've caused you nightmares, I want to apologize. That wasn't very nice of me, was it? Listen, if you still have those letters, go ahead and burn them or tear them to shreds or use them to line the birdcage. I guess you can hold off on the last one.

I know you love birds, but I draw the line at keeping one inside.

Anyhow, I've just had a few really good days and I wanted to tell you about them.

The other day we opened up a makeshift clinic and let some of the locals come to get a little medical care they might not otherwise have. I let the real doctors take care of giving shots and pulling teeth. What I got to do was play games with kids while they waited to see the nurses or when their folks were receiving treatment.

It sure didn't feel like being in the Army and for a little while, I was glad to be right where I was.

I've been reading my Bible a lot more lately. On days that are especially hard, it just seems to help me breathe again. Did you know Oma sent me a pocket-sized one a couple of months ago? It's been a real life saver the past few weeks.

Anyway, I was reading and a certain verse stuck out to me. I've never in my life written in a Bible. I just thought it was disrespectful, I guess. But I took the pen right out of my pocket and underlined that verse and wrote the date in the margin.

"The people that walked in darkness have seen a great light: they that dwell in the land of the shadow of death, upon them hath the light shined."

This is a terribly dark place, Annie. And it's real easy to get lost in that darkness. But even in the worst days and the terrors, I can see a light. I swear to you, I can.

It seems real corny to say, but when I think about that verse, it just seems like God is so close. Like I can reach out and grab hold of him.

I don't know if I'm explaining this right at all. I guess what I'm trying to say is that I feel at peace. Whatever happens over here, even with a war exploding all around my ears and death everywhere I look, I know that God is with me.

Everything is going to be all right. I just know it.

Happy New Year, sis.

Love,
Mike

PS: I know this envelope is thick and you might think I wrote all of this just to you. But I didn't. Sorry to get your hopes up. I wrote something to everybody (you, Joel, Mom, Frank, Oma, Grandma, Bernie, even our sweetie pie Auntie Rose). If I don't make it out of here, I want you to make sure they each get their letter.

Can you promise me that?

And I'm going to ask something really hard. Don't

read them unless, well, you-know-what happens. Can you do that? Put these in your sock drawer or hide them away in the attic or whatever you have to do to keep them safe.

They're important.

Dear Mike,

Happy New Year! Can you believe it's already 1968? Golly, this decade is speeding past in a hurry, huh? It seems like just yesterday we were little kids, sneaking downstairs to hide behind Mom's chair and watch Guy Lombardo ring in 1960. Do you think she knew we did that?

The Legion put on a boss party this year. It was a real gas. You would have been really proud of our baby brother. His band played two songs and didn't even get booted off the stage when they played the Stones.

Maybe when you get home we'll throw a bash and they can play for it. They really aren't half bad.

I wish we could sit at the kitchen table with a couple bottles of root beer to talk about all things. Truly, I don't mind you telling me about the dark days. Not really. Sure, those letters rattle me a bit, but I'm sure not nearly as much as they do you. Don't ever feel bad about writing those kinds of things to me.

But, I don't mind saying that hearing good news from you makes me happy. I've always loved that verse that you wrote about. Your take on it reminded me of something that happened a few months ago.

I sat on the public access dock, watching a storm that raged from miles away. The clouds loomed large, white hot lightning splintering from them followed by the crash-boom of thunder. The sound of it echoed across the water.

No rain fell where I sat. From the way it seemed, I

didn't think the wind would press the storm my way. It was all far off, distant.

I didn't tell anyone this because I was afraid it might not make sense to them. And it seemed a special moment that I didn't want spoiled because someone thought I'd lost my marbles. Something tells me you'll understand, though.

As I watched that storm, I just kept thinking, "That's how God is."

Sometimes he feels so far, as if to never reach us. We call for him, we beg him to come. And when he seems to stay away, we might even ask where he is.

Then we see his power on display and remember, he has gone nowhere. And he's lost not one bit of his strength.

I don't know if that makes any sort of sense to you at all. If it doesn't, just don't tell me or look at me funny.

Just remember, there's a light in the darkness. The darkness cannot understand it. But that light isn't for the darkness. It's for you. It's so you can find your way home.

I love you.

Annie

PS: The letters for the family are tucked away in my drawer. I hope that's where they stay forever.

59

Frank had written to tell me that he wouldn't be able to come home for my birthday dinner. He had loads of work to do and it was an awfully long drive.

"The end of January is a busy time around here, believe it or not," he'd written. "But I'll make it up to you next time I'm over that way. I promise."

It seemed like any other reasonable newly turned nineteen-year-old would understand. That she'd be a grown-up about it and not pout. For the most part, I did well with it. And any pouting I did do was in private so no one would see how immature I was.

Mom picked up burgers on the way home from work, and Oma made me a cake with whipped cream frosting. Joel set the table and David brought a bouquet of flowers. They sang to me and Mom turned off the lights so the candles could flicker in their fullness of beauty before I blew them out.

All in all, it was a good day, even with Mike and Frank not there.

•

Oma and David had long since gone home and Joel had gone to bed. Mom sat in her easy chair and I on the couch, each with a cup of hot cocoa and a second slice of cake.

"Why not?" Mom asked, serving them up. "My girl only turns nineteen once."

"Do you want to watch the news?" I said.

"Sounds good."

"David picked out pretty flowers for you," she said.

"He did." I glanced at the bouquet of daisies and carnations with a little bit of baby's breath here and there. "I've never gotten flowers before."

"It was sweet of him." She took a bite of cake.

"Mom?"

"Hm?"

"How do I know if we're going steady or not?"

"Oh, I don't know how kids do it now." She put down her fork. "I knew I was Frank's girl after he knocked Bill DeVries's lights out."

"He punched Dr. DeVries?"

"Well, to be fair, Bill wasn't a doctor yet." Mom smiled and got a faraway look in her eyes. "They were fighting over me. Bill said something about how a nice girl like me wouldn't choose to be with trash like Frank."

"I just can't imagine Frank hitting anyone."

"Oh, he was a bit wild." She shook her head. "It was that fire in him that I fell in love with. Oma, though, wasn't too fond of what she called his 'ill temper.'"

"And Dr. DeVries didn't have it?"

"Heavens no." She covered her mouth when she laughed. "If Frank was fire, Bill was room-temperature water."

"That's not flattering," I said.

"I guess not." She took a sip of her cocoa. "As far as David goes, he brought you flowers on your birthday and endured a meal with all of us. I'd say that's all the evidence you need."

"You think so?"

"I do," she said. "And you have my blessing. I saw the way he looks at you. He'll treat you well, I can tell."

"I didn't tell you about New Year's Eve."

"Did he kiss you at midnight?"

"He kissed my hand." I blushed and shrugged. "It was nice."

"His mother must be an incredible woman to have raised such a young man."

I nodded. "We should turn on the TV or we'll miss the beginning of the show."

She reached out from her seat, changing the channel to NBC.

But it wasn't Johnny Carson on the screen. Instead, an announcer with a larger-than-life voice said, "NBC News presents 'Viet Cong Terror: A Guerrilla Offensive.'"

"What's this?" Mom whispered, turning up the volume.

A man with silvery white hair and dark-rimmed glasses spoke of raiders and terrorism and snipers. The communist violence was widespread. Ten provinces, at the American embassy in Saigon, air bases, in civilian areas.

Two-hundred-thirty-two American soldiers dead. More than nine hundred wounded.

". . . the bloodiest two days we have known in Vietnam thus far," he said. "And while we were meant to be under seven days of truce for the Vietnamese new year, otherwise known as Têt, it appears the Viet Cong and the North Vietnamese

Army have broken the truce with offenses that span the whole of South Vietnam."

"Did you hear about this?" Mom asked.

I shook my head. "I haven't had the television on all day."

She put her plate on the end table.

The footage of men running across streets or crawling over grass was blurry at best. I had to squint to see what was happening. But the sounds of gunfire were clear, and there was a lot of it. As hard to see as it was, I knew when I saw men carrying stretchers to an ambulance or a body lying on the ground.

A man slouched among the American GIs, gun pointed in a window of what I imagined to be the embassy, shooting at whoever he could hit inside. He moved with no hurry from window to window, shooting in through the bars.

At one point, he held the shoulder of a kneeling soldier, steadying himself as he went to shoot through another window. It seemed the most normal thing for him to do, firing a gun into a building. If I hadn't known better, I might have thought he was spraying poison into a wasp-infested shed, for how casually he went about it.

The picture changed to a zoomed-in image of a man I assumed to be dead, lying in a fountain. Then more dead, lying on the ground.

"All of the Viet Cong terrorists, nineteen of them, were killed," the reporter said.

"They had lots of ammunition," a man in fatigues told the cameraman. "Had enough to snipe at helicopters and airplanes as they flew overhead."

A helicopter hovered nearby and the man pointed at it. Squinting, I hoped to see if it was Mike on it, even though I was sure there were hundreds of machines just like that one. All I could manage to see were shadows of men on board.

"These attacks," the reporter went on, "were meticulously planned and extremely well-coordinated. It may be that the communists are not winning this war, as we're told by the Pentagon. However, they are not losing it, either."

Mom turned off the television and picked up her plate and cup, headed for the kitchen.

"We won't lose," I asked. "Will we?"

"I don't know, honey," she answered. "We haven't lost a war yet."

"What would happen if we did?"

"Let's not think about that right now, all right?"

As hard as I tried, I couldn't put the idea out of my mind.

Mike: This is Mike Jacobson and the date is January 19, 1968.

Annie! Happy Birthday, you sweet, smart, and supercilious sister of mine. You've somehow managed to singlehandedly improve the past nineteen years of my life. Although, I can't remember a thing from before you came along, I'm quite certain I was miserable until I first met you.

Now, this next part is to all of you. Mom, you'll have to make sure Grandma and Frank get a listen to it too. All right?

The care package of goodies came. Before Christmas Day, even. Oma and Annie must have spent a month making all of those cookies. But the guys in my hooch say thank you. After this whole thing is over, you might have a couple boys knocking on your door for a cookie and a glass of milk. I told them you wouldn't mind that, Oma. And, Annie, I told those fellas to keep their distance from you. You're too good for any of them.

Background voice:

Hey, what gives, Jacobson?

Mike: *I'm recording over here, Smitty. Keep the lan-*
guage clean. (pause) Sorry about that, folks.

Ahem.

Great news! I've passed the halfway point of
my six months as a combat medic. That means
in just three short months I'll be in a hospital
somewhere for the rest of my time. Won't that
be nice? I'm holding out for Japan. I think that
would be keen.

I don't have long, I'm using my buddy's ma-
chine and he wants to make a recording for his
girl back home. But I wanted to let you all know
that I'm doing all right. I've gotten my bearings
here for the most part and I know I've saved at
least a few lives in the process.

Since I had no choice in the matter, I guess
this is the best situation for me. I'm making a
difference, even if just a small one. But, then
again, I'm sure the boys' parents back home
think it's a big deal, having their sons alive, even
if not in one piece.

I love every single one of you. Mom, Annie,
Joel, Frank, Oma, Grandma. I even like Bernie
some too. I think he'd clobber me if I said I loved
him, even if it's true.

Take care. I'll see you all before you know it.

This is Michael Francis Jacobson signing off.
(click)

60

Bernie was in an especially foul mood that Saturday morning. It was something about the grill not firing up correctly, although I hadn't really understood his grumblings fully. I hadn't asked him to clarify, either.

All I knew was that any orders I took would require him to cook on the stove top or in the oven, which made more work for both him and Larry, not to mention longer waits for our customers.

"Just tell them we're only serving baked goods this morning," he grunted at me. "We'll have to shut down for lunch, I suppose."

"I'm sorry," I said.

"Did *you* break it?"

"Well, no."

"Then stop apologizing so much," he said with a grunt. "You make me crazy for all the things you're sorry about."

"Sorry?"

"Very funny."

Fortunately, most of the people who came for breakfast

were happy to eat a doughnut or even a piece of pie in place of a fried egg and hash brown potatoes.

"Just as long as you have coffee," a few of them said.

Right around ten that morning, the breakfast crowd thinned and David came in, sitting at his usual table. He had the paper in front of him, open to the Marmaduke comic, chuckling to himself.

"What's that silly dog up to today?" I asked, walking up to his table.

"Same old, same old." He folded the paper. "I was thinking about going to see a movie today."

"Oh you were?"

"The new Jimmy Stewart one," he said. "It's a Western. Would you like to go with me?"

"Sure." I looked at the clock on the wall. "I get out early. We're not staying open for lunch."

"Sounds fine."

"If you don't mind, I'd like to go home and change my clothes."

"All right. Maybe I'll get you around two o'clock?"

I told him that would be fine and he asked if he could have a doughnut and a glass of milk. Behind the counter I put a fresh pastry on a plate for him, using the can of whipped cream to make it into a smiley face. I poured his milk and turned to go back to his table.

That was when the bell over the door jingled.

The man who walked in was in full dress uniform. Deep green jacket and pants, lighter green shirt beneath. Shiny brass buttons and badges on the breast of the jacket.

"Hello?" I said, still holding the plate and glass. "Can I help you?"

"I hope so, miss," the man said. "I'm looking for an address."

"Just a minute." I took the glass and plate to David, not feeling if I put it on the table or not. Then I went to the soldier. "What's the address?"

I swallowed hard.

"I have it here in my pocket." He reached into his pants pocket, pulling out a slip of paper and unfolding it. "It's on Lewis Street."

My body felt light, as if it might float away without me even realizing it. I looked at the paper.

Jacobson.

"David?" I said. "Tell Bernie I went home."

"Miss?" the man beside me said. "Are you all right?"

"Bernie will give you directions."

Without another word, without taking off my apron or grabbing my coat, I ran out the door.

The cold air shocked me back to awareness.

I had to get home.

61

Joel was in the living room, playing Opa's old guitar on the couch in his stocking feet. He looked up at me when I came in through the front door.

"Where's Mom?" I closed the door behind me, careful not to let it slam.

"Doing laundry," he said. "Golly, Annie, are you all right? You look sick."

"Joel, you have to go."

"What are you talking about?"

"You have to go to the store for Oma." I dug a dollar in tip money from my apron pocket. "You need to get her some flour. The big bag, all right? And you need to go *right now*."

"Why right now?"

"Because she needs it right now." I shoved the money into his hand, closing his fingers over it. "Hurry."

"Okay."

"Where are your shoes?"

"In my room."

I opened the closet off the living room. There were a pair

of Mike's old work boots. I tried not to think, tried not to feel. I grabbed them, putting them in front of Joel.

"Wear those. They'll fit."

"They're too big."

"That's okay. Just hurry."

My heart pounded and I couldn't draw in a deep breath for the life of me. I checked out the window as he tied the laces and then pulled his coat off the hanger. A dark blue car turned down our street, moving slowly toward our driveway.

He can't find out this way.

"Go out the back door," I said, pushing Joel in that direction. "Cut through the yards to get to her house."

"What about the flour?"

"Just forget it," I said. "Just go to Oma's."

"Why are you acting so weird?" he asked, struggling against me.

"You'll understand later."

"Fine, just don't push me anymore."

He went out the back way, Mike's boots clonking on the floor with every step.

As soon as he closed the back door behind him, I heard the car door close from our driveway.

"Mom," I tried to call, but my voice was too weak.

●

He sat in Mom's chair. Mom and I were next to each other on the couch. She held my hand. She nodded as he spoke, holding herself together with such courage, I could hardly believe it.

He said a lot. Not one word of it made any sense to me. His voice was garbled, unclear, like the times when Mike and I would dunk our heads under the surface of Old Chip and yell at each other, then we'd try to guess what the other had said.

But with that Army man, I didn't want to guess what he was saying. More than that, I didn't want to be right about what I thought it was.

"Thank you," Mom said after he'd stopped talking. "May I ask you something?"

"Yes, ma'am," he answered.

"Were you over there?"

"I was, ma'am."

"This is harder than being at war, isn't it?" She leaned forward.

"Yes, ma'am. I'd take a battle over this any day."

"I'm sorry you have to do this." She reached for his hand. "What a truly difficult job you have. But you do it so well."

"Thank you, ma'am." He met her eyes. "And I could not be more sorry about your son."

"Me either." She pushed her lips together tightly, as if catching a sob. "You can go. You'll forgive me if I don't see you out."

"Of course, ma'am."

And, just like that, he was gone.

"Mom," I said, my voice sounding as if it was coming from all the way across the room. "What do we do?"

"I don't know," she said.

62

I didn't remember moving off the couch and to the floor on the other side of the room and I couldn't recall who made me a cup of tea or having sipped any of it. Somehow Oma was there, holding Joel's head to her shoulder where he sobbed. The minister and his wife sat with Mom at the dining room table.

I noticed that, not only did I have tea, but it was also in my favorite cup. The one with the rooster cock-a-doodling into a sunless morning.

David came from the kitchen, right toward me, putting his hand out to me. "Let's get you off the floor, huh?"

I let him help me up, and I took a seat in Mom's chair. He squatted beside me, still holding my hand.

"Bernie's in the kitchen making some soup," he said. "In case you wanted to eat some."

"Okay," I answered, feeling as if in a fog. "I don't know."

"That's all right." David let go of my hand and pulled a straight-back chair from the corner and sat on it right beside me. "Is it okay with you if I stay for a little bit?"

"Don't leave."

"I won't."

"I'm so tired," I said, turning toward him. "That's all I can feel. I'm just tired."

"It would be all right if you closed your eyes." He took my hand again.

I shut my eyelids.

●

When I woke, Frank had taken Oma's seat next to Joel. My brother was leaned over, holding his head in his hands. His fingers worked through his hair that had grown into a mass of long curls.

"Like Bob Dylan's," Joel had said just the day before when Mom had complained about it.

Just the day before.

Before.

Frank caught my eye. He held his jaw clenched, his eyebrows lowered. But his eyes were watery and red.

"You came," I whispered.

He nodded.

"Then it's real?"

He looked away from me before nodding that time.

"Why?" I tried to ask, but no sound came out except a groan. "Why Mike?"

"I don't know," Frank said.

●

We sat at the dining room table, sipping the soup Bernie had made, more out of politeness than hunger. But the hot broth seemed to awaken me from the numbness in my chest.

As much as I hated to feel the terror and heartache and loss, it was better than suffocating in the void.

Elbow to elbow, none of us complained about being tucked around the table so tightly. It was as if the nearness was important, as if it was what kept us from falling to pieces right there in the dining room.

"Frank, do you remember the day Michael was born?" Mom asked, her voice shaking.

"I couldn't forget it if I tried." Frank gave her his half grin. "It's the same day I got this."

He angled his face upward and pointed at a scar that cut through the stubble on his chin.

"You fainted when I told you it was time for him to come," Mom said, laughing even as the tears collected in her eyes. "I thought I'd have to drive myself to the hospital."

"Five stitches," Frank said. "If only you could have experienced the agony I suffered that day."

"Oh, you." Mom cringed, grinding her teeth together and letting out a sob. "He was the most perfect baby, wasn't he?"

"He was. I couldn't take my eyes off him."

"He didn't like to sleep," Oma added. "I remember Gloria coming to my house and crying over how tired she was because he cried all night long."

"And you didn't believe me," Mom said. "You told me all babies did that."

"So I took your invitation to come spend the night." Oma shook her head and laughed. "He cried from dusk until dawn."

"Unless Frank had him," Mom said. "He loved being with his daddy."

Frank's brows gathered in the middle and he looked into

his nearly empty bowl of soup. "He was protecting a wounded soldier," Frank said. "He shielded him with his body. He saved that boy's life. That was what the officer who came to my house told me."

"They didn't tell me," Mom whispered, then covered her eyes with her hand. Leaning down, she rested her elbow on the table.

"Why would he do that?" Joel asked. "He was supposed to take care of himself so he could come home. Why would he risk it?"

"It was the right thing to do," Bernie said. "It was his duty."

"But why's it right that the other boy gets to live and Mike doesn't?"

"Joel," I said. "You know how Mike is. Always putting somebody else before himself."

"Then he should've thought of us," Joel said. "Shouldn't he have? Aren't we important enough?"

No one answered him. Maybe that was because there wasn't an answer to give.

63

I slept in fits and starts, finally giving up on trying somewhere around four in the morning. Sitting up in bed, I turned on my lamp and grabbed my glasses. My closet door was open from the morning before when I'd dressed for work.

Looking down, I realized I still had on my work clothes. At least I'd had enough sense to take off my apron.

I walked to my closet and took a fresh blouse off one of the hangers, feeling of its starched collar and deciding that it was the last thing I wanted to feel on my skin. Not even bothering to hang it back up, I tossed it on top of my dresser and opened the drawer that housed all of my T-shirts.

Bending down, I pulled open my pants drawer, picking up my pair of bell-bottoms. A whisper of paper against paper caught my attention and I squatted down. There, at the bottom of my drawer, were the letters Mike had sent, "Just in case."

Dropping the jeans and shirt to the floor, I picked up the stack of envelopes and sat at my desk, pushing aside my journal and a few books to make room. I set them out, making rows of envelopes, seeing all of our names in Mike's handwriting.

Annie Banannie.

I brushed my fingertips across the letter, feeling the lines and curves of the name Mike had called me when we were little. Picking it up, I turned it over.

Don't duck and cover, pal, he'd written on the back. *Keep your eyes open.*

I broke out in a smile at the memory before my eyes filled.

Using a nail file, I cut open the top of the envelope, careful not to mar the slightest bit of handwriting. I hadn't held many treasures in my life, but I knew one when I did.

My hands shook and I worried that I'd tear the letter before I even got it out of the envelope. After setting it down, I rubbed my palms together, blowing warm air on them from my mouth.

Don't duck and cover. Keep your eyes open.

The papers slid out of the envelope, and I unfolded them, smoothing them against the top of the desk, my hands still trembling.

Dear Annie.

To read more was to admit that it was true. To believe that Mike's body didn't move anymore, his heart no longer kept the rhythm of pumping blood, and his lungs had no more need to take in air. Letting my eyes move beyond my name was to know that Mike was dead.

Hands in my lap, gripped together so hard it hurt my knuckles, I resisted folding the letter and slipping it back into its envelope. I fought the urge to stack them all and hide them in my bottom drawer.

Don't duck and cover.

I read until my vision was blurred with tears. Then I wiped my eyes and kept reading.

And in that reading, I knew that it was true.

Mike was gone.

He wasn't coming home.

Dear Annie,

Good for you! I'm proud of you for being brave enough to read this far. I can't imagine what this day has been like for you. Or, if you've delayed reading this, I can't imagine how this time has been like for you.

If you need to take a breather, I understand. But, listen, chum. Don't quit reading it altogether. Remember, I spent time writing this and thinking about what exactly I wanted you to know. It would be a shame if you didn't finish.

You asked me a while ago if I'm scared. If I remember correctly, I answered that I was all right. I spent a lot of time trying so hard to not be afraid. There's certainly a lot of macho posturing around here sometimes.

I don't know if you've realized it yet, but I stole a book from you, bringing it in my pack all the way to the other side of the world. Forgive me, sis, will ya? Gosh, it sure takes a long time to read a whole book around here with all the business we get into. But I remembered that you'd told me to read it, so I thought I'd give it a whirl.

Guess what it was.

A Wrinkle in Time.

Surprised?

It was a little hard for me to get into with Mrs. Whatsit and such. But I kept going. Then this certain line stuck out at me.

"Only a fool is not afraid. Now go."

Every morning, I get up and before I even put my soles

on the dirt floor of my hooch, I feel that stab of fear. But then I remember what Mrs. Somebodyinthatbook said and I get up anyway. And all day long, I ask God to keep me going.

So far, he's pulled through for me.

Well, until now, when you're reading this.

I'm sorry, Annie. I tried to make it. I swear I did.

But, you know what? Neither of us has to be scared anymore. Not really. If you're reading this, then the very worst has happened. It can't get harder than this. Right?

Don't duck and cover, sis. Keep your eyes open because even though this is really hard right now, there's still so much good going on around you. See it, will you? Notice it in that special way you have of observing the world.

And on the days when it just seems too hard, do it for me, will you? Remember it all. Because when you get to heaven, I'm going to want you to tell me all about it.

Keep your eyes open, Annie.

And know that you were the best of the world to me.

Love,
Mike

64

The telephone had barely stopped ringing all day. It stood to reason that an announcement was made at church, the prayer list altered so that everyone would know about Mike. We'd stayed home that morning, and I was glad for it. The last thing I could have handled was a hundred pairs of eyes watching to see if I'd crack.

Undoubtedly, I would have.

As soon as Aunt Rose arrived, she played secretary, answering the calls and writing down messages on slips of scrap paper from our junk drawer. It was a wonder, watching her work, hearing her insist that we were not able to come to the phone at the moment.

Never in my life did I think I'd find myself so thankful for her.

"You got a few calls already," she said, handing me little pieces of paper. She pointed to the top one. "He had a nice voice."

I nodded. "Next time he calls, I'll talk to him."

She made a note of it on a tablet. "Annie wants to talk to David. Got it."

"And if Jocelyn Falck calls," I said. "I'll take it."

"Sure thing, sweetheart."

"Thanks." I stepped back half an inch, unsure of what to make of her term of endearment. If anything, Aunt Rose wasn't known for her affection.

"Your brother's been on the porch for nearly an hour," she said, nodding toward the front window. "I don't think he has a coat on."

"I'll check on him."

"Annie," she said, putting her hand on my shoulder. "I really am sorry. Mike was a good boy. I know how much you loved him."

I nodded and turned from her, feeling as if she'd stuck a hot poker into my chest. The burning radiated through my torso and into my arms, legs, neck. Gasping, I tried to breathe deeply enough to expel the heat, but it only seemed to make it worse.

I know how much you loved him.

I did. She was right.

You loved *him.*

But not in the past tense.

Loved.

My love for my brother hadn't ended. It wasn't over. It wouldn't stop.

"Do you know how much I love him still?" I wanted to scream. But there was no fight in me.

"Annie?"

Oma was at my elbow, her arm wrapped around my waist. Concern lined her face. Lack of sleep circled red around her eyes.

She muttered something in Dutch that I only understood

partially. The few words I picked out had to do with *that woman* and *no good*.

I knew she meant Aunt Rose.

●

Oma took me into Mom's room and closed the door, even going so far as to turn the lock so no one could come in.

"What did she say to you?" she insisted.

"That she knows how much I loved Mike," I answered.

"And?"

"That was all."

She sat on the edge of Mom's unmade bed and patted the mattress for me to sit beside her.

"Is it wrong if I still love him?" I asked.

"Well, I don't think so." She took my hand. "Are we not made for eternity?"

I nodded.

"Then Mike still is," she said. "Even if he isn't here in this house or riding a helicopter over the jungle or doing who knows what, he still is."

My shoulders curled down but Oma caught me, her arms stronger than I ever expected them to be.

"You can love him," she whispered through my crying. "It's right to."

I let her hold me, her words stuck in my head.

Mike still is.

65

Mom had a new pack of Luckies on the kitchen table. Half of them were gone and the saucer she'd used for an ashtray was full. Little flecks of gray were scattered around it. She sat at the table, resting her forehead in her hand.

"Are you all right?" I asked.

She shook her head. "I had too many. Now I'm dizzy and sick."

"You shouldn't have any." I picked up the saucer and dumped the ash into the trash can. "Who bought those for you?"

"Rose," she answered. "Just throw these away too." She handed me the rest of the pack.

"Is she gone?"

"Just for the night." She glanced up at me. "She and your grandmother are staying at the inn."

"And Frank?"

"Joel talked him into staying in his room."

"That should be interesting." I tossed the pack into the garbage. "No digging these out, okay?"

"I never want to touch those things again."

"Tea?" I held up the kettle.

"Please."

I nibbled on a cookie while the water boiled. It was the first thing I'd eaten all day. Maybe even since Bernie's soup the day before.

"Tomorrow Frank and I meet with the people to make arrangements," Mom said.

"For the funeral?" The cookie had turned in my stomach and I put the last half of it on the counter.

"Among other things." She sat up. "There's a lot to figure out."

I nodded and turned off the heat, pouring the water into two cups. "Do I need to be there?"

"No," she said. "I asked David to take you to a movie or lunch."

"He has to work." I put her cup in front of her.

"I guess he took the time off."

I sat opposite her, watching the water darken as I dunked a tea bag below the surface.

"What about Joel? You won't make him go to school, will you?"

She shook her head. "He's going to a friend's house."

"Don't fight with Frank, all right?" I said. "When you're making arrangements."

"I'll try not to." She blew on her tea. "He's just so darned stubborn."

"Hm." I lifted one eyebrow at her.

"I know. I have no room to call the kettle black."

"How long is he going to stay?" I got up for the rest of my cookie. "Do you want one?"

"One of the chocolate chip ones, please." She sighed. "Frank hasn't said when he's thinking of leaving. It can take a while for the remains to arrive."

I shut my eyes and swallowed hard.

"It's not a nice thought, I know," she said. "I'm sorry."

"Have you talked to Joel today?"

"A little. He's angry, which I expected." She took the cookie from me. "I hope he'll talk to Frank. Sometimes what a boy needs most is his father."

Six months earlier and I would have had some snide comment to make about boys needing their fathers. But, then again, six months earlier Mom would never have said such a thing.

●

It was just past ten o'clock when I went to bed. The door to Joel's room was ajar and I peeked in. He sat on the edge of the top bunk, his legs dangling off the side. Frank stood beside him, his hand resting on the bed frame.

When I saw the tears on my little brother's face, my instinct was to rush in. To climb up beside him and put my arm around his shoulders. To tell him that everything was going to be all right even if I wasn't sure that was the truth.

I put my hand on the door to push it open when I saw Frank step up on the ladder to pull Joel's head to his shoulder. He wrapped his arms around Joel's neck.

I went to my own room, careful to turn the knob when I shut the door.

The last thing I wanted to do was disturb them.

—————◆—————

Dear Gloria,

Forgive my handwriting. The nerves have taken over and I can't seem to keep my hand steady.

You asked me today how I was holding up and I didn't say anything. If I'm honest, I don't know how to answer that question. The closest I can come is to say that I'm miserable and I have many regrets.

Most of all, I regret missing Mike's life.

I don't want to miss another day of Annie and Joel's.

It may be foolish, but I don't think it's too late for me to try and be a father to them. The father I should have been all this time.

Still, I'll never forgive myself for what I've done. My only hope is that someday they'll be able to forgive me.

Frank

Dear Frank,

I don't know why I can't bring myself to say this to you in person. Maybe it's just that there are too many people around or that I'm afraid it would come out wrong. Writing it seems easier, even though I've written and rewritten it at least half a dozen times.

For years I had myself convinced that the kids didn't need a father. That I could fill all the holes you'd left us with. I taught them how to fish and paddle a boat, I took the boys to Scouts and taught Annie to sew. When they fought, I broke it up. When they were hurt or sick, I took them to the doctor. When they were upset, I comforted them.

I did this because I had no choice, Frank. You'd left me very few options when you went away.

But now I see their need for you.

It's so hard for me to ask, but please don't disappear again.

Gloria

66

The days before the funeral passed by in a haze. Hours either sped away, spent before I realized it, or dragged along, seeming to never end. Some days I couldn't remember if I'd eaten or gone to the bathroom or when I'd last showered. Others, I was aware of every moment I'd been awake.

A few days in the interim Frank had gone back to Bliss to "tie up loose ends." Mom went to work. Joel attended school and I popped in for a few hours here or there at the diner.

The world continued to spin, carrying us along with it whether we liked it or not.

Suddenly and finally, the night before the funeral arrived. Mom had set up her ironing board, pressing all of our black clothes for the next morning and starching Joel's button-up shirt. She had her hair in rollers and cold cream smeared on her face.

"Your dress is hanging up in the laundry room," she said. "You'll need a sweater to wear with it."

"Thank you." I took my dress off the hook, walking with it to the foot of the steps.

"Do you think Michael would hate us for making such a fuss over him?"

Facing her again, I shook my head. "I don't know."

"Frank wanted the whole shebang." She stood the iron on its end and moved the shirt she was pressing. "The honor guard and the salutes and 'Taps.' All of it."

"It will be nice."

"Nice?" She scowled at me. "None of this is nice. Nothing about this is nice."

"Mom . . ."

"I didn't want any of this for him. I wanted him to go to college so he could get a deferment. I wanted him to be safe." She lifted her arms, palms up. "I worked so hard. Still, he went. And now look at the mess we're in."

She yanked the plug of the iron out of the wall and ripped the shirt off the board. The way she fit it on the hanger, I feared she'd tear the sleeves right off.

"This wasn't supposed to happen," she said, her voice raised an octave. "Not to my son."

She placed her hands on the ironing board and breathed in and out through her mouth.

"Mom?" I said, taking one step toward her.

"I don't know what to do. I can't fix this."

Rushing past me down the stairs, Joel made his way to Mom. Without a word, he put his arms around her and she didn't fight him.

"It's all right, Mom," he said. "It's all right."

She didn't argue with him and she didn't push him from

her. Because, I thought, she knew that what he meant was that it was all right for her to let go, to not try to be so strong.

It was all right.

I sat on the bottom step, my funeral dress still in my arms.

There was nothing else I could do.

67

We'd followed the hearse from the church to the cemetery. Mom sat in the passenger's seat of her station wagon and Frank was at the wheel. Joel sat between Oma and me in the back. Behind us was a line of cars carrying most of the residents of Fort Colson, Michigan.

They'd come to honor Mike. To welcome him back home.

The honor guard was made up of six veterans from our little town. Bernie was among them and I was glad to have someone I trusted bearing the weight of my brother.

Their movements were slow, methodical, as if they were in no hurry to carry the casket to the grave already carved out of the earth.

The funeral director ushered us from the car to the wooden folding chairs less than a foot from where Mike lay in his casket. I couldn't tell if the burning in my lungs was from the freezing cold air or panic.

Don't duck and cover. Keep your eyes open.

"Would you like a blanket?" the funeral director whispered. "For your laps?"

"That's so kind of you," Mom said from her seat beside me. "Thank you, Clive."

He helped us tuck up under the black, fleecy cover. "I hope that helps a little."

His kindness made me cry and I nodded, hoping he'd understand my gratitude.

"Just a little bit longer, honey," Mom said, taking my hand.

Frank sat on the other side of me and put his arm around my shoulders. He didn't say anything, but that was all right. Joel, from the other side of Frank, leaned forward and looked my way, giving me half a smile.

Remember it all, Mike had written.

I took notice of all the people fitting in close to the graveside. Jocelyn was there and so was David. Larry and his mother stood beside the Vanderlaans. They'd come for Mike. They'd come for us. I observed the way no one spoke, paying silent reverence. How Mom shook during the opening prayer and let me put my head on her shoulder. I heard the minister speak, his voice muffled by the wind that whipped around us.

"Jesus told his disciples in the garden on the eve of his death, 'I am not alone, because the Father is with me. These things I have spoken to you that ye might have peace. In the world ye shall have tribulation: but be of good cheer; I have overcome the world.' Christ has overcome death and the grave. While we may mourn today, we are not left alone. The Father is with us and praise be to him who gives us the victory through his Son, Jesus Christ."

Remember.

I kept my eyes open, trying not to flinch with the three-volley salute of gunfire. And I did my best to listen closely to the bugle as it played "Taps." I paid attention to the way Frank cleared his throat and sniffled right after, the way Mom's hand tightened around mine.

The honor guard folded the flag, attentive to every crease, keeping the stripes straight. Tugging and smoothing, they started the triangular fold with the greatest of care, tucking the end under the blue field and the perfectly white stars.

An officer knelt in front of Mom, presenting the flag to her, reciting words in his deep voice. She nodded, holding the flag on her lap on top of the fleecy blanket. Her jaw clenched.

"Thank you," she whispered to him. "You have all done a fine job today."

"It's been my honor, ma'am," he answered before rising and saluting her.

When it was time, we left the fleece blanket on the chairs and walked away, Mom holding the flag to her chest with both arms. Frank at her side, holding her elbow in his cupped hand. Joel and me behind them, my arm linked through his.

I turned and looked back over my shoulder, hating to leave.

68

The Army had delivered a box of what they called Mike's "personal effects." It sat, unopened, in the middle of the dining room table.

"I'm not entirely certain I'm ready to open it," Mom said, looking at Frank where he sat across from her. "My hands are shaking."

Oma brought a plate of cookies in from the kitchen, handing it to Joel. "If you want to wait, that's all right, dearest."

"You might as well get it over with." Grandma crossed her arms.

"I agree," said Aunt Rose.

"Whatever you want, Glo," Frank said.

She nodded at him. "Will you open it?"

Frank stood, lifting the top off the box and looking down into it. One item at a time, he passed it to Mom. A stack of letters from home, a pouch full of coins, my copy of *A Wrinkle in Time*, the Bible Oma'd given him, a can opener, and a few odds and ends. He hesitated when he picked up Mike's dog tags and the St. Michael medallion, closing his fingers over where they rested in his palm. He cleared his throat, handing them to Mom, and reached into the box one last time.

"And his camera," Frank said, sitting. "He has at least six rolls of film in there."

Mom stood and peeked over the edge. "I'll take them in first thing in the morning."

●

It took more than a week to get the photos back from Mike's box. By then Frank was back in Bliss, Grandma and Aunt Rose were at home in Grand Rapids. Mom had decided it was better anyway, just the three of us getting to look through them first.

"We can take our time," she said, sitting in the middle of the couch.

Joel and I sat on either side of her.

My heart beat fast when she broke the seal on the first envelope, pulling out a stack of square photographs. The topmost one was of a little boy kneeling on the ground, holding a puppy to his chest. The next six or more were of a green field, most of them blurry.

But then was one of Mike wearing his grin, standing in front of a helicopter with a red cross painted on the side. Then one with him and three other men, all with serious faces. He'd taken pictures of a bunk that I assumed to be his, a few buildings I guessed were on the base.

Stack by stack, we found pictures that told part of the story he'd lived in Vietnam. Him with a nurse or sitting on his bunk, writing a letter. Who had taken the pictures? I doubted we'd ever know. But I certainly was grateful.

"Just one more," Mom said, opening the last envelope. "Oh, Michael."

It was of our Christmas together, the night before he left. He'd spent every shot of that roll on us. The picture of all of us together. One of Oma smiling sweetly. Bernie and Frank with arms crossed, not looking at each other.

"Look at this," Joel said, pointing at a picture of him playing his guitar.

"You look so grown up." Mom handed it to him. "Oh, and I took this one."

Mom held up a snapshot of Mike and me sitting on the floor by the Christmas tree, face-to-face, laughing about something. How seeing that picture made me miss him.

We kept flipping through them, then Mom stopped on one of her, holding her cup of tea and smiling prettily into the camera, her head tilted and one foot kicked up to the side. Behind her, Frank looked at her, the sullenness gone from his face and replaced by his full smile.

"That's a nice one, Mom," Joel said.

"Yeah," she answered, her voice soft. "It is."

The last was of the three of us, my brothers and me. They'd put me in between them, both of them giving me a kiss on either cheek. If my smile could have gotten any bigger it would have surprised me.

"Oh." Mom sighed. "I wish I could have that evening back."

Joel put an arm around her. "Me too, Mom."

"And to think I got after him for taking all these pictures," she said. "I wanted him to save the film for Vietnam."

"He never was very good at doing as you said." I laughed. "The stinker."

"How I love him." She blinked. "I love him so much."

We looked through all the pictures one more time before putting them away for safekeeping. Mom said she'd buy an album at the five-and-dime the next day.

It was late, but we didn't go to bed. And we didn't turn on the news. We just sat together, missing Mike.

Epilogue

SPRING, 1968

The loons came back to Chippewa Lake the last week of
March. They announced their arrival with a night concert
of tremolos and yodels. Frank had come back to Fort Colson
that week too. His reentry was quieter, just a man in a rusted
pickup truck full of his few earthly belongings.

He'd sold his business in Bliss and rented a cottage a block
or two from us, promising not to bother us too much. Still,
he came for supper most evenings.

Mom had decided against taking Frank's offer of divorce.
But she did accept his invitation to the occasional Friday evening movie or Sunday afternoon drive. She made no promises
of happily ever afters. But she also didn't refuse to entertain
the possibility.

Not long after Frank moved back she started wearing her
wedding ring again.

We'd visited Mike's grave every week since his funeral.
Oma had planted tulips on either side of his headstone, bulbs

she'd brought with her from the Netherlands. Each time we went, the searing pain of losing him lessened, replaced by an aching longing for him.

Even a million years wouldn't heal that. I wouldn't have wanted the cure anyway.

On the last Saturday of March, I borrowed Bernie's boat and rowed out to the middle of Old Chip. It seemed like a year since Mike and I had sat in that boat together. I felt of the oar handles, the sides of the boat, remembering my brother.

I believed that, as Oma had said, we were meant for eternity. That life on this side was a prelude to the real life ahead of us. At least that was what I hoped for.

Mike is.

Those two words in her thick accent had gotten me through more than a handful of really tough days.

I spotted the loons gliding along the surface of the water, tucked away in the safety of their usual cove. Lifting Mike's camera to my eye, I took a picture, hoping that it would come out clear, crisp once it was developed. I snapped a second just in case.

Taking the camera away from my eye, I saw a waving motion in my periphery. Turning, I saw David, his arms in the air. I slipped the camera strap around my neck before grabbing the oars and rowing back to the public access.

"Hi," I said, letting him take my hand to help me up on the dock.

"Hello," he said back. "No life jacket?"

"It's not that deep."

"You do know that somebody can drown in a teaspoon of water."

"That's not true." I pointed to the loons. "They're back."

"So I heard." He helped me tie the boat to the dock. "Do you think they're the same ones that were here last year?"

"I don't know," I answered. "I like to think so."

We sat on the dock, side by side, looking out over the water. I put my hand on my thigh, hoping he'd catch the drift that I wanted him to hold it. I wasn't disappointed.

"My mother's coming for a visit next week," he said. "She wanted to make sure she'd get to meet my girlfriend."

He peeked at me sideways with a silly grin on his face.

"You mean me?" I asked.

"Of course I do."

"I'm your girlfriend?" I couldn't help but smile. It felt so good to be happy.

"If you want to be."

"Sure I do."

He leaned toward me and I took in a sip of breath before he pressed his lips against mine. It was short but as perfect as I could have ever imagined. When I opened my eyes, his face was still so close. I couldn't help but giggle a little.

"Was that all right?" he asked, touching my cheek.

I answered by grabbing a handful of his shirt and pulling him in for just one more kiss. It was longer than the first, but only slightly. I still wasn't sure if I was doing it right.

"I sure do like you, Annie Jacobson," he said.

"Why?" I asked.

"Because you are unlike anyone else in all the world." He winked at me. "I mean that in a good way."

He stood and took both of my hands, raising me to my feet.

Mike would have approved of David. I had no doubts.

"Do you want to come over for dinner?" I asked. "Frank's grilling burgers."

He nodded. "I can walk you home."

"All right," I said. "Just give me a minute, okay? I'll be right there."

He let go of my hands and I watched him walk to the end of the dock.

From where I stood I could see the house we'd lived in when I was a little girl, the dock jutting out into the water. I imagined my younger self sitting there, beside Frank, each of us with a cup of coffee in hand. His black and mine mostly milk and sugar.

Then I pictured my little-girl self alone, waiting for him to come back. I still felt the loneliness of those days, just after Frank went away.

All those years later, on that late March day, I realized I'd never been alone after all. My Father had been there all along, smiling sunshine at me from behind the clouds.

I turned, joining David at the end of the dock.

Author's Note
and Acknowledgments

I was a snoopy child. Once in my rummaging I happened upon an envelope addressed to my mom, written in my dad's unique penmanship. The envelope was different, one sent via airmail. I knew straightaway that it had been sent from Vietnam.

I didn't read the letter. Somehow I knew that the words weren't for me. Even in a family of six, there needed to be some things kept sacred. Tucking it back in the box was the right thing to do. It wasn't long before my curiosity became captivated by something else and I'd forgotten about that letter.

In 2015 I was in the midst of edits for a Dust Bowl–era novel that was to release and dreaming up what might be next after I finished a trio of stories about a young girl from Oklahoma. That was when I picked up a book called *Dear*

America: Letters Home from Vietnam compiled and edited by Bernard Edelman.

As I read, I remembered the letter I'd found—long gone by then, I was sure. I thought about how young my dad was when he'd sent it, how young many of the boys who fought in Vietnam were, and how they each had families that worried and prayed from home.

It was then that I knew my next story would find its setting in 1967.

My stack of books reflected my curiosity into the events of the Vietnam War: *In Pharaoh's Army* by Tobias Wolff, *After the Flag Has Been Folded* by Karen Spears Zacharias, *The Things They Carried* by Tim O'Brien, *We Were Soldiers Once . . . and Young* by Harold G. Moore and Joseph L. Galloway, among many others. I watched countless documentaries, chief among them being *Vietnam in HD* and *The Vietnam War* by Ken Burns and Lynn Novick.

Fortunately, it wasn't by my efforts alone that *All Manner of Things* became the story you hold now. I owe a debt of gratitude to so many for the part they played in making the Jacobson family's story come to life. This isn't just a book I wrote, it's a novel that belongs to all of us. I cannot imagine a greater community to share it with.

Bruce Matthews: Your knowledge of all things loony (of the bird variety, of course) helped add a layer of meaning to this book that I could not have come up with on my own. Thank you, too, for your encouragement and checking with me often to see how the sixties novel was coming along.

Karl Rewa: Sitting with you over cups of coffee to talk about your time in Vietnam and life after gave me such insight, particularly into the characters of Frank and Walt.

Whenever I sat down to write their characters, I remembered what you said. "Tell them that what went on over there, what we had to do, it's not who we are. It's something that happened to us. That's all." Thank you for that.

The Pipping family: Gerri, I will never forget sitting at your table to hear your story of immigrating from the Netherlands. If I'd not met you, I doubt I could have written the character Oma. Gary and Adria, I so appreciate your insight into what it means to be Dutch American. Beth, thank you for sharing your family with me. They really are the sweetest.

Nancee Marchinowski: Much love, my friend, and lots of thanks for sharing about your life in 1960s West Michigan. You are a treasure to me.

Mom: Thanks for letting me pick your brain about details from how you did your hair in 1967 to what it was like to watch footage of the war on the news. I sure hope I got it right. And thanks for refining my musical taste by playing Simon & Garfunkel, the Beatles, and Aretha Franklin, to name a few. You introduced me to the soundtrack for this novel. You sure are peachy keen.

Dad: I can't think of any other father who would write up his war memoirs to help his daughter research the way you did. I can't tell you what that means to me. It's a document that wasn't just helpful in the writing of this book, but is a record of our family heritage. Thank you for sharing it with me.

Tim Beals: A million thanks for believing enough in Annie's story to pitch it on my behalf. Your enthusiasm for this project has been such an encouragement to me. Thank you.

Kelsey Bowen: As soon as I learned that I would have the opportunity to work with you as my editor, I knew that it would be a special relationship. You have not disappointed, my friend. Thank you for believing in me and loving the Jacobson family every bit as much as I do. Here's to many more stories told together.

Kristin Kornoelje: Your eagle eyes caught more errant commas than I'd like to admit. I appreciate your discerning edits. You certainly make me look smart.

Gayle Raymer: When I wrote Fort Colson into being I never imagined that a cover designer could capture my daydreams quite as perfectly as you have done. Because of you, I sure hope readers judge this book by its cover.

Michele Misiak, Karen Steele, Hannah Brinks and the rest of the wonderful Revell team: I hope you all know how dearly I love you for working so hard to get this novel into the world. It has been a joy to work with you from the very moment I signed the contract. I count myself blessed.

Chris Jager, Darron Schroeder, Sue Smith, and the rest of my Baker Book House family: You give me a place to sit and write, you give my books space on the shelf, you make me smile when I'm feeling the stresses of deadlines, you are cheerleaders of the best sort. Where would I be without all of you?

My friends: Your prayers, notes, hugs, and emails have kept me going. Alexis De Weese, Anne Ferris, Ash Nibbe, Betsy Carter, Catie Cordero, Jocelyn Green, Karee Mouw, Michelle Alvarez, Nicky Bower, Sarah Geelhoed, Shelly Hendricks, and Sonny Huisman. I can't imagine life without each of you.

Elise, Austin, and Tim: Thanks for jamming out to the Beatles, Jimi Hendrix, and Aretha Franklin with me. I'm convinced that you three are the coolest kids on the planet.

Jeff: You always have and always will be my favorite reader. I love you.

Finally, to Jesus, who knows our grief and suffering, our sorrow and longing yet offers us the promise that all will be well. Maybe not today, tomorrow, or for a long time. But someday. This is our hope.

Jesus should be #1

John 3:16, read+believe

Susie Finkbeiner is the CBA bestselling author of *A Cup of Dust*, *A Trail of Crumbs*, and *A Song of Home*. She serves on the Breathe Christian Writers Conference planning committee, volunteers her time at Ada Bible Church in Grand Rapids, Michigan, and speaks at retreats and women's events across the state. Susie and her husband have three children and live in West Michigan.

Meet Susie

SusieFinkbeiner.com

THE PAST IS NEVER AS PAST AS
We'd Like to Think

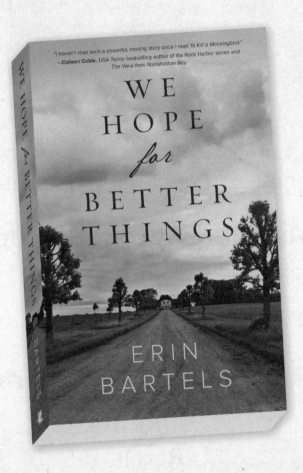

In this richly textured debut novel, a disgraced journalist moves
into her great-aunt's secret-laden farmhouse and discovers that
the women in her family were testaments to true love and courage
in the face of war, persecution, and racism.

Revell
a division of Baker Publishing Group
www.RevellBooks.com